Praise for

DEAN MAYES

"A riveting read! All you can think about is turning the next page!" ~ Georgina Penney, Author of Fly In, Fly Out; Irrepressible You; Summer Harvest

"Mayes's characters inspire sympathy, and I kept reading to learn more about them." ~ San Francisco Book Review

"Gifts of the Peramangk is an achingly beautiful story about perseverance and hope that I wished would never end. Dean Mayes clearly cares deeply about his characters, and his dedication to them shines through. I highly recommend this tale." ~ Long and Short Reviews

"It has been a long time since I read a book that made me think about life and about serious issues instead of just escaping into a good story. (It was a good story too.) And a longer time still since a book made me cry because it was so wonderfully written and contained such a powerful, moving story." ~ Once Upon A Dream Books

"Dean writes so beautifully that you can hear the music playing. You feel the emotions that are poured into compositions from the artists. I felt like I was back in orchestra, listening to a playback of a performance." ~ Books Complete Me

"A poignant, thought-provoking novel that deals with the real issue of racism, and with characters that are so well developed, I wept for them and I cheered for their triumphs, however tinged they may be with diversity and hopelessness." ~ Minding Spot

THE RECIPIENT

Dean Mayes

Cover Design: Michelle Halket
Cover Images: Courtesy & Copyright iStock: alenchi

Published by Central Avenue Publishing, an imprint of Central Avenue Marketing Ltd.
www.centralavenuepublishing.com

Published in Canada
Printed in United States of America

1. FICTION/Thrillers - Psychological 2. FICTION/Horror

Library and Archives Canada Cataloguing in Publication

Mayes, Dean, author
The recipient / Dean Mayes.

Issued in print and electronic formats.
ISBN 978-1-77168-038-7 (paperback).--ISBN 978-1-77168-039-4 (epub).--
ISBN 978-1-77168-050-9 (mobipocket)

I. Title.

PR9619.4.M49R43 2016 823'.92 C2015-906277-2
C2015-906278-0

For Xavier & Lucy

Who asked me a whole lot of questions...
and then helped me to answer them.

And I'm gonna ride this feeling as far as it goes.
I'm gonna ride this feeling.
I don't know, I don't know,
Whether I'm flying or falling,
But I'm gonna ride this feeling.

~ Kate Miller-Heidke and Keir Nuttall

CHAPTER 1

He occupied a region of consciousness somewhere on the edge of sleep—but not quite. He was still aware. A jumble of disconnected thoughts swirled inside his head. He could make no sense of them and it maddened him.

In the depths of the night he lay in his bed, listening to the sounds around him that prevented him from succumbing to sleep. He cursed silently. There was the quiet tick-tock from the alarm clock on his bedside table. The soft, audible breath of his wife sleeping beside him. The sound of his own heart beating. They melded together in the darkness, tormenting him. He could feel his anger rising. The battle to quiet his mind was futile.

With these sounds was another, more pervasive sound—the rhythmic hum that came from a pump in the hall just outside. It delivered oxygen into the adjacent bedroom via a long, thin tube connected to a port on the pump's surface, along the polished timber floorboards of the hallway and through the doorway of the bedroom where it terminated at the soft plastic prongs of the nasal cannula that sat just under the nostrils of the petite figure who lay in the bed.

It was a young woman. It was his daughter.

Peter Schillinge's eyes snapped open. He ground his teeth together. The unwanted realisation that he couldn't fall asleep dawned upon him and, hissing in frustration, he sat up and swung his legs over the side of the bed. He rubbed his eyes as his anger peaked. Peter rarely slept very well anymore. Night after night he waged the battle with himself. He had come to accept that it was one he couldn't win.

He finally rose, reaching in the darkness for a T-shirt that lay on the floor. He stumbled around the edge of the bed while pulling the shirt over his head. He cursed aloud then shushed himself as his wife stirred. Thankfully, Edie Schillinge did not wake.

In the hall, he felt for a lamp on a table and flicked it on, squinting in the soft light as he tiptoed to the doorway of his daughter's room. Rubbing the sleep from his eyes, he peered in.

A middle-aged woman with a kind face sat adjacent to the bed in a comfortable chair. She held a china cup and read a magazine. Looking up, she smiled. Sensing that he did not wish to speak or that, perhaps, he couldn't, the nurse remained silent as he stood in the doorway.

He gazed at his daughter.

She was pale, and painfully thin. Her hair, once a lustrous light brown—almost blond—framed her features. It had been lovingly shampooed by her mother the previous evening. The tubing from the nasal cannula sat on the powdery skin of her high cheek bones, which made subtle movements as she worked her jaw. It seemed she was in the grip of a dream. Occasionally, her petite nose wrinkled as the ends of the oxygen tubing tickled her nostrils. Her lips were dry and cracked; remnants of lanolin had been licked away or absorbed. She lay propped up slightly on pillows, arms across her chest, her ribs visible and prominent. They rose and fell under the thin cotton of her singlet with each breath she took. In the light from her bedside lamp, he could see her pulse visible on her neck, flickering rhythmically with each beat of her heart.

Her heart.

That failing heart continued to beat inside her chest, oblivious to everything but its biological programming. It continued to beat, but for how much longer nobody could be sure. Diseased and swollen, the malfunctioning organ stubbornly refused to fail. No one knew when it would. It was a time bomb whose detonation could occur in the next twenty seconds or the next twenty days.

He leaned against the door frame and tilted his head so that it rested on the timber. He gazed at her, his eyes becoming reddened and swollen with tears.

Peter Schillinge had watched helplessly as Casey had been ravaged by the effects of the disease that she had unwittingly contracted. Even now, after all this time, he still couldn't pronounce it properly.

Loeffler's Endocarditis—or so the literature said.

A condition caused by a worm called a helminth that inhabits tropical climates.

His eyes drifted from his daughter to her bedside table and mirror, upon which sat many of Casey's favourite things.

Prominent among the pretty scarves, jewellery, skin care products and assorted ephemera sat a group of photo frames. They were photographs of Casey from what seemed like another lifetime. Vibrant and healthy, the beautiful young woman in the images seemed like a stranger now.

There was Casey in the midst of a lacrosse match, her lithe frame compact in contrast to her tall competitor. Armed with her lacrosse stick, she was poised in staunch concentration. There was Casey receiving a national mathematics prize from a bookish-looking man in a rumpled suit. Casey at her university graduation, posing in a traditional cap and gown with himself and Edie proudly standing on either side of her. Casey's smile was a thousand watts—beaming forth her proud achievement. Alongside these framed photographs were other, more recent images.

Casey, grubby and sweating in hiking gear, posing with a group of her close friends at a jungle camp site, a lock of her auburn hair hanging down the side of her face from underneath her cap. A close-up shot of Casey, her hands resting on either side of an elephant's trunk as she nuzzled against it, grinning broadly. Casey standing at the tiller of a long boat on an expansive Asian waterway, her large, green eyes taking in the sheer limestone karsts which jutted vertically from the emerald water on all sides of her. Visual mementos from a backpacking trip through South East Asia.

The source of her troubles.

They could never have anticipated it.

After four long but rewarding years of study at university where she had achieved high distinctions in her dual degree in mathematics and computer science, Casey had treated herself to a once-in-a-lifetime chance for travel, soaking up the beauty of Vietnam, Cambodia and Thailand with a group of her uni friends.

She was happy, carefree and smiling in every photo. From hiking through a thick rainforest to riding on the back of an Asian elephant and sitting in an open, long boat travelling down a river, those experiences belied any hint of trouble for Casey.

On her return to Australia, her arrival at the airport signalled to her parents right away that something was not right. She'd lost weight and she looked dishevelled, unwell. Casey dismissed it as a flu; a gastrointestinal complaint that would soon pass.

But it didn't pass.

The lethargy, vomiting, and diarrhoea worsened. Her weight plummeted. She eventually succumbed, collapsed and was rushed to hospital. The diagnosis was confirmed quickly. Their worst fears were realised. Acute and irreversible heart failure.

Without a transplant, their daughter would die.

Though they were quickly put onto the heart transplant waiting list, they were under no illusions that the prospects for Casey were anything but grim. Donor rates in Australia were incredibly low and there were no guarantees of anything happening quickly.

Casey's doctors stabilised her as best they could; after which, there was little more they could do for her at the hospital. With supports in place, Peter and his wife brought their daughter home.

Home to wait? Home to die?

In the half-light, Casey stirred and coughed. The nurse got up from her chair while Peter remained where he stood, seemingly unable to move.

The nurse supported Casey into a sitting position so she could cough some more.

"There, there," she whispered softly. "Take your time, love. Let it pass, let it pass."

Casey leaned into nurse, resting her head on her shoulder until the coughing passed, then she lay back down into the pillow.

She blinked and looked across in her father's direction. She guessed it was him, though she couldn't focus enough to see him clearly.

Casey opened her mouth to speak. Snapping himself from his trance, Peter kneeled at her bedside and gently placed his fingers on her cracked, dry lips.

"Sssh," he whispered tenderly, lifting his hand to stroke her forehead. "Just rest, sweetheart."

His voice was as ragged as his emotions. They overwhelmed him. His anger, frustration, and powerlessness raged at having to watch his beautiful daughter die before his eyes. He cursed the unfairness of it all. He wanted to lash out with his fists and punish whatever invisible force it was that had done this to Casey.

The moment and the torment passed. He focused on his daughter's fragile face.

The nurse placed her hand on his shoulder.

"What say I go and put the kettle on? Make us a cup of tea. I know I could use another one."

Peter nodded absently then glanced at her.

"Yeah," he ventured in a whisper. "That would be nice, Bernie."

The nurse rose and turned from the room while Peter picked up a small tube of lanolin from the bedside table, opening it and squeezing a small, shining globule onto the end of his finger. He coated Casey's lips tenderly.

It was a small task, but it was much appreciated. Casey relaxed under his gentle touch.

His eyes went to a clock on the bedside table next to the photo frames.

1:25AM.

Too many hours until morning, he thought wearily, rubbing a knot of tension from the back of his neck.

Suddenly the sound of the telephone cut through the serenity, causing Peter to stiffen. He cocked his ear but couldn't react right away. He could not be sure that what he was hearing was real. Not until Bernie appeared at the door.

Peter hesitated as his eyes met hers and a jolt of electricity passed between them.

Peter stumbled to his feet and charged through into the hallway. He went to the telephone and lifted it to his ear.

His throat was so dry that he couldn't greet the voice at the other end. He croaked out an incomprehensible sound; his voice catching on the edge of his tongue.

Bernie steeled herself, watching him expectantly.

Peter forced his jaw to work. "H-hello?"

"Mr. Schillinge? Mr. Peter Schillinge?"

"Yes."

"Mr. Schillinge, it's Verity Goodall, Transplant Coordinator at the Medical Centre."

"Yes."

"I've just been advised, sir. We have a heart. They've found a heart. I've mobilised an ambulance to you. They should be arriving at any moment."

The muted sound of an ambulance siren sounded from the other end of the house, while the familiar blue and red flashes of light splashed across the hallway walls.

Bernie was compelled to action. Ignoring the whistling kettle, she rushed down the hall to the front door, leaving Peter standing in the darkened living room. He was frozen with the handset to his ear.

"Peter? Can you hear me?"

"Yes. I understand. I understand."

He could hear the front door opening, the rattle of an ambulance gurney being wheeled through it, the familiar green uniform of ambulance officers as Bernie directed them to the bedroom.

Bernie met Peter's eyes and she saw something in them that she'd thought she would never see: hope.

We have a heart.

Edie appeared in the hallway. Peter snapped back into the moment. He clutched the receiver to his ear once more.

"We're on our way," he said, and hung up. He went to his wife.

Edie Schillinge held her breath as Peter embraced her and smiled. It was the first smile she'd seen in what felt like an eternity.

"Was that the hospital?"

Edie regarded Peter carefully, in quiet contemplation.

Peter nodded, kissing her forehead.

"They've got a heart, darl," he said. "We better get our bags."

The paramedics had already lifted Casey onto the gurney and were strapping her in while Bernie made sure that her travelling case was ready and stationed it in the hallway. She then rushed to turn off the screaming kettle and gather both Peter's and Edie's bags.

"Peter, you ride with Casey," she said, meeting them in the living room once more. "I'll follow you with Edie, all right?"

Peter and Edie nodded and quickly dressed while the paramedics loaded Casey into the ambulance.

This was it.

The realisation reverberated in his mind. The long months of agonising wait evaporated in an instant. It was too much to comprehend.

Gathering his keys and wallet from his bedside table, he stood as Edie entered the bedroom. He met her steady gaze.

"This is really happening."

"Yes," he rasped. It was all he could manage.

"Central. This is Unit 24 en route, Oakford Avenue, Brighton to the Alfred with lights and sirens."

The voice echoed, as though distant. Casey couldn't determine where it was coming from.

She felt hands moving across her body as belts were tightened, holding her in position. There was vibration and movement. The rumble of an engine spluttering to life. The sound of a siren.

With a great effort, Casey opened her eyes and tried to focus. She tried to speak but couldn't.

Through the haze of light, the familiar shadow of her father hovered as he sat down beside her and took her hand in his.

"W…wha…happen—?" she uttered in a barely audible croak.

"They've found you a heart, honey," Peter said into her ear. "We're taking you to the hospital right now."

Casey tilted her head. "A...heart. But that's good news."

Peter clucked and wiped his eyes. Tears were streaming down his cheeks.

"It is, love. It is indeed."

The ambulance reversed out of the driveway and raced towards the city that twinkled with light. Casey thought she could hear a distant pattering above her head. "Is it raining, Dad?"

Through his tears, Peter smiled, feeling a rush of emotion. Even now, with her hold on life so tenuous, she was still aware of the smallest things in the world around her—as though they mattered.

He squeezed her hand and nodded. "Yeah, love."

Edie stood before a window, thumbing her gold necklace as she gazed thoughtfully at the cityscape. Rain pattered against the window. Rivulets of water snaked down the glass creating distortions of light and rainbows of colour.

Peter sat holding a foam cup in his hand. He swirled the liquid inside it absently. A silent TV hanging on the wall of the waiting area flashed the early news. The only sound in the waiting area was the distant pattering of the rain. Peter debated whether to swallow the last of the caterer's blend, but decided against it. Screwing up his nose, he set the cup down on the floor underneath his seat.

He glanced up at a clock on the wall. They had been here for almost fourteen hours.

Edie felt she'd barely had the opportunity to say anything to Casey before she went in. She had rehearsed speeches over and over. She had thought about this moment for so long. She'd promised to hold her hand. When the moment arrived it was all too rushed, too urgent. She had said nothing. Edie couldn't remember if she had held Casey's hand.

Peter studied Edie as she stood with her back to him. She was still as beautiful now as when they first met. Tall and stately, with fine shoulders and thick chestnut hair that hung stylishly to the top of her neck. She stood, serene at the window, though he knew she'd be wrestling with the guilt of not having spoken to her daughter before she was wheeled away. Edie was a perfectionist. She had planned for this moment, knowing that Casey needed her to be strong. It was a blessing and a curse. She had missed her opportunity to say anything of value to her. Though he knew she shouldn't punish herself, Peter knew better to try and sway his wife from her guilt. She would have to come to peace with it in her own time.

As if on cue to this very observation, Edie's shoulders relaxed. She turned to her husband. Her eyes were red. Her features lined with exhaustion. She was still beautiful.

She came and sat. She leaned against him and rested her head on his shoulder.

Smiling, Peter noticed that she was holding a photo of Casey as he took her hand.

Edie gazed down on a photo of her daughter—an image from her Asian holiday. With the sun setting off to her left, Casey's eyes were focused on the photographer. Worldly, youthful, inquisitive—they were Casey's strongest features, her most beautiful. There was comfort in those eyes.

"Indestructible," Peter mused, his voice filled with emotion.

For the first time since they'd arrived, Edie managed a wistful smile. "She always grabbed the world with both hands."

"She will again," Peter replied. "I know it."

Edie craned her neck to look up at her husband.

"Will she?" she questioned. Her eyes were plagued by doubt. "Will she really, Peter?"

Her question caught him off guard and he studied her for a long moment. It was as if she resented his faith in their daughter.

"You're not sure?"

"I don't know," she responded. "There's so much that can go wrong—so much that she has to *contend* with." Edie's voice faltered. There were no guarantees. She had read the literature. Not only was the transplant surgery itself not without risk but risk would remain for the rest of Casey's life. Casey would not be able to live the kind of life she had lived before.

The door to the waiting room clicked open and Peter and Edie looked up to see a man dressed in green scrubs and a theatre cap step inside quietly. He was tall, with tanned skin and a kind, handsome face. Dark sideburns were visible, poking out from the edge of the theatre cap. This was one of Casey's surgeons, Dr. Francis Arlo. Both of them stood anxiously as he nodded in greeting.

"How are you both?" he said softly.

"Good, Doctor, we're good," Peter said hurriedly, his eyes searching Arlo's face for an immediate indication of what was happening.

The surgeon placed his hand on Peter's shoulder and gestured for them to sit as he sat down beside them.

"We've finished the surgery," Arlo said, a weary but victorious smile spreading across his face. "She made it through. Casey has a brand new heart."

Edie gasped as an involuntary squeak caught at the back of her throat and she whipped up her hand to cover her mouth. Her emotions spilled forth all at once.

Peter put his arm around her and held her close. He reached out to Arlo with his free hand and squeezed his shoulder, his gesture filled with gratitude.

"When can we see her?" Peter asked raggedly.

"Fedele is just closing up now. In a few minutes we'll wheel her through into the recovery suite. She will have a breathing tube in place and she'll still be asleep, but I'll make sure you get a few moments with her. Okay?"

Peter nodded while Edie took a tissue from inside her bag and wiped her eyes.

Arlo took his cue and stood. He turned to leave when Edie looked up suddenly.

"Doctor…" she called after him, her voice shaking.

Arlo turned and regarded her warmly.

"What about her donor? What will happen to the…"

Her voice trailed off as she suddenly felt self-conscious at having asked the question.

Arlo nodded with not a trace of scorn or disapproval.

"The donor will be cared for, then released back to the family. They will all be looked after."

He turned from them once more.

"Please," Edie said, "Thank them."

Pausing at the exit, Arlo smiled.

"I will."

A THEATRE NURSE led Peter and Edie towards a large bay, occupied by several beds. Nurses and doctors manned each bed space, all of them attending to their patients.

Entering the bay, Peter began searching the faces in the beds as they were led over to a corner cubicle. A bed stood in the centre, flanked by various machines, IV poles, and monitors. So overwhelmed by the activity that was taking place, Peter failed to recognise the patient who lay in the bed. It wasn't until they were standing before it did he realise.

It was Casey.

A second nurse, stationed beside the bed, turned and acknowledged both her colleague and Peter and Edie.

She appeared so small, Peter thought. She was inclined, so that she was almost in a sitting position. A breathing tube protruded from Casey's mouth. The blankets rose and fell with each breath that was generated by the ventilator beside her. IV lines exited from a port on her neck, leading to a trio of nearby pumps that whirred rhythmically as they delivered fluids into her body. A myriad of coloured leads snaked out from underneath the blankets and joined a single cable that led up to the monitor upon which Casey's vital signs were displayed. Numbers flickered beside rhythmic wave forms on the screen. Edie's eyes were immediately drawn to the familiar green ECG trace of her daughter's heartbeat and she tilted her head curiously at it.

The waveform was vital and bright on the screen, accompanied by a beep that was steady and strong.

Her heart, Edie thought. Her new heart.

Casey's nurse turned and smiled warmly as she stepped out from beside the bed and set her chart down on a nearby workstation.

"You can step closer if you like," she encouraged in a pretty Scottish accent. "Talk to her. Let her know that you're here."

Edie hesitated, looked to Peter who seemed equally unsure. Casey's eyes were closed. She appeared peaceful.

"Go on," the nurse said. "It's all right."

Together, they approached Casey.

Edie reached out with a hesitant hand and touched her forehead, moving a limp few strands of hair from her brow. Casey's skin was warm—warmer than it had been in a long time. Edie felt a surge of hope.

Peter felt under the blanket for his daughter's hand and took it. Casey's fingers flinched under his touch. He felt them search for his and he looked into her face.

Her eyelids fluttered opened. Instinctively, Peter leaned in closer as Casey fought to focus on her parents.

She grimaced, aware of something foreign in her throat. A flash of panic passed through her as she worked her jaw instinctively. The nurse signalled to her colleague who nodded and turned to one of the pumps.

"I'm just giving her an extra dose of medication, to help her relax," she explained. "We're allowing her to wake up slowly. She's breathing largely on her own but we just want to be sure."

Casey sank back into the pillow. The panic washed away and she closed her eyes. Edie stroked her brow once more.

Through the fog of the sedatives, Casey recognised her parents. And though she couldn't express it, a font of joy welled inside her. She felt her father's fingers entwined in hers and with as much effort as she could muster, Casey squeezed them.

"Rest, darling, just rest," Peter whispered. "You made it, kiddo. You pulled through. Just like we said you would."

Peter was rewarded when Casey's mouth stretched around the breathing tube and, for the briefest of moments, formed a smile.

Her expression, as fleeting as it was, sent a surge of love through him and, in that moment Peter felt, for the first time in a long time, that everything was going to be all right.

Edie reached across the bed and squeezed Peter's free hand. She smiled through tear-filled eyes and they leaned in close to their daughter, touching their heads to her own.

The disembodied but steady beep, beep, beep from the monitor sounded in Casey Schillinge's ears and she wondered where the sound was coming from.

12 MONTHS LATER

HER RHYTHM WAS steady, her stride confident. She had set the treadmill to challenge herself, increasing the speed of the machine incrementally until she ran with considerable speed. Beads of sweat speckled her forehead and ran down the sides of her face. She felt a satisfying ache in her legs and arms as her athletic body approached its anaerobic threshold. She savoured the intensity; she revelled in it, feeling confident in meeting the challenge.

Though the music from her phone played loudly in her ears, her consciousness was detached from it—a distant echo in her mind. Instead, a much more organic sound jockeyed for her attention and won it.

The rhythmic beating of her heart. Or, rather, the heart that had been gifted to her.

Its beat was strong, vital—a healthy organ that was now very much a part of Casey Schillinge, even though it was not born from her. This was a concept she still wrestled with, all these long months since her surgery.

Casey powered herself onward, her breathing steady as she fed oxygen into her body. Into her bloodstream. Into the heart.

Then, turning a dial on the control panel, she slowed herself to a jog. She took a towel from the hand grip and wiped the sweat from her brow. She smiled broadly.

Placing her hand to her chest, Casey felt a powerful thump against it. She enjoyed testing it, pushing it as hard as she could, to see where its limits lay.

All at once, an intense pain exploded from the centre of the heart and spread out across her chest. It was strong enough to take her breath away, to cause her to stagger on the machine. She stopped on the treadmill, grabbing at the side rail with her free hand while she clutched at her chest. The pain grew in strength, holding her captive for several moments until, finally, it began to subside, reducing itself to a dull ache.

Casey became aware of something new. A sensation? No, a feeling. An emotion. It was a darkness that seemed to emanate from within the heart itself, bringing with it a sense of unease—and fear.

Shaking herself from the moment, she stepped off the treadmill, tossing her towel on the rail. Looking back at the machine, Casey Schillinge felt that potent dark sensation remain.

It chilled her.

CHAPTER 2

3 YEARS LATER

A MASCULINE FIST RAPPED THREE TIMES AGAINST THE GREEN METAL OF A HUGE industrial door that faced onto a darkened corridor.

The owner of that hand, a tall and angular middle-aged male dressed in an expensive grey suit stepped back, crossed his hands low across his front, and waited patiently.

He couldn't be sure if he could hear anybody behind the door, though a cursory glance at the floor revealed a thin shaft of light coming from inside.

Waiting patiently, he was distracted by the faint aroma of cinnamon that seemed to surround him here in this dark and dingy hall. A single light globe that dangled from a cobwebbed cable above his head flickered in the gloom, illuminating the remnant of a painted sign on the brick wall beside him.

Mitchell & Sons Granary Supply, in a faded, antique font, was declared proudly over an image of a pair of Clydesdale horses. They were hauling a vintage wooden wagon, piled high with what the man assumed were sacks of grain. Curiously, the visual cue touched off an olfactory hallucination within him. He thought he could detect the scent of oats—a hint to this building's long forgotten past.

He checked the face of his Tag Heuer watch and scowled. It was 10PM—a ridiculous time to be conducting business, he thought. He had been given little choice, however. His superiors' instructions to him were explicit: Be at this address no earlier than 10PM and no later than 10:05PM.

His lips shifted into a fleeting, ironic smile.

He would bet his left testicle that the instruction had come not from his superiors, but from their contractor. And that very contractor had earned a reputation for a being a hard arse.

Suddenly the green door groaned on its track and rumbled sideways, revealing a petite young woman. Her tousled wet hair was a dark nut-brown. He thought he saw hints of red in it, but he couldn't be sure. Upon first glance, it appeared to be a short bob tied back in a pony tail, but he noticed that both the back and sides were shaved close to the skin. A long fringe hung low over her large green eyes. Those eyes were ringed by liner that made her appear almost Gothic. Though her features were attractive and feminine, her powdery visage was stony, dangerous even.

She wore a grey, long-sleeved Lycra gym top that hugged her lithe figure and ended at the waist.

His eyes, almost involuntarily, scanned downward as he noticed that she wore bikini bottoms only; her long legs and slender feet were bare.

The corner of his left eyebrow raised appreciatively.

"What do you want?" the young woman snapped, jolting him from his procession of impure thoughts.

She folded her arms across her chest and leaned against the door frame suggestively, maintaining an interrogatory glare at the stranger before her.

"Schillinge?" he queried, shifting uncomfortably.

She nodded once.

"Is it done?"

Wordlessly, she reached down to the elastic waist of her bikini bottoms and plucked forth an object.

The man watched as she flipped the shining golden object into her palm and held it up for him to see. It was no bigger than a stick of gum; an ingot that was perfectly smooth and shining in the half-light.

With a flick of her hand, one end of the ingot suddenly swung open on a hinge revealing its true nature as an ingenious, delicate container.

The man leaned in closer to see and found himself gazing down on the small ingot. His brow furrowed. Squinting in the low light of the darkened hallway, he attempted focus on something printed on the high capacity USB key, but all he could make out was a symbol—a single octagon etched into the golden surface.

He looked up at Casey. "Is that it?" he questioned incredulously. Casey merely shrugged.

Slowly, the man reached up to take the key from her when, without warning, the lid snapped shut and she whipped it away before he even registered what she had done.

"Money first," Casey snapped as the man blinked at her.

Brushing down his jacket, the man reached into his inner pocket and took out a thin rectangular box. He held it out and she took it, stuffing it into the elastic of her bikini bottoms. Without taking her eyes off him, she handed over the golden key.

The man took it and pocketed it, then glanced down at her hip, at the shining rectangular tin tucked there.

"You're not gonna check it?" he queried.

She allowed herself a smirk.

"I designed your people's system, remember? You fuck me over, all I have to do is press a key."

The man grinned. "They told me that you're a hard-on," he leered. "So, all they have to do is plug this in?"

Casey nodded. "It'll do the rest. Deployment should take a half hour at the most. Your entire network will be upgraded to the new protocols, as per the contract."

The man raised one eyebrow, impressed. "Sounds good."

Casey watched as he turned on his heel and disappeared down the stairs. Once he was out of sight, she retreated into the semidarkness of her warehouse apartment, locking the heavy green door behind her.

In stark contrast to the dingy hallway outside the door, Casey Schillinge's apartment was an altogether different environment. The converted granary and flour mill offered a spacious living space that was modern and comfortable while incorporating elements of its historical past. A fully equipped, yet minimalist, kitchen lay to her right while a luxurious living area occupied the space to her left. Two leather sofas sat facing one another, watched over by a large, flat panel TV and entertainment centre. Up a steel staircase that was bolted to the exposed brick wall was a mezzanine level populated by a master bedroom and bathroom. Casey hardly ever went up there. It acted as little more than storage. Near a large window and balcony that extended the full width of the building, the space had been converted into a stylish bedroom that was divided from the main living area by a tall, Gothic-styled wardrobe.

It was an item in the centre of the apartment, through which Casey passed now, that presented the most divergent example of decor in the otherwise stylish home. A large architectural workbench with a tempered glass surface stood in middle of the room. On it sat an LCD screen and a keyboard that had been fashioned from a piece of glass. The light from the LCD screen accounted for much of the apartment's illumination presently, bathing everything in its immediate proximity in a turquoise light. The work bench, the screen, and keyboard were her tools of trade.

She set down the metallic cash box and she regarded the LCD screen fleetingly. With a quick tap of the glass surface adjacent to the keyboard, the screen went dark; its unearthly glow vanquished for the time being. Casey considered opening the case, but she decided to leave it untouched.

Having performed work for this particular client several times before, she knew they were good for the money. And she knew the payment was considerable.

For the past three years, Casey had employed her remarkable skill set—gleaned from her double degree in mathematics and computer science—and directed it into a career in which she operated on the edge.

On one hand, she contracted herself out to big businesses, providing her expertise in constructing and maintaining security systems and network infrastructure that was considered second to none. On the other, Casey performed work for various underground groups who would be considered an enemy of the legitimate corporate interests from which she earned her considerable living.

She was a "grey hat" in every sense.

A grey hat who was, finally, in between jobs.

This latest contract—the construction of a particularly complex security system for a prominent investment firm—had consumed her life for the past three months. It had involved writing a state-of-the-art encryption language from scratch, deploying it across a vast network, then testing it for weaknesses and flaws which she then had to eliminate one by one, before testing the system again. She put in long hours, had rarely left her apartment and had thought of little else other than the contract. Now, with the exchange of her signature gold-plated USB key with the company's representative, she had nothing left to apply herself to—at least for now. Casey could finally relax.

But therein lay a unique and difficult dilemma.

Casey turned from the desk and faced the exposed brick wall that separated the living area from the en suite bathroom. Hanging from the bricks there, bathed now in a soft orange hue from a street lamp outside, was a painting by the impressionist master Modigliani.

The woman in the painting looked down on Casey with overtly large, expressive eyes and lips that curled upward ever so slightly in a smile that could, for all the world, have been meant for Casey herself. Auburn hair hung down on either side of her elongated features. There was a beauty about the woman in the painting, who Casey knew to be Jeanne Hebuterne, Modigliani's lover and muse.

Though not an original, the painting was Casey's favourite possession: a gift from her grandparents on her twenty-first birthday. Her grandfather often said that she reminded him of a Modigliani painting. Casey smiled at the recollection, then absently clutched at the back of her head, feeling the short, sharp bristles of her dark hair. It had once been as long and as beautiful as Modigliani's muse.

It seemed like a lifetime ago.

Touching a hand to the glass that protected the print inside, Casey went to the fridge in the kitchen and plucked out a bottle of wine. A long-stemmed glass was already waiting for her on the adjacent countertop and she poured a generous lug of the sauvignon blanc into it.

Time to celebrate, she thought wryly.

Walking past the workstation, bottle and glass in hand, Casey looked over to the entertainment centre, locking her eyes onto a familiar looking object there: a voice activated R2-D2 toy from the Star Wars saga. It was one of Casey's little indulgences.

"Hey, R2," she commanded.

The little droid's flashing red and blue light winked to life and its domed head swivelled in the direction of her voice.

"Play music."

A door on the barrel chest of the droid flipped opened and an extendible arm appeared from inside.

This was not an accessory that came "out of the box" when Casey purchased it. Rather, its presence was a result of some considerable tweaking and customising by Casey herself.

The little droid rolled over to the front of the entertainment centre and aimed its arm at the infrared pick-up of the sound system.

In an instant, the frenetic rock music of the Foo Fighters filled the room. Casey allowed herself a satisfied smile.

Setting her glass on the edge of the work bench, she peeled her gym top off and tossed it at her treadmill in the corner of the room where it landed on one of the handles of the machine. The cool air of the apartment caressed her skin, causing her nipples to stand erect and she shivered, invigorated by the sensation. Reaching up, she massaged a knot of tension from her left shoulder. An intricate tattoo of a Japanese cherry blossom adorned her left shoulder blade, its pink flowers catching the light from the street.

For a moment, Casey considered remaining topless, but she opted instead to take a linen shirt that was hanging on the corner of her wardrobe. She quickly threw it on.

Collecting her glass and the bottle and opening the glass sliding door, Casey stepped out onto the balcony of her apartment. Immediately she felt the balmy summer evening air on her skin and she sighed.

She set the wine bottle on a table and sipped from her glass as she surveyed the bustling scene below her from the balcony railing.

This was the Esplanade, the main thoroughfare of the beachside suburb of St. Kilda. The street was thick with Saturday night traffic, both pedestrian and automotive, as people made their way to and from the myriad eateries and entertainment venues that lined the strip. To the north, Casey could see the lights from the iconic Luna Park fun fair, as well as the equally famous Palais Theatre, where large groups of people were milling about its entrance, waiting to be admitted to whatever gig was playing tonight. Further on, she could just see the famous Espy Hotel, another St. Kilda landmark that routinely drew large crowds most nights of the week.

The sight of so many people below caused Casey to shiver. She could feel an unpleasant knot of tension in the pit of her stomach.

She hated crowds as much as she hated being outdoors. The very thought of being trapped down there in the throng of Saturday night revellers filled her with dread.

Taking a larger gulp from her glass, Casey pulled her eyes from below and cast them out across the inky waters of Port Phillip Bay. A collection of flickering lights emanating from various ships and boats captured her focus, taking it away from the chaotic throng below. Her anxiety abated. Her breathing relaxed, the heartbeat slowed.

The heart, she thought darkly as she retreated from the balcony edge and sat down on a lounge chair.

Balancing her glass on her knee, Casey closed her eyes and closed out the sounds of the street until there was nothing but the sound of the beating heart inside her chest. Its thump was vital and strong.

Casey reclined on the chair, lifting her feet and laying her head back on the cushion. She placed her glass on the table beside her and reached towards the buttons of her shirt, undoing a couple of them, allowing the balmy summer breeze to caress her chest, her almost perfect skin. A single blemish resided there, dark red in the half-light. A thick, raised scar that ran down her sternum, perfectly centred on her chest.

She hated that scar more than anything.

Though it was from a life-giving surgeon's cut made in order to deliver the heart she now carried, it served as a permanent physical reminder of the journey she had taken from the edge of death, an abyss from which she thought she would never escape.

She was alive.

Whoop-dee-fucking-doo.

She was alive but she was imprisoned by the realities of a life post-transplant. The ongoing medical support and treatment and medications were an omnipresent, oppressive fixture in her daily existence. The regular visits to her doctors, the constant tweaking of her medications, the continual tests to ensure that her new heart remained functional and optimal. The medical team had inserted themselves into every aspect of her life, observing how she ate, how she drank, how she slept, how she worked. They were constantly advising her and counselling her.

She hated it.

Casey felt like some bizarre human experiment, destined for an eternity of analysis and scrutiny.

But there were also the other unanticipated things that no one, least of all she, could have predicted. Her insomnia was foremost. There were frequent periods where Casey could be trapped awake for days at a time, unable to calm her mind. It was a phenomenon that only existed since the surgery and it had not abated.

In order to function, Casey developed inventive strategies.

Work was one method. By taking on the most complex jobs she could find, jobs that would occupy as much time as possible, she would render sleep a luxury. So long as she was working, constructing, testing and problem-solving she could avoid dealing with the negatives of her insomnia. Medications helped too—and not the type that were sanctioned by her medical team. Casey had done enough research on the myriad of available stimulants and depressants to know what she could take safely, and in what combinations, if there was such a thing.

Despite this, Casey knew there was a limit to staving off sleep. Her body eventually called time-out and she had to succumb.

Then she dreamed. It was the thing she hated most of all.

With the completion of the contract and no new work on the horizon, she had run out of excuses to avoid sleep.

She drew the glass up to her lips again and sipped. Alcohol would numb her, but only partially.

Looking down, Casey spied a small wooden box on the table. Setting her glass down, she reached for it and balanced it on her knees as she opened it. Inside was a small metallic pipe and a Zippo lighter, both of which were surrounded by balled-up wads of green. She plucked up the pipe and pressed one of those wads into the conical spout, then lit the marijuana, taking a long drag. As the effects of the drug worked almost immediately, she reclined and smiled. Her muscles relaxed, the tornado of her thoughts dissipated.

If her physician knew what she was doing right now, he would have a shit-fit.

His drug-addled heart transplant recipient.

Fuck him and his rules, she thought acidly. *This is what changing my life gets you.*

Her life had indeed changed. It had shifted tectonically. No longer was Casey Schillinge the wide-eyed, optimistic young woman. The goody-two-shoes suburban daughter. The high achieving, straight-A university student.

The heart had changed everything. It had taken as much away from her as it had given her.

For now, the wine would anaesthetise her, but the weed would knock out her subconscious and give her what she so desperately craved: long, dreamless sleep.

CHAPTER 3

THE SHARPENED BEVEL OF THE NEEDLE TOUCHED DOWN ONTO THE SKIN AND pressed inward, puckering the surface until it punctured it. A small bead of red blossomed, clinging to the shaft of the needle. The nurse winced at the sight of the blood; fearing she had missed her target, but she opted to persevere. Angling the needle downward slightly, she flattened its trajectory as she searched for the invisible target beneath the skin.

Casey watched as the nurse shifted on her stool. Telltale beads of sweat formed on the nurse's brow as she squeezed her eyes shut and opened them again, refocusing to try once more.

Must be a newbie, Casey thought darkly, doing all she could to hold back a scowl. Instead, she kept her expression flat, watching the nurse like a hawk.

The nurse drew back with the most delicate of pressure, and her eyes brightened as a flashback of blood appeared inside the clear tubing that was attached to the needle. Reaching for a nearby vial, the nurse attached it to a barrel at the opposite end, and watched as a thin jet of Casey's blood flowed into the vial under pressure. She repeated the process with a second and third vial.

Withdrawing the needle, she pressed a ball of cotton wool to the entry site and Casey lifted her arm up, compressing the cotton wool against her skin.

"All done," the nurse said, her voice filled with relief.

Casey slipped her feet into her shoes, then grabbed a nearby pen and scrawled her signature on the form that lay on the bench.

"Thank you," she said quickly, leaving the room before the nurse could say goodbye.

THE GENTLE WHIR of motors vibrated underneath her as the platform on which she lay slid backwards, entering into the circular tunnel of the Magnetic Resonance Imager.

Adjusting her head on the pillow, Casey closed her eyes and tried to focus on her breathing, rather than the intensely claustrophobic environment. An ominous thrum surrounded her and she bit the inside of her lip. For a moment, she felt a faint niggle of pain in her arm from where the nurse had taken blood earlier, and she focused her attention on that in an effort to quell her anxiety. Casey supposed she had the inexperienced nurse to thank now for providing her with a means of distraction while she was temporarily imprisoned in this technological monstrosity and she smiled inwardly, if a little bitterly, at the irony.

The earbud headphones Casey wore crackled with static, then a male voice sounded in her head. "We're about to begin," it announced with cold detachment.

Casey nodded without responding, knowing that the source of that voice could see her via the camera situated inside the tunnel.

The shrill sound of classical music filtered into her headphones while, all around her, the hulking innards of the MR Imager rumbled to life. Its huge magnets began to spin, creating a bizarre, hammering cacophony that drowned out the music.

Casey couldn't decide which sound was worse.

She reflexively tried to put her hand to her head but stopped when the male voice crackled in her earphones. "Please keep still!" It ordered harshly.

In a booth outside the MRI unit, detailed images of Casey's internal anatomy began to appear on a screen in front of the radiographer. His thin fingers danced over a keyboard, tapping a series of commands as the front-on images became a series of transverse, top-down slices of Casey's chest. He regarded them blankly, behind impossibly thick glasses and scratched his neatly clipped beard thoughtfully.

Inside the tunnel, Casey grimaced, trying to close out the unnerving racket as well as the tinny classical music. She drifted into her thoughts, using an exercise that she employed whenever she was outdoors.

Casey touched a distant silence beyond the cacophony and rode on it for the final few minutes of the test. Then, suddenly, she felt the bed slide out from inside the machine. She blinked, looking up to see the radiographer and his assistant.

"We're finished, miss," he said flatly. "You can get dressed."

He turned on his heel as his assistant, who flashed a disapproving glare at him, took her hand and helped her into a sitting position. Scowling at the back of the man's head, she swung her legs over the side of the bed.

"He was different," Casey remarked dourly.

"New guy," the assistant replied. "Not really a people person."

Hopping down from the bed, Casey slipped her feet into her shoes and retrieved her bag from a nearby chair.

The radiographer appeared in the doorway of the MRI suite armed with a large envelope. "Here are your hard copies. Your consultant will have electronic ones in a few moments. The images aren't bad but you shouldn't have moved inside the imager."

Handing Casey the envelope with about as much emotion as if he were handing her a drive-through hamburger, the radiographer left the room without another word.

Casey lay on an examination bed in a darkened room, waiting impatiently.

An ECG machine sat beside her, its leads connected to adhesive pads strategically placed across her bare chest. She lay there now, covered only by a paper sheet, grinding her teeth. The machine was switched on and an annoying fault alarm was issuing from it.

The technician who had been attending to her had been trying to rectify whatever error the machine was experiencing, but she had failed miserably and had gone to seek help. That was nearly five minutes ago. No one had come back and the stubborn alarm continued to beep.

Looking across at the machine, Casey grasped an orange power cable that protruded from its rear and yanked it.

The machine's display went dark. The alarm silenced.

She sighed with relief and lifted her wrist to look at her watch.

Where are these people?

"Come on," she snarled.

As the words left her lips, the door to the room clicked open and Casey snapped her head up. Her eyes grew wide as Francis Arlo entered.

"Hello, Casey," he greeted warmly. "How are you?"

Blinking in surprise, she nodded at the young surgeon, offering him an awkward smile. "I'm okay."

Her frown was obvious, but Arlo ignored it as he sat down on a stool beside the bed.

Though it wasn't unusual to encounter the members of her original transplant team here in the clinic, she didn't expect to see Arlo—one half of the surgical team who had saved her life—performing duties that would usually be carried out by nursing or technical staff.

On reflection, however, she realised it wasn't that much of a surprise.

Francis Arlo was undeniably attractive. His Mediterranean ruggedness combined with his soft-spoken, friendly manner made him a popular figure in the transplant clinic among both staff and patients. Casey had to admit to having something of a crush on him. While he was first and foremost a surgeon, Arlo—like his superior, Fedele—often consulted at the clinic so that he could remain up-to-date and connected with the progress of their various patients.

Turning his attention to the recalcitrant machine, Arlo began pressing buttons on its control pad.

"The girls seem to be having all sorts of problems with this unit today," Arlo said.

"Apparently," Casey replied bashfully, reflexively lifting a hand up underneath the sheet to cover her breasts. "I ahhh, had to take matters into my own hands."

She gestured with her eyes at the cable on the floor. Arlo grinned knowingly and picked it up, plugging its end back into the socket. Powering it up, he waited for a moment then turned towards Casey.

Seemingly unaware of her embarrassment, Arlo leaned in and gently drew down the sheet so that he could examine the cables. In the process, he inadvertently brushed his forearm over her breast.

She shivered and blushed.

Oh God, please hurry up!

"Sorry," he apologized, examining the cables underneath her breast. "I better take a look at the cables. These machines never do what you want them to do."

"It's all right," she replied.

Turning to a trolley beside him, Arlo found a box of adhesive ECG pads.

"You're seeing Fedele today, I take it?" he inquired, inspecting each of the cables in turn.

Casey nodded. "This afternoon at three. Just gathering the usual data for him to pore over."

"Oh that'll be *fun*," he commented with a knowing smile. "I take it you've been running to and fro here."

"Oh, sure. It's been a real party," Casey retorted dryly. "It seems like this entire bloody hospital is filled with people who are in desperate need of a personality transplant."

Arlo chuckled pleasantly. "This place tends to breed eccentric personalities,

I'll grant you. But, you appreciate the importance of all the tests."

Casey clicked her tongue. "As you say…"

"He does like his data," Arlo finished for her. He raised an eyebrow and both of them laughed. Casey noticed that his mischievous smile had broadened.

"You wouldn't be taking the mickey out of him, would you?" she remarked. "You're skating on thin ice there."

"Never," Arlo retorted jokingly. "He's my mentor and inspiration. I couldn't *possibly*."

Casey giggled at his mocking tone, appreciating that it helped to put her at ease.

"You're doing well?" he asked, changing the topic.

"I am," Casey said. "I could do without all of this attention. It's no fun feeling like Fedele's personal voodoo doll. But, I'll survive. I guess."

Casey was surprised when Arlo's eyes glinted with sympathy.

"I can appreciate how disruptive it must be. It won't always be like this though."

"Here's hoping."

Arlo took the last of the cables, the one attached to her shoulder, and examined the alligator clip attached to the adhesive pad.

"Looks like we've got a faulty clip," he said, swivelling on his stool and retrieving a replacement from the wall cupboard. "Luckily, it's easy to fix."

He swapped out the removable clip from the cable, then replaced the dot before reattaching the cable. Glancing at the ECG display, he hissed triumphantly as the missing wave form finally appeared on screen.

"Ahhh," he mused. "Okay, I'm going to ask you to take a deep—"

Before he could finish his sentence, Casey filled her lungs with air and held it. Arlo grinned and keyed a series of buttons on the ECG machine. Casey watched the screen, waiting for a small 'complete' icon to appear. She didn't have to wait long. A printout began to emerge from a desktop unit nearby.

"All done," Arlo said. "You can get—"

Casey didn't wait for him to finish. She sat up and began peeling the sticky pads from her chest as quickly as she could.

Arlo retrieved the printouts and placed them into a clear plastic folder. By the time he turned back to Casey, she was fully dressed.

"I've emailed these over to Fedele," he said. "But hang on to these just in case."

"Thank you." Casey took the folder.

"It was good to see you, Casey," he said warmly. "Give my best to the boss, won't you."

She nodded. "It was good to see you too, Arlo."

Arlo's eyes narrowed slightly, but he maintained his smile. "How many times have I told you? It's Francis."

"Right," Casey blushed. "Francis."

Flipping him a jaunty salute, Casey turned and left the examination room.

The consulting suite was a world away from the cold and clinical confines of the hospital. Though it was a modern and minimalist environment, there was a surprising sense of warmth. Casey sat on an L-shaped, cream leather sofa centred in the expansive suite, looking out through a floor-to-ceiling window that took in a view of Melbourne's leafy eastern suburbs and the skyscrapers of the city itself. Though there were a couple of art pieces on the pale, wood-panelled walls on either side of her, the scenery beyond the glass was artwork in itself.

Her hospital experience had faded, becoming just another one of her bad memories.

They weren't even bad memories really. Just a trio of awkward experiences she would relegate to the periphery for another month until, inevitably, she would have to drag herself back to do it all over again.

For now, she let go of the tension that had gathered in her and relaxed. She could do so because of the environs she found herself in now.

This was the office of her chief surgeon, Simeera Fedele, one of the most celebrated heart transplant specialists in Melbourne, if not the entire country. His reputation as a leader in the field of transplant surgery was renowned worldwide and his expertise was routinely sought from around the globe.

Of all the clinicians she had consulted with or who had some hand in her care, Fedele had been with her since the beginning, not only as her chief clinician but also as a type of mentor and confidant.

The charismatic surgeon was especially known for forging close professional relationships with his patients. He did not see them as just another case file. Each of them were important and valuable individuals and Casey had to admit that she held a grudging respect for him.

It was hard for her to see him as just another intrusive member of the medical profession wanting to pick her apart and examine every corner of her body. Fedele's interest in her seemed purely centred on her total well-being: mental as well as physical and, unlike everyone else, it did not focus solely on the heart she carried.

Not to mention that his taste in interior design was impeccable.

Twisting in her seat, Casey regarded the shelving behind the desk, noting a considerable collection of books: medical texts mainly, along with a smattering of other academic titles. There were also a number of photographs featuring Simeera Fedele posing with other esteemed scientists and medical colleagues, some of whom Casey was familiar with through her own experience. There were a couple of pictures featuring prominent community figures, in particular refugee and human rights advocates.

Fedele was a noted humanitarian who had worked for a number of causes. There were high-level state and federal politicians in the photos, including the Federal Minister for Immigration and even the Australian Prime Minister.

Simeera Fedele was also known as a shrewd political operator, particularly when it came to lobbying on behalf of his medical and humanitarian causes. Casey also noted a couple of medals housed in custom frames. Community medals she assumed, although one of them appeared to feature the Rising Sun motif that was synonymous with Australia's armed forces.

Soft music was piped into the room from expensive speakers embedded in the ceiling. A mid-century modern desk sat facing the sofa. Crisp white and lacking any decorative flourishes, the piece appeared to have been handcrafted. Casey guessed it would have cost a fortune.

Fedele's receptionist had seen Casey through into his office and had ensured that she was comfortable. A cup of herbal tea had been brought to her and sat on a glass-topped table just in front of her. Aromatic wisps of steam curled up into the air from the liquid. She leaned forward and lifted the cup, cradling it in her hands.

On the table was a single photo frame housing a somewhat incongruous image for this kind of ultramodern office. The black and white photograph depicted two soldiers, adorned in heavy field gear, embracing one another in the desert with wide smiles across their dusty visages. Casey had seen the photograph before and it had intrigued her. Leaning forward, she reached out and drew the frame closer to her, squinting as she inspected the name patches on each soldier's breast pocket. The soldier on the left was J. Sonmez. The solider on the right: S. Fedele.

Her Simeera Fedele.

A decorated soldier as well, she mused absently, shifting the photograph back to its original position.

Leaning back in the sofa, Casey twisted and looked out at the panorama before her. She inhaled calmly, filling her lungs. The last vestiges of tension came out with that expulsion of air and she smiled inwardly. She sipped from the cup, appreciating the expensive herbal tea.

Behind Casey, the door to the office clicked and opened and she stood at the sound to see a tall figure enter. He smiled upon seeing Casey.

Simeera Fedele stood nearly six feet three inches tall, with flawless olive skin and a dark, ruggedly handsome face, the most prominent feature of which was piercing blue eyes. His head was shaved completely bald which only added to his intensity. He wore an expensive shirt over his muscular frame. The sleeves were rolled up and the neck was open. A pair of slim charcoal trousers finished the ensemble. He was holding a thick bundle of mail in one hand. He appeared relaxed, as though nothing ever bothered him.

He held up the bundle of mail fleetingly, revealing an elaborate logo on the envelope that was facing towards Casey: a crimson bird's wing, edged with gold, that swept around in a circle to form an *e*. It caught her eye and she lingered on it for a moment.

"It'll take me until the middle of next year to wade through all of this," he said as he set the bundle down on the edge of his desk. "My mail seems destined to consume more of my time than my patients."

He approached Casey and offered his large hand to her, which she took. His grip was firm, confident, and she returned it in kind. Fedele smiled again. When he spoke, his voice was smooth and accented; hints of his Parsi background melded with his British upbringing.

"How are you, Casey?" he greeted warmly. "You look well."

Casey nodded as Fedele gestured towards the sofa. "I am, thank you," she replied simply, if a little nervously.

Fedele strode to his desk and gathered up a thick folder from the surface. He put it under his arm while he rolled his desk chair around to position it opposite Casey.

He sat down and opened the folder, lifting the first sheet of paper from inside.

"I've had a chance to review all of your test results and I am pleased to say that the picture looks very good."

Fedele lifted a finger to his mouth and touched the end of it to his tongue then turned over another sheet.

"MRI showed normal heart size, good ventricular function and pulmonary flow. Your ECG shows a remarkable sinus rhythm and an almost perfect set of complexes—comparable to that of an athlete, in fact."

Casey nodded, then hesitated as Fedele's expression seemed to harden, so subtly that she almost missed it. She knew what was coming, even before he opened his mouth to speak.

"Your mother…called me this past week," he began cautiously, wringing his hands together as he leaned forward.

Casey's hackles bristled and she dug her fingers into the leather arm of the sofa. *Fucking hell*, she fumed silently.

"She is concerned that you're continuing to use."

"I'm not," Casey snapped; the lie sounded hollow, even to her.

Fedele's piercing eyes drilled into her; the emotion projecting from them was a mixture of concern and disappointment.

"Your blood work tells a different story."

His words hung in the air. Casey shifted uncomfortably, her anger and embarrassment fluctuating wildly. Her gaze faltered and she looked down at her lap.

"Levels of tetrahydrocannabinol detected in sufficient quantities to indicate recent usage of cannabis," Fedele read from the report in front of him. His voice was flat and cold enough that it chilled Casey. More than any other time today, she felt exposed, naked, laid bare.

He set the report down and reclined in his chair, steepling his fingers in front of his mouth thoughtfully.

"I don't understand, Casey," Fedele said, lowering his hands, palms out on either side. "You are recovering from a significant scare to your new heart, a diffuse histological response indicating an acute rejection of the organ. That was barely six months ago. Now, you've remained compliant with your medication regimen. You've achieved effective immunosuppression that has prevented any sign of a recurrence. It is clear that you're exercising and committing yourself to a balanced diet. Yet, you continue to use cannabis in sufficient quantities that they are detectable in your drug screen."

Fedele leaned forward, resting his elbows on his knees. Casey retreated further into the sofa, unable to meet his eyes.

"Casey," he began. "You're an intelligent young woman. I know you're aware of the highly dangerous effects using marijuana can have on the heart, especially a transplanted heart."

"Cannabis interferes with the function of immunosuppression therapy and greatly increases the risk of fungal infection from spores carried within the marijuana," Casey's voice was monotone as she recalled information that she had committed to memory.

Fedele's eyes widened in question and he held his hands out, palms open.

"So, what is it? *Why* is it? Ever since I've known you, you have never appeared this troubled."

Casey began fidgeting. Fedele sensed the defensiveness in her posture; the subtle hints that there was something, some piece of information she was holding close. Information that she was unable, or unwilling, to reveal.

"What?" he repeated once more, hoping that she would respond. Casey gulped, looked down at her hands.

The door to the office quietly snicked open and Fedele's receptionist stepped into the room.

Fedele looked away from Casey and up at her. "What is it, Stephanie?"

"I'm sorry, but I have Elyria Medical Services on line two. They say it's urgent but I can stall them if you like."

Fedele's lips tightened as he considered the information. He nodded quickly. "Tell them to wait."

Stephanie nodded and retreated from the room.

Finally, Fedele relaxed back in his chair and closed the folder in front of him.

"Okay," he said softly. "Look. I am going to tweak your tacrolimus prescription and your steroid, just as a temporary measure to get you across this hump. But..."

Fedele's voice dropped away as he thought about his next sentence. "You *have* to stop using, Casey. It is imperative. If you begin to show signs of rejection again, I am certain that we will not be able to arrest the damage the next time." He paused once more, allowing the import of his words to reach her. "And if we can't stop the damage to your heart and you find yourself back on transplant list, your drug use will be looked upon very poorly. In fact, I cannot guarantee that you will even qualify."

Casey dropped her head once more. She nodded, giving him the clear impression that she had at least heard his words.

Fedele reassembled the folder and stood. He returned it to his desk then stopped and turned at the door to his office.

He saw that Casey hadn't moved from the sofa. He waited quietly until she was ready.

Finally, Casey stood, brushed her dress and slung her handbag over her shoulder. Making her way over to the door, she stopped before Fedele and looked up at him.

She hesitated, as though she was about to speak. Fedele's eyes narrowed in expectation, then hope, but at the final moment Casey faltered and she retreated from the office.

"I'd like to see you again in a week," Fedele called after her. "I'll send you the appointment time."

Casey glanced back and nodded as she hurried from view.

Fedele closed the door and turned back towards his desk where he touched his hand to Casey's medical file.

He shook his head slowly as he moved his fingers from the folder to the bundle of mail. He touched the embossed crimson logo, the winged *e*. Underneath it were the words Elyria Medical Services.

He scowled.

From his perspective, Casey Schillinge was his most successful recipient. Her initial recovery had set new benchmarks and she had been a dedicated, willing participant in her own journey.

This recent turn of events, however, underpinned a troubling change in the young woman. Something that was totally out of character for her.

And he was damned if he knew what it was.

CHAPTER 4

Removing her leather flats, Casey looked out across the beach towards the cool waters of Port Phillip Bay then stepped down onto the sand. The warm granules shifted between her toes and she glanced up at the late afternoon sun that shone down on Mentone beach.

A long pier in front of her was occupied by a smattering of elderly fishermen, casting their lines out into the languid ocean. None of them were really concentrating much on their angling as much as they were on their raucous conversation. There was a wide variety of people on the beach who strolled either leisurely or with purpose: hand-holding couples, dog walkers, joggers. The sunny afternoon had brought out a few families as well and Casey observed a few of them either playing cricket on the sand or gathered on picnic rugs enjoying an early take-away dinner. The aroma of KFC chicken wafted in her direction and her stomach responded with an envious growl.

Of all the outdoor places, this was one of the few that didn't cause Casey the kind of panic that her agoraphobia had gifted her. It was quite the opposite. Here, she felt a rare peace, a sense of safety and comfort that was unlike anything she felt anywhere else.

She stepped across the powdery sand, approaching the flat sea that lapped gently at the beach. Stopping just before the water's edge, she found a relatively dry, compact area of beachfront and sat down.

Shielding her eyes, Casey looked across the bay again, then lowered her head to the tops of her knees, holding her legs in place with her arms. She exhaled noisily between her clenched teeth.

Thank God that's done.

Her hand dropped to her side and she pushed it into the pocket of her shorts. She felt the sharp edge of a piece of cardboard there.

Scowling, Casey pinched the edge of the card and extracted it, lifting it up before her. Blocking the sun from her eyes, she read the familiar print on the card.

Geddie Kirkwood - Clinical Psychologist.

She flipped the appointment card into the palm of her hand and crushed it angrily. She then flung it as far away from her as she could. It landed several feet away on the sand just before the water's edge.

A cursory check of her watch reminded her that she had to be back at the apartment soon. Her father was likely there already, taking over her kitchen and revelling in his "newfound love of culinary artistry," as he called it.

Casey smiled wistfully and lifted her head towards the descending sun. Her father was retired now, though he kept himself busy with various pursuits that included running errands like grocery shopping for Casey, especially on days like today when she had been rushing to her many appointments.

Well, most of them.

The discarded appointment card on the sand in front of her tumbled away on a gust of wind that kicked up, pushing it closer to the water.

Good riddance, Casey thought acidly.

The sun's ellipse was hovering closer to the horizon now and, as it finally touched the edge of the sea, Casey slowly rose to her feet and collected her shoes and bag from the sand.

Time to go play nice with Dad.

As SHE HAD predicted, upon opening the warehouse door, Casey was greeted to rich aromas that wafted from her kitchen courtesy of the tall, middle-aged man who hovered over a wok on the stove while referring to an open recipe book that lay on the bench nearby.

Peter Schillinge turned as Casey stepped in and he smiled broadly at his daughter.

"G'day," he greeted cheerily. "You're just in time. Do you want to set the table?"

Casey grinned wearily as she set down her bag and keys and placed a kiss on his cheek.

"Happy birthday, sweetheart," Peter said lovingly as he leaned into his daughter's kiss.

"Thanks, Dad."

She cast a cursory glance at the wok on the stove and salivated at the sight of numerous plump chicken pieces sizzling away there.

"That smells amazing," she complimented eagerly, inspecting the luxurious chicken concoction he was nurturing. She drew in the fragrant aromas: a fusion of lemon, coriander, pepper and something else she couldn't quite put her finger on.

"What on Earth have you got going on in there? Cinnamon?" Casey asked as she set about retrieving dinner plates and cutlery, setting them on the centre bench.

"You bet," Peter confirmed as he chugged a mouthful from a nearby beer bottle. "And not that grocery store garbage either. This is real Kerala cinnamon that I picked up from the market just this weekend. Costs a small fortune."

Casey smiled as her father worked the ingredients around the wok with something of a theatrical flourish. "I reckon I have just about perfected this baby. I've been working on it for weeks but I wasn't satisfied with the results I was getting until I got this proper cinnamon. I'll just finish it off with my own, homegrown bok choy as an accompaniment and I'll be done. People'd pay big money for this in a restaurant."

"Whatever, Dad," Casey sneered as she fetched a beer from the fridge and used the nearby bottle opener to flick the lid off.

Peter's eyes flicked from the beer bottle in her hand to her face and then away quickly. He hoped she hadn't seen that momentary flash of concern in his expression. But she had.

"Don't even," Casey snapped, but only half-seriously. "After the day I've had, I've well and truly earned this."

Peter grasped his bottle and held it out towards hers in a peace-offering gesture, to which Casey offered hers and clinked it against his.

"Cheers," she said.

"I heard the Burnley tunnel was a nightmare," Peter offered, changing the subject as best he could. "Truck breakdown?"

Casey nodded, lifting herself up so that she was sitting in the bench adjacent to him.

"It wasn't so bad. I came through on the tail end of it so I wasn't delayed very much at all. I still felt like losing my shit though."

Peter chuckled as he concentrated on the wok while glancing at his daughter. He noticed a few telltale granules of sand on her feet.

"Stopped by the beach, huh?" he ventured happily.

Casey nodded and tilted her head. "It was quiet, just nice. Old Barney and Claude were at it again, dissecting the footy instead of catching fish. I really don't think they've ever caught anything off that jetty."

"It's nice that you can still go there, you know, without feeling overwhelmed by the outdoors."

Peter caught his daughter's gaze for a long moment and he held it, concerned that he might have overstepped. He knew that Casey was acutely embarrassed by her agoraphobia. "Mentone has always been a friend to me," she smiled.

Peter flashed a wistful smile of his own. "I remember when you were a little tacker, we could never get you or your brother off that beach, especially when your grandfather was around."

Turning to the stove, Peter began serving up his culinary creation.

"We were difficult to keep a leash on," Casey responded lyrically. "Pa was as bad as we were. He was the one who encouraged us to keep playing cricket until well after sunset when we could hardly see. God, that seems like such a long time ago."

Peter frowned then, pausing with a full plate in his hand.

"What do you mean, a long time ago? You're only twenty-six now."

"It's not the years though, Dad," Casey said laconically, tapping the centre of her chest with a balled fist. "It's the mileage."

THEY SAT TOGETHER at the counter laughing and chatting as they ate their meal, which was indeed a culinary triumph. They shared a bottle of Riesling that complemented the dish perfectly, a treat that Peter brought with him each week.

Jazz music, Peter's favourite, played on the stereo system. The last remnants of stress from the day had been neutralised by the time Casey took her last mouthful and she sat back on her stool, nodding approvingly.

"That was a master stroke, Dad," she declared. "Very well done."

Peter nodded as he finished and gathered their plates together. "Not bad for a birthday meal?"

"Not at all," Casey agreed, raising her glass.

"So, twenty-six, eh? Three full years since the change-over," Peter remarked, as he finished loading the plates into the dishwasher. "How does it feel?"

Casey shrugged then grinned at his reference to the transplant.

"Like it's twenty-six? I don't know. How am I supposed to feel?"

Peter considered her question for a moment and then shrugged.

"I dunno. Like any twenty-six-year-old I suppose. I've forgotten what it was like being twenty-six. I think I read somewhere that it is the first year that you can legitimately call yourself an adult. Anything before that doesn't count."

"Gee thanks, Dad. *I think*," Casey chuckled. "So I guess that means it's all downhill from here."

"Not at all. I haven't behaved like an adult for thirty years and I don't intend to start now."

"Retirement seems to agree with you," Casey observed.

"Now that I've got you kids off my hands and have commandeered the house the way I've always wanted to, I'm enjoying something of a renaissance. Edie's fears about me becoming a whinging old fart have been turned on their head, well and truly."

The mention of her mother's name caused Casey's smile to fade and she nervously sipped from her glass to conceal herself from her father.

Peter, pretending he hadn't noticed the sudden change his daughter's disposition, stood and ferried the dinner plates and cutlery to the dishwasher.

"How is she?" Casey asked, realising now that she couldn't avoid the proverbial elephant in the room.

Peter thought about his answer for a long moment.

"She's good," he answered curtly. "Still doing legal aid stuff for Slattery and Gerard. Their immigration work seems to be kicking along quite a bit. I swear, it's like she's keeping longer hours than I did when I was working."

Casey didn't offer anything more and Peter went on stacking the dishes. Eventually he returned to the bench and sat down across from Casey. His expression was tinged with concern. "She asked after you."

Casey set down her wine glass, agitated, and circled the rim with her finger.

"Did she." She responded flatly to her father's white lie. Peter gulped, knowing that his daughter had caught him out. He was a terrible fibber.

"Look, love. She cares about—"

"Don't, Dad," she growled warningly.

Casey flashed an icy glare at her father which stopped him in mid sentence. "I know what Mum has been up to. Who she's been speaking to. Fedele told me today that she had been in touch with him."

Peter held himself, taking a sip from his own glass, as he thought about what he was going to say next.

"She just worries about you, Casey," he began. "I worry about you. You can't keep abusing your body the way you do, especially after that scare. You can't expect us to stay silent."

Both Casey and Peter were surprised by the sudden vigour of his observation and both of them blinked in the middle of the silence that followed.

"You don't go anywhere or see anyone," he continued, emboldened. "You never come to the house; there's three months worth of mail piling up there, including potential job offers. Instead you hole yourself up here for weeks at a time, working ridiculous hours for God-knows-who. I mean, when was the last time you had any sort of time off?"

Casey clutched her wine glass and glared at her father, unable to respond. Peter sat back, withdrawing from a potential confrontation.

"Your mum just wants you to be okay," he continued, adopting a more gentle tone.

"Well then, why doesn't *Edie* tell me that herself?" Casey challenged, her facade cracking.

"Because she—" Peter began.

"Because she doesn't approve of my life," Casey pressed, answering her own question. "She doesn't approve of where I choose to live or the work I choose to do or the people I choose to associate with. She would rather I be back at home, in my sickbed where she can be in control. She's hasn't come to grips with the fact that I have carved out a life for myself, that I can take care of myself now and I don't need her to care for me 24/7!"

Peter sat silent across from Casey, digesting her defence, but unsure of what to say next. He knew that she was at least partly right about her mother.

Sensing her father's awkwardness, Casey softened her expression. "Look, I'm good, Dad. *Really* good," she said. "I've just finished a big contract and I'm going to take some proper time off."

"A legitimate contract?" Peter probed, cocking one brow for effect.

Casey levelled her own brow into a frown. "Yes, Dad," she retorted. "A *very* legitimate contract."

"It's just that…Prishna Argawaal has been sniffing around again," Peter said solemnly. "She thinks you've been involved in some illegal stuff."

Casey paused in the middle of lifting her glass and studied her father.

On more than one occasion, Casey's reputation on both sides of the cyber fence had aroused suspicion within the ranks of the Victoria Police—despite the fact she was one of their most valuable assets in an ongoing war against cyber-crime.

The mention of Argawaal's name was enough for her to grind her teeth.

"She would say that. Look, Prishna's just shooting blindly because she's got a problem finding a *real* bad guy."

"So…you're not involved in anything untoward then?" Peter ventured.

Casey narrowed her eyes. "Dad. How many times do I have to reassure you? I don't do clandestine anymore. I gave that up. You're starting to sound like Mum."

Peter smiled and shook his head. "All right, all right. I'll let it go. But if Prishna is going to keep bugging us, you know?"

Casey nodded confidently. "I'll deal with Prishna. I've given the Cyber-Crime Unit more assistance than just about any other consultant out there. I think I've proven myself more than enough with them."

Though his doubt lingered, Peter chose to let it go. Reaching for the wine bottle in the middle of the counter, he poured himself another glass.

"How has your sleep been?" he asked.

Casey blinked at the sudden change in subject.

"It's okay," she stammered. "It'll be better now that I've finished this job."

Her response was unconvincing. She saw his concern and she looked away. There was no doubting how well Peter knew his daughter.

He reached into his pocket, fishing around until he clasped a pair of keys. He lay them down on the counter and slid them towards Casey.

"Take these. Drive yourself up to Hambledown and hide out at the beach house for a couple of weeks. Go see your grandparents. Get some fresh air into your lungs again."

Casey regarded the keys in front of her and managed a weary smile at her father.

She got up from the bench, rounded it and planted a tender kiss on her father's forehead.

"Thanks, Dad. I am okay. I *will* be okay."

He nodded, even though there was a clear sense of doubt etched into his features.

Casey turned to one of the kitchen drawers behind him, opened it and took out a familiar red box containing a deck of *UNO* cards.

She tossed it to her father, who quickly caught it.

"Best of ten?" she challenged, taking up her seat once more.

Peter chuckled at the sight of the cards and he took the deck out as Casey sat down in front of him and rubbed her hands together eagerly.

"Best of ten," he echoed as he began shuffling. "But we'll play for real this time around. *Moneybags.*"

CHAPTER 5

In the depths of night, Casey ran at a steady pace on her treadmill. Her eyes were closed in concentration as she exercised her arms and legs, tuning her mind to her muscles while she balanced her body in full stride. She listened to her breathing, regulating her respirations in time with her strides so each intake of air filled her lungs and emptied out in a satisfying, effortless rhythm.

The heart pumped in synergy with the rest of her body, receiving blood from her extremities, pushing it on to her lungs, where it was re-oxygenated before returning to the foreign cardiac tissue. The heart beat, ejecting her blood back out and into her body once more; the perpetual cycle that sustained Casey.

She was in tune with her body. Yet, she felt incomplete. An unnerving darkness clung to her from within.

She fought to ignore it. But, no matter how hard she tried, the beating of the heart pounded in her ears, carrying with it a taunt that demanded her attention. It was as though nothing could compete with the sound of the foreign organ beating inside her, and it angered her. Without realising it, Casey had dramatically increased the intensity of her exercise. She ran harder and faster. The machine responded to her effort. The longer she ran, the more intense her anger became.

Already, Casey was regretting her decision to take a self-imposed vacation. It had only been a week and she hated not having anything to do, no work to keep her mind engaged. A restless mind like Casey's was a dangerous thing.

She'd looked for any activity she could find. She'd started out by moving all of her furniture and stripping the timber floors of her apartment, re-lacquering them and moving temporarily downstairs into the garage while she waited for them to dry. After moving everything back in, Casey turned her attention to her computer hardware.

With the precision of an army sniper, she stripped the machine down to its component parts then rebuilt it. She rewrote the customised operating system—her own design—and loaded it, spending hours testing and retesting it, losing herself in the code.

She cooked. She cleaned. She rearranged. She watched old movies she had seen a dozen times before. She ran on the treadmill. But there were only so many times she could repeat these tasks.

Though Casey considered it, she hadn't taken up her father's offer of the beach house. The thought of leaving the protective cocoon of her apartment was too much. Her fear of driving, of being on the open road in the wide open spaces beyond Melbourne's urban sprawl gnawed at her. Her agoraphobia had gotten the better of her before she'd even challenged it.

All the while her thoughts played upon her. Her fears. The most worrying of them was the apparent silence from her clientele.

She had put it out there, via her usual lines of communication, that she wouldn't be available to take on any new work for a month or so. Casey didn't expect that they would take her at her word. They hadn't in the past. When she had gone off the grid, she would still find herself bombarded with requests for her services. This time, her inbox remained starkly empty. Her smartphone remained quiet. The message boards she frequented were strangely silent. It worried her. Casey had begun to think that her last job had put off a lot of her regulars. The intensity of it, the nature of it, the hours she'd had to devote to it at the expense of additional work was now, seemingly, returning to bite her on the arse.

The worry fed her anxiety and her anger and all she could do was to focus that into her exercise. Casey wasn't just jogging now. She was running at a speed that verged on sprinting. She was running on automatic. Then, she realised what she was doing and it shocked her. Shaking herself back into the present, Casey fought to refocus on her activity. She immediately dialled down the intensity on the treadmill controls, wincing as her muscles ached in protest. Slowly but surely, she returned to a jog, then a walk, breathing long and hard. Grabbing the handlebar of the treadmill, Casey lowered her head as sweat dripped from her brow. Finally she stopped, exhausted and spent.

Casey felt the need to close her eyes and rest. As she stood on the now stationary treadmill, her head resting on her arms, the temptation to give into that need became increasingly pronounced. She could feel herself drifting on the very edge of sleep. But something made her flinch and she whipped her body into an upright position, blinking the sleep from her eyes.

"No," she muttered through quickened breaths and a surge of adrenaline.

She could not submit to sleep. Not now. Not here.

The chronograph on the treadmill's display read: 1:11AM.

Casey's lips creased into a smile.

Sixty-five hours, she computed. *Not bad.*

There was a world record for the longest period without sleep. Casey had looked it up. Attributed to an eighteen-year-old named Randy Gardner in 1965, he set the record by going eleven days: 264.4 hours. Though he had done it without the aid of stimulants of any kind.

Casey's smile faded as she recalled that last nugget of information. Casey had not managed even half that. The furthest she had been able to stretch herself was 118 hours but she'd had to rely on numerous drugs to keep herself awake and functional.

Stepping from the treadmill she peeled off her top, sighing as the cool air caressed her skin. Casey glanced across at the Modigliani print on the wall. The eyes of Jeanne Hebuterne studied her thoughtfully, questioningly.

And Casey responded.

"What to do," she ventured. It was less a question as it was a prompt to something that was already beginning to foment.

Daubing her face with a towel, she stripped naked then padded barefoot across the apartment to her work table.

Opening her leather smartphone case, she thumbed through a collection of business cards until she found the one she was looking for and plucked it out.

Scrawled in pen on the card was a curious but familiar name. Casey quickly keyed in the number then hit dial. It rang several times before diverting to an operator voicemail. She hissed between her teeth.

"Typical," Casey scowled, ending the call. She set the phone beside the card. She glanced sideways once more at Jeanne Hebuterne's portrait.

"Guess I'm just gonna have to go see him," she scowled. Casey tapped the card with her finger.

She whispered the name scrawled there into the darkness of the apartment, before turning toward the bathroom.

"Sasquatch."

The Blue Heeler Bar stood on a dark side street, several blocks back from the beachfront. The street was populated by a mixture of tall residential and commercial buildings on both sides. In the darkness, they appeared to close in on the street itself, creating a sense of protective encapsulation around Casey as she walked cautiously towards the old Victorian building. Architecturally, the

Blue Heeler Bar seemed more suited to a Parisian laneway than a Melbourne backstreet, with its tall arches, wrought iron balconies and outdoor eating areas that were nestled under broad canvas shelters. It was a much-loved bar that drew in a vast and eclectic clientele and catered well to them.

Thumping folk-rock music pumped out from inside the stained glass windows as she approached, loud enough that it almost deterred Casey from going inside. The popularity of the establishment as a live music venue was renowned and it was clear that renown had drawn a significant crowd tonight.

Though the Valium she had taken prior to leaving the apartment had taken a significant edge off her anxiety, the marijuana countered it with a weird surge of adrenaline. Her breath was quick. Her senses were acutely attuned. The heart beat fast. Yet, she remained singleminded in her purpose, so she could focus effectively and ignore the crowds inside. She needed only to complete her task and then get the hell out of there and back to her solitude.

Approaching from under the orange glow of a street lamp, a security guard on the door looked in her direction and recognised her almost immediately. He offered her a courteous nod and gestured with a subtle flip of his thumb towards a side entrance, down an even darker laneway that flanked the pub. Casey headed in that direction while the guard spoke into his head microphone.

One of the advantages of being a regular at this establishment was that it afforded Casey some measure of preferential treatment.

They knew why she was here.

Entering through the side door, Casey was confronted by a robust crowd: patrons mingling around circular tables adjacent to the bar or listening to the five-piece band on the corner stage to her right.

Through her marijuana-induced fog, the din threatened to overload her senses.

The noise of conversation, the clinking of glasses, the raucous music from the bandstand. She noticed the presence of the band and their instruments: acoustic guitars, a fiddle, a shining chrome banjo that reflected glitters of light back into the room, the caramel vocals from a pretty, young woman at the microphone. All of it thickened the atmosphere and assailed Casey's senses all at once. Though she struggled to contain the bubbling cauldron of panic, for the briefest of moments she had an incongruous image of a crowd of flamingos chattering away.

The smell of various brands of deodorant, aftershave and perfume mixed with sweat from scantily-clad bodies hit Casey's nostrils and she couldn't decide if the combined aromas repulsed her or aroused her. Her skin bristled as she pushed her way through the throng. She fought the adrenaline surge while fingers of panic crept up her spine. Casey squeezed her eyes shut until she reached the bar. Feeling for the timber surface and grabbing it, she opened them again.

In the darkness of the pub, the garishness of the lights pointed at the house band, and the soft downlights of the bar, she finally spotted the individual descending from a staircase. Relief flooded through her as she took a breath and pushed her way across the room.

Patrons parted as a bear of a man dressed in a dark shirt, dark pants, and steel-capped boots stepped off the bottom stair and approached. Standing over six feet four inches tall, his intimidating presence commanded respect, even reverence. Sporting huge, toned, tattooed arms that were anchored to equally massive shoulders, he strode confidently through the throng, his stone-cold eyes focused forward. His jaw was squared off by a thick, sand-coloured goatee. His expression was hard, giving no sense of his state of mind or his personality.

That was until Casey emerged from the crowd and stopped before him. With a suddenness that caught a few nearby revellers who were watching him, the man's poker face melted into a warm, almost beatific smile. With a glint of light flashing in his eyes, he held his arms out as Casey embraced him. She planted a kiss on his cheek.

"How are you?" she shouted above the crowd.

Drawing back, Casey looked up as his half-serious frown was quickly replaced with a cheeky grin. He gestured with a nod to the stairs behind him.

"Good. Let's get out of here," he suggested in a heavy Scottish accent.

He shepherded Casey towards the stairs and together they disappeared.

The rooftop garden was significantly less raucous, though a large group of patrons was scattered across the various lounge areas and bars. At least here, Casey could hear herself think.

The smell of pizza wafted across from an ornate stone oven being tended to by a pair of enthusiastic kitchen staff who were entertaining the group seated around it. Casey felt her stomach rumble. She realised she hadn't eaten anything for at least a day.

Her companion gestured towards a small gazebo situated in a quiet corner, away from the main entertaining area that was occupied by a pair of wrought iron chairs and a matching table. As they passed the open bar, Sasquatch gestured with two fingers towards the girl serving there. She nodded, fetching two beers from a refrigerator.

Casey and Sasquatch settled into their seats and nodded as the server set the bottles down on the table along with a bowl of mixed nuts. Casey dove her hand into the bowl and tossed a handful into her mouth.

The photo ID card he wore clipped to the lapel of his polo shirt identified him as Scott, without any mention of the nickname that Casey used.

It was true that there were only a handful of people who could get away with calling Scott Taylor by that nickname. In the six or seven years that she had known him, Casey had never given any consideration to the consequences that might befall someone who wasn't welcome to refer to him by that honorarium because the nickname itself felt so natural to her.

Settled away from the throng, Casey's panic was quickly dissipating. In the presence of a man she could call a genuine friend, she felt at ease.

"So," Scott began, taking a long swig from his bottle. "What brings a crazy person like you to a place like this?"

Casey chuckled. Before she could speak, she caught his questioning frown.

"Aren't you supposed to be off the grid?" he probed.

Casey nodded slowly, as she swallowed a generous lug of beer.

"Allegedly. That is the rumour doing the rounds presently."

"I've heard those rumours," Scott replied. "I've been relaying that to various interested parties who've been making inquiries of late."

Casey's eyes flicked up into Sasquatch's own and he could see the worry reflected at him.

"Really?" she ventured hopefully. "Inquiries?"

Thoughts of the silence from her email account, her cell phone and the message boards returned.

"Mmm-hmm. I followed your directions and told them they'd have to wait for a while."

Casey slumped back in her seat, the disappointment clear on her face, which only made Scott's frown more pronounced.

"I-I thought that's what you wanted!" he exclaimed. Casey nodded slowly, a bitter smile creasing her lips.

"It is what I wanted," she responded with resignation. "But…"

"But you're having a hard time taking things down a gear," he ventured, confident from reading her body language that he knew what she was thinking.

Casey met his eyes. His perception was impeccable. "Am I that transparent?"

"Well, I knew it from the minute the boys downstairs gave me the heads-up that you were here. But there's no harm in listening to a friend's problems before making a guess."

Laughing softly and bitterly, Casey took a swig from her bottle.

"Scott, it's driving me fucking crazy," she blurted. "It's only been a week and already I'm going looney-tunes. This whole taking a holiday thing is... it's...I can't rest! I'm no good at this. I need to work!"

Her reaction caught Scott off guard, more so for the fact that she had referred to him by his first name than the revelation of her state of mind.

"I thought you were gonna tick off up the coast for a while," he said. "Get yourself out of the city and breathe for a bit. Lord knows you need it."

Casey tried to loosen the tension gathered between her temples.

"You sound like my father," she observed dejectedly.

Scott chuckled and drew his finger through his goatee. "How is Peter?"

Casey shrugged. "He's good. *Fatherly* as per usual. Not that I need any more of that."

Scott pursed his lips and whistled through them with an exaggerated expression of mock hurt, to which Casey could only laugh at. He considered her dilemma for a long moment.

"Look...what sort of work are you after?" he asked. "Are we talking above board or, perhaps, something a little more spicy? Bearing in mind that I thought you were playing the straight arrow these days."

"I have no idea," Casey ventured, shrugging her shoulders. "*Anything* that will keep me from going nuts. Who's active right now?"

"I'm not gonna lie, a lot of it is strictly black hat work," Scott admitted. "Not the sort of work I would've thought you'd be comfortable with. Most of your tier are pretty well set."

The thought of venturing into illegal territory to secure work right now did not appeal to her. Especially given the question marks that were increasingly being attached to her. Though she could probably handle herself, the assurances she had given to her father niggled at her conscience.

"You're sure there's no one who could use a hand? The Coops? Maynard? Steev? What about Pink? He's always in the shit with his programming and coding."

Scott chuckled and tilted his head, considering his thoughts. "Look, there maybe one or two possibles that could subcontract. Leave it with me. I'll check in with the Bastardos and see if there's something we can get you."

A brief quiet settled over them and Casey noticed that Scott was shifting uncomfortably in his seat.

Scott scratched his cheek, then gestured hesitantly at her chest. "How's—ahh—things there?"

Casey looked down and tousled the fabric of her shirt. When she looked back up at him, she wore a sarcastic expression.

"Are you still trying to cop a look at my tits?" she challenged before laughing at him.

Scott flushed pink and cowered behind his beer bottle. "I'll take that as an 'everything is okay' kinda explanation," he commented.

Casey reached across the table and squeezed his big, meaty hand. "Just get me some work, Sasquatch," she pleaded gently. "I know you've had my back since uni. You're one of a very small group of people that I can count on and I know I come to you a lot but I promise, I'll make it up to you."

A loud rapping on the warehouse door woke Casey from her sleep. She flinched where she lay and screwed her face up at the sound before opening one eye and checking the clock on her bedside. It was the following day. And it was nearly 1PM.

Groaning, she shut her eyes against the bright glare of the sunshine streaming through her window.

A further salvo of loud rapping peppered the door, reverberating in Casey's ears.

"I'm coming!" she called out gruffly, scrambling drunkenly from under the covers. She searched for a T-shirt and shorts to pull on over her naked form.

A third volley of knocking caused Casey to squint incredulously at the door.

"I'm coming! *Jesus*!"

Padding barefoot across the floor, Casey rubbed the sleep from her eyes as she went up to the door and peeked through the peephole.

She recognised the woman standing on the other side.

"Dammit!" she hissed.

Hesitating before the door, she eventually flipped the lock and grabbed the handle. Sliding the rumbling door aside, Casey revealed the woman standing there, one arm leaning against the door frame while her other hand remained raised, ready to knock again.

Dressed in a grey pantsuit, her raven hair pulled into a bun, the woman wore a dripping smile as Casey levelled a glare at her.

"What do you want, Prishna?"

Casey's eyes dropped down to the woman's waist; she saw the gold of the detective's badge glint in the sunlight from the window behind her.

"Nothing special," Detective Sergeant Prishna Argawaal replied. "Just thought I'd drop by and see what you were up to."

"I'm sleeping," Casey shot back, standing against the door, her arms folded.

Prishna took her hand off the door frame and inspected her watch. "At 1PM? Wow, things must be good in your line of work."

Casey rolled her eyes. "Moderately good. But you can't expect me to rely solely on the work you guys send my way."

"Hmm," Prishna's eyes narrowed slightly. "I'll grant you, our budget doesn't stretch far to remunerate you more generously. I see you've been making some influential friends in the corporate sector. They speak highly of your skill set."

Casey stared at Prishna.

Checking up on me again.

"*Others* are delivering similar praise," Prishna continued.

Casey clenched her teeth. She didn't respond.

"I've been working hard too, Casey, and making some friends in interesting places. You'll recall our talks in the past about this mystery hacker called Octagon."

"Cracker," Casey hissed, correcting Prishna. She hated it when people who should know better referred to the common misnomer that was applied to her kind.

Prishna laughed haughtily. "My mistake. I really should know better, shouldn't I. Well, the *cracker*—Octagon—has apparently been active in the underground again."

Casey nodded curtly. "Interesting."

"And we've managed to secure some fragments of the work," Prishna continued. "I've been showing it around and the consensus seems to be that the programming language is rather shall we say…*unique*. No one seems able to interpret it, however your name keeps coming up as someone who might."

"You want me to look at it?" Casey asked.

Prishna shrugged.

"Possibly. There is something curious about it, though. I've been doing a little comparison study of my own."

Here it comes.

"The programming language appears to have many of the characteristics of your own."

Casey retracted her head. A sardonic smile lifted her lips. "Look, Prishna, I'll ask you once more: what do you want?"

"I'm just thinking out loud, I suppose. I like you, Casey, and I know that you've been one of our finest assets. You have helped us solve more cases this year than we have at any other time in Cyber-Crime's history. But…I'm not convinced that you're completely untainted."

Prishna stepped forward into the doorway until she was very close to Casey's face. "I think you and this Octagon have more in common than anyone is willing to admit," she whispered menacingly. "You might have the favour of the Commissioner right now but I'm going to see about changing that. You will slip up and when you do, I will be there. Your parents won't be able to help you." In an action that she knew would antagonise Casey, Prishna reached out with a slender finger and ran it down the centre of Casey's T-shirt, right over the scar that lay underneath.

"You leave my parents alone," Casey snarled, slapping Prishna's hand away.

Prishna smiled as she turned on her heel. "I'll be in touch."

"I mean it, Prishna!" Casey shouted after her, unwilling to step through the doorway. "Leave them alone!"

Prishna was already gone.

Retreating back into the warehouse, Casey closed the door and held onto the handle, frozen where she stood as she tried to process what had just happened.

With a sudden snarl, she banged her fist against the door.

CHAPTER 6

It begins with utter blackness and silence.

A cocoon that envelops everything and reveals nothing.

But it does not last.

A low, rhythmic thump becomes audible, rising in volume. A beating heart. It exudes comfort and security.

Soft white light coalesces, bending and separating, forming distinct shards that pierce the blackness, spreading out across colourless clouds, absorbing light and transmitting hues of blue.

The awareness of herself emerges from the sound of the beating heart. She is comfortable and safe. She allows herself to exist.

Her awareness expands to include her body. She moves her arms and legs. She floats, unrestrained by gravity. She does not know where she is but she is completely free. It is invigorating.

She stretches her arms wide, spreading her fingers as far as she can. She uncurls her legs, extending them out before her; stretches her toes and lets herself go. Soft tendrils of light caress her naked skin, the tips of her fingers, the soles of her feet. She feels a tactile warmth and pleasure that gently tickles her and she laughs silently. Her hair crackles. Her skin prickles.

It is a pleasure unlike anything she has felt before.

Where is she?

It is not water. She can breathe comfortably here. But it is neither air nor space. There is density to her movements as she twists her body around, tumbling and turning gracefully in this cloudscape.

Is she even alive?

Blinking at the cloudscape, she watches as one of those billowing forms shifts, sending out a long, finger-like projection that approaches her, seemingly sentient and aware. It spirals inquisitively around her body.

She extends her hand towards the fluffy blue mass.

A crackle of electricity flickers from her fingertip and dances across the billowing form and it recoils sharply, retreating as though startled.

The colours in the clouds shift abruptly. Black tendrils stream from her finger and quickly slither across the mass, consuming light and colour. She blinks again, this time in alarm. Dark tendrils expand greedily across her field of view, heralding this new malevolent presence.

Hues of yellow and orange seep from the mass where they coalesce and bind themselves to the cloud forms, darkening and transforming into deep and thickening reds.

It is happening.

Her body is grasped by a force unseen. It brings her into an upright position, then she feels herself descending.

The heart beats faster, louder.

Her naked skin twitches and shivers. Biting cold replaces the serene warmth. Clothing coalesces over her body: harsh denim that scratches her skin. A starched cotton singlet that quickly becomes sopping. The wet clothing clings to her cold skin, and looking up, she realises it is raining.

Her bare feet touch a hard surface and she looks down, seeing bitumen all around her. She is standing on a road, a lonely outback road in some desolate wasteland that is unfamiliar. She looks around her, searching for a landmark, something familiar that will identify her surroundings. Another disembodied flash lights up the sky nearby and thunder rumbles through the thickening clouds. In that moment, she sees a road sign—not on the road before her, but in her mind's eye. The lightning reflects off it so brightly, the lettering is too difficult to interpret. Squinting in the fading light, she tries to see.

'Laster…' is all she can make out before darkness swallows the image.

Searching around her, she tries to find the sign as it exists in her immediate environment. But it is nowhere to be seen.

Eruptions of light flash from within the cloud mass above. Rain falls harder, denser. It splashes against her skin and runs sticky and viscous, like honey.

Dread seeps into her.

The thunder rumbles towards her again, carrying with it a deep, guttural moan that vibrates through her. Her breath quickens. For the first time, she is compelled to move.

She turns, stretches her legs, tries to run. But gravity bears down, making movements incredibly heavy.

A flash of light erupts and in the moment of disorientation that follows, she witnesses something: a scene from her mind plays out in front of her.

A lone figure, shrouded in shadow, stands there—an evil presence. Unnaturally tall, masculine but unidentifiable in the dissipating flash.

The low moan gains in volume and pitch. It is filled with torment and pain.

FLASH!

The shrouded figure steps forward and slaps her with an outstretched hand. She crashes heavily to the road, opening wounds in her shoulder and legs. She cries out, but it is a silent cry. She tries to get to her feet but slips on the slick bitumen that streams with the falling rain.

The figure pounces, pinning her body to the road. She feels her hands being lifted above her head in the grip of the stranger who remains shrouded in darkness. Again, she cries out in pain as her hands are shoved against the road.

The figure sits back on its heels. With its free hand, it reaches out and hovers over them both for a moment. Then, balling it into a fist, the figure smashes it down, striking her chest with all the force it can muster.

FLASH!

She screams as pain blossoms through her entire body.

The thunder and the moan meld into what is clearly a female voice. It cries out in terror. Is it her own voice?

The hands disappear into the cavity in her chest. Her fractured mind is curious, despite her terror. She struggles against the grip of the figure. The bitumen tears at her skin as she flails impotently. The hands of the figure squelch about inside her. The moans grow more shrill now. They are wails. They are screams.

The viscous rain turns a deep, ruby red and she tastes the metallic flavour of blood. She lifts her head skywards. The sky is bleeding.

The screams become unbearable and then she realises that it is she who is screaming.

The hand retracts from her chest and hovers above it. The assailant leans forward to show her the contents within. A disembodied cackle rips through the air, swallowing the horrified screams. Rivulets of crimson course down over a masculine jaw.

She is consumed by terror. Drenched in blood, too paralysed to move.

Then, suddenly, she is free.

She is now standing a few feet away from the figure, yet it is still straddling someone underneath.

She looks at her hands, staring at them. She cannot understand. She wants to turn and run but the figure's silent magnetism holds her in thrall. The figure turns its face towards her, but the darkness shrouds its features.

The figure beckons with what is held in its hands.

She leans forward to see.

It is a heart. A beating and bloody heart, crawling with maggots so numerous that she can hear them squelching over the muscular tissue. A black slick oozes from the severed arteries and veins that feed into the disembodied organ and drips over the hands that hold it.

Lightning flashes and in that instant, she becomes aware of the presence beneath him.

That presence is moving on the ground between her and the figure, struggling to free itself—as she had struggled just moments before.

She tilts her head, confused.

Her eyes drift down.

A face, contorted in anguish, disfigured by ragged slashes, thrusts itself towards her and howls in terror.

The face of a woman.

"HELP ME!"

Casey erupted from the nightmare and thrust the blankets from her as she scrambled back into a sitting position, punching at the air with her fists. She screamed into the darkness as she fought against disorientation and fear. Her breaths came in ragged gasps and her pulse was racing. Suddenly, nausea gripped her and she whipped her hand up to her mouth just in time to catch the bolus of vomit that shot forth, which then sprayed onto her singlet.

The last vestiges of the nightmare dissipated and Casey realised that she was in her own bedroom in the apartment and safe. She was free from the grip of the horrible dream—yet another horrible dream.

Feeling pins and needles prickle her hands and fingers, she fought to slow her breathing and she blinked into the darkness, afraid to close her eyes again in case the nightmare returned. Slowly, steadily, she prevailed. She brought her ragged breaths to heel. She began to think again.

Flipping on her bedside lamp, Casey cast a cursory glance down, spying the mucous vomit that now clung to her singlet. She scowled in disgust.

"Fuck."

Gingerly lifting her arms, she prepared to extricate herself from the offending garment when she froze and looked across the tousled blankets she had thrown off just moments before. There were blood stains all over them.

The nausea threatened again as Casey looked about herself in desperation, searching for the source of the bleeding.

Scrambling from the bed, she went through into the bathroom and peeled off her top, tossing it aside as she flicked the light switch and approached the mirror.

A series of angry welts criss-crossed over her sternum and oozed blood, despite most of it having congealed and dried.

Casey gasped, lifting her hands up and inspecting her fingers, her nails. There was blood on them, caked and dried around her fingertips and underneath. There were ragged tags of skin as well, her own skin.

Gazing into the mirror at her own reflection, fingers of horror crept up her spine as full realisation dawned.

Slowly, Casey reached out to the tap and turned it, filling the basin with cold water. Taking a flannel from a rail she dipped it into the stream of water then touched it to her chest, wincing as she wiped away the caked blood. Then she began to shake involuntarily and felt her head begin to spin. Trying to concentrate, Casey dipped the flannel into the basin. Ribbons of blood billowed out in the water as Casey lifted the material and continued to clean. The shaking did not stop.

She leaned over the basin cradling her head in her forearms as she battled to calm herself.

She plunged her face into the cold water until her entire head was submerged.

In the ice cold, with her eyes squeezed shut, Casey saw incoherent flashes. Holding her breath, she allowed them to assail her all at once. Then, suddenly, an image from her nightmare emerged.

A face. A young woman's face.

As quickly as she'd plunged her head into the basin, Casey yanked her head up and blinked as rivulets of water streamed down her face. The image hit her like a blow to the gut. Her emotions froze. Her mind stopped.

A single question remained.

Who was that?

CHAPTER 7

The black Volkswagen sedan pulled up outside an attractive red brick house on a leafy, suburban street. Casey killed the engine and leaned back in her seat, surveying the house pensively. She held the key in the ignition, wrestling with whether to actually leave the car, until she slowly withdrew it; then she removed her sunglasses.

The house and gardens were immaculately groomed, largely the result of her father's labours. A freshly-painted cream picket fence with an ornate letterbox framed lush green lawns, the centrepiece of which was a pretty Japanese maple with deep red leaves. It was centred in a circular bed resplendent with colour. Completing the scene was a restored railway bench seat where she knew her father often sat to admire his domain. He was a proud man.

At this home, on this quiet street, the world had always seemed so much more vibrant and alive compared to the dark, cloistered warehouse Casey sought comfort in.

Casey rested her hand on the door handle. Her visits to her family home were rare now. If it weren't for the gentle prodding of her father, Casey doubted that she would bother putting in an appearance here at all.

She had conflicting memories of her life here.

The Oakwood Avenue house had been a tranquil childhood home, safe and nurturing. She'd been raised in a loving family. Her mother and father had both worked hard to provide for both herself and her brother Angus. They wanted for very little and were encouraged to pursue their dreams and aspirations. Accordingly, they had both flourished.

After Casey's surgery, that love became constrictive, suffocating. Her recovery presented challenges for her and everyone around her and her initial needs were so great, she could rarely leave the confines of this house. The walls quickly closed in on her. Her family's concern for her well-being became twisted by the realities of what she had endured and continued to endure.

While her father and her brother were able to recognise this and curtail their protective behaviour, her mother could not.

Perhaps due to an innate sense of motherly protection, Edith Schillinge took it upon herself to care for her daughter, to assist in every aspect of Casey's recovery. From researching and implementing a healthy diet, reading up on appropriate physical activity, ensuring she was up-to-date with her daughter's medication management to encouraging healthy living, Edie immersed herself in the minutiae, believing that whatever she could to do to assist Casey would be a welcome distraction.

In the beginning, Casey had welcomed it.

Over time, Edie's involvement became overbearing to the point of intrusion. For a young woman wanting to recapture some sense of normalcy and, more importantly, independence, Casey railed against it. Mother and daughter clashed bitterly. Casey refused to submit to the endless scrutiny of her health and well-being. She began to distance herself and fight for the freedom she so desperately wanted.

She decided to pursue the career she had put off for so long. Then she moved out of her home altogether—to put as much distance between her mother and herself as she could. While her father understood and supported that need, Edie could not. Their relationship fractured.

But her move opened up more problems.

The nightmares began; and they stayed, tormenting her night after night. Like they had done just last night. To even think about what had happened filled Casey with horror and disgust and she squeezed her eyes shut in order to banish the memory.

Bringing herself back to the present, Casey's eyes drifted across the front of the property to the carport. Her father's 4WD sat in the left-hand space. The right-hand space—where her mother's BMW would normally be—was empty.

Good, Casey thought. *Timed that well.*

A flash of resentment passed through as she recalled Fedele's revelation that he had spoken to her mother, but she batted it away, gripped the car's door handle and took a deep breath. She opened the door and climbed out just as her father came into view from the side of the house, armed with a wheelbarrow.

Upon seeing the VW, Peter stopped, waved and smiled broadly.

Breathing steadily, focusing only on her father, Casey locked the car and walked briskly around to the path. The exaggerated feelings of vast space around her threatened as she approached him. She quickened her pace as Peter held his hands out and embraced her warmly.

"Hello, love," he greeted, planting a kiss on her forehead. "This is a pleasant surprise. How are you?"

As he held her, Peter noticed the rapid breathing and sensed the crippling agoraphobia clawing at her. He'd worked out a long time ago how to keep Casey anchored, to stave off the panic so she could bring it under control. His patience was welcome.

She drew back.

"Good, Dad. I'm good," she responded quietly, standing away from him and holding herself straighter. She nodded, confirming as much to herself as to him that she had, for the moment, prevailed.

She glanced at the wheelbarrow filled with soil and then across to a neat, paved area against the fence where a similar pile of organic material lay.

"At it again, huh?" Casey observed with a sardonic grin.

"Of course. Got new vegetables to get in. I'm aiming for a champagne crop of cauliflower this year—even better than last year."

Casey laughed and nudged him in the ribs.

"Give me a hand. My back's killing me."

Casey took hold of the handles of the wheelbarrow, hefting it and rolling it towards the pile where she deposited the load. Peter watched her, smiling proudly, admiring her tenacity, her unflinching focus, knowing that the battle still raged inside of her. She'd always been like that, even before. Tenacity was a quality that had never changed, despite all the other changes.

She returned the barrow with a grin and set it down between them.

"Wanna have a look at what I've been up to?" he ventured hopefully, gesturing towards the rear of the property.

Casey glanced over his shoulder at the back gate, then she looked towards the empty space beside his 4WD.

"She's out," Peter said reassuringly. Casey could hear the tightness in his voice as he held up his hands defensively. "Don't worry. She won't be back for a few hours yet."

"C'mon," she nodded, relaxing a little. "Before I change my mind."

Picking up a shovel, Peter took the wheelbarrow and gestured to Casey to go on ahead of him.

They passed through the gate just as an apricot-coloured Cocker Spaniel bounded up to Casey, barking enthusiastically. It leapt up, planting its paws on her thighs and wagging its tail furiously.

"Hello, Sammy," Casey greeted, dropping to her haunches and scratching the dog affectionately behind his floppy ears. Sam was actually her dog, but Casey had long ago surrendered him to her father, knowing that the warehouse was no place for an active pooch such as this.

That Peter was not at all disappointed by her decision had assuaged much of the guilt she harboured about leaving him here. Holding her palm out flat, she motioned for Sam to lower himself and he submitted obediently. She grabbed the handles of the wheelbarrow from her father once more and hefted it forward as the dog fell into a measured step beside her and then bounded across the back lawn towards the vegetable garden.

"So," Casey began evenly. "Where is she?"

Peter eyed his daughter, surprised that she would ask the question. "Doing a few extra hours for Stephen today. I did suggest that you might call by today. But she was already committed."

"Probably a wise idea," Casey said simply.

An awkward quiet descended between them until Peter gestured towards his vegetable garden.

"What do you think?"

Casey looked upon four rectangular beds, each bordered by a timber box which Peter had built himself. The pungent odour of fresh compost rose from the soil which Peter had patiently collected over many months and had turned into each bed. Freshly planted seedlings poked up into the mid-morning sunshine, lined up in impeccably straight rows and spaced equidistantly. Stooping down, Casey dragged her fingers through the soil of an empty box and lifted her hand to her nose.

"This is beautiful soil, Dad," she remarked enthusiastically.

"My own concoction," Peter replied proudly. "Only the best organic matter—all of it composed of vegetable matter that I've grown previously."

It was clear how much effort he had gone to. The garden's presentation was indicative of his devotion to exacting standards; the right soil, sturdy construction, equal distances and straight lines.

Casey gestured towards the centre of the garden. "I see the cubby house bit the dust."

"Well, it wasn't getting any use," Peter explained. "Wood was rotting and the dog was paranoid about it. I half expected to come outside one day to find him crushed underneath it."

Casey smirked and folded her arms. "As usual, Dad, you've outdone yourself. I'm putting my hand up right now for some of that cauliflower. I have two or three dishes in mind I can put it into."

Peter chuckled as he bent down to retrieve a rolled up garden hose from a nearby tap. Rounding Casey on his way back, she stepped forward then turned to face the house. A sunroom, featuring large glass panels looked out onto the garden. It was another recent addition to the house which Casey had not yet seen completed.

"Wow, this has come up a treat," she commented, outstretching her arms. "Almost wish it had been here when I was still here."

Peter smiled at Casey, looking at her out of the corner of his eye. "Why don't you go and have a look?" he suggested.

Casey stiffened. "N-no. That's all right."

"Casey, the house isn't going to bite you," Peter coaxed her. "As I said, your mother's a good couple of hours away."

He shook his head sadly. His daughter's reluctance to even step foot inside was one thing he had trouble accepting.

"I do wish you could both bury the hatchet one of these days."

Casey flashed him an icy glare. "You shouldn't be mentioning hatchets, Dad," she warned.

Peter detected a subtle shift in Casey's posture. Her shoulders sagged and her resistance faded just a little.

"Look. I'll come in with you," Peter suggested. "That mail of yours is sitting on the table in the dining room. If you don't take it now, I'm gonna toss it in the recycling bin."

Placing the hose down, Peter gently cupped his hand under her elbow. She didn't resist. Together, they crossed the lawn and stepped up to the house.

At that moment, Sam sprinted past them and escaped through the side gate.

"Crap," Peter hissed.

He glanced at Casey.

"Go on," she gestured. "Go and get him before he gets squashed."

Casey opened the door and passed through it into the sunroom.

She had to admit, it was a gorgeous addition to what had once had been a simple, enclosed verandah. The engineered quality to the glass and steel construction had her father's fingerprints all over it. It said a lot that this extension had been designed and completed in the few short years since he'd retired from his career as a civil engineer.

The old bugger can't help himself, she mused.

Casey looked across at a dining table on which sat a shoebox filled with mail. Several mailer tubes sat beside it. She looked through into the kitchen and living room fleetingly.

Shaking her head slowly, she approached the table and put her hands on both sides of the box. She quickly inspected its contents.

God, what a mess, she thought ruefully.

She thumbed through the envelopes inside the box, inspecting them more closely, looking for any signs that they might have been tampered with—as had been the case in the past—but she saw nothing obvious.

On the far side of the table, Casey noted an assortment of documents and folders that bore the name of Slattery & Gerard, the law firm her mother worked for. They had been left in such a way that it appeared her mother had been working through them and had stepped out with the intention of returning to them. Her eyes drifted over and she noticed among them some documents carrying a familiar logo: a crimson bird's wing, edged with gold that swept around in an arc to form a large *e*.

Casey squinted and tilted her head curiously. She had seen that logo before, but she couldn't quite recall where.

"Hello."

Though the voice was soft, it still made Casey jump. She whipped her head up to find her mother standing at the entrance to the sunroom. Her silent defences snapped to life.

Edie Schillinge was still striking in appearance, though there was a weariness in the way she held herself. Telltale lines creased the edges of her eyes, her chestnut hair was flecked with grey. Casey couldn't be sure if that grey had been there the last time they had seen one another.

Mother and daughter stood before one another, neither able to offer up the next exchange.

"I thought you were working," Casey remarked, deadpan.

Edie shrugged, stepping around the table and setting her handbag down beside the documents.

"I had some errands to run for the office. It didn't take as long as I thought it would."

Casey's eyes shifted between her mother and the paperwork before her, which did not escape Edie's notice.

"This is going to keep me plenty occupied," she ventured.

"What is it?" Casey asked, her curiosity towards the familiar logo piqued.

"Just some pro bono work we're doing on behalf of new migrants to Australia. Slattery & Gerard have several clients on their books. We provide assistance with asylum claims, visa disputes, that sort of thing. Actually, we've got Professor Fedele to thank for some of this. He facilitated some of the work through some humanitarian consulting he does."

Casey bristled at the mention of her surgeon's name, but she held herself in check. Instead, she nodded at the logo, now remembering where she had seen it: on the envelope that Fedele was holding when she had seen him in his office.

"That's his organisation?"

Edie looked down and thumbed the document. "Well…not so much his organisation. One that he consults with. Elyria Medical Services. They conduct health assessments for new arrivals, asylum seekers."

"Boat people?" Casey ventured.

Edie nodded hesitantly. "Them too."

Awkward silence drifted between them. Casey shifted on the spot, wishing she hadn't spoken so much, hadn't expressed so much interest in her mother. Edie gathered up the papers on the table before her, placing them into the folder and closing it over.

"Anyway…it's all fairly mundane work," she said, dismissing it. "There's just a lot of it."

Edie nodded toward the box before Casey. "So, Dad finally convinced you to collect that. Seems like you've got your own work cut out for you."

Casey regarded her mail and nodded. "Mmm-hmm. I'm sure there's a whole bunch of bills in here that are well overdue."

Hesitating, she moved to pick up the box, her skin prickling with anxiety. She wanted to extricate herself from here as quickly as she could before things had the chance to turn.

"How are you?" Edie offered, setting aside the papers in her hand and stepping forward. There was a flash of hope in her eyes. "How have you been?"

Casey looked at her mother, her gaze shifting, unable to meet Edie's directly. "All right," she replied tersely.

Sensing her daughter's defensiveness, Edie nonetheless persisted. "Dad says you might head up to Hambledown for a bit. That would be good for you."

Casey looked down at her feet. "I might. I haven't decided yet. I still have a lot going on here."

Casey attempted to turn away. Edie stepped down from the doorway.

"I-I was just about to put the kettle on," she ventured hopefully. "Would you stay for a cup of tea? I have some of that chai you like."

"I better not. I have to get going." Casey stepped back from the table and turned towards the door.

Watching her daughter leave, Edie bit her lip, trying to search for something to say. "How was Prof. Fedele?" she blurted, trying to keep her daughter from leaving.

"Fine," Casey responded harshly. Her scalp bristled at the mention of his name.

"W-well, what did he say? Is everything going okay?"

Casey stopped at the entrance. She turned slowly and, for the first time, fixed her mother with an icy glower.

Edie faltered where she stood.

"What do *you think* he said?" Casey retorted angrily. "After all, you should know."

"I-I don't understa—"

"Oh, don't you dare, Edie! Don't you *bloody* dare!" The strength of Casey's rebuke was enough that Edie recoiled and had to stifle a gasp.

"He told me you called," Casey continued. "That you were *concerned* about the pot and the pills. So don't stand there and play all innocent with me."

"I-I'm not trying to," Edie responded breathlessly. "I'm just…I just want to know that you're okay."

With that, Casey flung the box from her hands, its contents scattering across the floor. She raised an accusing finger at her mother.

"No!" she shouted. "That's not it at all and you know it. This is about you interfering again. This is about you being unable to keep your nose out of my business. I can take care of myself."

"But *are* you, Casey?" Edie's sudden challenge stopped Casey cold. At once, Edie's demeanour shifted and she crossed her arms over her chest. "Are you really? I mean, look at you! You look like you haven't slept in days. You've got bags under your eyes. Have you spent any time in the sun?"

"You know I can't spend a lot of time outdoors," Casey spat venomously.

Edie ignored her daughter as she continued, suddenly emboldened. "You're still doing drugs, Casey. You know that's completely irresponsible in your condition. And what's that on your shoulder? Another tattoo? I mean, *who does* that to themselves?"

Casey blinked at her mother.

"I do, Edie!" she screamed, her blood boiling. "I do. I do what I fucking want, when I want and I don't need anybody's permission."

Casey couldn't believe she was in the eye of yet another confrontation. Her cheeks flushed pink. Her eyes became swollen and she brushed at them angrily in a futile attempt to prevent the tears from escaping. The last thing she wanted was to appear vulnerable in front of her mother.

Just then, Peter appeared in the doorway and positioned himself between his wife and daughter.

"What the bloody hell is going on here!?" he demanded. "Jesus, I leave you two alone for five seconds."

"You said she wasn't going to be coming, Dad!" Casey retorted shakily, her chest heaving. Edie looked helpless.

"Look," Peter said, casting concerned glances between both daughter and wife. "Let's everyone take a moment to calm down a little. This is doing none of us any good."

He glared at Casey, waiting for her acknowledgement. After a few seconds, she nodded affirmatively. He then looked at Edie. Her eyes were fixed straight ahead. Her expression was fearful.

She was looking at her daughter, but not at her face.

Peter followed her gaze down and then saw what she saw.

A billowing cloud of red on the white linen of Casey's shirt bore over her sternum, fresh blood that was seeping into the material from the wounds on her chest.

Casey frowned through her tears and looked down, realising that the dressing she had placed over the scratches on her chest had peeled away, revealing the angry, self-inflicted welts underneath.

She gasped and stumbled backwards. The only thing that prevented her from falling over was the door frame behind her and she felt desperately for it to keep herself up.

She felt dizzy. Her emotions were in turmoil. She couldn't let anyone see her like this—especially not her parents. Especially not her mother.

The walls of the house closed in on her. She had to get away from here, but her legs wouldn't allow her.

"I need the toilet," she croaked as nausea beckoned and the urge to vomit overcame her.

His shock melting into concern, Peter reached her to gently place a hand under her forearm but Casey brushed it away angrily.

Instead, she lurched forward and ran to the bathroom.

CHAPTER 8

The suite was a quiet and comfortable space, the centrepiece of which were two stylish sofas arranged around a wood cabinet that served as a coffee table. Two large bookcases stood behind in the corner of the office, filled with a comprehensive library of psychology texts, assorted self-help books and one or two fiction titles. These were offset by a number of photos of good-looking, happy people.

On the wall opposite, framed in imposing black timber, hung a Mark Rothko print. It was a large painting whose bold colours Casey found garish and ugly. The pairing of browns and oranges had been thrust together with an aggressive hand and Casey couldn't decide if it was meant to intimidate or simply scare anyone who came here. It was a difficult image to ignore.

This suite was far removed from the modernism of Fedele's consulting suite. French doors looked out onto a secluded lawn and rose garden, where a fountain and urn provided a haven for birds, a trio of which splashed in the water presently. Large rose bushes, their limbs filled with fat buds, surrounded the urn while a rambling rose grew along a fence farther out. It provided a soft backdrop to the scene that minimised the visual presence of anything manmade. A pair of cast iron chairs sat on either side of a matching table, providing the option for consultations to be conducted outdoors if the therapist and client so wished.

Casey couldn't remember if she had ever taken up that option. She sat on the sofa now, facing the garden and taking in the scene before her. She drifted on the nuances of what was taking place outdoors: noting the birds in the fountain, how the breeze tugged at the tenacious foliage of the rambling rose, how the shadows from the building fell across the lawn. She occupied her mind with the scene and added random thoughts to her stream of consciousness, so she could avoid having to deal with her situation in the room here and now.

"Casey."

The voice, though soft and measured, jolted Casey out of her reverie. She jumped in her seat and turned in the direction from which that voice had come.

The woman sitting across from her was middle-aged with cropped, sandy hair and large eyes that were framed by a pair of stylish glasses. Her face, faintly lined, was still youthful and projected patience and openness: a willingness to listen without foisting expectation.

Geddie Kirkwood sat in a leather recliner with cushions bolstering her small frame from behind. She wore a brightly patterned scarf that paired well with her soft green blouse—an expensive one, Casey surmised. She rested a clipboard on her knee that held a lined notepad. An expensive fountain pen was intertwined between her fingers. It was her preference to make a lot of notes. She waited patiently.

Very patiently.

It had been two months since Casey had last sat in this room.

She and Kirkwood had danced this merry dance for almost three years. In the immediate period after Casey's surgery, they met for an hour on a weekly basis as recommended by the transplant clinic. Kirkwood also met individually with Casey's parents and her brother and also as a group as part of the process of transitioning and adapting to life post-surgery. As Casey's recovery progressed, the sessions stretched from weekly, to fortnightly, then monthly as Kirkwood reassessed hers and her family's needs.

Casey found it difficult to believe that she had once viewed these sessions as valuable. She had felt comfortable in her psychologist's presence and was readily able to explore and reflect on how she was coping with the changes that had shaped her.

But, as she had with everything else to do with her medical care, she soon came to resent having to submit herself to Kirkwood's constant scrutiny. She began to see these sessions in the same way she saw everything else: an intrusion. As she had done with her mother, so too did she begin withholding herself from Kirkwood by either refusing to talk in these sessions or by simply not attending them at all.

After yesterday's incident at her parents, however, her father's reaction had guilted her into coming here.

Casey had a way of bluffing her way through the meetings with lengthy explorations about her feelings of survivor guilt, a common challenge faced by transplant recipients. Or she would explore her feelings of fear that the organ might fail again after her most recent rejection scare.

But it was all fiction.

Casey had hardly felt any of the significant survivor guilt the research papers talked about. As for her recent rejection scare, Casey had avoided talking about it in any significant detail because she had skipped a multitude of sessions. When Kirkwood tried to visit her in the hospital, Casey refused to see her.

Casey was surprised that Kirkwood still seemed to buy all of it. Every time they met, the psychologist lapped up Casey's spiel without question and dutifully framed her "therapy" around addressing Casey's fictions.

For her part, Geddie Kirkwood had observed a significant and increasingly disturbing change in Casey Schillinge. The defensive posture Casey had adopted was stark enough and though she played along with Casey's conversations around her adjusting, Kirkwood knew there was something much deeper happening. She had access to Casey's medical files and had seen the toxicology reports. The drug use was clearly an increasing problem, one that had to have an underlying reason.

Casey sensed that Kirkwood was close to the truth. Which was why she had avoided these sessions as much as she could. The defensiveness she had to adopt was exhausting and Casey feared that if she continued to submit to Kirkwood's probing, the psychologist would eventually discover the truth.

The insomnia and the nightmares.

If Kirkwood discovered either of these, she would surely have Casey committed.

Thus, the game continued.

"Casey?" Kirkwood repeated softly.

Casey shifted on the sofa. She couldn't even remember what they'd been talking about.

"You were telling me you were concerned that the doctor had altered your dose of the anti-rejection medication again—that you felt that he was making too many changes too quickly."

Casey nodded, rubbing her forehead wearily with thumb and forefinger.

Bullshit. Bullshit. Bullshit.

"Yes," she responded quietly. She offered nothing more.

Kirkwood nodded, scribbling a note on her pad. "How's work?" she asked, changing the subject. "You're still consulting?"

Casey sat a little straighter in her seat and lowered her hand to her lap. She shrugged her shoulders.

"I am."

"And how is that going?" Kirkwood ventured.

"Good. It's good."

Kirkwood nodded. Casey fidgeted some more. More note-taking. Kirkwood's eyes flicked from Casey to the page as she peered over the rim of her glasses.

"Did you want to elaborate on that?"

There was no sarcasm in Kirkwood's voice, though she raised it just enough to imply exasperation at her patient's noncommittal answers.

Casey's features tightened; she was searching for something, anything, to answer with. It was clear from the way she held herself that she was agitated.

"I've just finished a job. A big one…enough for me to take some time off."

"And how do you feel about that? Taking time off, I mean. I imagine it'll be hard for someone who thrives on work the way you do."

Casey shrugged once more. "I'll manage."

"Manage?" Kirkwood echoed with slight puzzlement.

"Yes," Casey retorted, a little more sharply than she had meant to. "I am managing. Just like everyone else with busy lives is managing."

Kirkwood offered an empathetic smile. "Sometimes our lives can fill up with commitments quickly, can't they? I'm sure you're in demand."

Casey tilted her head. "It's a living."

"How are you sleeping?"

Casey shivered. Kirkwood noticed, but gave no indication that she had.

"What?" Casey faked nonchalance, pretending she hadn't heard the question.

"Your sleep. I can imagine it would be hard to switch off sometimes. Are you having any problems?"

"No," Casey responded sharply. She fidgeted with the hem of her skirt.

Kirkwood creased her brow and allowed silence to hang in the air for a long moment. "Your dad and mum? They're busy, too, I expect. Your brother?"

Casey's brother's face flashed in her mind. She very nearly smiled but quickly stifled it.

Again, her expression didn't escape Kirkwood's notice.

"Angus is well-established in London," Casey said simply. "His firm gave him a promotion recently. I got a call from him on my birthday. That was nice."

Kirkwood removed her glasses and set them down on the chest in front of her.

"What about your parents, how are they?"

Looking away, Casey pushed down a rising lump in her throat. Without realising it, she had reached into her top and rubbed at the dressing that was just visible above her neckline. Kirkwood noticed this.

"Dad is fine as always. Supportive...*unobtrusive.* He keeps things ticking along for me in terms of bookwork and accounts."

Kirkwood studied her, waiting for additional information, but Casey remained silent. Her eyes wandered nervously between Kirkwood and the garden outside. She reached again for the dressing on her chest and scratched at it.

"What happened there?"

Casey looked down and adjusted her shirt to cover it up. "N-nothing. Just an oil splash from cooking."

Kirkwood nodded. She lidded her pen and then set both it and the notepad down on the coffee table in front of her.

The hands of a clock on the wall opposite ticked closer to the top of the hour, indicating that they were close to the conclusion of the session. Both of them knew it.

"You didn't mention your mum," Kirkwood observed.

Casey looked away and down into her lap. "No. I didn't."

Kirkwood waited a few moments, opening her palms out towards Casey in silent encouragement.

Casey remained silent

Both knew they had achieved very little. Only one of them was concerned.

Kirkwood looked at her notebook, at Casey and then at the wall. The hands of the clock reached the hour.

"We're going to have to leave it there for today, Casey," she said.

Immediately, as though a school bell had rung, Casey stood and brushed herself down, while Kirkwood also stood and closed the notepad laying on the coffee table. Casey was already heading toward the door when Kirkwood spoke again and the psychologist almost had to skip to try and catch up with her.

"Could we make a time for you to come and see me again in a week or so?"

Casey opened the door and glanced back at Kirkwood.

"I'll call you," Casey dismissed, passing through the door and striding down the hall, not bothering to wait for Kirkwood.

Kirkwood considered following her, but paused at the door to her office and watched Casey go.

She sighed heavily, noticing her next client waiting for her expectantly. Kirkwood acknowledged the man with a nod.

"Just give me a moment, Bill," she said, retreating back into her office and closing the door behind her. She stood there, holding the handle, attempting to process her thoughts. She looked over at the notepad on the coffee table.

Geddie Kirkwood sat for a moment on the arm of her chair and skimmed the myriad notes she had made during the session. There were more words on the page than both she or Casey had spoken during the preceding hour.

Kirkwood had written a number of descriptors as she observed and listened to Casey Schillinge. Concerns about the current treatment regimen. Depression indicators secondary to survivor guilt. Fear about current health trajectory and future. All of them had been crossed out by Kirkwood and adjacent to each, she had written: 'Not currently relevant.'

Further down the page, she looked over another grouping of notes.

Agitation. Excessive fidgeting. Worsening withdrawal with an unwillingness to volunteer information, particularly about mother (? Conflict worsening in this area). Lethargy with signs of insomnia (medical notes indicate continued use of barbiturates).

Below all of these notes and scribbles, near the bottom of the page, Kirkwood had inked a question mark followed by the following sentence:

Casey is hiding something.

CHAPTER 9

She was perched on the stool in front of her workstation. Her arm was extended across her knee and her fingers held a joint. Long, languid wisps of smoke curled upwards in the darkness towards the ceiling.

It was the last one, Casey realised ruefully. She had not heard from her supplier in days now. Her calls to his number had gone unanswered which meant that he'd probably gone and gotten himself in trouble again.

Another idiot to contend with.

Cursing silently, her hand shook as she lifted the joint to her lips. She inhaled the smoke as economically as she could, then she reached for the glass of scotch—neat—that sat on the glass tabletop.

Casey hadn't moved from this spot for hours. Her emotions were fractious after the session with Kirkwood. As she had predicted, talking with Kirkwood yesterday had done little to help.

She was sick of everyone's fucking advice. She wished she could be left alone. And yet, there was a part of her that didn't want to be left alone. That made her angrier.

Even her apartment no longer felt safe. The walls here felt as though they were closing in, suffocating her and yet, to step outside right now would feel a thousand times worse.

Casey glanced at the clock.

It was 10PM.

She glanced at the painting of Jeanne Hebuterne and smiled bitterly.

"Thirty-six hours, Jeanne," Casey remarked with a slurred and scratchy croak. The Randy Gardner world record flashed in her mind. "Wanna try for the record again?"

Casey gazed at the portrait as if expecting a response, but when none came, she exhaled in disgust. She considered pitching her glass at the wretched print but she hesitated, then relented. She was too stoned to be bothered.

The weight of her self-inflicted sleep deprivation bore down on her, yet she fought it by recruiting as much anger as she could, forcing a battle within herself that released her reserves of adrenaline.

Dangling the joint from the corner of her lip, Casey reached across the table, tapped a key on her laptop and checked her cloud folder.

Empty. Maddeningly empty.

Still no requests for her services had come. Just like the empty folder on her cloud storage, her post office box—where a lot of her work usually came to—had also remained stubbornly empty.

She sensed Prishna's hand in this, manipulating events in the hope it would trip up Casey. If Prishna had made contact with Casey's underground associates, they would be running a mile from any potential attention they might attract. The consequences were not worth the risk of dealing with her.

There had to be something she could do. Checking the clock again, a plan began to form in Casey's mind. Launching from her stool, she grabbed her keys from the kitchen counter and made for the door of the apartment.

Scott made his way downstairs, scanning the crowd in the front bar. He'd received Casey's text message and was concerned; it had seemed agitated, off balance. It wasn't like her. Stepping into the crowded bar, it didn't take long before he spotted her.

Something was off. Casey appeared dishevelled and she was clearly stoned. She gripped a beer bottle and lifted it to her mouth, emptying it. Approaching her, Scott noticed a male patron in a business suit leering at her. He immediately stood in between the sleazy patron and Casey.

Casey jumped as he tapped her arm. When Casey turned and glared up at him, Scott could see that everything about her was tense.

"Come on," he said, nodding towards the stairs. "Let's go and have a talk."

Once they had settled into their usual table up on the rooftop garden, Scott set a glass of water down for her and a beer for himself, which did not escape her notice.

"So. You wanna tell me what's going on?"

Unexpectedly, Casey began to shake. "Oh, everything," she choked, fighting tears. "Everything. Where do I start?"

"How about at the beginning," Scott suggested evenly, watching as Casey fished in her pocket for the remaining portion of her joint. She held it up and attempted to light it with her Zippo, but Scott snatched it from her grasp and crushed it in his fist.

"What the fuck!" Casey exclaimed angrily.

"Jesus, Case, you can't go lighting up that shit in a public venue," Scott shot back. "Do you want me to lose my job, *yer midden.*"

Casey's expression lurched between hurt and shame. She slumped back in her seat, wiping angrily at her eyes. "I need *something,* Sasquatch. I'm going out of my mind sitting around and pretending like I'm enjoying taking all this time off. I'm desperate."

Scott shifted uncomfortably. "Look. The thing is…I've *asked,* Casey," he began apologetically. "It's just that there's nothing out there. I put the feelers out—more than once—but the usuals are being cautious. They're not willing to offer much just now. Because…"

His voice drifted off and Casey glowered at him. The way he said that last sentence caused her to bristle.

"*Because why*?" she challenged, much more forcefully than she intended.

"There's been talk, Casey. About you. You've been in Cyber-Crime's pocket for a long time and the word is getting out. That detective friend of yours—"

"She's *not* my friend." Casey cut him off.

Scott continued, undeterred.

"Well, she's been sniffing around. And it's gotten a few of the grey hats nervous. A lot of them suspect that you've been double dipping. Playing both sides."

His last sentence, in particular, stung Casey.

"That's not fucking true and you know it!" she blurted viciously, causing numerous patrons nearby to turn in her direction. "You know I've always protected the Circle."

Scott held his hands out in an attempt to placate her.

"*I* know it's not true, Case." He lowered his voice and sat forward in his chair. "Believe me, I know. But look…until things settle down…maybe it is best that you continue to lay low for a while."

He allowed the import of his words to register with her. But Casey seemed to grow more agitated by the minute.

"Look at yourself," he said, exasperated. "You look like shit. Why don't you take your old man's advice and get yourself out of here. Go catch some sun and reboot."

Casey's expression twisted and she gripped her glass so tightly her knuckles turned white. "I'm so sick of everyone giving me advice!"

He flinched as her spittle struck him in the eye.

Her pupils dilated and she snarled at him. "You sound just like everyone else. Why don't you all just go and fuck off!"

Bolting upright, she slammed the glass down on the table and it cracked in her hand. Both of them blinked and looked down to see a rivulet of blood sliding down the glass from underneath her grip.

She immediately regretted her words. Staggering back from the table, Casey knocked over her chair. She felt an awful snapping inside her head as she glared at her speechless friend.

The rooftop garden began to spin. Her eyes darted left and right. Everywhere she turned, Casey was confronted by the faces of patrons staring at her in shock.

Her drug-fuelled fog was beginning to fade and tendrils of panic began to finger the back of her neck.

"I'm..." she stumbled, letting go of the glass which toppled onto its side before rolling off the edge of the table and smashing on the ground. Looking down at her hand, she saw a deep gash in her palm. Without thinking, she wiped the hand against her top, smearing blood all across it.

Casey turned and stumbled from the rooftop garden and down the stairs, disappearing to the street.

Slamming the industrial door shut, Casey slapped the locking mechanism across and shoved the padlock securely in place.

She was panting, her mind reeling from having verbally assaulted her best friend. She couldn't believe she had behaved so awfully and choked at the recollection, bringing her bloodstained hand up to her mouth.

The metallic taste caused her to recoil and she looked at the thick laceration she had inflicted. Tears streamed down her cheeks, distracting her from cleaning the wound. Instead, she fumbled with her phone. She wanted to call Scott right away, apologise to him, try and make things right, but she had no idea what she would possibly say. Faltering with the device, she set it down on the kitchen counter. As she did so, it began vibrating and she blinked at the screen.

It was Scott calling.

She shook her hands wildly, afraid to pick up the phone.

I can't!

Reflexively, Casey slammed her thumb down on the touch screen, hitting the dismiss button and she slapped the phone away. It shot across the counter and clattered noisily to the floor on the far side, out of view.

She went to the kitchen cupboards, throwing open the doors above the stove and spilling their contents at her feet. She dropped to her haunches, searching for the tin box in which she usually stored her marijuana. The box had toppled to the floor along with containers of flour, rice, bread crumbs and other assorted condiments and she looked down, identifying the upturned container with its lid open, in the mess. Her stomach plunged. The box was empty, as she knew it would be.

"Fuck!" she cursed out loud.

Undeterred, Casey sprang drunkenly to her feet and fumbled her way up the stairs to the mezzanine level, throwing open the door to the unused guest room.

Stumbling over a maze of boxes, disused furniture and a queen bed that was covered in plastic, she identified a bedside cabinet on the far wall. Leaping over the bed, Casey fell to her knees in front of the cabinet, tearing the drawers from it. She desperately picked through the contents, picking out several plastic zip-lock bags, searching for one that was filled.

Again, she was thwarted. There was nothing here either.

Her anger peaked and she clutched at the handle of one of the discarded drawers, flinging it across the room. It struck the opposite wall and shattered into a dozen jagged pieces.

Screaming at the top of her lungs, she grabbed another drawer, and then another, hurling them and watching them obliterate in a similar fashion to their counterpart. Then she was on her feet, upending cardboard boxes, another bedside table, the bed itself. She destroyed anything she could get her hands on. Her anger could not be assuaged and she relished in it.

Exhaustion quickly crept upon her and all at once her remaining energy left her. She stopped abruptly and fell to her knees. Blinking at the destruction she had wrought, Casey suddenly laughed out loud.

She lurched to her feet, swaying back and forth. Her laughter disintegrated into loud, wracking sobs and her legs buckled. She collapsed to the floor, oblivious to the chaos. Shards of broken glass from a small vase cut into her lower legs and the tops of her feet. Blood bubbled forth from the wounds.

She was oblivious to any pain.

Without warning, a loud rapping at the door downstairs broke through the silence in the apartment. Casey jumped, gasping in the darkness. A moment or two passed before the knocking repeated itself, followed by a voice.

"Casey!"

It was her father.

Shit! Shit! Shit!

Shaking her head, desperately trying to clear it, Casey staggered and lurched forward, tripping over the disaster zone as she made for the door and then the stairs. Stumbling down them, she darted across the living area to her bathroom.

"Casey! Are you in there? Open up!"

Outside, in the corridor, Peter tested the door. This wasn't like Casey not to answer. She must have heard him.

He cocked his head, listening for signs of life from within. "C'mon, Casey! What's going on?"

Finally, her voice sounded from the other side. "Just a minute, Dad."

Casey splashed water over the cuts on her legs and her hand, cursing the tenacious blood that continued to ooze.

Patting them dry as best she could, Casey straightened her top and glanced at her reflection. She was repulsed by what she saw but there was no time to do anything more. She couldn't put her father off.

What was he doing here at this hour anyway?

Unlocking the door, Casey slid it aside and looked up at her father who recoiled upon seeing her.

"Christ, Casey!" he gasped, pushing past her and into the apartment. He spied the mess on the floor in the kitchen and noted her smartphone nearby. It was vibrating again with an incoming call from Sasquatch.

"What the bloody hell?"

"What are you doing here, Dad?" she shot back. "It's gotta be like, *ridiculous* o'clock?"

Peter paced around the kitchen bench, retrieving her phone from the tiled floor. He held it up, revealing a cracked screen through which she could see Scott's caller ID.

"Scott called me," he replied angrily as he tapped the answer button on her phone and took the call.

Casey stood awkwardly, hands on hips as Peter reassured Scott that he was with her now, glaring at his daughter as he spoke. She couldn't do anything except wait.

Finally, Peter ended the call and set the phone down on the counter. He continued to glare at her for a long moment. Then, he closed his eyes and breathed in and out audibly, calming himself. His expression morphed accordingly; his anger replaced by grim concern.

"What's going on, Casey?" he repeated. "Seems you made a hell of a scene over there."

Casey felt her cheeks flush and she looked away from him. She reached for the door and slid it closed as she tried to come up with something, anything, to answer him.

"It was nothing, Dad," she answered weakly. "A disagreement."

"A disagreement? Casey, Scott was pretty shaken when he called me, and he wouldn't call me if it was just a disagreement."

Lifting a hand up to her forehead, Casey closed her eyes, trying to remain calm even as her defensive hackles threatened to stand up in the presence of her father's questioning.

"Look," she blurted. "I can't give you any other explanation. We had a fight…an argument. Friends do argue sometimes, Dad."

Peter shook his head. "Bullshit. You and I both know that Scotty is the least argumentative person we've ever known."

"C'mon, Dad," Casey retorted in exasperation. "Don't pressure me, please. It's late."

"You're damned right it's late! It's nearly midnight. But, I'm not going to stand here and listen to you blow me off this time. Jesus, Case—look at you!" Peter thrust his hand out, gesturing to her appearance.

His forceful observation caused her to blink. For his part, Peter felt terrible for having said what he did and his shoulders slackened, adopting a less intimidating posture.

"I'm worried sick about you…your *mother* is most certainly worried sick about you. Whatever it is that's eating you up…it's starting to show."

Casey watched her father begin to falter. Try as she might, Casey could not completely dismiss him because she knew, deep down, that what he said was true.

Peter set his keys down on the counter and slowly took out a stool. He sat down and rested his arms on the surface.

"I've been willing to accept, for a long time, the thing between you and your mother has been more about her not being able to let go of you—to let you get on and make a life for yourself."

Casey watched her father as a weariness descended over him.

"But I'm beginning to understand the worry she has for you, Casey. You're so *withdrawn.* So solitary. And what's with those cuts?"

She couldn't meet his eyes. Instead, she looked down at her hand, at the congealing blood and grimaced. Slowly, she went over to the sink, turned the tap and ran cold water gently over it.

"Dad, it's not what you think," she said softly. "I'm not try—"

"Well, *Jesus,* Casey, what is it then!?"

Peter's voice caused her to jump. She turned to face him.

"I'm tired, Dad," she said, turning off the tap and reaching for a dishcloth to press to the wound. "Tired and frustrated. I just...*can't relax*."

"Well, what does Geddie think about all of this? Surely she would have some idea how to—I dunno—fix it."

Casey stiffened at the mention of Kirkwood and she closed her eyes tightly.

Peter, however, was unmoved. "No, no, Casey. Not this time," he growled. "You're not going to keep blowing me off whenever I ask you about her."

"What's there to tell?" Casey protested, as she bent down to clean up the broken glass on the floor. "The sessions are boring, Dad. She offers nothing but typical feel-good *bullshit* about living as a recipient and...I don't want to keep being reminded that I'm a bloody recipient!"

"Why do you keep going to see her then?" Peter challenged. "Why not find another therapist?"

"Because I don't have much of a choice, Dad. She's been assigned. She's the transplant clinic's go-to *screw*!"

Looking down at the mess from the cupboards, she shuffled across and stooped down, picking up the spilt containers.

Peter watched her, grimacing as he wrestled with what to say. "I'm scared, Casey," he offered finally. "For what you might do if you don't stop isolating yourself."

Reaching into his wallet, Peter took out a photograph and handed it over to her. Casey gazed at the image of herself, taken years ago on her Asian trek. Sweat drenched tank top, grubby hiking shorts, her backpack laying at her feet, she was standing on a summit overlooking a lush rain forest, a hiking stick in her muscular arm; the other hand rested on her hip. She stood tall and proud, her expression confident, her smile victorious, eyes wide and beaming.

It was as if she was looking at a stranger.

"What happened to that young woman, Casey?" Peter whispered. "Where did you go? Why did you go?"

Casey began to weep as she clutched the photograph.

"I can't..." she began to say through quiet sobs.

"Look," Peter wept. "I don't care about this rubbish with Prishna and I don't even care about the kind of company you might be keeping. But *something* is eating away at you, Casey—something deep down. I know you might not believe it, but whatever it is—we can work it out...together. You and me and your mum. But you've got to *allow* us."

Casey seemed very small. "I don't know."

CHAPTER 10

THUNDER RUMBLES ALL AROUND. THE DEEP GUTTURAL MOAN IS CARRIED ON ITS BACK.

She is here again.

The road stretches before her. Rain peppers the inky bitumen while disembodied flashes of light erupt across a blood-red sky above.

Dread seeps through her.

She knows what is about to happen.

Searching around in the darkness, she tries to orient herself, tries to remember.

Forks of electricity tear at the fabric of the sky, and in her mind's eye she sees the road sign, its reflective surface illuminating like a beacon in the darkness. She squints, tries to focus, but the flash makes the writing on its surface impossible to interpret.

She curses as the darkness swallows up the image.

Rubbing her eyes with her hands, she becomes aware of someone nearby. Shivering, she stands and turns. The shadow of the human figure stands behind her, several yards away, shrouded in fog.

She squints through the mist, trying to focus.

There is an object behind the figure. Metallic. Man-made.

Is it a vehicle? A car?

Beams of light puncture the darkness from that direction and she thrusts her hand out against the blinding white.

The assailant steps forward. The moan rolls across the sky and the assailant breaks into a run.

Flinching, she turns and tries to flee.

Inertia weighs against her but she fights it, pumping her legs as fast as they will carry her.

The assailant is gaining. She panics and screams into the darkness only to be taunted by the moaning and the thunder above her.

A lightning flash erupts and she thrusts out her arm in an effort to shield herself until it dissipates.

When she draws her arm down, her eyes go wide. The assailant is front of her.

She screams as she crashes into him and is thrown backwards like a rag doll.

The low moan gains in volume and pitch, filling with torment and pain.

FLASH!

The assailant is on her in an instant. He pins her arms above her head with a giant, gloved hand. With the other hand, he wrenches at her jeans, grabbing them at the waist and tearing them from her as if they were paper.

She screams, writhing impotently in her assailant's grip as he pins her pelvis to the ground with his knee. He tightens his grip on her wrists before reaching down, between her legs. With a sickening realisation, she feels him clawing at her inner thighs.

FLASH!

She cries out in protest, her voice melding with the moan from the sky and she draws power from it. She recruits it, channels it into every single muscle fibre. As the fingers begin to penetrate, she unleashes a massive convulsion, so powerful that she lifts herself from the roadway and upends her attacker, throwing him backwards.

The effort has spent her. She flails wildly, unable to get to her feet. The clouds above shift and belch, turning the rain once more into a deep, ruby red. The metallic flavour of blood stings her lips.

FLASH!

The assailant pounces again, throwing himself at her and pinning her to the bitumen. His gloved hand slams down over her mouth, preventing her from screaming. He raises a fist above his head. Her eyes go wide.

The fist crashes into her chest. Blood, bone and tissue spray upward before them as his fist disappears into the cavity. Though there is no pain, the screams from above intensify, becoming unbearable in her ears.

The arm retracts from her chest. The hand holds a bloody, beating object.

A maniacal grin. A disembodied cackle. Rivulets of crimson course down over a masculine jaw.

Insane with terror, drenched in blood, she is too paralysed to move. Yet, an inexplicable strand of curiosity anchors her in this moment.

The beating and bloody heart, crawling with maggots. A black slick oozes from the severed arteries and veins and drips over the hand and down into the cavity the figure has made.

FLASH!

An onrush of images assails her, flickering and flashing like a poorly aligned film reel.

The road before her. The figure, shrouded in darkness. The vehicle, stationary by the road. The road sign, illuminated by headlights so bright, the writing on it is too hard to see. The rain. The blood. Her blood. Her screams. The heart.

The face…

As the screams lash the darkness all around, the face of the young woman, contorted in anguish and disfigured by ragged slashes, thrusts itself towards her, howling in terror.

"HELP ME!"

Casey screamed into the darkness, writhing in her bed as she tore herself once more from the nightmare. Tendrils of the dream clung to her, refusing to surrender as horrifying imagery continued to flash before her. The screams in the dreamworld melded with her own here and now along with the taunting, disembodied cackle.

Casey struggled to open her eyes. Terror consumed her. The heart beat inside her so forcefully she could feel it thumping against her chest. Clawing at the darkness, Casey's hand found the thick body of her bedside lamp and she clutched it with a vice-like grip. She ripped the lamp from the table causing the electrical wire to snap taut like a whip.

She flung the lamp at the nightmare, obliterating the images as it sailed through the air before striking the edge of the wardrobe. The glass shade shattered into dozens of glimmering shards. The ruined body spun in the air as it fell to the floor.

The sign on the road. That face. The scream. Her scream…

Casey bolted upright, swatting at the air in front of her but the nightmare clung to her, suffocating her. Her mind reeled, tumbling toward the edge of madness.

With a sudden burst of superhuman strength, Casey sprang from her bed. Her body slammed into the brick wall adjacent, her face striking the door frame so hard that she vaguely heard the sound of bone snapping. A vicious cut opened up beside her nose. She would not be stopped.

The nightmare would not be stopped.

She scrambled on her hands and knees into the living area, as though the nightmare were chasing her. Thrusting outwards, she batted at the air, trying to stop it from catching her. She was wailing now. Tears streamed from her unfocused eyes as she begged silently, desperately for it to stop.

She collapsed to the floor then rolled onto her back, feeling the warmth of the blood that oozed from her nose and the gash on her face.

Somewhere in her fractured mind, Casey touched a spark of anger. Anger at the nightmare that refused to yield. Anger at the terror of the unfamiliar face that cried out to her, begging her for help.

Enough!

Casey recruited that anger and nourished it. Adrenaline surged and she used it to consume the terror. A single, pure thought replaced it.

Springing to her feet, Casey whipped her head around, flinging a long, thin spatter of blood across the room. It splashed across the portrait of Jeanne Hebuterne.

Letting out a final scream, Casey rushed blindly forward in one last attempt to obliterate the nightmare.

The sign on the road. That face. The scream. Her scream...

Raising her arms over her head, balling her hands into fists, Casey flung them downward with all the power she could muster.

She crashed through the glass pane of the sliding door, causing it to explode in a shower of jagged shards that tore at her skin, her face and her arms. Blood splattered everywhere, melding with the cascades of ruined glass. Casey screamed into the night, so loudly that passing pedestrians on the street below stopped and turned in the direction of the sound to see glittering glass billowing from the balcony.

Casey crumpled as she hurtled forward, finally wrenching herself from the grip of the nightmare.

The barrier of the balcony rushed towards her. Her forehead slammed into the rendered surface. As flashes of light popped before her eyes, she clung to her consciousness before the world turned sideways.

THE AMBULANCE SPED through the night, swerving in and out of the midnight traffic, slowing only to run a series of red lights as it raced towards the city. Red and blue lights flashed. Sirens wailed urgently.

Inside the vehicle, a pair of paramedics struggled with a single, bloodied occupant. She was thrashing wildly, screaming through a sedative haze as she tried to slap away the oxygen being held over her face. Her screams drowned out the ambulance's sirens. The female paramedic holding the mask ducked and weaved, trying to avoid the blood spatters that Casey was spitting in her direction, while her counterpart struggled to secure her wrists so that she couldn't hit either of them. He continually kept lifting his own gloved hands up and away as Casey wheeled her forearms free. Blood streamed from dozens of wounds on her skin, some of which had shards of glass protruding from them.

Frustrated, the paramedic held back and watched her swinging arm, waiting for an opportunity to grab her wrist. He met his colleague's eyes and he scowled. Spying an opportunity, he darted forward and snapped his wrist around Casey's, gripping it like a vice. With a great effort, he finally managed to shove her arm down and he secured the leather strap around it.

Finally, he thought, hissing air out from between his teeth.

Without pausing, he repeated the action with her other hand, then slumped back.

Casey screamed as she pulled against her bonds, desperately but impotently.

"Miss, calm down," the female paramedic pleaded with her. "Please calm down. You're safe here. We're taking you to the hospital."

"Nooooo!" Casey wailed underneath the mask. "Pleeeasee noooo!"

The woman looked worriedly at her colleague sitting across from her. "Can we give any more sedative?"

The male paramedic shrugged. "I've already given enough to knock out a horse."

They both looked down at Casey's wrists and arms. The muscles in her forearms were so taut that they were quivering. The fabric of her restraints was very nearly cutting into her wrists. The whites of her knuckles stood out.

The female paramedic grimaced, watching Casey fight as hard as she could to keep from submitting to unconsciousness again.

For it was there that the nightmares lay in wait.

She blinked furiously at the woman holding the mask over her face, trying to reach her with her eyes. She looked at the name patch on the paramedic's breast pocket: Mel.

"Pleeasse, Mel," she cried, weeping uncontrollably. "Don't let me dream."

Something in her voice caught Mel's attention and she met Casey's eyes. She expected Casey's pupils to be unfocused pinpricks by now. Instead, they were abnormally wide and focused. They chilled Mel to her core.

"Screw it," the male paramedic muttered, swivelling in his seat and grabbing at a box on a shelf.

He quickly drew up a vial of sedative into a syringe and attached a needle to it before plunging the syringe into Casey's thigh.

Casey cried out in protest. Then, an overwhelming warmth flooded through her. Her resistance collapsed. The struggle left her and her muscles let go. Gurgling underneath the mask, Casey's eyes fluttered and closed.

Mel turned towards the driver. “How long, Brian?”

“Five minutes,” came his determined response. “We're almost there.”

“Floor it,” Mel snapped urgently. “We don't have five minutes.”

The ambulance skidded to a halt in front of the Emergency Room entrance of the hospital. The rear doors were thrown open. An attending team of medical personnel gathered like a swarm of bees, helping the gurney from the back of the vehicle. One of the team barked orders at a crowd of people in the immediate vicinity. Mel remained at Casey's head, holding the mask in place as she shouted information to one of the attending doctors.

“Twenty-six-year-old female. Found alone in her apartment.”

Casey could hear everything that was being said through her sedative-induced fog, although it came to her consciousness as fractured and incomplete.

“Multiple life-threatening lacerations to face, arms and hands as a result of impacting with a plate-glass window. Multiple foreign bodies found in those wounds and several old wounds to her chest.”

Somehow, Casey was able to register horror at what Mel was describing to the others about her own body.

“Apparent suicide attempt…”

Casey's mind screamed in protest.

No! I wasn't!

Darkness descended like a veil.

THE FIRST THING she became aware of was a sound. A familiar sound, a rhythmic beeping that echoed, bouncing gently off the walls of her consciousness. The beeping became foremost in her awareness. She knew that sound all too well—a sound from her past.

Where am I?

As her awareness grew, she attempted to open her eyes. At first, her lids would not yield. They twitched once, then twice before fluttering wildly.

Slowly, Casey opened her eyes.

The room was softly lit. Her vision slowly spiralled into focus and she blinked to help steady what she saw around her.

The first thing Casey saw was the monitor that hung from an armature. She grimaced, noting that her head was turned way over to the right hand side, but also that her neck was painfully hyper-extended. As she further awoke from her deep sleep, she realised why this was so.

Her entire face felt swollen and puffy. She tried to draw a breath through her nostrils but she found that she couldn't. Her nose was packed full with something, some kind of wadding. In fact, her entire head felt this way and she screwed up her face in protest. Casey immediately regretted it. Intense pain knifed through her face, strong enough to take her breath away and she instantly felt nauseous.

Turning her head slowly, Casey attempted to lift her hand to her nose but she was prevented from doing so by a thick fabric cuff that held it firmly at her side. Repeating the same action with her other hand yielded the same result.

Confusion and anger billowed.

Then she remembered.

With an effort, Casey lifted her head off the pillow. She was in a room, closed off from the outside by a thin curtain. Beyond the curtain she could hear the distant thrum of activity: a hospital's accident and emergency department, the sounds of calls being announced over a public address system. Casey listened for any sign of someone approaching, but it did not seem as though anyone was in any hurry to get to her.

Then, Casey understood why.

She became aware of a presence in the cubicle with her.

Casey's eyes fell across the slight figure of Geddie Kirkwood, curled up in a chair, her arms folded tightly across her chest. She was fast asleep.

Casey recoiled as much as her shackled body would allow. The noise she made caused Kirkwood to stir. She opened her eyes.

"Well, hello there," Kirkwood greeted, sitting up and stretching her arms out before her. "Welcome back."

Casey scowled and flinched painfully; as she did so, the intense pain in her nose stabbed her. She glared in Kirkwood's direction. "What do you want?"

"How are you feeling?" Kirkwood asked, ignoring Casey's question.

"Why are you here?" Casey shot back.

Kirkwood stood and approached Casey's bed.

"I just came by to see you and your parents. They're just getting something to eat so I promised I would stay until they returned."

Though Kirkwood's explanation seemed genuine enough, Casey sensed that she was not telling her the full story.

She shook her wrists in the shackles. "What's with this?" she spat.

Kirkwood frowned. "You have been detained under a section of the Mental Health Act," Kirkwood explained in a neutral tone. "Your parents agreed to this and have allowed you to be held involuntarily until you've been deemed to be a risk neither to yourself nor to other people."

Casey's cheeks reddened. Her jaw shook with barely contained rage. "I want out of here right NOW!"

Kirkwood nodded sadly and turned, pacing slowly toward the end of the bed. "I can't do that. Casey…don't you remember what happened?"

She paused to see if Casey would answer. She remained silent.

"Two nights ago you threw yourself through a plate-glass door. You completely trashed your apartment. There was blood all over place. It looked like a murder scene in there."

Kirkwood turned back towards Casey and gestured at the thick fabric shackles.

"When you were brought in here, you assaulted a nurse and a doctor."

"Bullshit!" Casey retorted.

"They've decided not to press charges but it was touch and go for a time," Kirkwood continued, ignoring Casey. "Look at yourself—right now."

Casey's wrists and forearms were flexed so tightly against the shackles, her arms shook.

How dare they hold me here!

"How long have you been planning this for?"

The question caught Casey off guard and she glowered at Kirkwood, who calmly sat down and drank from her coffee cup.

"What? What do you mean?"

Kirkwood held her hands out, palms up and shrugged.

"It's all there, Casey. I haven't missed anything. Neither have your parents. The withdrawal, your unwillingness to talk. The alienation from your family and friends. The evidence of self-harm. It is clear to me that you've been building up to this for a while. I'd just like to know, how long have you been planning this?"

Casey was apoplectic. She could not believe what people thought she was. But the implication was clear. She struggled once more in her bonds.

"I haven't. I *wasn't.*" She twisted her wrists in the shackles, trying to gain purchase on the Velcro flaps.

Kirkwood watched her. "You weren't what, Casey," she challenged softly.

Reaching the zenith of her struggle and realising the futility of it, Casey slumped back into the mattress of the gurney, defeated. Her efforts had worn her out enough that she was panting profusely.

"You weren't what, Casey?" Kirkwood repeated, more urgently this time.

Casey turned her head and looked at Kirkwood again. The fire had gone from her eyes.

"I wasn't trying to kill myself," she said.

"The state of your apartment—and yourself—would suggest otherwise."

Kirkwood's remark touched off an awareness of herself then, as her face throbbed from the pain of the bruising.

"I *wasn't* trying to kill myself," Casey hissed, through clenched teeth.

Kirkwood sprang from her chair and leaned in close to Casey.

"Then what were you trying to do?" she probed, forcefully enough that it caused Casey to blink. "Look, we've been playing this game for years. You come and see me and we sit in silence session after session. We achieve nothing. I've watched you slowly withdraw, Casey. I've watched an intelligent, vibrant young woman with the world at her feet become a shadow and you won't—or can't—tell me why."

Drawing up to her full height, Kirkwood kept her eyes focused upon Casey. "But you don't need to tell me why, Casey. Because I already know."

Kirkwood extended a finger and touched it lightly to Casey's temple.

"You're hiding something. Something frightening. Something that has you waking in the middle of the night, screaming into the darkness and *scaring the shit* out of you."

As she spoke, Kirkwood watched Casey's expression change: from defeat to anger, then fear. Casey did not attempt to blink away the tears that formed. She turned her head away from Kirkwood and shut her eyes.

"You need to say what frightens you so much, Casey."

Kirkwood waited for several moments then, calmly, she stepped back, turned on her heel and left the room.

Outside, Kirkwood stood in the hallway. Frustration gathered within her. She turned to the door, flirting with the idea of marching back in there and demanding that Casey speak. Instead, she hesitated, forcing herself to relinquish her anger at the situation. No good would come of confronting Casey now. She sensed a breakthrough was coming. Kirkwood would wait.

She had waited this long. She could wait a little longer.

CHAPTER 11

Fedele sat on a stool, quietly preparing items on a trolley beside him. Casey sat on the edge of her bed in front of him. She was hunched over, her head tilted to one side. Her eyes were diverted down and away from him. They were glassy and unfocused. Fedele had been told the amount of sedative she carried on board was considerable. Yet, despite this, Casey held herself somewhat defensively. She was shaking slightly, and did not resist him as he applied a tourniquet to her outstretched arm. Any ideas of protestation that Casey might have harboured had been significantly blunted.

Fedele stole glances at her, hoping he could engage her in conversation but, in the short time he'd been here in this locked room, she had said nothing. She'd barely acknowledged his presence. While he had been made aware of her state before coming here, he was still quietly shocked by just how traumatised she appeared.

Donning a pair of gloves, Fedele shifted the trolley then lifted the butterfly needle with a syringe attached.

"Okay," he said softly. "You know the drill. I'm just going to take a blood sample."

He hesitated, waiting to see if she would respond, but Casey remained submissive, gazing down at the floor through red-rimmed eyes.

He punctured her skin with the needle and saw the immediate flashback into the tubing. Casey did not flinch. He took the required amount of blood into this first vial, then he set it aside, quickly attaching a second. As Fedele kept a cautious watch on her, he flicked his eyes surreptitiously in the direction of a single large mirror behind her. He raised his brow at his own reflection.

Standing behind that one-way glass window, Arlo watched Fedele with silent admiration. Though he knew Fedele couldn't see him from inside the room, Arlo nodded in response.

He was in awe of his mentor's quiet way, his attentiveness. It was highly unusual for a surgeon to perform a task many would consider menial, yet Fedele had never considered it beneath him. Arlo wasn't surprised. Simeera Fedele's investment in each of his patients transcended the norm. He had made it his mission to travel with them through each phase of their journey. His ways were considered unorthodox and the subject of much discussion and even controversy within the surgical fraternity but Fedele would have none of it. He cared deeply and Arlo knew that Casey Schillinge's plight, in particular, affected Fedele. Fedele would be feeling a sense of responsibility for her situation, a sense of failure for not intervening sooner. He knew for certain that Fedele wouldn't give up on her.

Once he had collected what he needed, Fedele released the tourniquet, then he turned his attention to the samples. He had filled several vials, labelled, dated and signed them, then sealed them in a clear zip-lock bag.

Fedele clasped his hands together, resting his elbows on his thighs.

"The staff tell me that you're not getting much sleep," he said softly.

Casey's expression remained blank. Fedele's expression filled with concern.

"Sleep is important, Casey, most important. Surely you must know that if you are well rested then it will be that much easier to overcome this."

He let his words drift between them, hoping that, somehow, they were getting though. She gave no indication that she had heard him.

Fedele rubbed his chin. "Look, I know it is hard, being in here. But it is not unreasonable for us to ask what has happened to you. To try to help you."

Casey's eyes turned in his direction, though she made no effort to turn her head.

"You are one of my greatest successes, Casey. You are better than this. You have a fire inside you that is unlike anything I have ever seen. Do not allow that fire to be put out."

Fedele tapped his own temple for effect. "This torment that has kept you a prisoner. Free yourself from it. I know you can."

There was a slight quiver at the edge of her lips; an unmistakable tension in her jaw. Her eyes moistened but she held herself taut.

Fedele stood, wheeling the intravenous trolley over to the door where he swiped his card over the scanner beside it. The mechanism clicked and he paused, turning back to her.

"You have a strong heart, Casey—and I don't just mean the heart that beats inside of you." Fedele slipped out, ensuring the door locked behind him.

He waited for a moment as Arlo approached him from the antechamber. "What do you think?" Arlo asked.

Fedele put his hands on his hips. The lines on his forehead furrowed deeply. "I don't know. She is very traumatised. Whatever it is that has scared her, it must be considerable. I can't reach her."

Arlo scratched the back of his head. "I've never known her to be like this. She hasn't indica—"

Fedele whipped his hand up, silencing Arlo. He stepped to the door to Casey's room.

Fedele put his ear to it and listened.

He could hear soft sobs coming from inside.

Prishna Argawaal alighted from a lift and scanned the corridor. Consulting her smartphone, she checked the screen with a sign that hung from the ceiling up ahead to her right. Satisfied that she was in the right place, she pocketed her phone and headed in the direction marked by the sign and soon found herself outside a pair of locked doors.

She noted an intercom with a small camera on the wall adjacent to the doors and she stepped up to it and pressed a button.

"Can I help you?" A tinny, metallic voice sounded from the speaker.

"Yes, you have a patient here, Casey Schillinge. I'm hoping to see her."

There was a moment of pause before the intercom speaker clicked and popped.

"I'm sorry, are you family or a clinician?"

Prishna frowned and pressed the button. "I'm neither, I'm—"

She was interrupted by a crackle of static from the intercom as the voice cut her off.

"Only clinical staff and immediate family are allowed to see the patient at this time. You'll need to make arrangements with them."

Shaking her head, Prishna reached into her jacket and pulled her badge from her belt. She raised it to the camera before her and turned her head towards the doors.

A high-pitched buzz sounded, followed by a click from inside the doors.

With a knowing smile, Prishna took the handle and pushed inward, entering the secure psychiatric ward. She saw the nurses' station ahead and made her way to it.

Prishna had heard secondhand that Casey had been brought here, which accounted for the fact that she had been unable to reach her at home. And though it wasn't unusual for Schillinge to be difficult to contact, Prishna had thought it odd that she'd seemingly disappeared. Likewise, her parents' home had been uncharacteristically empty on the drive-bys Prishna had made in recent days. Whatever enmity Prishna might have had towards Casey, it had been replaced with a genuine concern, in light of what she had been told.

Approaching the glass-enclosed nurses' station, a young, casually dressed woman looked up and recognised Prishna from the exchange she'd just had via the intercom. Prishna smiled as the nurse stood.

"I'm sorry," she started, raising her face slightly toward an opening in the glass that separated them. "I didn't kn-know we were expecting anyone else from the police."

Prishna waved her hand, brushing away the nurse's concern as she showed her badge and identification once more.

"You weren't to know. I'm not here as a part of the enquiry into Miss Schillinge's detainment. I am Detective Sergeant Prishna Argawaal. I know the family. I'd just like to make sure she is okay."

"Well," the nurse began, pointing over Prishna's shoulder in the direction of an open doorway behind her. "Her parents are actually here at the moment. They're in the lounge. I can ask if they'd like to see you."

The nurse glanced at a colleague as she stepped through a locked door and came out to where Prishna was waiting. Gesturing towards the lounge, the nurse walked in that direction. Prishna followed closely.

Just as they reached the entrance, Peter appeared in the doorway. The anger in his expression was unmistakable.

"Mr. Sch—"

"What are you doing here?" he growled, cutting the nurse off mid-sentence.

"I heard about Casey," Prishna said, raising her hands. "I was concerned. I wanted to see if she was okay."

"How do you *think* she is, Prishna? How dare you turn up here?"

Peter flushed red and he stepped forward abruptly, balling his hands into fists.

"You've got a bloody cheek," he spat. "Thought you'd catch her at her weakest? Thought she'd drop some piece of information into your lap that you can use against her?"

Edie appeared behind Peter. Her eyes met with Prishna's as she moved to calm her husband, placing her hand on his shoulder.

"Peter," she implored as quietly as she could.

Peter shrugged her off angrily, then glared at the nurse. "Get her out of here now! You should never have allowed her in."

His eyes glazed. Prishna gulped, knowing that the situation was spiralling out of control.

"Peter," she began, trying to placate him. "I just wanted to know if she was okay."

Peter lunged towards her until his face was mere centimetres from Prishna's own. She stood her ground, though her heart was pounding.

"If you don't leave," he hissed, "I'll throw you out of here myself."

"Peter!" Edie gasped.

Peter felt her hand on his shoulder again and he glanced sideways. Edie was standing just behind him, looking at Prishna.

"Peter," she whispered softly. "Don't do this. It's not worth it."

Something in his mind clicked and he realised just how he was standing, how he was holding himself. He glanced down through his tears at his fists and shuddered, shaking them loose before looking up at Prishna once more. He stepped back, awash with shame. He struggled to work his jaw.

"Get her out of here," he whispered at the nurse before turning away and retreating into the lounge.

CHAPTER 12

Peter and Edie sat in silence.

Across from them, Francis Arlo sat on the arm of a chair.

An oppressive thickness hung in the air. Peter and Edie had been unable to look at one another or speak for several hours. They didn't know what to say.

Arlo had tried to buoy their spirits by conversing about the mundane, but he was feeling increasingly awkward. Yet, he felt as though he couldn't just leave them.

Edie eventually looked across at him.

"You look exhausted, Arlo. Why don't you go and get some rest?"

Arlo smiled wearily. "I'm on days off now, Edie. I've got time to spare for you both. Fedele would be here also but he's got a large theatre list today."

Edie reached out and squeezed Arlo's hand.

They waited anxiously for something—anything—to happen. But, as the hours passed and days melded into one another, it was becoming evident that their daughter had locked herself away from the outside world for reasons known only to herself.

Edie had purposely refrained from seeing Casey, reasoning that her presence would only make matters worse. Even Peter—whom everyone figured was best placed to communicate with her—could not break through to his daughter. Casey was as much a stranger to him now.

He sat forward, resting his arms on his knees and rubbing his hands together. His features were stony as he struggled to hold himself together. His eyes were raw. He swatted at fresh tears in muted anguish, not wanting his wife to see.

Edie regarded him with something akin to sorrow but outwardly, her expression remained flat and lifeless.

She was well aware of the turmoil raging inside her husband. She had reached that point long ago. After months and months of trying to reconnect with Casey, of battling against her growing alienation, she had realised bitterly that her daughter was lost to her. Edie didn't know this person that had stepped into Casey's shoes.

Edie had grieved and moved on.

She could only surmise that Peter was now arriving at the same realisation. It was his turn to grieve; yet she did not seem to have the energy to support him.

Peter looked up and saw her dispassionate expression. Through his tears, he furrowed his brow. "How can you just si—"

"Sit here?" Edie interrupted him.

She felt a flash of anger but she let it go.

"This has been coming for a long time," she offered with grim resignation. "Maybe you haven't seen it. Or maybe you have and you've just refused to acknowledge it, but I've known that we would be sitting here eventually."

"But she was never like this," Peter protested breathlessly. "She's always been so pragmatic. A problem solver."

Peter's eyes drifted across the coffee table upon which sat his wallet, car keys and phone. He reached for his wallet and took it, unfolding it as he brought it close to him.

His eyes fell across a photograph inside, secured in a transparent sleeve. It was Casey.

She stood on a cliff-top overlooking a beautiful, lush jungle vista. Dressed in a grubby singlet, hiking shorts and a small backpack, she stood with a hiking stick, tall and proud. Her head was turned towards the camera, her face was haloed by the setting sun. She wore an enthusiastic, almost triumphant, smile.

Glancing at Arlo, Peter offered the image to him. Arlo took it and gazed at the photo. He bowed his head respectfully.

"She's always been so determined," he offered softly.

Peter nodded slowly.

Dawning realisation taunted his conscience. The young woman in the picture was indeed gone. He wept openly now.

Edie's facade began to crack. Tears came freely, more for the grief she could see in her husband than her daughter's predicament.

"What is it that has damaged her so much?'" he whispered.

The glass door to the lounge clicked. Edie and Arlo looked up to see Geddie Kirkwood standing there, hesitating.

"Should I come back later?"

Edie stood. "No, no," she said. "It's all right. Please, come in."

Peter didn't look up as she entered, but nodded absently in support of his wife. His eyes remained unfocused, staring downwards as Edie motioned for her to sit. Arlo stood and sidestepped as Kirkwood passed him. They greeted each other with a silent nod. Arlo set the photograph down on the table as Peter tried to compose himself.

"Sorry, Geddie," he apologised, squeezing his nose between thumb and forefinger to stop it from dripping.

"No need to apologise," Kirkwood responded sympathetically.

"Has there been any change?" Edie ventured flatly, almost reluctantly.

"No," Kirkwood replied solemnly. "She continues to eat a little. Her doctor reports that she is, otherwise, physically well. She just refuses to speak."

Peter leaned back shaking his head. He hissed in frustration. "Six days. Six *bloody* days."

"I know this is an impossible situation," Kirkwood said. "But we can only review her current orders when—and if—she decides to speak. Until that time, I can't establish whether she will be a risk to herself."

"I just want to understand why," Peter whispered.

Kirkwood gestured to the photograph on the table. "Do you mind?"

"No, of course not. Please." Peter slid the image closer to her hand and she picked it up.

Normally, Kirkwood would have put on her glasses to examine a photograph as small as this one but there was no need. Even in the soft light of the lounge, she could make out the image of Casey.

"She is indomitable," she remarked.

Peter raised his eyebrows at her. "*Is*?"

Edie was as equally surprised by her remark.

"Mmm," Kirkwood mused. "Anyone who can go a week without giving ground to any questioning from me must have an incredibly strong will."

"What are you getting at?" Peter asked with a hint of exasperation.

"Casey is doing her level best to prevent anyone from getting inside her head. That doesn't strike me as someone who is weak, or dare I say it, suicidal."

Edie reacted first. She glanced at Arlo then lifted her hand to her forehead, rubbing it in frustration.

"How can you say that? Your saw her apartment…what she tried to do to herself. How can it be anything other than a suicide attempt?"

Kirkwood nodded, then smiled sadly. "Because it was so chaotic. Casey is a methodical person, right? I heard you say it yourself, she's a problem solver. If Casey were going to attempt something so drastic as suicide, I'm betting she would plan it down to the finest detail. It's not in her nature to act so randomly."

Peter and Edie exchanged bewildered glances. Edie shook her head.

"It's a long bow, but I'm asking you to trust me on this. I've worked with her long enough now to know what she is and what she isn't. I don't believe she tried to commit suicide."

"Well, what was she trying to do?" Peter asked, trying to remain calm, to allow himself to go along with Kirkwood's line of thought.

"We've suspected that Casey has been avoiding sleep, haven't we?" Kirkwood ventured. "You've said it yourself, Peter. You've told me that Casey has often hinted to you that she doesn't sleep well and, in all likelihood, hasn't done so for at least a year."

Peter nodded. "Yes, but she's a workaholic. She always has been. It's a personality trait she's picked up from me."

"And that is, in all probability, quite true, but don't you think there is something wrong about it? You've surely seen the signs. The sleep deprivation, the mood swings—not to mention the use of drugs, stimulants especially. She's not using them to keep herself working."

Kirkwood paused.

"I think she's using them because she's *afraid to sleep*."

Peter felt a rush of conflicting emotions as he digested Kirkwood's theory. On one hand, there was relief that Kirkwood didn't think this was an attempt at self-harm. At the same time, he felt a perverse sense of curiosity as he began to search for the possible scenarios that her hypothesis opened up. Yet, as he did so, those scenarios also compounded his confusion and then his fear.

"Do you think someone has spooked her?" Arlo ventured curiously. "Threatened her perhaps? A stalker?"

Kirkwood seemed to consider Arlo's suggestion, but she shook her head. "I don't believe so. I think this is something more visceral. Something within herself."

A pager inside Kirkwood's bag vibrated and she retrieved it, checking her watch. Inspecting the pager's display, she looked at Arlo, Peter and Edie apologetically.

"I'm sorry. Looks like I'm going to have to leave you for now. Have you given any further consideration to finding someone outside of your immediate circle here in Melbourne who might be able to help us in encouraging Casey to open up? You mentioned your son?"

Peter shifted uncomfortably. "We haven't told him about her being in here. Angus has just settled into his job in London and we didn't think it was fair to put him into the middle of this. Even if we could set something up, a video conference or something similar, he would rather get on the first flight home. Angus and his sister have always been close. But, with things as bad as they are right now, we're not even sure that he could get through to her either."

Peter stood and walked aimlessly around the table, stopping before a window that looked out onto the city.

Kirkwood watched Peter as she collected her bag, slinging it over her shoulder. Her eyes drifted to Edie.

Though Edie's eyes were glazed, she had tilted her head suggesting that she was thinking through something. "There may be someone."

Peter turned around and Kirkwood paused at the door.

Edie looked across at Peter and held his gaze.

"There *is* someone."

PETER MADE HIS way along the bustling arrivals hall of Melbourne airport's domestic terminal, heading towards a gate midway along the thoroughfare.

His troubled mind had refused to relent on the drive out here. Since Edie had put forward her suggestion, he'd wrestled with it.

Bringing further unpredictability into the situation carried a huge risk and Peter wasn't at all sure that this was the right course of action. He feared the damage it could do, yet he'd driven out here anyway. His inner voice told him to go with it.

Approaching Arrival Lounge 8, Peter scanned the crowds to see the first passengers disembarking from the evening flight. He took a moment to collect himself, realising that he'd hurried from the car park more quickly than he'd intended. He brushed the droplets of water from the sleeves of his windbreaker and dragged his fingers through his wet hair. Peter noted that the rain was falling heavier than it had been when he'd set out from the hospital.

"Welcome to Melbourne," he mused darkly.

The individual he'd come for stepped through the entrance into the lounge and immediately scanned the crowds with something of a bewildered expression, but when he spied Peter he smiled warmly and waved.

His thinning, silver hair was combed neatly back. His tanned, leathery face boasted jowls that had grown slightly more prominent with age, yet they did not fully consume his visage. He was dressed in a suit jacket, shirt and tie that was paired with moleskin jeans and leather boots. As he stepped around a group of passengers, Peter noted how put-together his father-in-law looked, despite the little time he'd had to prepare.

They approached one another and offered their hands simultaneously.

"Hello, Peter."

"How are you, Lionel?" Peter offered in return before embracing his father-in-law warmly.

Lionel Broadbent slung the strap off his shoulder bag with his thumb and lowered it to the floor.

"I'm well," he chuckled gruffly in a pleasant British accent. "Melbourne has turned the weather on, predictably."

Peter nodded, distracted. "I take it it's all sunshine in Hambledown, as per usual."

"Is it ever not?" Lionel asked sarcastically. "I was in shorts and flip flops before I left this morning. I packed accordingly. Thankfully Ruth checked the forecast before we left for the plane."

A moment of awkward silence crept in between them, then Peter crouched down to pick up Lionel's bag.

"Is this…ooof!" Peter grunted as he hefted the bag up. "Jesus, what did Ruth pack into this thing?"

"Bare essentials, apparently," Lionel replied as they walked toward the arrival hall. "Although her definition of essentials varies greatly from mine."

"Apparently."

The SUV cruised along the slick Tullamarine freeway, untroubled by the downpour. Through the rain-peppered windshield and the wipers swinging rapidly back and forth, Lionel watched the approaching skyline of the city grow more prominent.

"How long has it been?" Lionel asked.

"A week," Peter replied with a soft gulp. "*Physically*, there's nothing wrong with her. It's just that she won't talk."

The dashboard lights threw an unearthly glow up onto Peter's features. Lionel noted deep lines of tension across his forehead. He could see that he was thoroughly exhausted. Peter appeared twenty years older.

"And you think it's because she's hiding something?"

"That's what her psychologist thinks. I don't know what to think anymore," Peter's shoulders slumped. He leaned back into his seat.

"*Psychologists*," Lionel remarked acidly. "They're more trouble than they're worth."

Looking out the window, Lionel shook his head slowly.

"And no one has been able to reach her?" he asked.

Peter didn't respond. His eyes remained forward, unable to look at his father-in-law. Lionel noted that his eyes were glassy and his lip trembled as he struggled to keep himself from breaking down.

Lionel chewed the inside of his lip, trying to think of what to say next.

"She's so *bloody stubborn*," Peter said finally, his voice trembling with anguish.

"What makes you think I'm going to be of any help?"

Peter managed a bitter half-smile.

"I don't," he said, turning to look at Lionel sympathetically. "Sorry…"

Lionel frowned.

"You were Edie's suggestion," Peter added simply.

At this, Lionel's eyes went wide and he took an audible intake of breath. "*Edie*. Good Lord."

CHAPTER 13

Do I knock?

His leathery hand, balled loosely into a fist, hovered near the white door. Lionel cocked his ear, hoping to hear something from behind it. He shook his head.

Silence. Too silent.

Looking back over his shoulder and glancing down the corridor, Lionel realised he was alone. Of course, that was how he'd wanted it to be, but now he wasn't so sure. This wasn't, after all, just anyone he'd come to see.

What am I going to find?

Lionel pushed through his doubt and rapped on the door three times, then lowered his hand to the handle. He opened it and quietly stepped into the room. Its starkness assaulted him. The walls were painted a crisp white. Though a high window allowed light and the colour of the grounds beyond into the room, a cold and clinical feeling enveloped him—and it wasn't pleasant. There was a single bed. Actually, it wasn't even a bed. Rather, it was a large, vinyl-encased piece of foam with a pillow, sheets and a quilt.

No metal or fittings that could be used as a weapon to harm—or to inflict self-harm, Lionel thought.

A single large mirror was embedded in one wall, and underneath stood a small wash basin. There was another door opposite.

The room was sparse, unsympathetic.

Casey was neither on nor in her bed, nor on the single plastic chair provided. In fact, Lionel almost made the mistake of thinking there was no one in the room at all. As his eyes wandered however, they fell across the pathetic form huddled up in the corner on the other side of the bed.

He gulped upon seeing her—stifling a gasp.

Despite Peter and Edie's warning, he was nonetheless shocked by his granddaughter's appearance.

Her hair was matted and flat to her head. Her skin was pasty. Her eyes were sunken and ringed with dark circles. Her cheekbones were disturbingly prominent. The singlet and shorts she wore were crumpled and stained with what Lionel guessed was fresh vomit.

He couldn't be sure that Casey even registered his presence. Only the twitching of her eyelids betrayed her otherwise catatonic state. Her eyes did not turn in his direction. Rather, they darted in every direction but his. As Lionel quietly closed the door Casey flinched, causing locks of her stringy fringe to fall down over her face and she drew her knees closer to her body.

Lionel shifted, somewhat awkwardly, unsure of whether to remain standing or whether to take up the chair next to him. He continued to study his granddaughter, contemplating whether to speak first or sit.

Did she even realise it was him?

Taking the folded newspaper out from under his arm, Lionel lowered his hand to the chair and drew it towards him.

"You might w-wanna wipe that down," Casey slurred suddenly from underneath her curtain of fringe. Her voice was gravelly, clearly affected. "I think I peed on it earlier."

Raising an eyebrow, Lionel regarded the chair then leaned in close to it. There didn't appear to be any offensive detritus evident but, just in case, he saw a hand towel hanging over a tap behind him and he reached for it. Quickly wiping the seat down, he tossed the hand towel into the basin then positioned the chair and sat without giving Casey's warning another thought.

He crossed his legs casually, then he leaned back. He continued to study her but he said nothing. In truth, he wasn't entirely sure of where to begin. Instead, he unfurled the newspaper he held and took out a pair of glasses. He began to read.

For her part, Casey struggled to maintain a discreet eye on her grandfather through her sedative-induced haze.

What is he doing here? More to the point, why is he reading the newspaper?

Casey tried to clear her head, unsure whether she was hallucinating.

Part of her couldn't believe he was here and it took all of her resolve to prevent her from springing to her feet and rushing to him: her beloved Pa. The other part of her seethed with anger at what she suspected was a ploy, hatched by Kirkwood and her parents—a push to get her to talk.

With a blunted expression of incredulity, Casey looked out from under her hair at Lionel as he casually read the newspaper. Though her vision was blurry, she recognised the masthead of the *Hambledown Reader*.

"W-what are you doing?" she slurred in annoyance.

Without looking up, Lionel licked the end of his finger and turned the page. "Catching up. I didn't have the chance to read this on the flight."

Casey blinked.

"Weather's beautiful in Hambledown right now," he continued as composed as he could. "Can't believe I left it for the rubbish that's coming down outside. Mind you, it does seem rather poetic given the circumstances."

Casey turned her head. "It's a-always beautiful in Hambledown," she said softly.

"The meadow above the beach is looking more lush than it has in years, you know. The Braithwaites have cattle grazing on it right now in fact. It's turned into quite the little earner for Sonya and Andrew. Sonya sends her love by the way."

Casey squeezed her eyes shut, still not convinced that this was real, that Lionel was here.

"They've not long gotten back from America. Catching up with Andrew's family, touring about, that sort of thing. It's wonderful to see actual—"

"What are you doing here?" Casey snapped abruptly.

Lionel looked over the edge of the newspaper. She'd brushed her hair aside and was now staring at him with piercing eyes. A smile tugged at the corners of Lionel's mouth.

Lowering the newspaper, he sat forward. "I'm told you're in rather a predicament."

"How did, how could you have kno…"

Her voice trailed off; a flash of understanding managed to register through her fog and a bitter smile appeared.

"Dad asked you to come here, didn't he?"

Lionel turned the page of the newspaper without looking up and went on reading. "No. Your mother did actually. She thought I might be able to help."

Casey shrugged petulantly and leaned her head against the wall.

"Your parents are sick with worry. What is this business about not eating or talking to anyone?"

Casey didn't answer.

"Surely you can't think that is healthy," Lionel observed, frowning.

"I don't know," Casey said dismissively, holding her shoulders up as she fought a wave of dizziness. "I wouldn't want anyone misinterpreting me. There s-seems to be a lot of that going on lately. Especially from Edie."

Lionel didn't react to her invective.

"Why do you believe that everyone is conspiring against you?" Lionel ventured.

"You've seen the reports, yes?" Casey countered. "Young woman tries to throw herself out of her window at two in the morning. People tend not to trust the words of someone who's tried to off herself."

Casey's lip began to shake. Her eyes glazed and she looked away from her grandfather.

"Were you? Trying to off yourself?"

Casey shook her head defiantly. A single tear trickled down her cheek.

"No," she whispered.

"Well," Lionel said cautiously. "Why don't you tell them that? Talk to them and tell them."

Casey wiped her face angrily. "They don't w-want to listen. They d-don't want me to leave here. Kirkwood. Dad. E-Edie, especially," Casey spat. "Now that I've gone postal, everything can be as they've always wanted it to be."

Again, Lionel frowned. "Do you really believe that?"

"They're all happy because they think I'll be forced to reveal myself to Kirkwood and her *mind-fucking.*"

"What's there to reveal?" Lionel asked.

Suddenly, Casey lurched to her feet and staggered as she fought to maintain her balance. Her defiance had returned. Lionel remained seated, unflinching as Casey paced back and forth.

"Dad's happy because he won't have to put up with Edie's bloody nagging." She waved her arms angrily, ignoring his question. "He won't have to check in on me to make sure that I'm *behaving* myself."

"What is there to reveal?" Lionel repeated, adding a harder edge to the question this time.

Casey shut her eyes. "Edie's happy because she can finally have me exactly where she wants me—wrapped up in cotton wool—just like she's always fucking wanted!"

"Oh, don't be so *bloody* ridiculous!" Lionel shot back with considerable rancour. Casey shuddered where she stood.

Lionel sat straight in his seat, his eyes boring into Casey with a potent fire.

"No one wants you to stay here, least of all your mother," he hissed. "They do actually want you to be well but unless you drop this ridiculous charade, you're going to find yourself locked up in here for the foreseeable future. And who knows how long that could be?"

Crossing his arms, he let his words hang in the air between them. His gaze remained unrepentant.

"What are you afraid of, Casey?" he probed. "It's obviously significant enough to have caused you to change so dramatically. I don't even recognise you." Lionel stood, placing his hands in his pockets. "Do you think I or your grandmother haven't noticed? Sure we may not be around as often as we used to be but we've seen it. You look different. You never seem happy. You haven't ventured north to see us in what, two years? Hambledown was your favourite place to come to spend your holidays, even during your university years."

"People do change, Pa."

"Do they change so much that they want to end it all without there being some underlying reason? I don't believe they do. So what is it? What are you hiding?"

Casey's features tensed. Her eyes grew wide and her jaw quivered. "I wasn't *trying* to hurt my—"

"No? Then what?" Lionel interrupted her. He leaned against the far wall, hands still in his pockets, studying her. "What's going on with you?"

Casey looked away from him and rubbed her forehead, agitated.

Of all the people to press me, why did it have to be my Pa?

"Tell me what it is," he said forcefully. "Everyone has been treating you with kid gloves for far too long but it's time to stop. You have to start facing up to this, Casey."

Outside the room, Kirkwood and Peter stood before the one-way viewing window, watching Lionel and Casey. Kirkwood was biting the inside of her lip. She was clearly tense. She turned to look at Peter who, by contrast, was surprisingly calm.

"We're taking an awful risk," she remarked with concern. "I don't know if it's wise for someone untrained to push her so hard."

Peter breathed in slowly. "Lionel's had thirty years in the Victoria Police," he said softly, looking at her. "He used to this sort of stuff. He's an old-school copper."

Kirkwood shook her head slowly.

Casey backed herself further into the corner and wrapped her arms around her legs tightly.

"Don't, Pa," she whispered through gritted teeth.

"Don't what?" Lionel retorted. "I'm not the one playing games. Tell me what you're afraid of. What's with those awful wounds on your chest? Is it your heart? Is there something wrong with it? They say you haven't slept properly in months. Why is that? Is there something you fear about sleeping?"

She felt a pounding in her head as Lionel's questions peppered her. Her anxiety grew, seeping into her lungs, suffocating her. Her eyes darted fearfully from her grandfather to the floor.

Sensing an opening, Lionel stepped forward.

"Tell me," he demanded.

In her mind, flashes of imagery pierced through a dark veil and she gasped. Glancing around the room, Casey could not determine whether she was awake or caught in the nightmare once more. She threw her hands up in front of her face but she was unable to stop the images hurtling towards her.

The road. The car. The lone sign in the darkness.

"Tell me!"

Casey lifted her hands to her head, grasping her scalp hard. She hissed angrily as the images came faster.

The shrouded figure coming towards her. She was running as though caught in a thick soup, her face a mask of terror.

"TELL ME!"

In her mind, Casey saw herself standing before a towering wall. Large fissures had opened up in the structure. Mortar crumbled and turned to dust, allowing the nightmare's images to slip free like nebulous apparitions. Her scream was silent as she flung herself against the structure, pushing with all her might to stop her fortress from collapsing, even as large columns of stone all around her cracked and crumbled. The wall shook and sagged. She cried out, but her screams were swallowed by the chaos. Tears of blood streamed from her eyes and fell at her feet.

"No, no, no, NO!" Casey screamed in the confines of her hospital room as she balled her hands into fists and pounded ferociously at her temples. She hissed through her teeth, squeezing her eyes shut against the torrent.

But it was no use.

Lionel's shoulders dropped at the same moment as his features. He looked upon his granddaughter in horror and shame as she continued to beat on herself, rocking back and forth and slapping her feet against the floor.

Shatterpoint, he thought ruefully.

Lionel was canny enough to know when a subject had been pushed too far. There was nothing left he could do. He could only extricate himself from the room as quietly as possible without causing further trauma.

Slowly, his hand enfolded a piece of paper in his trouser pocket and he drew it out, looking down upon the picture card of Jeanne Hebuterne. He hesitated momentarily, then stepped forward and set it down on the edge of her bed. He turned and went towards the door.

"Don't leave!"

Lionel stopped at the sound of Casey's voice through wracking sobs and slowly, he turned back to face her. Casey's hand was on the picture card before her.

"Don't leave," she pleaded again, her tear-filled eyes fixed upon him.

He did not move.

"I can't make them stop," she seethed desperately. "They keep c-coming for me and I can't make them stop."

Lionel turned back to face her while keeping his hand on the door handle.

"What, Casey," he whispered urgently. "What can't you stop?"

Unfurling the index finger of her left hand and tapping angrily at her temple, she steeled her jaw and ground her teeth together. Her body shook once more in reaction as she prepared to let go of that which she had held onto for so, so long.

"The…the…" Her face became a mask of anguish. "The nightmares."

As the revelation spilled from her lips, Casey sagged against the wall and began to wail uncontrollably.

Swiping his own tears away, Lionel dropped to his knees and took her into his arms. He held her tightly as her entire body seemed to crumple in his embrace.

"It's all right," he soothed gently. "It's all right. Let it go, Casey."

"I can't make them stop, Pa," she heaved desperately. "They've been with me for so long and I can't make them stop. I've tried so hard to fix this on my own. I couldn't fix it, Pa. I couldn't fix it!"

Adjusting himself on the floor while not letting her go, Lionel looked over at the mirror on the wall opposite and nodded. Behind it, Kirkwood and Peter stood silently, unable to look at each other immediately.

Finally, Kirkwood turned her head.

She was visibly shaken.

"He got to her."

CHAPTER 14

In a pretty flower garden, in a quiet corner of the hospital grounds, Casey sat on an ornate bench. Her legs were drawn up, her arms wrapped around them and she held them tight against her body. Her eyes were closed as she rested her head on her knees, luxuriating in the warmth of the sun on the back of her head.

It was a beautiful morning. To Casey, having realised she'd lost count of the days she had been held indoors, it had an almost hyper-real feel to it. A light breeze tugged at the upper branches of nearby shade trees, whistling through the foliage in such a way that she felt she could hear the crinkling of each individual leaf. It caressed the hedgerows behind her and the rosebushes surrounding her. Birds twittered on the lawns and splashed in a nearby fountain; it sounded as though they were right beside her.

The brightness of the morning necessitated sunglasses, even though Casey knew instinctively it was just an average sunny day. Colours appeared so much brighter. Then there was the presence of others around her. People—other patients—walked or sat nearby, either with family or hospital attendants, engaging in conversation or, like her, revelling in the solitude the gardens afforded. Casey felt unsettled by their proximity.

Lifting her face, she felt the luxurious warmth of the sun and she smiled. For a moment, Casey almost felt free.

At least the illusion was nice.

She could not deny that she felt a release from the psychological imprisonment that had tormented her for so long. She was grudgingly appreciative of her grandfather's persistence. In its place, however, was far less certainty. There were now more questions.

And she did not know where to begin answering them.

Glancing to her left, she spied a hospital attendant pacing nearby. Though he was keeping a respectful distance, there was no doubt he was keeping a close eye on her. She smirked.

Casey looked back towards the main building of the hospital and spied Kirkwood approaching her from across the lawn. As their eyes met, Kirkwood hesitated and seemed to consider leaving her be. Casey sat forward in expectation and gestured with a small wave. Acknowledging her, Kirkwood continued forward, closing the short distance to the garden seat.

"Gorgeous morning," Kirkwood greeted. "How are you feeling?"

Casey nodded. "Awake. But not in a bad way."

Lowering her legs to the ground, Casey shuffled aside in a silent invitation.

Kirkwood looked across at the hospital attendant as she sat and nodded subtly at him. She set the clipboard down beside her.

Casey noticed their silent communication. "Was the chaperone *really* necessary?"

"Well, this *is* your first time out in nearly two weeks," Kirkwood observed. "As much as we'd like to give you the space you want, we're obligated to ensure you are safe."

"Afraid I was gonna run?" Casey mocked gently. "I don't think I'd get very far if I tried. I still feel like a zombie."

"Quite an eventful past couple of days," Kirkwood remarked. "I have to admit, your grandfather? I did not see that coming."

"Lionel is a tough cookie," Casey said. "Always has been."

Kirkwood raised her brow. "Tough is right. I'm thinking of offering him a job on staff."

"He's an old-school detective, and a fiercely independent one. He would probably break every rule in your text books. Any lesser patient would have shattered in that room." Casey raised her eyebrows and allowed a smirk.

Kirkwood smiled knowingly. "You may be right. Between you and me, he would do more good for the patients here than most of my colleagues."

"Did Edie really suggest bringing him here?"

Kirkwood nodded. "Your mother knows you better and loves you more than you want to believe."

Casey bit her lip angrily at that observation. She looked away again.

"Well...I can't say that I'm *not* glad to see him." She bowed her head slightly. "I've missed him. My brother and I used to spend a lot of time with him and Nana when we were growing up."

Kirkwood turned to the clipboard beside her. Her hand hovered over it. "They sound like good people. Kind people. Your grandfather is very concerned about your well-being."

Casey's smile faded. "I guess I should add him to the list then."

Another moment of quiet passed between them. Casey fidgeted with a piece of loose thread at the edge of her dressing gown.

"Shall we pick up where *he* left off, so to speak?" Kirkwood ventured.

Casey stiffened. "Don't push it," she said warningly.

"Well," Kirkwood nodded, maintaining her posture. "How about we start somewhere else?"

Casey frowned wearily.

"Look. You've made real progress. Probably the most significant progress in all the time I've known you. Don't you want to try to build on that?"

Casey glanced sideways at Kirkwood. As much as she might have tried to deny it, Kirkwood had a point.

"When did it begin?" Kirkwood ventured, sensing Casey was open to her questioning. "The sleepless nights. The insomnia?"

"That's pretty obvious, don't you think?" Casey said flatly, nodding at Kirkwood's folder. "I'll bet you can pinpoint exactly when it began."

Kirkwood nodded. "My guess is that it was around a year after your transplant. There was definitely a tipping point where I felt you were beginning to withdraw. You're saying that was when the nightmares began?"

"At first I was just shocked by it." Casey's eyes drifted down across the grass. "It was so…*violent*. Disturbing. I'd never had any sort of dream like it before. I remember being so unnerved that I didn't go back to sleep that night. But, it seemed like it was just that one time. It didn't come back and I put it out of my mind. I didn't think anything more about it." She sat forward, straightening her back and she took a breath. "It came again, maybe two weeks later. Same nightmare but much more intense. More detail. More violence. I didn't sleep for days afterwards. But it caught up with me eventually and, as soon as I did sleep…" Slowly, Casey removed her sunglasses and rubbed her eyes. "It happened again and again. Not every time I slept, but close to it. The same nightmare. The same violence. More powerful each and every time."

Kirkwood watched Casey closely. Her eyes revealed a deep pain. Gone was the defiance, the defensiveness that had so characterised Casey Schillinge. In its place, Kirkwood saw resignation. Casey would give her the answers she sought. There was no sense in holding onto them any longer.

"I couldn't predict them. I didn't want to. I began skipping sleep as much as I could. Working helped. I had enough work to keep me going for days at a time. But, eventually I exhausted myself and I'd fall asleep on my feet. The nightmares would come. So I began looking for other ways of avoiding sleep."

"Drugs," Kirkwood said flatly.

Casey nodded.

"What are you seeing in the nightmares that frightens you so much?"

Casey shivered. "I'm on a road...*somewhere.* I don't know where. It's isolated and remote."

"And what's happening there?" Kirkwood pressed cautiously.

"I am running, trying to get away. Someone is coming after me. Chasing me."

"Do you know who it is?"

"It's always too dark. I never see their face."

"Why are you running? What has the person done to you?"

Casey began rubbing her hands together. "I'm being...attacked," she whispered raggedly. "Beaten and...*mutilated.* I don't know why. I try to get away but I can never escape. I'm forced to the ground. There's blood everywhere. It's all around me. It's coming from me."

Casey turned to face Kirkwood. Her eyes were filled with anguish. Tears trickled down her cheeks. Kirkwood reached out and placed her hand on Casey's shoulder. She squeezed reassuringly.

"What happens when you're on the ground, Casey?" Kirkwood pressed, suppressing a rising lump in her throat. She feared she knew what was about to come next.

Casey drew her hand up reflexively and she gasped. The pain of revealing herself was searing.

"Like I said, I'm being attacked," she hissed. "Violated and tortured. But..."

Casey paused involuntarily as her voice caught in her throat. Her eyes flicked left and right as if she were trying to understand something within the memories of her dream. Kirkwood leaned in closer.

"What is it, Casey?"

"*It's not me.*" Casey agonized.

Kirkwood's blinked. "Not you?"

Casey began to shake. "It's as though I'm there and experiencing it. But at the same time, I'm watching as though it's not me."

Casey faltered and covered her mouth with her hand. Her gaze drifted, as though she were trying to comprehend what it was that was happening in the dream.

"It's okay, Casey. Take your time."

"There's someone else. A third person. I'm watching someone else being attacked. I don't know who it is. Every time I get close to seeing them, I wake up."

Casey squeezed her eyes shut, trying to calm herself, realising that she was beginning to panic.

Kirkwood carefully processed what Casey had just told her. She did not know what to make of Casey's description of the nightmare or why she was having them, but seeing her acute distress, after only ever witnessing her defensiveness in the past, quickly pushed those questions to the background.

"You must have felt very isolated," Kirkwood offered sombrely.

"I could never tell this to Dad or Edie," Casey replied bitterly. "They would never have understood. Jesus, I don't understand it." Casey rubbed her eyes. "I spent so long trying to regain my independence after the transplant that if I'd revealed any of this, it would have been fuel for my mother to argue I'm not well enough live my own life."

"And now that you have?" Kirkwood posited.

Casey flashed a bitter smile that faded almost the instant it appeared. "Well, I'm here already, aren't I? Seems I'm buggered either way."

"I don't know about that," Kirkwood countered. "You're not nearly as crazy as you think you are. The question is…what to do about these nightmares."

"I want them to stop," Casey retorted angrily. "How do I do *that*?"

"Well," Kirkwood began, considering that very question. "It would be useful to know why it is you're having them in the first place. There's nothing in your history to suggest you've ever been the victim of a sexual assault or systematic abuse."

Casey whipped her head around and glared at Kirkwood. "Definitely not! Jesus!"

Kirkwood tilted her head. "It *may* be, that the answer to this lies within the dream itself."

Casey frowned, watching as the psychologist pondered her statement silently, then her eyes widened. She understood where Kirkwood was heading with this but she wanted to hear it from Kirkwood herself.

"What are you suggesting?" she questioned worriedly.

"I'm suggesting that there may be a way," Kirkwood said.

She looked at Casey with an expression of burgeoning confidence.

"A way to find out what is going on inside your dreams and maybe, to stop it."

Casey sat across from Kirkwood in her hospital room. The cold and clinical chunk of foam that had been originally assigned to Casey had been replaced by a proper bed, with comfortable and attractive linen. A table and chairs had also been brought in, along with a small sofa and a television set. The lighting in the room was considerably softer now that Casey was no longer on intensive watch.

Lionel sat nearby, having been invited by Kirkwood to sit in on this session, much to Casey's relief. Having him present made Casey feel more at ease than she otherwise might. It also lent a legitimacy to what she was about to subject herself. She couldn't believe what she was going to do—what Kirkwood was encouraging her to do—nor could she believe that her grandfather was supportive of it.

"Okay, Casey," Kirkwood began. "In a moment, we'll begin. Remember, myself and Lionel are here with you. If you feel overwhelmed or frightened, we'll stop. Okay?"

Casey rubbed her hands over the tops of her legs and exhaled. She nodded, glancing at Lionel who smiled at her. His expression betrayed him. She could see the hesitation in his eyes—a sense that he wasn't convinced of the benefit of what was about to happen.

Kirkwood nodded, then stood and walked over to the window. She lowered the curtains, further softening the light in the room.

"Are you ready?"

Casey smiled. "No."

Kirkwood smiled and sat down, resting her hands on her knees. "Remember. You'll be able to control the imagery in your mind, almost as if you were controlling the playback of a movie. You'll be able to fast forward or rewind or pause or even stop it. I'll keep talking to you and ask you to interpret what you see."

Kirkwood lowered her voice, adding a softness and evenness to it that was calming. Casey leaned back into the chair and nodded.

"Close your eyes. Slow your breathing. Listen to my voice and let your body go. Starting with your head, allow all the muscles in your body to release."

Slowly, Casey lowered her head and closed her eyes. She followed Kirkwood's instruction, relaxing back into the seat.

"Feel the muscles in your arms, your hands and fingers. Let them go loose. The muscles in your chest and torso, moving down to your legs, your calves and ankles. The soles of your feet. Your toes. Release the tension in them."

A warmth washed through Casey. She could feel the individual muscles slacken. Casey could hear the sound of her own breathing and with it, the beat of the heart.

As her concentration focused inward, Kirkwood's voice guided her toward a calm centre.

"Clear your mind. Empty your thoughts until there is nothing."

Casey appeared serene. Kirkwood looked across at Lionel and nodded subtly, indicating that she was ready.

"Now remember, I am here to listen, Casey. All you have to do is describe what you see. Nothing or no one can hurt you. You are safe. You are in control."

Casey nodded slowly, silently.

"We're going to enter your dream now."

Through the familiar black shroud that covered her vision, a pinpoint of light flickered and danced. Casey tilted her head, curious as it began to draw closer, growing in size and shape, becoming a gelatinous mass that swallowed the darkness, revealing the familiar cloudscape to Casey. Soon, it surrounded her on all sides. She felt herself floating. The heart beat softly.

"What can you see?" Kirkwood asked, taking up her notepad and pencil.

"Clouds," Casey responded. "Everywhere. I'm floating in them."

"Can you see anything else? Look down."

Casey tilted her head.

Far below her, through breaks in the cloud formations, Casey could see a thin ribbon of bitumen, marked with white lines.

"A road," she whispered. "The road. I-I'm far above it."

"Can you reach it?" Kirkwood asked.

"I think so."

Casey turned her body over and angled herself, using her arms to propel herself downwards. The ground rushed towards her and she spread her arms, slowing her descent. Casey extended her legs, stretched out her toes and touched down gently onto the bitumen. Almost immediately, rain began to fall and she shivered instinctively—both in the dream and in the room.

Lionel straightened his back and looked to Kirkwood, who nodded reassuringly.

"What is it, Casey?" she probed.

"It's raining," Casey responded. "I'm wet and cold."

"Okay. Let's try something here," Kirkwood ventured. "I want you to imagine that you're completely dry. The clothes you're wearing are comfortable and warm. The rain can't reach you. You're surrounded by a bubble of air. It's protecting you."

Casey looked down and watched in amazement as her sopping clothing twitched against her skin. All the water in them was suddenly pulled out and she was completely dry. She turned her head up to see the falling rain bend as it splashed against an invisible shield that surrounded her.

Casey stepped forward hesitantly, watching the bubble move with her and she couldn't help but smile. Lightning crackled across the sky, lighting up the landscape around her, revealing the familiar landmarks. The collapsing stone fence to her left. The line of shattered pines up ahead to her right. She made a note of them as she moved forward.

"What can you see, Casey?" Kirkwood pressed gently.

"I see a stone fence. It borders a paddock—a large paddock. It's desolate… no pasture. There is a line of pine trees that have been stripped of their foliage. It's like they're dead."

Kirkwood scribbled on her pad.

"You sense death here?"

Casey nodded, quickly this time.

Deep thunder rolled across the landscape, carrying the guttural moan that always reverberated through her. She cocked her head and stiffened as dread seeped through her pores.

"It's happening," she breathed.

"Remember, you are in control of this, Casey. All you have to do is stop the flow whenever you want to. I'm right here with you."

Casey turned in the dream looking for Kirkwood but she could not see her. She could however, feel her presence, as if she were standing right beside her.

"Look around you and tell me what you can see."

Casey nodded, stifling a lump in her throat. She looked into the darkness and continued. The bitumen was slippery under her feet.

A second fork of lightning erupted and Casey spotted the road sign, its reflective surface shimmering. Casey instinctively quickened her pace towards it, looking up as she got closer.

"The road sign."

"Can you see what's on the sign, Casey?"

As the lightning strike dissipated, Casey squinted into the darkness, trying to see.

"Remember, you can back it up if you need to, just like controlling a piece of video footage."

Casey nodded and cast her eyes skyward, watching as the lightning above her flashed back into being, crackling in reverse from the point at which it had previously disappeared. When the light was at its brightest, she looked back at the road sign again.

"It's too bright," she cursed between clenched teeth. "I can't make it out!"

Her frustration caused her to lose her grip on the progression of the dream and she was propelled forward, past the sign and into the shadows of the devastated pine trees.

The moaning grew louder and with it, dread and fear beckoned.

Ignoring it and focusing ahead, Casey saw the outline of the car, stationed at an angle. Its headlights punctured the darkness. Casey raised her arm against the glare.

And then she saw him.

Standing in the middle of the road over a crumpled form beneath him.

"It's him!" Casey hissed. Her chest heaved and she felt herself stumbling back.

"Remember, Casey, he can't hurt you," Kirkwood's voice sounded, distant this time.

Casey didn't acknowledge her.

The shrouded figure dropped to his haunches over the stricken human form.

The moan grew louder until it transformed into a horrified scream. Casey slapped her hands against her ears.

The shrouded figure snapped his head up and forward, looking directly at Casey. She could not see his face underneath the wide brim of his hat.

Without warning, he plunged his hand down between the legs of its victim and Casey jerked in pain and terror on the couch.

"Nooo!" she screamed.

"Control it, Casey. You can control it."

Lionel launched out of his chair and prepared to go to his granddaughter but Kirkwood held out her hand desperately to stop him.

"Just wait," she whispered urgently. "It'll be all right."

Lionel relented, filled with anguish.

Kirkwood rose from her chair and moved over to sit beside Casey, who was panting harshly, hyperventilating.

"Can you hear me, Casey?"

Casey nodded rapidly, through clenched teeth. "Make it stop!"

Her head snapped forward just as the assailant prepared to pounce. He launched himself at her. She thrust out her palm in front of her, pushing a pressure wave toward him that distorted the air around them. The pressure wave crashed into the assailant, stopping him in mid stride—frozen. The maelstrom around her ceased. Everything fell silent. Droplets of rain hung stationary in the air.

Slowing her breathing, Casey visibly relaxed and Lionel backed away from her chair.

"It's okay," Casey said softly. "Everything has stopped."

She blinked into the lights of the car ahead and tilted her head, trying to see around the immobile assailant in front of it.

"I see a car…a sedan of some kind. I can see him. He is or was over me? Not me. He's over someone."

Casey squinted harder. "It's a w-woman. I can't see her. But I can feel her. I can feel what she's feeling."

"Can you get closer?" Kirkwood queried, glancing at Lionel. "Can you see who she is?"

Casey screwed up her face, as though trying to focus on the scene before her.

"I can't. I…" she paused, trying harder. "I can't see her yet. I can't see her until it…until…"

Kirkwood nodded, understanding. "What about him; can you make out anything that identifies him?"

"No. He is just a shadow. He's always been a shadow."

"What is he doing?"

"He's frozen. I've stopped him."

Kirkwood made more notes on the page in front of her, then placed the pad and pencil down. She contemplated what she had written for several moments.

"Okay. Let's stop there, Casey. I don't want to push you any further. I want you to back away from the scene now. Let yourself relax. Let your mind go blank."

On the road, Casey blinked as though disoriented. She turned away from the scene before her, feeling the sense of warmth and comfort return. She crossed her arms over her chest and clasped her shoulders. She began to walk away from the frozen assailant, his stricken victim, the desolate pine trees. The sense of death.

"Leave this place," Kirkwood's voice guided her. "Return here with me and your grandfather, where it is safe."

Casey's mind began to drift. Her eyes began to lose focus. She turned her head slightly, spying the road sign passing on her right. Distant light pulsed from somewhere behind her and she stopped.

"Wait," she said aloud, looking around for Kirkwood but remembering that she was alone.

The road sign loomed and she fought to retain her focus.

Casey turned and tried to run toward the sign. Her legs felt heavy.

No!

In desperation, she thrust her head up and reached out towards the sign.

Nothing.

Casey…

"Casey?"

Her eyes fluttered open and Casey found herself back in the office with Kirkwood sitting beside her and Lionel sitting opposite. She felt completely calm, relaxed—more relaxed than she had felt in a long time.

She blinked and looked at Kirkwood.

"How do you feel?" Kirkwood asked.

Casey thought for a moment, realising that her mind was empty. She suddenly didn't know where she was.

She looked down at her hands and then across at Lionel who continued to watch her expectantly.

"Casey?"

Suddenly, Casey gasped. Her features contorted into an expression of shock. Then realisation.

"What is it?" Kirkwood said, worried.

Casey fixed her eyes on Kirkwood and drew her hand away from her mouth.

"Lasterby Road," she whispered.

CHAPTER 15

Casey stepped through a pair of large glass doors and paused at the top of the steps. A stone path led away from the Victorian-era hospital building, across the manicured lawns toward a nearby car park. Beyond a high fence was the outside world.

Hesitating, Casey turned and looked back over her shoulder, ensuring that Kirkwood and Lionel were close behind. Lionel carried her small travelling case, which he used to gesture at the doorway.

Anxiety prickled at the back of her neck as she walked along the path. Her mind cast itself back to the day she had left that other hospital, after her transplant. She recalled the same sense of fear. Here and now however, she quickly dismissed it as absurd, reminding herself that this place had been a prison that had, albeit temporarily, stifled her freedom and forced her to open herself up to far more scrutiny than she had ever wanted.

She was yet to determine whether that had been a wise thing to do, given that another reality began to emerge as she walked out from the shadow of the building. She would now be subjected to another type of prison: her parents' home and the suffocating scrutiny of her mother. She bit down hard on her lip at the thought of it.

As they approached the car park, Casey looked ahead to see her parents approaching from the far side of a group of vehicles that included not only their 4WD, but Casey's own Volkswagen sedan. She glanced questioningly at her father. He managed an awkward smile but Edie's taut expression betrayed an obvious discomfort.

Stopping before her car, Casey looked down and away from them, unable to meet their eyes. Peter embraced her awkwardly, planting a kiss on her forehead.

"Good to see you, love," he offered, as though reciting a scripted line.

As he drew back, Casey nodded over his shoulder at her Volkswagen. "What's with my car?"

Peter glanced at Edie, then across at Lionel who allowed a subtle smile to tug at the corners of his mouth.

"We thought it would be a good idea if Pa drove you back to the warehouse…and perhaps stayed a while there. You know, just until things settle down."

Casey raised her brow in surprise and she turned to her grandfather. "Is that right?"

Lionel nodded as Peter then Edie stood in stony silence.

"Your father and mother and I felt that it would be better for you to get yourself back into a routine as quickly as possible. I suggested I might stay with you, if that's all right. You do still have that guest room upstairs, don't you?"

Casey cast a conspiratorial glare at both Lionel and her father. One corner of her lips pulled upwards in a smile and she could not help but flick her eyes towards Edie. Her mother turned her head away stiffly.

Peter placed his arm around Casey's shoulder and gently steered her away from her mother.

Lowering his voice, Peter looked into his daughter's eyes.

"Look. Think of this as a way to keep Mum happy. She'll accept that you're not on your own and you'll be able to get yourself right again in your own space, albeit with a fairly innocuous chaperone. Agreed?"

Casey gave her father the pretence of considering what he had said, even though she already knew that what he was suggesting was a win-win for everyone…except Edie.

She nodded finally. "I won't argue with that."

Kirkwood, who had been standing at a respectful distance, approached and handed Casey an envelope. "You're all set. I've made a time for you to come and see me on Friday, okay?"

Casey nodded. "Thank you."

Kirkwood gently squeezed her hand. "You've come a long way, Casey—a *really* long way. But there's more to do."

Casey smiled softly and turned towards her car. Out of the corner of her eye, she noted her mother's expression had changed subtly, having witnessed that last exchange with Kirkwood.

It had softened.

As Casey climbed the stairs to the warehouse ahead of the others, she had a flicker of panic, having realised that she hadn't seen it since the night of the accident. No one had mentioned the state that it had been left in when she had been taken by the ambulance, so she had no idea if anyone had thought to clean the embarrassing mess she had caused.

As she alighted onto the corridor outside the industrial door she froze. The corridor was clean—and not just a little bit clean, *a lot clean.*

The flickering light bulb above her head that she had ignored for so long had been replaced. In fact all three of them had been replaced so that the entrance to the warehouse was now significantly more inviting. The faded granary poster seemed more vibrant, just with the amount of light that played across it. A potted plant stood just outside the big green door below a high window that allowed bright sunlight into the corridor.

This window had been boarded up for years.

Casey paused before the door and glanced conspiratorially at Lionel and her father. Slowly, she drew her keys out from her shoulder bag and slid it into the lock, sensing that she knew what she was about to find inside.

Hauling the great door aside, Casey looked in on the apartment and simply nodded. It had been completely cleaned from top to bottom. The shattered glass from the window had been swept away and indeed the window itself had been repaired. Her bed had been made up with fresh linen. There was nothing of the trauma of her accident. It now seemed so long ago.

Setting her keys down on the kitchen counter, Casey surveyed the handiwork with appreciation while Lionel drew aside the large curtains and opened the door out onto the balcony. A fresh sea breeze filtered in from outside and Casey drew it in.

"I'd almost forgotten how wonderful that view is," Lionel remarked as he set Casey's case down on her bed. Casey turned and gestured with a nod towards the mezzanine.

"I'd show you where the guest room is," she said. "But I guess you've probably worked that out already."

"I did endeavour to respect your privacy."

"There's nothing but junk up there anyway," Casey smiled warmly at her grandfather. "The company will be good."

"Do you want me to hang about and cook something?" Peter offered. "I know it's a little early."

Casey rebuffed him with a smile. "Thanks, Dad, but we'll be all right. You deserve a break and besides, you'd better get Edie home."

There was a moment of awkward silence at Casey's acknowledgement of her mother's absence. Edie had decided to remain in the car.

Peter shrugged. He leaned in and planted a kiss on his daughter's forehead. "The kitchen has been stocked. Just let me know if you need anything."

"I will."

Casey nodded to Lionel, then walked her father downstairs to the path leading up from the street. Casey glanced across at the 4WD, saw the shadow of her mother's profile behind the darkened passenger window. A knot of sadness tugged at Casey's stomach and Peter noticed her shoulders droop slightly.

"She's never going to accept all of this," Casey said sourly.

Peter followed Casey's gaze.

"You've taken some big steps. She'll come around. Just give her time."

"I've given her time, Dad. *Too much bloody time.*"

"You're getting yourself together. Sooner or later, she'll see that."

Casey offered him a sad nod, then turned back toward the warehouse.

"Talk to you soon."

Casey found Lionel sitting on the edge of the sofa when she returned, holding a tea cup in one hand, gazing upon the portrait of Jeanne Hebuterne.

He nodded at the countertop, upon which sat an identical cup. Languid wisps of steam rose from the cup and, as Casey turned to it, she caught the sweet scent of chai rising on the steam. It was her and her grandfather's favourite.

"Mmm," she mused pleasurably, taking up the cup. "I knew you wouldn't forget to bring your stash."

Lionel chuckled as Casey joined him. He turned his attention back to the portrait. "I managed to get most of the stains out of the canvas without too much trouble. Though I'm still worried about one or two of them."

Casey squinted, trying to see what stains her grandfather was pointing out. "I can't see anything."

Lionel stood and approached the portrait, extending a finger out towards the right cheek of Jeanne Hebuterne, then beside it where long tresses of her red hair fell down over her shoulder. A trio of darkened splotches stained the canvas.

"They're stubborn," he observed gruffly.

"Like their owner."

Lionel glanced at his granddaughter. He couldn't help but smile at her dark humour.

"I remember when Ruth and I bought this for you," he said. "We'd trudged around Sydney for days searching for it. It became something of an obsession."

"Can't imagine where you got *that* from."

Lionel chuckled. "Your obsession with his art did seem to arrive out of left field. It was as though you had found Modigliani all at once," Lionel clicked his fingers for effect. "Suddenly, you just had to immerse yourself in him."

Casey tilted her head.

"It's rather a curious taste," Lionel continued. "For someone so wedded to the intricacies of information technology as you are. I can only imagine how…monochrome, all that code and programming must be. All those zeroes and ones."

Casey smiled at her grandfather.

"It's not that rudimentary, Pa."

Casey approached the portrait now, gazing up into the eyes of Jeanne Hebuterne. She had become somewhat central to Casey's love of the art of Amedeo Modigliani.

"You do have a point," she acknowledged. "All that code. All those equations. They're absolute. Linear. They are set out exactly as they should be. Where others see them as rigid and uninspiring, I see a kind of beauty in them." Casey paused, sipping thoughtfully from her cup. "But, I guess I've come to yearn for things that are different from what I do. This art is a perfect example. Modigliani's work…it lives and breathes. I love the stylisation. I love his use of colour. You put 'em together and there's something definitely stimulating about it."

As Casey gazed at the portrait, she let her mind wander. All of those things were true. Casey was drawn to something within the works of Modigliani—this work in particular—and it was something powerful.

Though she couldn't determine what that something was.

Casey reclined in her chair on the balcony and gazed out at the star-filled night sky. She sighed. It was good to be home.

Cradling a glass of water in her hand, Casey gently swirled the liquid within, watching how it caught the light from inside, then she closed her eyes. The sounds of Bach's "Goldberg Variations" piped through from the stereo, courtesy of her grandfather.

She smiled.

She loved Lionel's choice of music. It was soothing. It allowed her mind to drift.

Yet, no sooner than she found herself relaxed, a question began to tug at her consciousness.

What is that place?

She squeezed her eyes shut in an effort to crush the incessant question but it would not go away. It persisted. Then an image coalesced.

The road sign.

From the moment she'd latched onto that final, fragmented image from her dream during Kirkwood's session, it had needled her consciousness, nagging her for days. The last thing she wanted now, having just returned home, was to be pulled back into the nightmare.

And yet, the moment she closed her eyes, she was drawn involuntarily to it.

As if part of her actually wanted it.

"Fuck," she cursed under her breath, opening her eyes and drawing the glass up to her mouth.

Even with her eyes opened and focused on the sea beyond, she could still see the lone sign.

Lasterby Road.

Why is this place so vivid?

She couldn't recall ever having been to a Lasterby Road anywhere and yet, the image seemed as strong as a memory.

Though she felt the familiar echo of fear from her nightmares, her curiosity gathered momentum until it gained the upper hand.

She couldn't stand it any longer. Pushing up from her chair, Casey stepped through the doorway and into the apartment.

Lionel was tucked into one corner of the sofa, his head bowed over, fast asleep.

Tip-toeing across the room, Casey sat at her desk and booted up her computer. Her fingers danced across the keyboard as she initiated security measures, ensuring her network activity was secure behind her customised virtual private network, then she opened a browser window. She considered using the darknet, but decided against it and ran an open-web search for Lasterby Road.

Almost immediately, a slew of results flashed up and Casey examined them carefully. Though there were dozens of references to Lasterby Road, much of it appeared to be fragmentary data. Descriptions from news sites all around the world. Obscure references from various local government websites. A few message board postings. Some images. None of them appeared noteworthy. The results blurred into one another.

What am I looking for?

Is it even a question of what, rather than where?

Casey opened another tab and navigated to a satellite imaging service where she was greeted by a high resolution image of Australia, complete with a number of statistical overlays and option panels surrounding it. Touching the search pane with her finger, she hesitated momentarily, then typed in 'Lasterby Road' on the keyboard.

She was greeted with thirteen results for thoroughfares named Lasterby all across the world as the on-screen map zoomed out to reveal the locations her search had yielded. They included the United States, Canada, the United Kingdom, South Africa and Australia.

Lifting one leg up onto the seat and leaning into it, Casey retrieved her glasses and put them on. Manipulating the display with her finger, she appraised each of the pins on the global map.

She sighed. Frustration needled her.

Scrolling her finger across the map, she centred it over the land mass of Australia. If this were to be a question of where, she could start by ruling out all of the locations outside of Australia. If she was certain of anything at this point, she had never been to any of them.

Double-tapping the screen, she zoomed in on the five Lasterby locations in the south-eastern corner of Australia. One in rural South Australia. Two in New South Wales and the remaining two in her own state of Victoria.

Casey squinted, noting that the South Australian Lasterby Road was a dirt track that snaked across a ruddy and vast landscape: pastoral countryside. She recalled the sense of desolation from her dream. The environment in it was akin to rural farmland rather than the vast barren scrub on the screen here. In her gut, she knew this wasn't it.

She manipulated the map over the two New South Wales locales. One of the entries here was again a dirt track running through hilly terrain, close to a township and Casey lingered here for several moments, noting the presence of trees clumped together. The proximity of the township didn't feel right.

She moved away to the second location but when she clicked on the pin there, the description was for a Lasterby Street in what appeared to be a residential development close to the coast.

She homed in on the two remaining pins.

One hovered over a winding fire road in dense, mountainous forest well east of Melbourne's urban sprawl. The other denoted a long strip of bitumen, running in a roughly north-south line in the left-hand corner of Port Phillip

Bay.

She lingered here, zooming in on the pin. The landscape here appeared to be grazing country. A small mountain range overlooked acres upon acres of meadow from the northern edge. Again it was desolate, in a similar vein to her dream, but it seemed too desolate. There was nothing that looked familiar.

And then…

As Casey zoomed out, her eyes hovered over a thin dark line flanking a portion of the road at its southern end. Tapping her finger in the centre of the line, the image zoomed in, then shifted and flashed as it re-focused, revealing the detail. Trees with elongated limbs, dark, needle-like foliage and long shadows cast outward to the left of the line indicating an afternoon sun.

Pine trees!

The tall, devastated pine trees from her nightmare flashed in her mind and Casey felt her stomach plunge.

To the south of the line of pines, Casey spotted a dirt track that intersected with the bitumen. A few feet from that intersection, she saw a dark, L-shaped object: a fence.

An old stone fence.

Her eyes darted between the line of pine trees and the rubble on the opposite of the road, Lasterby Road.

Was this the place?

An isolated pocket of countryside in the south-western corner of Port Phillip Bay. Casey sensed, from the lay of the land and the lack of population surrounding it, this area was vast and open—the kind of place that would terrify her.

She gazed at the landmarks, trying to discount their significance. It couldn't possibly be right.

But deep down inside, she knew.

"Can't sleep?"

Casey jumped at the sound of her grandfather's voice. He was standing right beside her.

"What is this?" he queried, leaning in.

Casey reached forward and tapped the screen. An information panel popped up.

Lionel read the description.

"This is what you've been dreaming about? This place?"

"I have no idea, Pa," Casey lied.

Lionel tapped the screen, causing it to zoom out enough so that he could judge its proximity from the centre of Melbourne. It was a little over an hour's drive, despite the fact it was in the middle of nowhere. He looked at Casey's steadfast gaze. He sensed that her mind was working furiously.

"I thought you were scared of open spaces."

Casey looked up at her grandfather.

"I…I…" Her voice caught in her throat as she glanced back at the screen. "Something happened there," she said, pointing with a slender finger. "Something important. It's been stuck in my mind for so long, Pa."

Lionel nodded in understanding. "Then we'd better go and see if we can find out what it is."

THE BLACK GMC van cruised along the country road, heading toward a strip of azure ocean that filled the horizon beyond the miles of farmland that surrounded them.

Casey sat in the rear passenger seat, holding onto the seatbelt strap as she tried to avoid gazing out at her surroundings. Instead, she concentrated on a comical 'Sasquatch' bobble head figurine that danced crazily on the dashboard. They had been on the road for a little over an hour and she felt she was doing pretty well in keeping her agoraphobia at bay.

Lionel sat up front, watching the rolling countryside through his own window, while occasionally stealing a glance at the mountainous figure driving the van. Lionel was still coming to grips with Scott's intimidating presence—his elaborately tattooed arms, huge hands—and yet, Lionel had been taken by Scott's gentlemanly demeanour from the moment Casey introduced them to one another. On the drive out of the city, he had noticed the quiet way in which Scott made sure Casey was okay, distracting her from her agoraphobia by having her navigate using his smartphone.

Now that they were in the vicinity of the road they were looking for, Scott again stole a glance at Casey, bringing her attention back to her assigned task.

Looking at the screen, Casey spied a blinking chequered flag near the top. It was steadily descending toward the cursor in the middle of the screen as they approached their destination.

"It's just ahead," Casey said, peering over Lionel's shoulder. She scanned their surroundings, comparing them with the satellite image. The familiar landmarks she'd identified last night were there.

Scott slowed as they approached a turn on their left. A crooked pole rose up from a patch of overgrown grass. Attached to it, was a green sign with white, reflective lettering. All three of them gazed at the sign as they drew nearer.

Lasterby Road.

Scott pointed south, toward a distant line of trees. "Let's go have a look."

Casey sat forward now, holding onto the back of Lionel's seat, the gnawing anxiety of her agoraphobia pulsing in her temples as they drove onward down the isolated stretch of bitumen.

A temporary fence that had been erected to block access to the road had collapsed long ago; its remnants lay across the roadway. Scott slowed as he drove over it, then he continued on cautiously. The road was pocked with shallow craters and the surface was cracked in places, indicating that it hadn't been used in some time.

A cold knot settled in Casey's stomach.

The road rose slightly, obscuring the landscape ahead, but as they levelled out Casey felt as though she had received a sucker punch. On their left, no more than a dozen yards away, a straight line of tall pines came into view.

Imagery from the nightmare flashed in concert with what she saw here and now. The pines were tall and healthy specimens, in stark contrast to the devastated branches from the nightmare.

This was the place.

Scott glanced over his shoulder, his expression filling with concern as he noted the colour had drained from her face.

"Keep driving," she instructed stonily.

The van slowly passed the pines while Casey kept her eyes forward. Her breath had quickened, her pulse pounded, but she remained focused.

Ahead, Casey spotted the second landmark she knew so well. She didn't want to believe it.

The tumbled-down remains of the stone fence came into view at an intersection. It was very nearly concealed by overgrown weeds. A dirt track branched off to the west and led away toward a trio of distant hills. Here, again, a sign denoted the road. Casey reached forward and placed a hand on Scott's shoulder.

"Stop," she said softly.

Scott angled the van over to the side of the road. Even before he'd brought it to a complete stop, Casey had clicked open the side door and stepped out. Both Lionel and Scott exchanged looks as Scott extinguished the engine and the two men got out.

Casey walked slowly forward, craning her neck to appraise the sign as she passed it.

The veil of her nightmare descended.

The darkness surrounding the sign. The glare from the headlights on its reflective surface.

She could barely comprehend it, yet there was no doubt.

This was the place that had haunted her for so long. Everything appeared exactly as it did in her nightmare.

Casey's legs became heavy. Her hands began to shake.

Her eyes darted forward, along the road to the place next to pines where she had witnessed—and had been a victim of—horrific acts of violence.

But I haven't!

"I've never been here!" she screamed.

Her nightmare leached from her mind, the dream world melding with the real. Anguished screams resonated as Casey recalled the violence she had observed and experienced. And then, she was sucked from that experience. She was standing before the all-too-familiar scene, reality replaced by fantasy, as she watched the woman screaming, crying out to Casey.

She thrust her face out towards Casey, pleading through blood-soaked tears, clawing at the air between them with her free hand.

No!

The heart thumped furiously inside Casey's chest, sending shards of pain through her. She clutched at her shirt. Her legs buckled and she collapsed to the road, consumed by the pain and the noise and the chaos in her mind.

Lionel and Scott rushed to her side. Lionel dropped to his knees and grabbed her shoulders. With the touch of his hands, the chaos ceased abruptly. She was returned to the present, to the quiet.

Casey looked up at Lionel through unfocused eyes and blinked as though she did not know where she was.

"Casey?" Lionel shook her gently, trying to reorient her. "Casey!"

She squeezed her eyes shut, then opened them again. Her tortured expression slackened, melting first to confusion, then calm.

And then determination.

"It happened here," she rasped, raising a finger to her temple and tapping it hard. "Whatever it is that's going on up here, it began on this road."

"I don't understand, Casey," Lionel shook his head.

"All this time, I've been dreaming that something happened to me right here."

Lionel helped her to her feet and she brushed herself down. She held her arms out before her, palms down, as if feeling a magnetic force rising from the road before her.

"But, it wasn't me at all."

Lionel glanced at Scott who was equally perplexed.

Casey stepped forward, her mind working anew as she took in the scenery around her, assessing it. Approaching the pines, Casey inspected them, trying to see if there was anything significant about them.

The car was there, in the darkness, stationed at a crazed angle on the road.

Realisation began to foment and Casey looked down, touching her hand to her chest. Through the ragged scars, she could feel the heart beating fast, yet steady.

She turned to face Lionel and Scott.

"I think I know what happened."

CHAPTER 16

The apartment was quiet. Though the sounds of the street and beach filtered through the open door, it wasn't loud enough to distract Casey.

On the drive back from Lasterby Road, the image of the young woman had remained firmly planted in Casey's mind.

She was pleading with Casey, reaching out from underneath her assailant with a single, free hand, clutching desperately towards her.

Casey felt the stranger's terror; a visceral echo. It caused her to shiver.

Casey sat at her computer. A browser window was open, with a page of search results on it. She had been at it for several hours, ever since Scott had dropped her and Lionel back at the warehouse. Lionel had decided to head out and fetch a few grocery items and visit her parents.

She knew it was to give her some space with her thoughts.

She smiled wanly, thinking of his consideration and thankful that he trusted her to not do anything rash.

Her eyes refocused on the screen. A page of images was displayed in front of her, images of countryside in the vicinity of Lasterby Road and some of the road itself.

Until now, the most compelling snippet of information she had discovered on Lasterby Road was the reason for its apparent closure: a scientific report chronicling geological instability in the area surrounding it.

She hissed as she scrolled angrily through the images.

You know…

"Rubbish, rubbish, rubbish."

Returning to the search pane, Casey paused and stood, going over to the kitchen and pouring herself a glass of water.

Again, the face of the girl appeared in her mind.

Her anguish. Her torment. Their torment.

Casey squeezed her eyes shut then turned to the screen.

A voice inside taunted her.

You know what to look for…

Her hands hovered over the keyboard and she wiggled them nervously; she was fighting against herself to get them to type that which she sensed deep down was the key.

Finally they descended. Casey keyed in 'Lasterby Road' then, beside that, a date.

March 17, 2012

This time, she filtered the results by news items only. She tapped 'Enter.'

Instantly, a page of news headlines flashed up: the first of which was an item from the Australian Broadcasting Corporation.

Young Woman Found Critically Injured On Country Road Following Apparent Hit/Run.

Casey felt her stomach lurch as she clicked into the story.

Police are appealing for any witnesses to come forward after a young Melbourne woman was found abandoned with critical head injuries on an isolated rural road two nights ago, the apparent victim of a hit-and-run.

The story was brief, giving little additional information or images. Casey backed out of that story and went to the second item in the results:

Police Race Against Time In Search For Answers To Baffling Hit/Run On Lasterby Road.

Victoria Police have been unable to find any clues to the circumstances surrounding a tragic hit-and-run accident involving a twenty-two-year-old student from Melbourne's inner northern suburbs.

She clicked back then tapped the next item. This time, she gasped as the page flashed up.

Young Woman Lies In Induced Coma As Detectives Continue Their Inquiries After Hit/Run.

Melbourne's public is snapping to agonised attention at the plight of a young Melbourne woman and the mysterious circumstances surrounding the hit-and-run which left her in a coma. Twenty-two-year-old student Saskia Andrutsiv lies in an induced coma with life-threatening head, abdominal and pelvic injuries after being found close to death by a local farmer on Lasterby Road near the beachside township of Queenscliff.

Police have been unable to find any witnesses of this tragic accident. Preliminary enquiries point to Miss Andrutsiv's presence at a music festival at a Queenscliff beach in the hours prior to her discovery but no other details have come to light as yet.

To the right-hand side of the text, a grainy black and white image had been posted of a young woman, to which Casey's eyes zeroed in.

It was her!

Reaching out from underneath her assailant with one free hand, clutching desperately at the air.

Casey fumbled underneath the glass surface of the desk, searching for a notepad and pencil. She flipped the pad open and slapped it on the desk, scribbling down the name of the girl, then returned to the computer screen. Clicking back into the search results, Casey scrolled down the page further. The headlines began to blur into one another, though the name Saskia Andrutsiv, the road and the mention of the music festival continued to feature in the subtext below each headline.

Casey was searching now, beyond those initial headlines and the dates on which they were posted, looking for the next logical item that she sensed she knew would come.

She found it.

Doctors Announce The Death Of Lasterby Road Hit/Run Victim. Family To Donate Organs.

Saskia Andrutsiv, the young woman at the centre of a baffling hit-and-run accident, has lost her battle. Doctors announced that her family has agreed to turn off her life-support this evening. Despite their best efforts to save her life, doctors have described Miss Andrutsiv's injuries as catastrophic and that her head injuries in particular were so severe that her chances of recovery were severely limited. In making their devastating decision, the family has agreed to donate Miss Andrutsiv's organs, saying that the opportunity to provide a life-saving gift to multiple patients was one that brought them great comfort at this tragic time. Formerly from the Ukraine, Miss Saskia Andrutsiv was described as a vivacious young woman, a loyal friend and a passionate student who was enrolled in an Art History degree at Melbourne University. According to a family spokesperson, it was Miss Andrutsiv's dream to become a gallery curator, preserving the works of famous European artists.

Casey's eyes filled with tears as she read through to the end of the news report. Here, a higher resolution image of Saskia Andrutsiv had been posted. This time, there was no doubt.

Her hand lifted towards her chest. The heart within thumped forcefully, its beat quickening, the longer Casey gazed at the image of the woman on screen.

The industrial door slid aside and Lionel entered quietly, armed with a pair of shopping bags. Upon seeing his distraught granddaughter, his eyes grew wide with worry and he placed the bags on the kitchen bench.

"My dear, whatever is the matter?" he asked, rushing to embrace Casey.

Lionel peered down at the screen. His own heart plunged as he scanned the information.

Casey wiped her eyes, slumping into her grandfather's embrace as a renewed torrent of emotion surged.

"She was my donor, Pa," Casey sobbed. "I've found my donor."

Casey stood before the window in Kirkwood's office, taking in the garden outside. A trio of birds frolicked in the urn, splashing water everywhere. She watched them intently, distracting herself from the emotions that swirled inside her.

"We can sit out there if you like."

Casey cocked her head, considering Kirkwood's offer. Instead, she turned back into the room. "No, that's all right."

Kirkwood nodded, then regarded the yellow envelope that Casey had set down on the table. "Did you have something to show me?"

Casey sat down in the armchair opposite Kirkwood and clasped her hands together. "I do. And, I think I need your help."

Kirkwood cocked an eyebrow and offered an inquisitive smile. "Well, that's something I've been eager to hear for a long time."

Casey did not smile in return. Her gaze remained fixed. It was steely, serious.

"I know why I've been having the nightmares," she said. "I don't quite understand *how*—but I do know why."

Kirkwood sat forward.

"I know who my donor was."

Kirkwood blinked, shock registering in her features. She watched as Casey opened the envelope on the coffee table and drew out several A4 printouts. She regarded them as a fleeting moment of doubt threatened. Then she held them out for Kirkwood.

"Saskia Andrutsiv," Casey began, "was struck down by an unknown vehicle four nights before my heart transplant in 2012. It happened on a country road just outside of Queenscliff. A Lasterby Road."

Kirkwood lifted her reading glasses into place. She studied the news articles one by one.

"She was discovered by a farmer who reportedly heard her scream and found her on the road, left for dead. He called an ambulance and they took her to a hospital where she lay in a coma. The doctors tried to save her, but her injuries were too serious. They were…*catastrophic*."

She looked down at her hands, fidgeting nervously.

"Saskia Andrutsiv was declared braindead on the 17th of March, 2012. Her family made the decision to donate her organs."

"March 17th," Kirkwood said softly. "The day of your transplant."

Casey nodded. "No one ever came forward and admitted to having been involved in the accident. There were no witnesses to it and the police were never able to find anyone responsible. It became a cold case."

Kirkwood was concerned. Though it was not unheard of for organ recipients to discover who their donors were, it was uncommon and expressly discouraged.

"Casey," Kirkwood began cautiously. "You know very well that there are strict laws in place to protect recipient and donor families. In any case, h-how can you even be sure that this woman is your donor?"

Casey bowed her head and nodded at the floor, acknowledging Kirkwood's point.

"Why then? Why would you want to know?"

"Her death was no accident, Geddie," Casey declared calmly.

Kirkwood blinked as Casey's expression became even more determined. It didn't escape her notice that Casey referred to her by name—possibly for the first time ever.

"The nightmares—*my nightmares*—I thought it was me being attacked in them. But it wasn't me at all."

Casey leaned forward and pointed to the A4 sheet in Kirkwood's hand, the image of Saskia Andrutsiv.

"It was her," she said, her voice dropping to nearly a whisper. "It was her that I've been seeing. It is her heart that I'm carrying inside me." Casey balled her hand into a fist and tapped the centre of her chest.

"She was murdered on the road that night…and she has been trying to tell me ever since."

Kirkwood sat up straighter in her chair and set the printouts down on the table. She exhaled through her teeth, clearly uncomfortable with Casey's theory.

"Casey, I can't possibly know where to begin with all of this. What you're telling me is not rational. It's the s-stuff of *fiction*."

"It's not fiction!" Casey snapped defiantly. She stood abruptly. There was a fire in her eyes that alarmed Kirkwood enough that she gripped the arm of her chair.

Casey quickly relaxed her shoulders.

"Look. I've never sought to find out who my donor was before now. I've never wanted to. You've been trying to get me to talk for years, Geddie—to tell you what's going on inside my head. Well, *this* is what is going on!" Casey pointed sharply at the news article.

"I know it sounds completely crazy. But Saskia Andrutsiv is the face I've been seeing in my nightmares and I *promise* you, I've never seen her anywhere else."

Casey paused as the woman's face echoed in her mind. Tears began to well and she wiped her eyes with her knuckles in frustration.

"She has been trying to reach me—to tell me the truth—and I wasn't listening," she continued shakily. "But I am listening now."

Kirkwood listened and considered.

Her rational, analytical mind would never entertain such a scenario. Then again, Casey Schillinge was no ordinary patient. Kirkwood was aware of literature, often regarded as fringe, concerning cellular memory: the idea that donor organs contain some sort of neuro-chemical "memory" of the individual from which they'd been harvested.

"You believe this to be true, without *any* foundation to support your theory?" Kirkwood ventured.

"I know it sounds ridiculous. But yes." Casey's gaze drifted through the window. She crossed her arms. "I'm not crazy. I *know* I'm not."

In that moment, Kirkwood saw something in Casey that she doubted she'd ever seen more acutely.

Determination. Resolve.

"Well," Kirkwood ventured cautiously. "I'm not entirely sure how we can go forward with this."

"I want to re-enter the nightmare again," Casey replied softly. "Like we did before. I want to see if there is anything else—a clue—something I can, I don't know, follow up on."

Kirkwood shifted uncomfortably in her seat.

"Casey, I don't know if that is a good idea. It could be very dangerous for you."

"Then why did you do it before?" Casey challenged, staring directly at Kirkwood.

Again, Kirkwood couldn't help but smile, but it was an awkward, reactionary smile at having been so comprehensively skewered. She studied Casey for a long moment and then nodded.

She was beginning to see where Casey was heading. "You think that by solving her murder, the nightmares will stop."

Casey shrugged. "I don't know. Yes. *Maybe?*"

Without speaking, Kirkwood rose from her chair and went over to the window, drawing the blinds across. She then switched off the main light and turned on a lamp that sat on the corner bookshelf behind the sofa. The light in the room softened considerably.

Casey sat down on the sofa.

"Make yourself comfortable, like you did before," Kirkwood instructed hesitantly.

Casey kicked off her sandals and set them to one side, wriggling her toes and rubbing her feet on the soft carpet. Adjusting her top so it flowed freely, she relaxed back and looked across at Kirkwood expectantly.

The doubt on Kirkwood's features was unmistakable.

"I *want* to do this," Casey said confidently. "I *have* to do this."

Kirkwood bunched a cushion behind her back and rested her hands on her thighs.

"Okay," she began. "Like before, you'll control the imagery. Fast forward or rewind, pause or stop. All I'll do is keep talking to you and ask you to interpret what you see."

Kirkwood lowered her voice, adding the familiar softness to it that calmed Casey. She leaned back into the sofa.

"Close your eyes. Focus on my voice and let your body relax. Starting with your head, allow all the muscles in your head and your neck and your shoulders to let go."

Casey complied and breathed deeply, feeling air moving in and out of her lungs. Several minutes passed as she further relaxed and drifted slowly into a lessened state of consciousness. She felt herself heading into darkness and Kirkwood's voice came to her as a disembodied echo.

"Find your way to the road," Kirkwood guided. "Let me know when you get there."

Casey opened her eyes and looked along the length of Lasterby Road. Rain fell all around her but she was protected from it. She was fully clothed and she was dry.

"I'm here."

The familiar pall of fear enveloped her but, this time, Casey shrugged it off. Glancing to her left, she saw the road sign and regarded it fleetingly.

This time, this was not what she had come here to see.

Casey brought her arm up to shield her eyes from the glare of the headlights up ahead.

The guttural moan metamorphosed into anguished cries.

The assailant and the victim struggled on the slick bitumen in front of the car. The terror of the moment shook Casey but, again, she brushed it off as she focused on what she was seeing, rather than what she was experiencing.

"Tell me what's happening," Kirkwood said, trying to maintain an even tone. "What do you see?"

"I see *them*," Casey started. "In front of me."

"Remember, Casey, you control the imagery. Slow it down or even stop it, if you need to. Can you see the attacker?"

Casey squeezed her closed eyes tighter. "I c-can't. It's too bright."

Kirkwood's eyes narrowed and she sat forward in her chair. "Why is it so bright, Casey? What is making it so bright?"

Casey lifted her arm reflexively, both in the dream state where she squinted against the glare of the powerful beams and here in the room before Kirkwood.

"H-headlights. The headlights of a car."

Kirkwood leaned forward, reaching for her notepad and pen.

"What can you tell me about the car?"

Casey tilted her head, squinting to see around both the assailant and his victim, trying to overcome the glare.

The body struggled against the brute force that held her. Casey was distracted as she felt herself weighed down—as if she were underneath the violent predator, even though she was standing at least fifty feet away. She snarled at him. She would not allow herself to be distracted this time. Suddenly, the assailant raised his hand above his head, balling it into a fist.

Her stomach lurched with an all-too-familiar horror, knowing what was to come.

"I-I can't," she gasped. "*T-too bright.*"

"*Focus, Casey,*" Kirkwood urged, her voice echoing in the hurricane of Casey's nightmare. "Close out as much as you can and just focus on the car."

The assailant thrust his arm down, striking the victim in the middle of her chest with crushing force. Excruciating pain ricocheted through Casey's own chest, accompanied by a wave of dizziness so intense that the world tilted to one side. She felt the air being sucked from her lungs and a jet of blood shot from her nostril, but Casey wiped it away angrily. She steadied herself on the bitumen and glared at the car beyond.

Through the blinding light, Casey was able to discern the low-slung rectangular orbs of the car's headlights, below which sat a pair of cat-like fog lights whose beams punctured the darkness. The main lights tapered towards the centre of the vehicle where they ended on either side of the centre grille: an upside-down trapezoid ringed in a highly-polished chrome.

The assailant struck again, battering his victim with a metal bar in his hand. Fountains of blood blossomed from her chest. The victim struggled underneath him, managing to partially free herself from the assailant's grip.

The face, contorted in anguish, disfigured by ragged slashes, thrust itself towards Casey and howled in terror.

Grabbing her chest, Casey did all she could to ignore Saskia. She grimaced then staggered forward, eyes on the car behind them, on the grille between the headlights. Casey's eyes went wide as she began to see the detail there.

A symbol!

On the seat across from Kirkwood, Casey stiffened and Kirkwood flinched.

"What is it, Casey?"

"*I see*!"

"Tell me what you see?"

Lifting her arm, Casey extended her finger and began to rotate it in the air.

Kirkwood rose quickly from her seat and plucked a pencil from the table, placing it into Casey's fingers.

"Draw it for me."

Casey complied and gripped the pencil in her fingers as she lowered it down before her. Kirkwood slid a sheet of paper underneath as the pencil touched the surface. She crouched before Casey, watching and waiting expectantly.

Casey squinted in the light, fighting to keep her focus on what she saw before her, ignoring the violence that continued between her and the car.

On a piece of paper, Casey drew a single circle, then added a second circle whose left-hand curve sat slightly inside the first. She drew a third, then a fourth circle and then allowed the pencil to clatter to the floor.

"That's it," she wheezed.

"Okay," Kirkwood nodded. "I'm going to bring you out now. I want you to turn away from there."

Casey went slack on the sofa, her shoulders slumped. In the nightmare, she repeated the same action while letting her eyes drift away from the blinding light and over the desperate face of Saskia.

She reached out with her hand towards Casey. Her lips slowly formed words. "Help me."

Casey met her eyes for the first time and felt a calm wash over her.

She nodded confidently. "I will."

Casey's eyes fluttered open and she found herself sitting in the calm quiet of Kirkwood's suite once more. She blinked, disoriented for a moment then sat forward looking at the piece of paper on the table before her.

Four perfectly-drawn circles, each sitting slightly inside the other.

"What does it mean?" she questioned.

Kirkwood reached into her handbag which was sitting beside her chair and lifted a ring of keys from within.

She turned the keychain over so Casey could see, revealing a metallic symbol to her.

"I drive one myself," Kirkwood said. "It's an Audi."

CHAPTER 17

LIONEL APPROACHED THE TOWERING ST. KILDA ROAD HEADQUARTERS OF Victoria Police and stood on the sidewalk for a long moment, taking in the monolithic structure of glass, steel and concrete. He had almost forgotten how intimidating the building appeared.

Ten years, he mused. *Has it really been that long?*

A convoy of squad cars, pursuit vehicles and prisoner transports were parked kerbside in front of the building. Despite having spent much of the latter part of his career stationed at this very building, Lionel had always found it to be an intimidating environment. He had much preferred the smaller station houses to the big city department. Having been away from Melbourne for well over a decade since his retirement from the force, his feelings of uncomfortable awe were only heightened and, for a brief moment, he wished he were back at the Hambledown General Store.

Having parked opposite to the headquarters in the leafy grounds of Melbourne Grammar, Lionel scanned the four lanes of St. Kilda before him for a break in the traffic. Spying an opening, he hurried across and into the shadow of the police building. He stopped before the steps leading up to the main entrance and glanced up at the symbol of the Victoria Police Force: an inverted, five-point star with the motto, 'Uphold The Right.'

Lionel had worn that badge for close to thirty years, first as a uniformed police constable, having been recruited from the London Police Force as part of an exchange programme, then as a detective in the Homicide Squad where he had finished his career as a decorated Senior Sergeant. That he was considered something of a legend within the Force was a reputation with which he had never felt entirely comfortable.

Given his presence here now and the reason for which he had come, he quietly hoped that reputation was a card that he could put into play.

Entering the building and approaching the reception desk, Lionel clutched at his tie, adjusting it absently before stepping up to the desk itself. A pretty, young receptionist looked up from her computer terminal and regarded him politely.

"Can I help you, sir?"

"I'm here to see Detective Senior Sergeant Farnham Whittaker. He is expecting me."

The receptionist frowned slightly and turned to her computer screen. "Your name, sir?"

"Lionel Broadbent."

Behind her, a uniformed officer turned his head and studied Lionel quizzically.

"I-I'm sorry, sir. I don't seem to have your name in his appointment schedule."

"Oh."

Lionel couldn't help indulge in a knowing smile.

Typical Farnham.

"Perhaps if you could call up to his office and let him know that I'm here, I'm sure he'll…"

"I'll need you to take a number and have a seat in the waiting area," the receptionist interjected abruptly.

Lionel blinked at the young woman. "Look, I'm sure if you just let him know that I'm here."

"I'm sorry, sir," the receptionist interrupted again. "But you *are* going to have to take a number."

Lionel's jaw set and he glared at the receptionist with more rancour than he had intended.

The police officer who was watching the exchange stepped forward now, studying Lionel more closely as Lionel prepared to comply, albeit reluctantly, with the receptionist's instruction.

"Ahhh…excuse me," the young officer said. "But did you say your name was Broadbent? Lionel Broadbent?"

Lionel glanced at the officer, maintaining his perturbed expression.

The young officer, clearly having a flash of recognition, quickly pushed past the receptionist who was now glaring him with incredulity, and grabbed a clip-on guest pass from the counter. He gestured to Lionel.

"Please, Mr. Broadbent. Please come this way. I'm very sorry."

"Jeremy!" the receptionist hissed, trying to keep her voice low. "What are you—"

He silenced her with a glare and an exaggerated wave of his hand as he ushered Lionel through a secure door.

"Just follow the directions to the lift, sir," the young officer said, handing Lionel the visitor pass once they were on the other side. "Detective Whittaker's office is up on le—"

"Level five," Lionel finished for him with an awkward smile and a nod. "I know where to go."

"Sir, can I just say…" the officer began, rubbing his hands together in an excited child-like gesture. "I-it's an absolute honour to meet you. I studied your career at the Academy. I wrote a dissertation on your investigative techniques. I always remember what you said of investigation: Assume nothing. Believe nothing. Check everything. I've never forgotten that."

Lionel examined the young constable; his uniform, neatly pressed, shoes polished to a high shine. Lionel passed his eyes over his badge.

"How long have you been out, Constable Jeremy Delfey?"

"Twelve months, sir. I'm in Traffic Operations but I plan on applying for Homicide. I want to become a Detective."

Lionel nodded. "You've quite a road ahead of you. I trust that you are aware of the commitment."

"Yes, sir. It's been my dream since I was a kid. Just to be here now in the uniform is an honour for me."

Lionel smiled warmly. "I'm sure you'll go far, Constable Delfey. I wish you good luck."

The young constable swelled with pride and stood tall, as though he were about to salute Lionel, his cheeks threatening to flush pink. Lionel stepped forward and offered his hand. The constable took it in his own reverently.

"Thank you," Lionel gestured with his head toward the door. "For helping me out back there."

He stepped back and turned towards the lift.

Alighting on level five, Lionel found himself in a beehive of activity. Uniformed and plain-clothed police rushed back and forth, worked at their desks, talked with colleagues, delegated tasks to subordinates. Phones were ringing off the hook. The chatter of the department assailed him, excited him and disoriented him all at once.

He'd definitely forgotten that buzz of HQ.

Lionel made his way through the expansive office complex. A few heads turned in his direction. A number of familiar faces greeted him enthusiastically as he passed, causing him to stop and exchange handshakes and pleasantries. Eventually, he reached his destination: a corner office suite with expansive windows that looked out across St. Kilda Road to the grounds of Melbourne Grammar and the Botanical Gardens beyond.

Approaching, Lionel could see a tall man seated at a desk on a telephone. Middle-aged, with scruffy, silver hair, the man was dressed in a navy suit jacket and tie. As he stopped at the entrance, Lionel noted a visible coffee stain on a portion of his white business shirt. Farnham Whittaker turned slightly in his seat and his face lit up upon seeing Lionel. He motioned hurriedly for Lionel to come in as he continued his animated conversation on the phone.

"I understand that you want that cleared up as soon as possible," Whittaker was saying in a voluminous Australian drawl. "But I just can't commit the resources to deal with your situation just now."

He closed his eyes and raised his head, clearly frustrated as he listened to the voice on the other end of the line. He then began nodding as Lionel removed his anorak and hung it on a hook before taking up a chair opposite.

"Look," Whittaker said, interrupting the caller. "I will try and address the situation later today and have an answer for you. I have an appointment that has just arrived."

He nodded with an exaggerated raise of his eyebrows at Lionel, as if seeking his approval.

"Good enough," Whittaker said finally as he drew the handset away from his ear and cradled it.

He let out a sigh of relief.

"Jesus bloody Christ!" he exclaimed breathlessly, leaning back in his seat and looking at the ceiling.

"Problems?" Lionel ventured, amused.

"Problems is right," Whittaker echoed. "Carol can't get away from court in time to pick up the girls from school and get them to tennis practice so, of course, the world is suddenly in crisis and I'm left to pick up the pieces."

Lionel frowned quizzically. "Carol? *Your* Carol?"

Whittaker nodded with mock indignation, then his expression melted into a warm grin. He stood up from his seat and quickly rounded the desk, his arms outstretched.

"Lionel Broadbent," he announced as Lionel got up just in time to be enfolded in a bear hug that was strong enough to make him groan. "How on Earth are you? What has it been—a year? Two years?"

"Since the last reunion dinner? Two years is right, I should think," Lionel replied bashfully, stepping back and smoothing down his jacket. "I wasn't able to get away from the store for the last one."

"Amazing," Whittaker shook his head, still smiling. "Well, it's bloody good to see you. Things haven't been the same here since you retired. A lot of changes, and not all of them good ones."

"I think the writing was on the wall when I called it a day," Lionel observed wryly. "The department has enmeshed itself too closely with government. It seems to have taken on some bad habits. Though, you've achieved some significant victories of late. I see the Carrington Task Force has made the news a number of times."

Whittaker grinned self-consciously as he went across to the office door and leaned out. He signalled to a secretary with a gesture that indicated a coffee cup and the secretary smiled and stood.

"Well, I had a good teacher," he continued, closing the door and returning to his desk. He held out his hand toward Lionel. "The best, actually. Most of this department owes something of its legacy to you, Lionel."

The compliment caused Lionel to squirm and he crossed his legs awkwardly. "Rubbish," he dismissed. "Policing is and has always been a collaborative pursuit—a team effort. I learnt as much from those under me."

"Always the modest one," Whittaker observed, sitting down. "How's things up in Hambledown?"

"Quiet. Just the way I like it. The general store is ticking along, although Ruth tends to run the enterprise more now. She's an obsessive organiser—can't help herself."

"I think we share some common ground there," Whittaker chuckled.

The secretary entered the office armed with a tray upon which sat a trio of cups, a plate with some sliced fruitcake and a pot of freshly brewed coffee. The aroma hit Lionel's nostrils and he felt his stomach leap.

He waited as she poured cups for all three of them, then delicately swiped up a slice of the cake and winked at Whittaker before exiting the office as swiftly as she had arrived.

"So, when did you arrive in town?" Whittaker asked, taking his cup.

Lionel's expression faltered a little and he tilted his head. "I've been here a couple of weeks."

Whittaker's eyes bulged. "And you didn't think to give us a call before now and organise a catch-up beer. *I'm hurt, Lionel.*"

Whittaker flashed yet another lopsided grin but it faded when Lionel didn't respond in kind. Instead, he seemed to retreat further into his chair.

"I've been a little…preoccupied, I'm afraid."

Setting his cup down, Whittaker regarded his mentor with concern, sensing that he was troubled by something.

"What is it?" he asked. "Is everything all right?"

"Yes," Lionel answered uncertainly. "Possibly."

"Would you like me to close the door?" Whittaker offered, making a move to stand.

Lionel turned in his chair and regarded the door, then nodded. "That would probably be a good idea."

Whittaker complied.

"Can I talk to you, off the record?" Lionel asked, sitting forward in his seat, cradling his cup in his hands.

"Lionel, of course you can," Whittaker responded, returning to his seat. "We've been friends for thirty years. You know you can come to me with anything."

Whittaker frowned quizzically, studying his old mentor, trying to gauge what it was that was on Lionel's mind.

"Is this about Casey?" he ventured. "That thing with Cyber-Crime?"

Lionel looked up at Whittaker at the mention of his granddaughter. He shook his head hesitantly.

"Look," Whittaker continued before Lionel could answer. "I'm aware that a couple of detectives have called Casey into question."

"Well, it *has* been weighing on her family and me somewhat," Lionel admitted. "One detective in particular seems to be keeping a close watch—Prishna? That's her name, I think."

Whittaker chuckled. "Prishna Argawaal. She's a girl scout. Good detective but she has a tendency to go after conspiracy theories."

"Well, she seems to have concocted one about Casey. About her having some sort of nefarious sideline career that runs counter to the work she's been doing for the Department."

"Don't believe it," Whittaker croaked dismissively. "Casey is one of our best assets. Hell, *I recruited her*—I'll vouch for her."

"I'm sure *you* will, Farnham. It goes without saying that I believe my granddaughter and I'll do anything to protect her from any sort of harassment."

"I'll have a word with Argawaal, Lionel. Tell her to turn down the enthusiasm knob."

Lionel hesitated before looking up at an expectant Whittaker who tilted his head.

"That's *not* the only reason you've come to see me, is it?"

"No. I wanted to talk to you about an old case. A cold case."

Whittaker nodded thoughtfully. "One from your time?"

"Slightly after actually. It goes back about three years, a hit and run down near Geelong. Young woman, early twenties, apparently hitchhiking back to Melbourne after leaving a music festival at Queenscliff."

Whittaker's expression remained neutral.

"You had some input on the case for a time actually," Lionel continued. "I saw your name in some of the press coverage."

Whittaker finally nodded, the wheels turning. "The name was Andrutsiv. Yeah, I remember."

Whittaker returned to his chair.

"A baffling case. Saskia Andrutsiv, twenty-two years old, found abandoned on some isolated road out in the boondocks. Horrible injuries but still alive. We never found a car. No one came forward. It was declared a major crime when the decision was made to turn off her…"

Whittaker's voice trailed off and he regarded Lionel with suspicion. "W-wait a sec. Why did you want to talk about this case?"

"I may have come across some new information."

Whittaker's eyes narrowed. "I see. So what they say about retired cops not being able to switch off their investigative minds is true then. You been looking for old cases to crack, Lionel? Can't let it go?"

"I haven't allowed myself to become *that* pathetic," Lionel retorted gently. "No, I've only just recently become acquainted with this case. But there may be one or two fresh leads worth looking into."

"Fresh leads," Whittaker responded, his eyes narrowing into an interrogatory gaze. "From where?"

Lionel managed a faint smile at his former colleague's demeanour. "Let's just say the information is credible. But I'd need to be sure that I'm across the specifics before I can be sure that it is worth pursuing."

Whittaker sat back in his chair then rotated slightly, turning his attention to an open laptop. He tapped at the keyboard with one hand while looking back and forth between Lionel and the screen.

"Organ donor," he said softly, reading from whatever information it was that had appeared on screen. His expression paled. "Saskia Andrutsiv's family donated her organs after she was declared brain-dead."

Lionel didn't meet Whittaker's eyes which narrowed as the detective swivelled to face him. Instead he nodded, looking down into his lap.

"Casey…received her heart transplant around the same time, didn't she." It was less a question than an observation. "You think it came from this girl?"

"We know it did," Lionel said flatly, looking down and picking at his thumb. "It's been confirmed."

Whittaker's lower jaw slackened. His eyes grew wide. "Jesus, Lionel! You do realise how many laws you've broken in obtaining that information?"

"Well, to be clear, it wasn't me who got a hold of that information. You do know how resourceful Casey can be."

Whittaker sat back stunned. He rubbed his hand over his mouth, clearly agitated.

"Why on Earth would Casey want to risk her hide by finding out who her donor was? Shouldn't she be focusing on living her own life with this gift she's been given and not worrying about where it came from?"

Lionel held up his arms, palms out, towards Whittaker.

"Look, let's just say that Casey's health has been precarious for some time. She's feeling significant distress about having this organ inside her—something that is not uncommon to organ recipients—and she felt she had to find out about the person who gave her a second chance. Unfortunately, she uncovered more than she bargained for. Casey believes that she has some new information about the case that may be significant."

"What do you think?" Whittaker questioned, extending his finger at Lionel.

Lionel thought for a long moment before answering. "I trust her."

"Well, okay. Let's get Casey in here. She can tell us what this information is and, I dunno, we can decide what to do with it."

"That sounds encouraging," Lionel responded bitterly. "You and I both know that VicPol doesn't have the resources of a dedicated cold case unit. The information will wither and die on the vine before anyone decides to look into it."

Whittaker feigned a hurt expression. "That's a bit harsh. Look I can shift a few things around. It won't be that hard."

Lionel sat still. He didn't respond.

Several moments of silence passed between them.

"What are you asking for, Lionel?" Whittaker probed.

"Just a look at the case file."

Again, Whittaker's eyes bulged and, for a moment, Lionel thought he resembled a bullfrog.

"Christ! You know I can't give you access to a case file! You, more than anyone, know the sort of shit that would get me into."

"I'm not asking you to *give* it to me. I'd just like thirty minutes in a quiet corner, out of the way, where I can read it and see if any of the established facts marry up."

Whittaker shook his head in bewilderment and held up his hand defensively. "I'm not going to have an old-aged pensioner and his granddaughter running around like Tango and bloody Cash!"

"Oh come now, don't be ridiculous, Farnham," Lionel admonished, giving his voice a ring of his old authority. "You know it's not going to be anything remotely like that. All I want to do is ensure that we're not wasting anyone's time. Do you think I don't remember all of the crackpots and charlatans that used to come forward with wild claims about old cases?"

"Lionel," Whittaker lowered his voice. "I don't care that you know the circumstances of this poor young woman's' death or even the fact that she was a donor to your granddaughter. The internet is that bloody pervasive now that I'm sure with a little effort you could find out as much as you want to about the case including the colour of the victim's undies the night she was hit. But, I'm not going risk the wrath of the Force, the Courts and a one-way trip to prison, just because you think you've got a whiff of something new."

Lionel nodded slowly and silently. Resignation set in.

He knew he was asking too much.

Slowly, he stood and retrieved his jacket from the coat hook behind him as Farnham stood and shuffled out from behind his desk. He met Lionel's gaze with a pained expression.

"I'm sorry. You taught me everything I know. I know you wouldn't come to me if you weren't absolutely sure of what you had. But that's the thing, you taught me *too well.* I can't bend the rules."

Lionel offered a curt smile and his hand, which Whittaker took.

"No, and nor should you. I'm sorry I've put you in this position. It was unfair of me."

Lionel turned towards the door and opened it.

"Wait, Lionel," Whittaker said falteringly. "Bring Casey in. We can talk and I'll see to it personally that it's handled."

Lionel left Whittaker's office and began walking towards the lifts.

"This information," Whittaker called after him. "Where does it come from?"

Lionel stopped in mid-stride. He lifted his finger and tapped it to his temple three times.

He exited the lift into the reception area and looked out through the glass entrance doors ahead of him. The trees on the far side of St. Kilda Road were swaying back and forth, caught in the aggressive grip of fresh gusts of wind. Grimacing, Lionel slipped his arms into the sleeves of his jacket and drew the collar up around his neck.

I suppose I deserve it, he thought darkly.

Approaching the doors, they slid aside revealing the full force of the blustering conditions outside. He noted the first drops of rain on the path.

"Lionel!"

The voice rang out from behind him and he turned to see Whittaker emerging from a lift beside the reception desk. Whittaker hurried across the reception area towards him and stopped a few feet away. He regarded Lionel uncomfortably.

"Come with me," he said.

CHAPTER 18

Shoving the heavy door aside with her foot, Casey lurched into the apartment grunting with the effort of carrying a heavy box of magazines in her arms. Sweat beaded from her forehead as she struggled through the living room and into the bedroom, where she practically tossed the box. As it hit the bed, its contents spilled out across it, with some titles falling off the edge on the far side. Casey shook her aching arms and blew air noisily up and over her face. Lifting loose strands of hair away from her eyes, she stood back, hands on hips and appraised the mess she had just created. She went back to the entrance where two more boxes sat in wait. She hefted each of these in turn into the apartment where she deployed them onto the bed in a similar fashion to the first. In short order, she had created a proper mess.

She grimaced.

Casey doubted she had ever seen as much literature dedicated to cars in her life: glossy print magazines, newsprint supplements, dealership catalogues, street machine magazines, classified almanacs. The volume of material dedicated to luxury cars in particular was astounding. There must have been at least a hundred titles here.

Since she'd left Kirkwood, the nebulous memory of the car had positioned itself front and centre in her mind. Having invested so much of her resolve in fighting against the recollection of the nightmare, Casey now found herself trying as hard as she could to hold on to the details.

The irony of this was not lost on her.

The mysterious car lingered in her consciousness, teasing her with fragments of clarity through a disconnected mist. She could see fractured detail. The low-slung rectangular headlights. A trapezoidal grille. Four polished, chrome rings in the centre.

Audi... Audi...

No matter how hard she tried, Casey couldn't sharpen her memory and it gnawed at her like an itch that she couldn't scratch. On a recommendation from Scott, she'd decided to hit up a secondhand bookshop that specialised in the kind of print ephemera that now graced the entire surface of her bed. Being something of a petrol-head, Scott often sourced auto magazines from there. She'd spent a good hour selecting boxes of back issue magazines, catalogues and newspapers that had, fortunately, been sorted into publication dates and years. While the average customer might have sought one or two titles from any given box, Casey had taken multiple boxes.

The man at the counter had regarded her as if she were nuts.

Casey examined her watch and, turning hesitantly, she retrieved a pair of scissors from the kitchen. From her shoulder bag she took out a large sketch pad, a roll of Scotch tape and a box of pencils she'd purchased on the way home.

On the way back to her bedroom, she stopped before the door to the balcony. The mid-morning sun streamed down onto the bay, the light chop on the sea's surface glittered with reflected light. Casey opened the door, allowing fresh air into the apartment. She smiled. Closing her eyes, she allowed the scent of the ocean to clear her mind.

In a moment of clarity, she recalled the car that so intrigued her. She recalled the road that so unnerved her. The scene of violence that so terrified her.

And she recalled something else, something elusive that had nothing to do with the car or the road or the violence.

She could not put her finger on it.

Casey returned to her bed, feeling a twinge of anxiety as she surveyed the massive pile.

She wondered if the magazine store guy was right.

Kicking off her shoes and climbing onto the bed, Casey crossed her legs and scanned the magazines, newsprint and brochures before her.

Opening the sketch book and taking out a pencil, she rested it in her lap and began drawing. She sketched and shaded, closing her eyes repeatedly and going into her mind to pluck out her clearest recollections of the car. Within an hour, Casey had produced dozens of detailed perspectives of the car. She had filled the sketch book front to back with incarnations of the vehicle's front detail, headlights, fog lights and grille with the eponymous rings of the Audi symbol a prominent feature in all of them. There was a sleekness to the shape of the car she had drawn. The lines felt ultra modern, suggesting a vehicle that was new or near-to new.

A killer with expensive taste.

Leaning back against her pillow, she looked over the pile again.

"Where to begin…"

The obvious place was with the big, glossy publications where she would, no doubt, find high quality images of Audis that she could stick on the wall in the hope that it would jog her memory.

Laying the pad down, Casey leaned forward and shifted the pile in front of her, lifting out a "Luxury Motor" magazine. The cover, ironically, displayed an image of an Audi, though this was an SUV model. She examined the date of publication in the bottom corner of the magazine.

December 2011.

Just a few months before her transplant.

Nodding, Casey opened the magazine and began browsing.

Almost immediately, she found a picture of a silver Audi sedan whose front detailing closely resembled her sketches in the pad beside her. Comparing the two, Casey decided this was an image worthy of further scrutiny. She lifted the scissors, cutting around the image, then lifted it from the page and fixed a piece of Scotch tape to it. Climbing off the bed, she stuck it on the brick wall beside her at head height.

Returning to the magazine, she turned a few more pages until she found another image—this time, a low-slung, dark blue convertible. The lights here were similar and were paired by a set of fog lights set underneath them. Casey extracted this picture as well and taped it beside the first on the wall.

She continued this process again and again, hour after hour. Working her way through the magazines, she sorted them by year of publication, ruling out anything whose publication date was any later than 2012. Something told her that the car from the dream was new, if not brand new. She browsed through each title, identifying Audis, comparing them with her sketches. If there was a definite visual correlation, she methodically cut out those images, checking that any available description for the year of manufacture fell no earlier than 2010 and no later than March 2012. She attached a piece of tape to them and added them to the wall. When she had finished with one magazine, Casey tossed it to the floor and retrieved another. She frowned at the growing mound of print material at her feet.

Morning became afternoon. The sun crossed over the top of her building and was now streaming in through the windows beside her, although Casey was only vaguely aware of the passing of time. She continued to work her way through the pile, cutting and taping and affixing pictures to the wall, looking for some hint of recognition in the ever-growing mosaic. Each time, she went into her mind and recalled the scene. Saskia's face flashed with terror and desperation…and something else.

Looking away from the wall, Casey bit the inside of her lip. Her eyes danced across the floor, as though she were searching for something.

Saskia's face appeared and she allowed it to stay there.

Was Saskia trying to tell her something?

She couldn't make sense of it. And then it seemed to slip away. Casey hissed as she lost her grip on the memory.

"Dammit!"

Some time later, Casey absently stood from the bed and she lowered the shades. The sun began its descent. Afternoon progressed towards dusk. Casey turned her head and saw the edge of the mighty orange orb touch the horizon out on the bay. She cast a glance at the clock on her bedside table.

Nine hours…

The wall opposite was almost entirely covered with images. Everywhere she looked, Casey saw Audi sedans—a dizzying array of sizes in both colour and black and white, from full-cover photographs to stamp-sized classified shots that she'd gleaned from the trade classifieds. She had surrounded the doorway leading into her en suite bathroom and had even covered the door.

Only a few brochures and newsprint publications remained before her, while the recycling bin adjacent was filled so full that the lid would no longer close.

Casey blinked. Slowly, she stepped off the bed and wandered along the length of the wall.

So engrossed was she in her examination of her work, she only vaguely heard the rumbling of the front door as it slid aside.

"Casey?"

Lionel's voice sounded but it didn't register with her. He slid the door closed and set his key down on the counter. He called out again. Casey flinched and shook herself from her stupefied daze.

"In here," she called.

Lionel appeared from around the corner and frowned quizzically at his granddaughter. She crossed her arms as she appraised the wall before her. At first, he didn't see what she was looking at, but as his eyes followed her own, they went wide as he looked upon the vast collection of images on the wall.

"You've been busy," he noted with a hint of bewilderment.

Casey's cheeks flushed as she nodded, embarrassed.

"I guess I have."

Lionel squinted at the collage. Casey couldn't help but notice his mercurial smile. She tilted her head.

"What's so funny?"

"Oh. Nothing really," Lionel hesitated, glancing sideways at her. "It's just that…the way you've arranged all these pictures. It reminds me, very much, of how I used to problem-solve certain things, pieces of evidence that baffled me."

Casey's shoulders slumped. "I've been at this for nine hours, Pa. I don't know *what* I'm doing."

Her eyes floated over the wall of images.

"You didn't think to use the computer?" Lionel ventured, gesturing with a nod towards the darkened monitor.

Casey shrugged. "I thought the magazines would be a better idea. Placing them on the wall like this gives me a better visual. But I don't know if I'm on the right track or whether I'm just complicating things by doing all of this."

She held out her arms, shaking her head.

"I can see some parts of the car clearly in my mind but, I'm worried that I'm confusing my memories by trying to force myself to see something that isn't there."

"Maybe you should leave it for now," Lionel suggested. "Take a break and try to empty your mind. Things will become clearer."

Casey exhaled and nodded. "I should get us something to eat."

Lionel smiled with a hint of mischief. "Let's get out of the house for a bit. I quite fancy some fish and chips."

THEY SAT ON a wooden picnic table overlooking the Mentone jetty, a generous serving of battered fish and steaming, thickly cut chips sat in a nest of butcher's paper between them. The setting sun had dipped below the horizon. The sky, a brilliant orange, reflected off the water as small waves rolled onto the shore providing entertainment for a group of children down on the sand who were riding them in on boogie boards.

Lionel licked his lips as he opened a small tub of tartar sauce and upended its entirety over a single piece of fish. Casey laughed affectionately at her grandfather.

"Don't you tell your grandmother," Lionel grumbled dryly, grinning sideways at Casey.

She scoffed at him, then plucked a thick potato chip from the pile and popped it into her mouth.

"Don't you tell my mother. No doubt she's been milking you for information about me every chance she gets."

"Of course she is. She wouldn't be your mother if she wasn't. She comes from a long line of busybodies."

Casey whipped her head up at Lionel, whilst trying to stifle a huge, knowing grin.

"That said," he continued. "She *does* act out of love—even if it is a little heavy-handed."

"*Are you kidding me?* Edie's got all the delicacy of a Mack truck. If anything, it's she who has driven me more nuts than…"

Casey caught herself when she was met by her grandfather's eyes. She detected a subtle hurt in them and she looked down between her feet.

"Sorry."

Lionel shrugged it off and continued devouring his fish.

"I just wish I could remember."

Casey went quiet. Her features tightened and Lionel could tell that her thoughts were drifting back to the conundrum of the car.

"Casey," he chided softly. "Give yourself some space."

"There's something I'm missing, Pa," she said. "It's something to do with the dream…with the event. But I can't work out what it is."

"Well. Is it the car? Another object? Something to do with the assailant?"

"No." She paused, trying to will her mind. "It's something to do with Saskia."

Lionel frowned and looked across the bay. "I think you should let it go. You look so tired. When was the last time you got any sort of sleep?"

Casey sighed tersely. "I don't know. Back at the hospital? A few days ago? I can't sleep, Pa. I'm scared to."

"It can't be doing you any good. Eventually you'll crash."

"I know, Pa," Casey nodded. "I guess I've gotten used to existing this way, but I know…"

Her voice trailing away, she turned to a bottle of water and picked it up, twisting the cap open.

"Remember how we used to come here as kids? You and Nana brought Angus and me here most weekends during the summer. We were hardly ever out of the water."

"You were a pair of water-babies. No doubt about it." Lionel smiled.

"This place, it's the one thing that hasn't changed. Even though everything else has. I can count on this place. You know?"

Casey squinted at Lionel who nodded, understanding.

"I feel the same way. I used to come here before you were born. I fished from that jetty. We need quiet places like this to escape to. To contemplate and reflect."

Another quiet drifted between them and hung in the air for several long moments.

"Why do you believe me, Pa?"

Lionel blinked at his granddaughter's sudden question. He tilted his head slightly, thinking of his answer.

"I see a lot of your mother in you," he began. Casey stiffened and her features hardened, which caused Lionel to hold up his hand to placate her.

"Just listen," he urged. "I mean to say that you have a pragmatic streak within you, which is very much like your mother. You've never been one to indulge in anything particularly fanciful or, in other words, believe in bullshit."

Casey frowned, not quite understanding where Lionel was headed with this train of thought.

"But I have noticed some things, subtle changes, ever since your operation. Your personality. Your likes and dislikes. The way you do things. Yet, you have remained the sensible and driven young woman you've always been."

Lionel paused, looking out across the jetty.

"I'll confess, I have often wondered whether you might have taken on some of the traits of whoever it was that gave you your heart."

Casey frowned. "What makes you say that?"

"Let's just say that I've witnessed things in my lifetime that led me to wonder about the very nature of human potential beyond our physical existence."

"I don't understand," Casey responded uncomfortably.

Lionel smiled wistfully. "Are you sure about that?"

Her grandfather's curious gaze drilled into Casey and she gulped softly.

"Okay," he said. "On a much more pragmatic level, I've been able to look at what is publicly known about this case. There were gaps in the original investigation. Enough gaps that I think are worth pursuing."

"Well, I think I've already run headlong into nowhere," Casey observed ruefully. She tapped her finger to her temple and continued. "Aside from whatever is going on up here, I don't have anything else tangible to go on. I don't know where else to turn. I haven't been able to find any details about where this girl lived or whether she has any family I can seek out."

"I wouldn't be so sure about that," Lionel said, tearing off another piece of fish from the paper between them.

"What do you mean?"

"I've spoken to an old colleague of mine at St. Kilda Road. You know him actually."

Casey gulped and stifled a feeling of dread.

"Not Whittaker," she groaned painfully.

"Yes Whittaker," Lionel shot back. "Despite what others might think of you, he regards you very highly. And he still owes me a favour or two."

Lionel wiped his hands with a serviette then reached into his pocket. Casey watched him curiously as he took out a piece of paper and unfolded it. He handed it to Casey.

"Your donor was living with her grandmother here in Melbourne, a Mrs. Lesia Andrutsiv. It seems the police didn't think it prudent to interview her at the time of her granddaughter's death, partly because Mrs. Andrutsiv was gravely ill herself and in no state to answer any questions."

Casey examined the piece of paper. Her eyes grew wide.

It was the address details for Saskia's grandmother.

"He gave you this?" she asked breathlessly. "Pa, he could lose his job over this."

"It seems he might just think there are enough questions that are still worth asking about this particular case. He just doesn't have the resources to commit to asking them."

"He's allowing us—"

"He's putting his faith in us," Lionel corrected her. "Aside from this, he won't be able to give me anything else," Lionel interrupted. "We'll have to do our own digging. If we find anything worth bringing to his attention, he'll look at it and decide whether to take it further."

"What about Prishna?"

Lionel flashed Casey a lopsided smile. "I don't think you'll need to worry about Prishna for now. I think this will be much more interesting."

CHAPTER 19

The van drew up alongside the kerb of a quiet suburban cul-de-sac. Rolling down her window, Casey scanned the relatively modern brick houses, all of which were nestled under a collection of towering gums. They stood in stark contrast to a quaint, clapboard cottage with a bull-nosed veranda, a clear relic from yesteryear. Though it appeared tired and in need of attention, the cottage boasted a number of pretty flower beds which were alive with colour. Several hanging baskets lined the veranda. A compact, grey Toyota hatchback emblazoned with the livery of a community nursing service was parked out front.

Retrieving a scrap of paper from her shoulder bag, Casey checked the address again and nodded. "This is it."

Moving the gear shift into neutral and extinguishing the engine, Scott sat back and discreetly looked Casey up and down. Her hair was clipped back from her face. The blouse she wore under her business jacket appeared overtly feminine compared to the usual attire he was used to seeing her in, but it definitely suited her. Paired with the skirt and the tan pumps she wore, Casey appeared for all the world like a journalist or lawyer. He couldn't recall ever having seen her dressed so formally. Though he would never say it out loud, he had to admit, she looked good—really good.

"You think you're ready for this?"

Casey quickly flipped her visor down and checked her makeup in the mirror—another addition Scott could scarcely remember having seen her wear.

"I dunno," she responded, fretting. "How do I look? Is my makeup too much?"

"Are you kidding me? The makeup is fine. Perfect actually."

Casey whipped her head around and glared at him. Scott's cheeks were actually flushing.

"Cut it out, pervert," she chided.

"Seriously though," he ventured. "You're taking a risk. I'm not sure this university graduate research thing is gonna fly. If this woman has any inkling that you're posing then you could be in big trouble."

Casey gazed at the tidy cottage across the street, then at the clear blue sky above. It was a cloudless morning with bright sunshine. She felt a wave of dizziness threaten her, but she shook it away. Clasping a clipboard folder with the Monash University logo on its surface, she opened it and examined a printout inside.

"If she's as ill as these notes say she is, I don't imagine she'll ask a lot of questions. She might not even capable of talking. But, I'm less interested about whether she can answer anything than I am about learning more of who Saskia was. She *lived* here, had a life here. There's gotta be something I can find."

"Well. I'll be waiting," Scott said reassuringly. "Be careful."

Casey nodded, then opened the door and stepped down from inside. She hesitated, her hand on the door handle. She turned around slowly.

"I never apologised for how I spoke to you that night. You know, before things happened. I treated you appallingly."

Scott regarded her warmly and brushed his hand at her. "Forget about it, Casey. I understand that things are tough on you. I know you didn't mean it."

"You're too good to me, Sasquatch."

Closing the door, she stood in the shadow of the van, taking a moment to adjust her clothing. She took a deep breath and stepped gingerly toward the cottage, promptly stumbling as she rolled her heel to one side. She cursed out loud but stopped herself from falling completely. Watching her from the van, Scott gasped at first, then whipped his hand up to his mouth to stifle a chuckle. Collecting herself, she shot him an angry glower then walked forward once more.

Approaching the cottage door, Casey lifted her finger to a doorbell and pressed it. It elicited a pleasant chime as she stood back and waited, biting her lip and glancing sideways at the window. She could see movement from within.

A lock turned and the front door clicked open. A plump, middle-aged woman with a pleasant face dressed in a nurse's uniform peered out and smiled at Casey.

"Good morning, can I help you?"

"Ahh, y-yes," Casey began nervously. "My name is Winnie Lextor. I spoke to somebody on…"

"Ohhh," the woman beamed. "Yes, that would have been me. I'm Raelene. I'm Mrs. Andrutsiv's carer."

Raelene opened the screen door and stood to one side to allow Casey access. Casey blinked in surprise and stifled an urge to look over her shoulder at Scott.

She found herself in a compact, homey living room that was furnished with antique timber cabinetry, a floral-patterned sofa and matching armchair, both adorned with hand-stitched cushions. The pleasant scent of lavender from an oil burner suffused the room. Casey's eyes were drawn to a collection of photographs on the walls. There were old and fading sepia images housed in ornate frames, mixed with more recent colour photographs that Casey guessed dated back to the 1970's. In a glass display cabinet to her left, Casey locked onto an even more recent image that caught her breath. It was Saskia, posing with an elderly woman in a park.

Saskia was wearing a summery blouse, knee-length shorts and sandals. Her long, dark hair hung down over her slender shoulders. Her pretty smile was warm, affecting. It lit up her face. The elderly woman, also smiling, sat in a wheelchair, and a crocheted rug was draped over her lap. The heart leapt and Casey whipped her hand up to her mouth reflexively.

"Lesia has been at me all morning, wanting to know when you were coming," Raelene said as she rounded Casey and took a moment to inspect her.

Though her smiling face appeared welcoming, Casey detected a hint of suspicion in the older woman's eyes. Raelene continued to stare, then she gestured toward the sofa.

"Have a seat. Lesia's in good spirits this morning. You've caught her on a good day."

Casey smiled and then sat as Raelene turned toward the hall. Suddenly, the clickity-clack of metal on timber sounded and Raelene stopped in mid-stride as a painfully small figure rounded into view, armed with a walking frame that she hefted with audible gasps and grunts.

"Speak of the devil," Raelene observed mischievously.

Casey stood up instantly as Lesia Andrutsiv issued a bell-like laugh, bobbing her head as she entered the room. Negotiating her way around a coffee table, she made for her armchair.

She was bent over the frame, her spine deformed by the cumulative effects of arthritis. Despite this, she moved into position and deftly effected a ninety-degree turn, then flopped herself down in the recliner.

"Good morning! Good morning!" Mrs. Andrutsiv greeted through a fit of coughing. She spoke in a lightly accented voice that ranged between a squeak and a whisper. "It is so lovely to have a visitor to my home."

Casey shifted in her seat and glanced sideways at Raelene, who folded her arms and leaned against the door frame. She continued to stare intensely as Casey resumed her seat.

Mrs. Andrutsiv raised a gnarled hand and clicked her fingers.

"Tea! We must have tea. You will join me—yes?" Her elfin eyes beamed at Casey. "Would you be a dear, Rae, and fetch us a pot?"

"That would be nice," Casey nodded quickly, watching as the nurse slowly retreated into the hall.

The elderly woman squirmed in her seat, adjusting herself until she was comfortable. Casey turned her attention back to her.

Mrs. Andrutsiv's thinning salt-and-pepper hair was tied back in a ponytail that hung all the way down her back. Her eyes were uncharacteristically bright, and twinkled with mischief through a pair of ancient spectacles. There was an undeniable wisdom in them, the sum of a long life and experience. Her face, though heavily lined and sporting prominent jowls and liver spots, seemed to take in Casey with a sense of childlike wonder.

"You said your name was Winnie, yes?" she asked curiously, shaking Casey from her silent observation. Casey nodded, noticing the old woman looking her up and down.

"That's right."

"Hmmphh. You don't look like a Winnie," Mrs. Andrutsiv remarked unexpectedly, looking at Casey over the rim of her spectacles.

If you only knew, Casey thought ruefully, trying not to react to the probing observation.

If there had been any doubt about the sharpness of this woman's mind, it had been trounced in that moment.

Casey nervously picked at the folder in her lap.

"I'm a student from Monash University. As I explained on the telephone, I'm involved in a research project looking at families of individuals who've been organ donors. I understand that you volunteered your details some time ago. They were given to me in confidence so that I might ask you a few questions about your granddaughter?"

The mention of Saskia seemed to make Mrs. Andrutsiv's demeanour brighten and though she smiled broadly, Casey did notice the old woman's eyes mist over.

"Ah yes," Mrs. Andrutsiv sighed wistfully. "My dear Saskia."

Reaching into the neckline of her dress, Mrs. Andrutsiv lifted out a gold chain with an oval charm hanging from it. Leaning forward, she worked her arthritic fingers along the edge of the locket until it snapped open, revealing a tiny photograph inside.

Casey leaned forward to inspect the photograph. It was a portrait of Saskia, a high quality, studio shot that had been shrunken to fit inside. She lifted her hand to hold the locket and felt a surge of electricity crackle through her chest.

"She had so much life ahead of her," Mrs. Andrutsiv said. "And she had already lived through so much."

Casey opened her folder and took up a pencil, ready to begin writing. For her part, Mrs. Andrutsiv relaxed back into her chair and nodded at the notepad.

"Tell me about this project of yours. What would you like to know?"

"Ah, anything really, Mrs.—"

"Lesia," the elderly woman interrupted. "Call me Lesia, please. You make me sound *positively* ancient."

Casey smiled and cleared her throat.

"My project is about the people behind organ donations. These anonymous heroes who give such a priceless gift. I want to tell their stories. These donors are sometimes the forgotten ones in this journey."

Lesia Andrutsiv raised her brow with interest.

"A worthy study. I am pleased to help as much as I can, though, I don't know very much about the medical things."

"That doesn't matter so much," Casey said. "It's…their personal stories that I'm interested in. Of course, everything we discuss will be treated confidentially."

Lesia nodded. Her eyes drifted beyond Casey out through the window.

"Saskia came from my homeland. She lived with her mother and father in the east just outside of Kharkiv. They did not have much but they were a proud family and they worked hard. Her mother was a teacher and her father served in the Ukrainian military. Very early on, Saskia displayed a gift for learning. As a young child, she read and read. It was said that you could not pull her face from a book. She had a hunger for knowledge and she loved language and art. That is why she came here."

Casey looked up from her notepad.

"Art?"

"Yes. Art history. The great painters. The great periods. Saskia was obsessed with them. She took after her grandfather—my husband. He was an art history professor. We came to Australia so that he could teach. Saskia devoured languages too. Studied them religiously. She could speak three languages by the time she was ten years old. It was her dream to study both art and language. She wanted to visit all of the great galleries of the world and to become an art curator."

"And she came to Australia?" Casey asked.

Lesia nodded slowly. Her expression become sombre. "Yes. Though how she came here happened out of rather tragic circumstances."

She paused and looked down at her hands cradled in her lap.

"Her father—my son—was a soldier in the Ukrainian Army. He was stationed on the border with Russia."

Lesia raised her hand thoughtfully and smoothed her skin on either side of her mouth.

"He was killed in an accident while on a patrol. They never fully revealed to us how it happened. In the aftermath, her mother feared they would be pushed into poverty. Her mother and I talked and we decided it would be best for Saskia to come to Australia. If she were to have any chance at a better life and to further her studies, we agreed she would come and live with me and go to university here. Together, we did everything we could to make that happen. Her own talent helped. Saskia was awarded a scholarship and she was able to come here on a student visa."

"When was that?" Casey asked as Raelene appeared from the hallway armed with a tray upon which sat a teapot, cups and a plate of cookies. She set it down on a little side table and began pouring a cup for Lesia and Casey.

"It was seven years ago," Lesia replied and nodded at the realisation that so many years had passed. "I was so happy to have her come and live with me. Since my husband died, I have lived in this old house on my own. I actually thought about returning home to Kharkiv until we began talking about Saskia. She b-brightened this place so much."

For the first time, Lesia faltered. Her emotions bubbled up, her lip trembled.

Raelene stepped forward this time, and knelt next to Mrs. Andrutsiv's chair.

"Lesia," she said concerned. "You don't have to do this."

Lesia brushed her away with a wave of her hand as she composed herself.

"I am fine. I am happy to do this," she said, sitting straighter in her chair. "Saskia was admitted to the University of Melbourne. She was nervous at first, of course, having come from so far away, but in time, she came into her own. She made friends. She was very happy."

Lesia's voice drifted away to silence and she lifted her cup to her lips and sipped softly from it.

"You obviously made her feel very happy here," Casey offered nodding toward the photograph of Lesia and Saskia together.

Lesia smiled and her cheeks flushed pink. Then, suddenly, as if a switch had been tripped, Lesia's eyes lit up and she drew her cup away swiftly.

"Would you like to see her room?"

Casey blinked in surprise and worked her jaw impotently. "I ahh..."

"I kept her room just the way it was the day she left it," Lesia continued, becoming more animated. "I could not bring myself to touch it. It was her... *haven.* Come, let me show you."

Raelene sucked in a breath as Lesia lurched forward, grasping the handles of her walking frame with her gnarled fingers.

"Come, come," she grimaced, pushing up and rising to her crooked standing position. "It will be good for it to have some air and to be visited again."

Lesia shuffled her way past Raelene who was clearly uncomfortable, though she held her tongue as Casey followed close behind. The two exchanged glances; Raelene's full of suspicion.

She knows, Casey thought ruefully.

Lesia paused at an open doorway at the end of the hall that led into a large, open sunroom at the rear of the house. Tastefully decorated, it looked out onto a back garden that, like the front, had been lovingly maintained. Lesia raised a hand from the walker and pointed to the right, at a white timber door in the far corner of the sunroom.

Approaching it, Lesia hesitated, resting her hand on an ancient brass knob. She glanced sideways at Casey, then turned the handle, struggling momentarily with the mechanism.

Casey gulped as she stepped inside. She felt dizzy and had to place a hand on a small desk to steady herself.

The room held a sense of familiarity even though she had never been here before. It was tidy and, like the sunroom, it had been furnished with a modern, feminine touch. Though it had not been occupied in over three years, it felt light and airy, with sunlight from outside filtering through a large window that faced onto the garden.

"She loved this little room," Lesia beamed, noticing Casey's languid gaze out through the window. "And the garden. She tended to it nearly every day. Saskia used to say that she felt safe there."

Casey turned her head towards Lesia. "Safe?"

Lesia leaned against her walking frame and shrugged. "Saskia did not like large, open spaces, or unfamiliar places. You could say that she *struggled* with them. Saskia used to suffer from awful panic attacks. She much preferred to stick to her own home."

Casey stifled a gulp, feeling painfully self-conscious.

A tall bookcase stood against one wall. It boasted a large selection of titles ranging from fiction to text books: art and art history, linguistics and dictionaries of several languages. Next to that was a wrought iron bed with a floral quilt underneath another, smaller window that took in the morning sun. A white wardrobe with a decorative border stood adjacent to it, facing the bookcase. A rucksack hung from one handle. Positioned between the bed and the wardrobe was a matching dresser and, above that, was a framed picture that took Casey's breath away.

She gasped, as though she had been punched in the stomach.

It was Jeanne Hebuterne, the same Modigliani portrait that hung in her own apartment.

Lesia tilted her head. "My dear, are you all right?"

Casey did not answer. She stepped forward, her eyes fixed upon the portrait she knew so well, her thoughts and emotions spiralling.

It couldn't be.

Lifting a hand to the portrait, Casey touched the cheek of Jeanne Hebuterne.

"You know Modigliani, child?" Lesia ventured with a hopeful lilt.

"Yes," Casey responded without turning around. "I do. His work is very beautiful."

"Saskia brought that print with her from Kharkiv. It is—was—her favourite. She was particularly drawn to the story of Modigliani's lover, tragic though it was."

"Jeanne Hebuterne," Casey whispered. "She was his muse, his principal subject. She devoted her life to him. When he died, she could not bear the loss."

Quiet lingered between them. As Lesia looked from the print to Casey, she could see a sadness betrayed in the young woman's features.

"You know her *very well,*" Lesia remarked.

Catching herself, Casey looked away and her eyes wandered over to the dresser. Here, too, were postcard-sized prints ranging from Van Gogh and Rembrandt to DaVinci and Picasso. Among these were items of jewellery, earrings, handcrafted necklaces with fancy charms and coloured beads. An ornate hairbrush sat, as if in wait, and Casey noticed strands of hair still caught between the bristles.

Finally, she turned towards Lesia who was holding a tissue in her outstretched hand. Casey blinked, realising her eyes were moist with tears and she quickly took the tissue.

"I'm so sorry," she whispered, embarrassed.

Lesia smiled. "I understand, my dear. To walk into such a place—one that still has so much life—it can have a powerful effect."

Casey lifted her folder and opened it, reminding herself of the pretence she had to maintain.

"May I ask how was it that Saskia decided to become a donor?"

Lesia shrugged her shoulders. A visible lump rose in her throat.

"She made the decision when she first arrived in Australia. Saskia had a deep sense of responsibility, felt that it was an important thing to do. Of course, I never believed that her wish would ever be carried out."

A pall of sadness descended over Lesia. Her eyes drifted away and into her memories.

"It was a terrible decision to have to make."

Casey gulped softly, building up the courage to probe deeper.

Though she did not need to confirm it, she felt she had to hear it.

"Could I ask you what happened?" she ventured, trying to hide her nervousness.

Lesia turned to the desk and pulled out the chair.

"It was an accident, a terrible accident. It happened just after a particularly difficult period for us both when we were just beginning to see some sunshine in our lives once again. Saskia had been studying so hard and she had been under a lot of stress because of my illness. I was very sick from the chemotherapy I was having. Even worse, Saskia had had some *trouble* with her student papers."

"Her papers?"

Lesia nodded absently as she struggled to recall the events.

"She kept a lot of it to herself. She did not want to worry me while I was in the hospital, but there had been a misunderstanding over her student papers. She'd had to make an appeal to the authorities. She had to sort most of it out on her own."

Lesia caught herself and stopped speaking. She averted her eyes, fidgeting nervously for several moments.

"Anyhow, it was a very trying few months," she resumed, more hesitantly. "When it all settled, her friends treated her to a weekend at the beach. A music festival, it was one of those big parties you young people love so much. It was called Pleasant Music, or something like that. Such an interesting name, isn't it?"

Casey moved to the bed and sat down on the edge of it, careful not to disturb the quilt. Lesia did not seem to mind.

"Saskia had such lovely friends. They cared about her a great deal. Especially Shelley."

"Shelley?" Casey echoed softly.

"Her best friend," Lesia answered, a wan smile returning to her features. "Shelley was the first school friend Saskia met and they quickly became inseparable. They did most everything together. It was Shelley who took her to the festival. They were going to camp down there on the beach for the weekend with a group from the university, enjoy the music, then return ready for classes refreshed and recharged."

Turning to the desk, Lesia lifted a photo frame and passed it to Casey. Inside the patterned frame was a photograph of Saskia and another young woman posing together. They were both dressed formally in flowing dresses. They were surrounded by revellers of a similar age on a dance floor, suggesting that it was taken at a university function.

"This is Shelley?" Casey pointed to the pretty young face in the picture.

Lesia nodded then, all at once, she faltered. Her shoulders slumped as though a great weight had descended on them. Her emotions threatened to overwhelm her, but she sat straighter in her seat and composed herself, refusing to let them prevail.

"I remember they left on a Friday morning. They were excited, yet even to the very last moment, I had to push her to go. Saskia worried about leaving me, worried about being somewhere unfamiliar but I wanted her to have some fun, especially because it was by the seaside."

Lesia retrieved a tissue from inside the sleeve of her cardigan and dabbed her dripping nose.

"That was the last time I saw her," she said, her voice shaking. Her hands shook in her lap and a single tear welled in her eye before it ran down over the deep lines in her face.

"They told me she had been hit by a car in the night. On some lonely road, far from the beach. I could never understand how it happened that way."

Lesia's voice cracked and faded to a whisper, but she was determined to finish.

"She fought for four days to live. But they told me her injuries were too grave. Another doctor came to see me. He talked to me about giving her organs to people who were very sick, who were close to death. I had to make a decision quickly, or else those others might not survive."

Casey sat in stunned silence at the elderly woman's brave recollection. In that moment, Casey felt sick with shame at having so blatantly intruded into Lesia's little home, into the tragedy of her granddaughter.

"The pressure on me to decide was so great." Lesia held her hands out and shrugged her shoulders. "But I said yes. I have struggled with that decision ever since. Even though I know that she lives on in others—that they have been given a second chance, my Saskia has been taken away from me."

Lesia lowered her head and wept softly. Casey was too moved to speak, to notice anything other than the frail woman sitting before her, recounting her grief. She failed to notice Raelene, who had suddenly appeared in the doorway, shaking Casey out of her reverential quiet.

Raelene held her arms out and placed them around Lesia's shoulders while fixing Casey with a malevolent glower.

"Come on, Lesia, you need to rest, my love. There'll be no more talk of this for you today."

"It's all right. It's all right," Lesia protested, as she struggled to her feet and submitted to Raelene's gentle corralling out of the room.

Casey stood, took a moment before she placed the photo frame back on the desk, then followed after them.

No sooner had she closed the door and made sure it was secure behind her, she turned to find herself confronted by Raelene, who stood, her arms folded mere inches from her face.

"What do you think you're doing?" she hissed, keeping her voice low.

Casey blinked and opened her mouth to respond, but Raelene whipped her hand up to silence her.

"I don't know who you are, but I've never heard of any student doing a kind of research that involves pumping a poor, defenceless woman for information about her granddaughter's death. Where are you from, really? The media? The police?"

Casey steeled herself against the woman's interrogation.

"Neither," she said, clutching her folder to her chest.

"Well, have you got any identification then?"

"Not with me, but you can check with the university. They'll confirm my credentials."

Raelene stared at Casey, considering her bluff.

"I think you had better leave," she said in a low and threatening voice. "I might just make that call."

Standing aside to allow Casey to pass, Raelene then followed closely as she walked through the house toward the front door. As she approached it, Casey hesitated and looked through an open door into Lesia's bedroom. She saw the old lady sitting on the edge of her bed, staring back at her. Their eyes met one last time as Raelene brusquely ushered her out of the house. What Casey saw in Lesia's grief-stricken face chilled her.

She opened the door and stepped out onto the garden path, not looking back as the door was shut loudly behind her. Instead, she kept her eyes forward, realising that Scott's van was nowhere to be seen.

"Shit!" she cursed, her breath quickening. She scanned the street, unable to find the van anywhere nearby.

Suddenly, she heard two quick bursts from a vehicle's horn and Casey whipped her head to her right to see the van turn into the street from the intersection. Kicking off her shoes and grabbing them up with a free hand, she ran toward it as Scott leaned across from inside and opened the passenger door for her.

"Jesus, Sasquatch, are you trying to give me a heart attack?" she snapped breathlessly as she climbed in and fastened her seatbelt.

"I thought it would be a good idea if I didn't draw attention by waiting out front," he replied defensively. "I had a feeling. You know?"

Casey flashed him a sideways glower, which was quickly replaced by relief and she rubbed her brow. Scott pulled away from the kerb and motored away from the cottage.

"You were right. There was a nurse and I don't think she bought my act for a second."

Scott winced. "Are we screwed?"

"She threatened to make a call, but I don't think she was serious. In any case, it doesn't matter too much for now. I think I've got something to go on."

Reaching into her bag, Casey lifted out her smartphone and thumbed to the gallery. Tapping a thumbnail, she brought up the full image. It was a snap of the photograph in Saskia's bedroom. Thankfully, it was a clear shot. Holding the phone up, Scott glanced across at the photo and frowned.

Casey's eye was drawn, not to the face of Saskia, but to the face of the girl beside her.

"Shelley," she said softly.

CHAPTER 20

Waving to Scott as the van pulled away, Casey dashed up the oil-stained path to the warehouse. She could feel anxiety creeping in the minute she stepped out into broad daylight, but she made it to the comforting shelter of the garage before it could overwhelm her.

Sidestepping around the Volkswagen, she paused to catch her breath beside the stairs. She reached out for the rail and was about to climb them when she heard a male voice grunting and cursing through an open doorway that led from the garage to the rear of the warehouse. Cocking her head with both curiosity and concern, Casey regarded the doorway and gulped.

She'd had enough of being outdoors for one day.

Nonetheless, she peered around the paint-chipped door frame and spied Lionel standing before a pile of timber that was leaning up against the warehouse wall in the far corner of the paved courtyard. Across from him, a dump bin had been positioned outside a large gate.

Casey blinked and noted that the bin was half-filled already. She turned back to appraise her grandfather. He was sporting grubby overalls, a wide-brimmed hat and a pair of canvas gardening gloves. A wheelbarrow sat beside him, partly filled with refuse.

Lionel stepped back from the discarded timber pallets and other refuse and wiped his dripping brow. His expression hinted at exhaustion but his demeanour remained determined.

"Dare I ask?" she ventured, studying him.

Lionel shook his head. "You can ask," he responded. He promptly turned his attention back to the timbers.

Casey smirked, watching as he made a second attempt at hefting a pallet. This time, he succeeded in wheeling it around and dropped it noisily onto the barrow. He staggered back but quickly recovered and smiled with satisfaction.

He winked at Casey.

"You don't have to do this, Pa," she said.

He dismissed her with a wave of his hand. "Think of it as a belated house-warming gift. You know, you could do quite a lot with this area. A courtyard garden, an outdoor retreat, entertaining space—just like on those nauseating renovation shows."

Casey pursed her lips and blew a raspberry at that.

"*Outdoor entertaining*? Christ, could you honestly imagine me as the perky hostess? I don't think so."

Lionel chuckled and rested his hands on his hips. He inspected his handiwork.

Casey had attempted to make something of this area in the past. A rusted barbeque stood in the far corner. She had bought it not long after purchasing the warehouse but had never used it. A similarly rusted and paint-chipped outdoor dining set—three cast iron chairs and a circular table—sat forlornly nearby.

Aside from the accumulated refuse, the rest of the courtyard area was populated with large stone pots boasting the remnants of Casey's failed attempts at growing trees and shrubs, an effort to bring some greenery to the otherwise austere industrial building and its grounds. In the time that she had been away, Lionel had achieved much in removing the worst of the rubbish she had been promising herself she would deal with for as long as she had been here.

Picking up a nearby towel, Lionel took off his gloves and wiped his hands and brow.

"So," he said. "How did you fare?"

Casey leaned against the door frame. She sighed, then tilted her head.

"Blah," she began, exasperated. "The whole student ruse started out okay but…"

Her voice drifted away to nothing as she remembered the morning's encounter.

"But?" Lionel pressed.

"Well," she continued. "Lesia Andrutsiv was more with it than I expected. She bought my act; was quite talkative actually. But, she had a personal nurse who saw right through me. She threatened to look into my credentials."

Lionel raised his brow. The disapproval was unmistakable. Casey looked up at him forlornly.

"So we can probably expect some blow-back from Whittaker."

Casey stood straighter and shifted nervously on the spot.

Lionel's features softened a little and he offered a smile. "Let's not worry just yet. Why don't we go upstairs," he said, tapping the wheelbarrow. "I could use a drink."

Slinging the towel over one shoulder, he headed for the doorway.

In the apartment, Lionel took the whistling kettle from the gas flame and turned to fill the cups he had set up on the counter. Immediately, the scent of tea wafted up on the tendrils of steam and into Casey's nostrils, relaxing her, if just for the moment.

"Do you think you can handle him?" she asked as Lionel slid a cup to her. "I mean, what exactly did you and Whittaker cook up?"

"He agreed to give us some breathing room…on the proviso that we don't do anything stupid," Lionel answered, setting the kettle back down on the stove. "I suspect that he has his own doubts about what happened to Saskia Andrutsiv. He'll consider anything we turn up so long as it is fresh. He didn't specify *how much* rope he would allow us but I wouldn't want to push it. I'll speak to him if it becomes necessary."

Casey sipped from her cup.

"I'm more interested in hearing what this Mrs. Andrutsiv had to say," he said, changing the subject. "Did you learn anything of value?"

Casey shrugged. "Not much. A little about Saskia's background. She was here in Australia on a student visa, was studying art history and linguistics at Melbourne University. She had dreams of furthering her studies abroad."

She paused and closed her eyes, revelling in the warmth and comfort of the tea.

"She filled me in on some of the detail about the weekend she went away to the Pleasant Festival. She had a friend at uni who drove them both down to Queenscliff."

Lionel paused as he was about to close his lips around the edge of his cup. "A friend?"

Casey reached into her bag, shuffling through it until she found her phone and the photo she'd taken from Lesia Andrutsiv's house. She handed it to Lionel.

"A good friend actually," Casey pointed over the top of the smartphone screen as Lionel took it and slid his glasses into place. "Her name's Shelley."

"Shelley?" Lionel echoed questioningly. "Shelley Agutter?"

Casey raised her head. "Yeah. How did you know?"

"She was mentioned in the case file," Lionel answered. "The police questioned her following the accident."

"What did she say?"

Lionel shrugged. "Not a great deal as it turns out. Understandably, she was in shock. According to the transcript of the interview, Shelley Agutter told the police that they'd travelled down to the festival and met up with a group of friends. They'd pitched tents at a camping ground, just a short walk to the festival itself. It seems they spent a lot of time drinking and partaking in a healthy amount of drugs."

Lionel retrieved a leather-bound notebook from the sofa.

"Shelley vaguely remembers that the group were together at the festival on the Saturday night," he continued, thumbing through the pages. "Saskia had decided to leave early and walk back to the campsite. Neither Shelley or the others had any idea how Saskia came to be on Lasterby Road. They were in the *party mood,* as it were."

Casey tilted her head from side to side, recalling the conversation with Lesia Andrutsiv. "Shelley blamed herself for what happened. She promised Lesia that she would look out for Saskia. Lesia said they were like sisters. Inseparable."

"Seems odd then, that if they were supposed to be inseparable, Saskia would choose to leave the group and walk back to their campsite alone?" Lionel mused, his eyes drifting.

"Especially since she was terrified of being outdoors, in open spaces," Casey added. "She didn't feel comfortable on her own."

Lionel regarded Casey with surprise. "Agoraphobia?"

Casey nodded.

"Did Mrs. Andrutsiv say anything else? Was there anything going on in Saskia's life at the time of the accident?"

Again Casey shrugged.

"Only that Lesia was battling cancer. She was undergoing chemotherapy. Saskia did pretty much everything for her grandmother and she still managed to keep up with her studies. She was a loner. She didn't go out much or mix with anyone outside of her small group of friends."

Lionel looked up. An awkward smile creased his lips but Casey diverted her eyes away, feeling embarrassed. She lifted a finger, remembering something else.

"Lesia *did* mention something about Saskia's papers. Some sort of trouble with her papers."

Lionel glanced up from the photograph. "Her papers?"

"Yeah. Mrs. Andrutsiv seemed vague about it but I guessed it might have had something to do with her student visa. She wouldn't, or perhaps couldn't, elaborate much on it but she did say that Saskia had to sort it out on her own."

"Hmmm," Lionel ventured, his mind working. "There was no mention of that in the case file."

"If it were something to do with her student visa, there would have to be something on file somewhere, right?"

"Perhaps," Lionel replied, making a note in his book on a blank page. "It would be good to talk to this Shelley Agutter. Get a feel for who she is and whether she might be willing to talk more about what happened that night."

"That might be a little difficult," Casey said, her expression faltering. "I pulled her details on the drive back from Mrs. Andrutsiv's home. She's not living in Melbourne anymore."

Picking up her smartphone, Casey navigated to the information she'd gathered.

"She's living up in Ballarat. Apparently, she deferred her studies after Saskia's death and left the city. She's pouring coffee at a cafe there and studying part-time at a private college."

Casey held up the smartphone. "I've got her class and shift schedule for the next two weeks."

Lionel's eyes twinkled. "Well, we can work with that. Ballarat isn't more than an hour's drive from here."

Casey shivered. "Pa…there's *at least* a hundred kilometres of open freeway between Melbourne and Ballarat. I haven't driven that sort of distance in years. You saw what I was like in Scott's van."

Lionel's eyes narrowed. "You don't have to do it alone. I can still, quite capably, drive a car."

Casey regarded her grandfather thoughtfully. She turned and lifted her smartphone and called up some notes she'd made on the drive back from Lesia Andrutsiv's house.

"It would be good to see if I can talk to her."

Casey considered Lionel for a long moment. She nodded hesitantly. "You're happy to do this? You don't think this is *crazy*?"

"A drive in the countryside would do us both good, don't you think? I think it would be rather fun."

A wry smile turned Casey's lips. "Yeah, I guess."

Lionel pointed out through the industrial door.

"I'll be downstairs. You can come help if you'd like."

Casey wrinkled her nose and brushed him away.

"No, no. I'm gonna put the machine on and have a run. Then I'm gonna have a shower. A long one."

After a two hour session on the treadmill, Casey emerged from the shower, enclosed herself in a thick robe and twirled a towel around her head. As she slid the bathroom door aside, she listened for her grandfather, ensuring that he wouldn't suddenly appear while she was changing. Thankfully, the apartment was empty.

Changing into a pair of briefs and throwing on a light cotton T-shirt, Casey tossed the robe back through the bathroom door where it landed perfectly on its hook. She gave a cursory glance at the collage of car images.

Tiredness taunted, beckoning her towards slumber, but it clashed with her fear of sleep and the dream world that lay there. Pressing her fingers to her temples, she pushed her weariness away and tried to focus.

She turned and paused. A dark cloud coalesced in her mind: a nagging memory from within the nightmare that she could not clarify.

She had washed away the frustration from earlier in the day and she was in no mood to revisit it now. Looking again at the wall, she snarled at the magazine images.

Saskia's face flickered before her eyes and she felt herself lurch sideways. With a sharp intake of breath, she quickly felt for the bed and sat down. Emotional echoes raced from within as the nightmare flashed across her conscious field of view. She couldn't stop it.

Casey saw Saskia's face and she blinked, trying to understand its presence.

Terror…Desperation…Pleading…

What was it? Was she trying to say something?

The memory reached its zenith, then it tumbled away from her.

The moment had passed.

Casey gripped the towel turban in both hands. She closed her eyes and began rubbing her hair vigorously.

She felt a renewed pull, an urge to turn around.

Something had caught her attention in the images on the wall. It was taunting her, silently coaxing her to look. Casey gripped the towel harder.

Casey relented and turned around.

Her eyes went straight to the images at eye level on the door. A navy blue convertible coupe, its soft-top pulled up, drew her attention first. Casey studied it, going straight to the lines at the front and the arrangement of its headlights and grille. She closed her eyes and allowed her thoughts to go into her memories of the car in her nightmare. The same lines. Same headlights.

But…

Something wasn't quite right. Opening her eyes, Casey stepped up to the door and pulled the magazine image of the coupe from it. She regarded it again for a long moment. Then, she screwed up the picture and let it fall to the floor at her feet. She then chose another. She took it from the door and studied it before screwing it up and dropping it.

Another.

And another.

The mosaic before her had begun to resemble a giant slice of Swiss cheese. A growing pile of paper balls grew around her feet.

"Fuck," she cursed to herself.

CHAPTER 21

CLOSING THE DOOR TO HER OFFICE, KIRKWOOD TURNED AND PICKED UP A folder from her desk. Casey was pacing back and forth in front of the coffee table, hands on hips.

She's clearly preoccupied, Kirkwood noted. *Agitated even.*

Kirkwood took up her usual position in her armchair and adjusted her cushions behind her back. Casey continued her intense gaze through the window, folding her arms across her chest.

"Bad day?"

Kirkwood's question caused Casey to turn her head sharply.

She blinked and, as though realising how she must have appeared, her cheeks flushed. Her shoulders relaxed. Dropping her head, she nodded.

"Not so much a bad day. Rather, a frustrating one."

"Well, let's *talk* about it?" Kirkwood suggested with gentle sarcasm.

Casey managed a self-mocking, pained expression as Kirkwood gestured to the sofa opposite.

Kirkwood smiled knowingly.

"It's okay," she said, adopting a reassuring tone. "We can talk about something else if you'd like. We can talk about anything. I'm just pleased that we have been able to talk."

Slowly, Casey turned and took up the seat.

"It's the dreams," Casey said softly. "It's always the dreams."

She looked down at her hands. She was picking at a chipped end of her fingernail.

"There's something that keeps coming to me—some kind of fragment—that I can't quite nail. It's right there on the edge and I think it's really important."

Concern tightened Kirkwood's features, which didn't escape Casey's notice.

"I want to go back in," Casey said, determined.

Kirkwood tensed and shifted.

"Casey, I thought we had discussed this."

Casey clasped her hands in her lap.

"I know, Geddie," Casey said, nodding. "But this thing, it won't let go. I think that...Saskia might be trying to tell me something."

When Kirkwood didn't answer right away, Casey continued.

"Look, you said it yourself that examining these dreams could be helpful to me in healing. *You* started this."

Kirkwood nodded awkwardly.

"Well, y-yes I did. But using them as a basis for searching for clues to a supposed murder? Do you think that is appropriate? It's preventing you from moving on."

Casey could feel her frustration gathering, but she surreptitiously squeezed her hand into a fist to keep it at bay.

"I know this is real. And I know that if I can understand it, then I can put the dreams behind me and I can move on."

Kirkwood bit the inside of her lip as she considered Casey's argument. She could not deny that since Casey's admission to her grandfather, Casey had been much more receptive to therapy.

"You truly believe that Saskia is trying to tell you something?"

Casey thought about that question for a long moment. She nodded slowly.

"I'm not sure," she answered. "I'll only find it once I'm in there."

Kirkwood set her clipboard down on the floor.

"Okay," she answered. She held up her finger. "But I'm only going to do this one more time."

Casey sat up straight, eagerly resting her hands on her legs.

"All right," Kirkwood began.

Casey didn't wait for Kirkwood's instruction. She had already closed her eyes.

"Just like before. Let's start with the relaxation technique and slow everything down. Empty your mind and find your way to the road."

Casey complied and allowed her body to relax into the leather sofa. Emptying her mind, focusing only on Kirkwood's voice, Casey drifted until she felt herself shift into the darkness of her dream state until Kirkwood's voice faded far into the background.

Slowly, from the nothingness of her senses, Casey could hear the heart beating steadily—soft and comforting.

And then...

"Let me know when you're there."

Kirkwood's voice barely registered as she felt herself descending toward the road. Looking down, Casey saw rivulets of rain running across the tops of her feet. Above her, the lightning erupted, illuminating the road.

And the scene before her.

Stifling the familiar surge of nausea, Casey surveyed her surroundings and nodded quickly.

"Yes," she said simply.

"Okay," Kirkwood's disembodied voice sounded. "Just like you did before. Examine the scene and tell me what you see."

Casey stepped forward, squinting against the brilliance of the headlights ahead of her, using her outstretched palm to shield her eyes.

"I want to see the car," she murmured.

Kirkwood tilted her head. Retrieving her clipboard from the floor, she quickly reviewed the notes she had made from their previous session.

"Let's leave the car for a moment. Tell me, what else can you see."

Casey's looked back over her shoulder into the darkness.

"I don't see anything else."

"What about her?" Kirkwood challenged. "What about Saskia? You said Saskia was trying to tell you something."

Casey stiffened. Her breath quickened. She balled her hands into fists and pumped them nervously.

"I…I…"

"Tell me what you see, Casey," Kirkwood pressed, sitting forward in her armchair. "Saskia is there before you, right now, with him. Surely you can get closer."

"I c-can't," she stammered fearfully. "I don't want to."

Lowering her voice, Kirkwood studied Casey carefully. "No one can hurt you here, Casey. Just step closer to Saskia and tell me what you see."

"But he's *on* her," Casey's voice came in ragged, horrified gasps. "I can't stop him. I can't help."

"You're just an observer here. You can't change what happened."

Gulping softly, Casey walked slowly forward toward the shrouded forms of the assailant and Saskia.

Saskia was struggling against the huge form that straddled her, wrenching her arms in a vain attempt to free them. She thrust her head up and away from the huge gloved hand that was clasped over her mouth. Though Casey could feel the impact of Saskia's scream, the scream was silent.

Suddenly, Saskia managed to pull her left arm free and she began clawing desperately at the road surface, searching for any purchase with which she could pull herself free.

The familiar horror assailed Casey as though it were she who was underneath the attacker and she gasped, fighting to orient herself.

It is not me. It is not me.

"What do you see, Casey?"

Casey was closer now than she had ever been to Saskia.

Balancing on the edge of panic, she fought the urge to flee. Casey forced herself to look ahead.

The hand of the assailant came down, smashing through Saskia's chest. A silent, sickening mixture of blood and shattered bone.

And still she fought to free herself.

Her head twisted around in a desperate effort to find a means of escape. And in that moment, Casey and Saskia were looking at one another.

Casey's legs buckled and she dropped to her knees. Blood erupted from the ragged cavity in Saskia's chest and spattered everywhere, mixing with the falling rain and forming rivulets of crimson that trickled down her skin.

Saskia thrust her free hand out, stretching her fingers as far as she could, searching in desperation for Casey's own hand.

"What do you see, Casey?" Kirkwood pressed, her voice echoing distantly.

"She's reaching for me," Casey gasped.

Kirkwood blinked as Casey jerkily lifted her left hand from her lap and reached out before her. In the dream, Saskia formed words which Casey could see and understand though she could not hear them.

Help me!

"She's pleading with me…"

As Casey instinctively reached forward, Saskia's pupils flickered and dilated and her hand snapped fast around Casey's wrist. With a surge of inhuman strength, she yanked Casey towards her.

Casey opened her mouth to scream but could utter no sound. Instead, her own eyes bulged as she looked into Saskia's face.

Saskia's lips began to move, forming words? No, letters? Casey couldn't be sure. She was trying to understand, trying to control her terror.

Saskia kept mouthing the words and Casey tried desperately to decipher them.

S…

Casey began moving her own lips in concert with Saskia's until she began to realise that they weren't words at all. Rather, they were letters and numbers.

X…

8…

0…

3…2…5…4…

Over and over again, Saskia repeated the letters and numbers and Casey spoke them back to her in silence until they were repeating them in unison.

S…X…8…0…3…2…5…4…

A fork of lightning flashed close, its effect causing Saskia to release her grip. All at once, a serene expression came over her face, so serene that Casey thought she saw her smile.

Then, without warning, Casey felt herself being yanked backwards. She cried out as her body tumbled and rolled violently along the road like a rag doll as Saskia's face, the car, the assailant disappeared into the gloom.

Clawing frantically at the air, Casey screamed, trying to stop herself.

But she couldn't.

She felt herself dragged into the night sky.

"Casey!"

Kirkwood's voice rang like a gong and Casey's eyes snapped open. She was back in the room with Kirkwood but she was no longer on the sofa.

Instead, she was writhing on the floor, grabbing at the carpet and a form that was over her. Blinking in terror, Casey realised that she was screaming at the top of her lungs. Kirkwood was trying to restrain Casey as she lashed out. Several blows had connected.

"Casey!"

Realising that she was no longer in the dream, Casey stopped. She withdrew her arms and scrambled into a sitting position, backing away, more to protect Kirkwood than to protect herself.

Embarrassment and shame flooded her.

"Oh God! I'm all right, I'm all right!" she croaked breathlessly.

Exhausted, Kirkwood scrabbled back on her knees and leaned against the sofa.

At that moment, there was an urgent rapping at the door and Kirkwood looked around.

She glanced at Casey.

"I'm so sorry," Casey gasped raggedly.

Kirkwood got to her feet and hurried to the door, opening it to find her receptionist standing there with an expression of terror on her face.

"It's okay. Everything's okay," Kirkwood calmed her as quickly as she could.

"What on Earth happened?" the receptionist probed urgently. "The waiting area has cleared out!"

Kirkwood nodded and held up her palm.

"I've got it under control, Stacy. Just give me a moment, okay?"

Closing the door, Kirkwood retreated back into the office to find Casey already on her feet. She was standing before the window, looking out, chewing nervously on her thumbnail.

"That was my fault. I brought you out too quickly."

Casey began to shake her head.

"You were beginning to panic," Kirkwood continued. "I *had* to do something."

"It's okay," Casey said softly. "I'm glad you did."

She looked down on the table where Kirkwood had dropped her clipboard. On the sheet of lined paper secured to the clipboard was a series of letters and numbers, hastily scrawled.

SX803254.

Casey bent down and tore the sheet away. She held it up. "She gave me this."

Kirkwood gulped. "You were reciting it over and over."

Casey blinked. "Saskia was reciting it to me. Over and over again, until I remembered them."

Folding the sheet of paper and holding it tightly, Casey stepped forward, retrieving her bag from the sofa.

"I've gotta go," she said softly.

Kirkwood's eyes grew wide. "*Casey!* We haven't finished. We can't leave it at this."

Casey headed towards the door.

"I have to find out what this is, Geddie. This is important."

Even though she knew Casey wouldn't be persuaded otherwise, Kirkwood followed, stepping around her to grasp the door handle.

"Please, Casey. Don't do this. We don't know what this means and it could end up being more damaging for you, if you pursue it."

Casey hesitated, considering Kirkwood's plea and the folded note in her hand.

"I'll come back, Geddie. *I will.* But I've gotta do this."

Kirkwood let go of the handle and allowed Casey to exit.

"I can't do this again," she said solemnly. "I can't take you back in."

Casey nodded. "Hopefully, you won't have to."

CHAPTER 22

In another life, Casey would have relished being in such picturesque surroundings as the leafy grounds of Ballarat's Gainsborough College. As she emerged from a line of trees near the entrance to the exclusive school, Casey found herself standing before an expansive, sunlit lawn. A Gothic-style mansion stood on the far side. Next to it, connected by arched cloisters, was a stone chapel that appeared ancient.

Her breath quickened and she gulped.

Small clusters of students were lounging on the grass and under the nearby trees. Some were engaged in conversation. Some were solitary, laying with their heads against their rucksacks or rolled-up clothing, reading or dozing. The odd couple could be seen snuggled up together and basking in the warmth of the mid-morning sun. Further afield, a group of young men kicked a football back and forth.

It wasn't so much the large gathering of people that caused her anxiety to ratchet up. Rather, it was the prospect of having to traverse the lawn in order to reach the buildings on the far side.

Casey cursed herself for having insisted that Lionel drop her here. Glancing back over her shoulder, she could see him standing beside the car, but his back was turned. She had barely coped with the long, scenic drive up here from Melbourne with miles and miles of open rural heartland to stare at; an agoraphobe's worst nightmare. She'd had to retreat to the rear of the car for the last part of journey, lying down on the back seat with a blanket pulled over her.

Here and now, she licked her lips, realising her tongue was as dry as sandpaper.

She wished Lionel were here with her.

Casey closed her eyes and concentrated on her breathing.

I have nothing to fear, she repeated over and over to herself. *I look just like any other student here.*

Outwardly, her appearance was as similar as any other student.

It was just a question of keeping herself from losing her composure. Then she would stick out like a sore thumb.

Scanning the mansion beyond the lawn, she noted a pair of leafy trees. Casey picked out the one closest to her, then drew in a deep breath. She adjusted her shoulder bag, then ploughed forward, weaving in and out of groups of people, marching at a speed that had her almost breaking into a run. A few heads turned in her direction as she passed, albeit with a fleeting interest only.

Crossing from the lawn onto a paved thoroughfare, Casey leaned against the trunk of the tree and exhaled loudly, realising that she had been holding her breath the entire time.

Thank God.

Wary of being noticed, she composed herself, taking a minute to slow her pulse. She then reached into her shoulder bag and retrieved her notebook.

Shelley Agutter had been "off the grid" since shortly after Saskia's death. Although with Casey's resources, it hadn't been difficult to establish her whereabouts. With a little help from Scott, who had some connections within the security community, Casey learned that Shelley had only recently enrolled at the privately-run Gainsborough School of Art & Design.

The school offered post-graduate courses in fashion, interior, and architectural design and it was the fashion curriculum that Shelley evidently had been drawn to. She balanced her classes here at the college with serving at a local coffee house in the town centre. Shelley had also struck a deal on behalf of the cafe, enabling her to run a small, transportable coffee cart right on campus.

Unfolding a printed map of the campus grounds that was stapled to the page, Casey examined it and the notes she'd scribbled hastily in red ink, then looked up and west of where she now stood.

Accompanying the mansion and chapel, which had once been a convent, was a smaller, Tudor-styled house situated on an adjoining property. It had been incorporated into the campus and was linked by a path that ran through a purpose-built quadrangle. This building housed the fashion design faculty, complete with classrooms and studios, and was the place where Shelley Agutter was purported to spend most of her hours.

Casey saw the beginnings of a long thoroughfare, known as The Walk, just a short distance away. Calmer now in the shadow of the towering mansion, Casey made her way toward The Walk and fell in with the light pedestrian traffic moving back and forth along it.

The air here smelled crisp and sweet. Long garden beds to her right, sheltered by huge Moreton Bay fig trees, had been freshly watered and the light breeze that wafted along the path captured the scents from the flowers, lifting them up where they mingled through the canopy above her head. Casey felt a pang of affection for her university days.

Up ahead, Casey spied a cluster of bright red outdoor umbrellas arranged inside a courtyard that also served as a thoroughfare bridging the smaller house to the mansion. The portable cafe cart resided in the centre of the courtyard, serving a sizeable cluster of people there. Beyond the courtyard, Casey could see the slate-tiled roof of the house itself.

This was it. This was where Shelley—according to the timetable Casey had—was likely to be.

Approaching slowly, Casey cast her eyes around, scanning the tables underneath the umbrellas. A loose line of customers was gathered adjacent to the coffee cart, waiting to be served. Shielding her eyes, Casey examined the servers beyond the waiting line, but she didn't recognise anyone.

Looking back over her shoulder, she noticed a constant stream of pedestrians moving between the house and the mansion. If her information was correct, Shelley should be working right now.

Casey felt inside her shoulder bag for her purse and checked to see if she had enough change for a coffee, which she did.

Approaching the line, Casey fell in behind a young couple who were holding hands and chatting happily as they waited to be served. Using them as cover, she peered around their shoulders. There were two servers behind the counter: an athletic young man with a chiselled jaw and an older woman with upswept greying hair.

Casey paused as a third server stood up into view from a crouching position behind the coffee cart. It was another woman.

Right away, Casey recognised Shelley Agutter.

Though she was around the same age as Casey, Shelley appeared much older. Despite this, her features were still soft, like they were in the photograph, but Casey noted a weariness to them too. Shelley moved efficiently, tending to the customers without engaging with them. Her sandy hair was held in place with a clip that also served as a placeholder for a pencil. She wore a fitted black T-shirt. A name badge was pinned to the material over her left breast, confirming her identity.

Casey lifted her hand to clutch at her shirt. An echo of familiarity clanged in her mind. She bit the inside of her lip.

Cut it out, she admonished herself. *You've never met her before.*

The line moved forward until Casey found herself facing Shelley.

Shelley smiled indifferently. "What can I get you?"

Casey didn't answer. She stared at Shelley without realising it. Shelley shifted and met her stare with narrowed eyes.

"What can I get you?" she repeated, more firmly this time.

Casey shook herself back to the present. "Sorry, I…ahhh…coffee please. Cappuccino and a muffin."

Casey pointed through a small, transparent cabinet between them and Shelley nodded, fetching a blueberry muffin and setting it down on a napkin. She turned to the coffee machine beside her while Casey waited. She continued to watch Shelley as she worked. She knew she couldn't talk to her here and start asking questions in front of all these people.

Glancing back over her shoulder, Casey saw the line behind her beginning to lengthen.

The lunchtime crowd.

Casey would have to bide her time.

Shelley turned back with the coffee cup and Casey quickly averted her eyes, which didn't escape Shelley's notice. She paused, frowned, then set the cup down beside the muffin.

"$5.80," she said with a hint of caution.

Casey handed her change over and retrieved the muffin and her coffee. She retreated from the cart, taking up a position at a table just out of view as the lunchtime crowd grew thicker. The line now extended far beyond the edge of the courtyard.

Casey drew the photograph out of her bag and examined it once again, ensuring that there was no doubt the Shelley in the image and the woman working the cart were one and the same.

Suddenly, her phone rang inside her bag and Casey set the photo down so that she could answer.

"Any luck?" Lionel's voice sounded, before she could speak.

"I'm sitting across from her as we speak," Casey said, keeping her voice low. "But I can't engage with her just yet. The lunch crowd really likes this coffee cart she serves at and I don't want to make a scene."

"Are you okay? Do you want me to come to you?"

"No, no. So long as I focus on what I want to do and forget about where I am, I'm fine. But I hope this doesn't take too long."

"Okay. I'll wait for you. Just call me if you change your mind."

"I will, Pa. Thank you."

Casey ended the call, then set her phone down so that she could pick up her coffee.

As she looked up, Casey saw Shelley leaving from behind the cart, armed with a large shoulder bag. She was waving goodbye to her colleagues as she passed in front of them, then she crossed the courtyard in the direction of The Walk. She disappeared from view behind a tree.

"Dammit," Casey cursed as she scrambled to gather her shoulder bag, knocking her half-empty coffee cup over and spilling liquid across the table top. A number of heads turned in her direction at the sound of her voice.

Grabbing a handful of serviettes from a holder, Casey tossed them down on the mess she'd created before abandoning the table and rushing in the direction that Shelley had headed.

Casey scanned The Walk. It was considerably busier now than it had been when she had first arrived. Large groups of people were moving back and forth in between several stationary groups of students who were mingling in her vicinity. She couldn't see Shelley anywhere.

She hissed.

Casey moved forward, urgently scanning her surroundings. Shelley was nowhere to be seen. If she lost her now, Casey would have to wait to do this all over again and she doubted she could stay out of doors for much longer.

As she felt hope slipping away, her eyes fell across Shelley. She was climbing a set of steps onto the wide verandah of the mansion, several dozen yards ahead of Casey, in the company of another student.

Great, Casey thought. *She's got company.*

She rushed along the path and skipped up those same steps, finding herself at an entrance to the College Administration. Through the pair of glass doors, Casey saw Shelley and her companion as they walked down a long hall, laughing and chatting. Casey slipped inside and noted a sign pointing to a lecture theatre in the direction she was headed. She followed at a safe distance, fearing that the two women were going to enter that very theatre, but both women passed the entrance and instead turned a corner towards a group of offices and a reception area.

Once there, they stopped before a counter, smiling at someone out of view. Craning her neck, Casey watched as Shelley shrugged the shoulder bag off her shoulder and reached into it, retrieving an envelope from inside which she then handed over. Casey inched closer, hoping that she might hear what Shelley was saying.

Suddenly, both girls stepped back from the reception area and turned in Casey's direction. Her eyes went wide and she ducked into an open doorway beside her.

She was sure they had seen her.

"Can I help you?"

Casey spun around to face a young woman who was sitting at a desk.

She could feel the heart in her throat. She could hear Shelley and her companion as they approached, then passed by the doorway.

"Ahhh," Casey stammered impotently.

They did not stop.

"I'm sorry. I think I'm lost."

Casey turned back to the entrance and cautiously peeked around the door frame into the corridor.

It was empty.

"Shit."

Lurching into the corridor, Casey rushed towards a junction and flicked her head to her right. The doorway where she had entered earlier was closed and didn't appear to have been disturbed. She glanced left just in time to see the two women exiting through a similar doorway leading out of the building.

She hurried after them, determined not to lose them again.

All the while, her mind was working furiously, trying to determine just how she would approach Shelley.

Leaving the building and onto a similar verandah to the opposite side of the mansion, Casey stopped abruptly when she looked across and saw Shelley and her friend standing under a tree continuing their conversation. Though they were turned away from her, Casey ducked out of view. Satisfied that she hadn't been seen, she watched them. After several minutes, they finally bade each other farewell, exchanging kisses before parting company.

Shelley watched her friend go then she bent down to run a finger along the inside of her canvas shoe. Evidently, she had picked up a small pebble. Flicking it out, she rose and turned toward a darkened arch adjacent to the chapel, disappearing through it. Casey gave chase, crossing the courtyard in the shadows of the grand architecture, and ducked into the darkened thoroughfare beyond.

She found herself under a line of grand arches that appeared like something out of a Harry Potter movie: the cloisters that linked the chapel to the mansion.

Shelley walked along the path several yards ahead, then turned right, passing out of view. Using the shadows cast by the imposing columns of stone, Casey followed swiftly. Turning right, Casey crossed under an even darker under-walk that was lit by Gothic light fittings that cast an orange glow on the ornate stonework above her head. It caught her attention, distracting her until she looked up to see the expansive paved boulevard open out ahead at the bottom of some steps. Beyond that was the huge lawn she had crossed over earlier.

Casey's eyes bulged, and she skidded to a stop at the top of those steps, recoiling at the sight of the open space before her. She felt something snap in her ears and she lurched sideways, taking shelter in the shadows.

Not now. God please, not now.

Squeezing her eyes shut, Casey forced herself to breathe, then she glanced across at the boulevard and the lawn beyond.

Shelley was nowhere to be seen.

"Shit," she hissed angrily, gripping the column and glancing desperately in all directions: the boulevard beyond, the cloisters and quadrangle behind her. She was totally alone.

I've lost her!

"Why are you following me!"

Casey jumped and spun around in reaction to the voice that came from beside her. She looked into the angry eyes of Shelley Agutter.

Shelley had silently emerged from behind an adjacent column, taking advantage of the moment when Casey was looking in the opposite direction. She now stood not more than a couple of feet away from Casey, glaring at her menacingly.

"Who are you?" she snapped.

Casey stumbled backwards and she raised her hands. "I'm sorry. I didn't mean to scare—"

"Who are you?" Shelley retorted, cutting Casey off menacingly.

"Look, I'm," Casey stuttered. "I was hoping to ask you some questions."

Shelley's expression shifted in confusion. She scanned Casey up and down. "Questions? About what?"

Casey blinked. She would have to think quickly. "I understand that you were a good friend of Saskia Andrutsiv."

Shelley's eyes went wide and she recoiled visibly at the mention of that name.

"Saskia," she whispered, as though uttering it felt like knives slashing at the back of her throat. She began to look about her in all directions fearfully. "Who are you? Why would you want to know about her?"

"I'm looking into her case and your name came up," Casey said quickly.

"Her *case*?" Shelley hissed incredulously. "Are you with the police?"

Casey shook her head quickly, too quickly.

"I'm not with the police," she said, trying to muster a reassuring tone. "My name is Casey. I'm doing some research into unsolved cases and Saskia Andrutsiv's came up."

Casey's voice trailed off. She knew her response sounded pathetic.

"*Unsolved*?" Shelley said bitterly. "How did you find me?"

She hefted the strap on her bag and began to back away in the direction of the boulevard.

"Look!" Casey croaked, reaching with one hand while keeping the other planted on the stone column. "I've come by some information about the night of her accident. You were interviewed by the police. You knew her. I was hoping you might be able to help me."

"I want to know who you are!" Shelley spat viciously.

"I'm a friend," Casey answered weakly. "My name is Casey. The information I have about Lasterby Road is new and I just wanted to ask you about it."

"Lasterby Road."

Without warning, Shelley began to shake. Her expression tensed and her eyes became glassy. Casey could sense her fear.

"I'm not going to talk to a stranger about Saskia," Shelley whispered shakily. "I c-can't be talking about this. And *you* shouldn't be asking questions."

At that, Casey's eyes narrowed. "Why not?"

Shelley blinked, startled by the question. Again, she glanced around them both, as though expecting someone else to emerge. She backed away from Casey and turned to leave.

"Please," Casey began as she stepped away from the column. Shelley broke into a jog, peeling away from Casey in the direction of the boulevard. She skipped down the steps and into the daylight.

The university grounds opened up before Casey, stretching away into the distance. She stopped at the top of the steps, stared at the wide, open space, unable to go any further.

"Please, Shelley!" Casey called as Shelley crossed over onto the lawn.

Shelley paused and turned back. She was about to speak, but something about the way Casey was standing at the top of the steps stopped her momentarily: the way this stranger was looking at her.

There was a hesitation in Casey's expression that felt familiar.

Shelley had seen it before.

Brushing the thought aside, Shelley pointed an accusatory finger at Casey. "Don't come near me again."

She turned on her heel and hurried away.

Casey retreated under the safety of the columns. She squeezed her eyes shut, fighting to regain control.

1...2...3...4... You're safe...you're safe.

Calm was returning. She nodded slowly to herself, then she opened her eyes.

And looked directly into the face of Prishna Argawaal.

"Hi there," Prishna greeted sarcastically, leaning against a stone column.

Casey baulked, realising who it was.

She rolled her eyes. "Jesus Christ."

Prishna adopted a look of mock hurt. "I'm not *that* frightening, surely."

Casey attempted to turn away but Prishna stepped forward and deftly shifted directly into her path.

Her expression hardened. "What are you up to, Casey? It's good to see that you're out of the loony bin, by the way."

"None of your *fucking* business, Prishna," Casey spat.

Prishna cocked an eyebrow. Her lips turned up in a knowing smile. "Oh really. Well, I wouldn't be so sure about that. It seems that you've been busy. Causing a little trouble for people. People like Lesia Andrutsiv and Shelley Agutter."

Casey turned away.

"It didn't make much sense to me, at first," Prishna continued. "It didn't fit with you. Then I did a little digging and, lo and behold, it turns out that you do have a little connection to them after all. Don't you?" Prishna nodded at Casey's chest. "If I were you, I'd be grateful for that heart, Casey. Don't go digging up the past, looking for something that isn't there. You're only going to cause them more heartache. Besides, you've got bigger problems to deal with."

Casey seethed. Her lips grew even more tighter. "Are we *done*?"

Prishna waited. Then she beamed a proud, satisfied smile.

Casey wanted to punch her.

Without waiting for an answer, Casey grabbed the shoulder strap of her bag tighter and marched down the steps. Prishna watched her go, her expression faltering somewhat at Casey's brush-off.

"I'm watching you, Casey," Prishna called after her. "Whittaker is watching you, too."

Casey didn't look back. Her anger pushed her on, keeping her fear at bay.

CHAPTER 23

Hello!"

Peter's voice sounded from the bottom of the warehouse stairs as he trudged up to the apartment, armed with a trio of grocery bags.

Receiving no reply, he frowned as he stopped before the industrial door and set the bags down, fishing his keys from his pocket.

He called again as he turned the key in the lock and slid the door aside to find the apartment empty.

"Empty," he mumbled under his breath, stepping inside. Depositing the grocery bags on the counter, he scanned the apartment, casting a cursory glance upstairs to the mezzanine, then through the windows onto the balcony. The curtains were open, framing the azure bay beyond.

Though she was usually home on a Tuesday afternoon, Peter supposed that Casey was out seeing Kirkwood or perhaps she was at the hospital. As for Lionel, he could have been anywhere. Probably catching up with old police colleagues, Peter figured. He decided he would just get to it, unpack the groceries and start cooking their curry.

Peter went over to the glass doors and opened them, stepping out onto the balcony, lingering for a moment with his hands resting on the rail. A flotilla of small yachts was cruising up and down the bay just in front of him.

He shook his head and smiled. *Sure picked a gem of a spot,* he thought.

Turning to head back inside, something caught his eye in Casey's bedroom. He frowned, trying to see through the reflection of the glass and what appeared to be a vast mural covering the brick wall. Slowly, he stepped inside and peered around her wardrobe.

Cars? he thought, puzzled.

The entire wall, from floor to just above head height, was covered in pictures, though he noticed gaps in the mural. In all of the images, Peter identified the familiar circles of the Audi emblem.

He drew closer, then looked down at the floor beside Casey's bed. A burgeoning pile of paper balls lay there.

Dropping to his haunches, Peter picked up one of those balls and unfurled it, revealing a glossy magazine picture of an Audi sports car: a midnight blue convertible with shining alloy wheels, its bright headlights punching the low light before it.

What on Earth?

He picked up another ball of paper and another, unscrewing them to see similar pictures, his confusion mounting and evolving into concern then worry, until an unpleasant knot tightened in his stomach.

Peter didn't hear the industrial door slide aside, nor did he hear Lionel's voice.

"Casey? Are you home?"

Lionel appeared in the space between the wall and the wardrobe.

"Peter?" he greeted.

Peter spun around and looked up at his father-in-law. He held up the magazine picture in his hand.

"What is this?" His expression was taut.

Lionel exhaled softly, turning his palms outwards towards Peter. "It's Casey's."

Peter's eyes narrowed. His nostrils flared.

"Casey's *what*?" he pressed, his voice rising in agitation. "Jesus. What is this?"

"Look, it's a part of her therapy," Lionel lied. "It's her way of trying to understand, I guess, what it is that is going on inside her head."

Peter's mouth opened slightly. His glare became more intense. "In her head? You mean those bloody dreams?"

Lionel shoved his hands into his pockets.

"Well, yes. Those dreams have been at the core of why Casey's been so troubled. She's trying to understand them and, hopefully, stop them from happening."

"*Bullshit*," Peter spat abruptly. "That's not it."

Lionel blinked as Peter screwed up the piece of paper in his hand and threw it to the floor.

"Prishna has been to see us again. She thinks Casey's up to something. Looking into an old case?"

Lionel was about to speak, but Peter cut him off. "Casey discovered who her donor was, didn't she? Some kind of hit and run?"

Lionel sighed wearily which served only to cause Peter's eyes to bulge. He shook his head incredulously, expecting more from Lionel.

"And now what? Casey's taken it upon herself to find out what happened? Because of this...*dream*?"

Lionel nodded, "Yes."

Peter could not believe what he was hearing. "Jesus Christ, Lionel!"

Peter pushed past Lionel and circled Casey's workstation. He placed his hands on his hips, pacing the living room, trying to keep himself calm.

"This is bloody ridiculous. Why are you letting her do this?"

"Because I believe her," Lionel responded, without turning.

Peter froze in mid-step.

"You *believe* her?" he hissed, stupefied.

Lionel gazed at his son-in-law. "I believe her. Casey is one of the most pragmatic people I know. Have you ever known her to go off half-cocked with anything?"

"What is *that* supposed to mean?"

"Think about it. All her life, Casey has been the ultimate pragmatist. She has always followed the rules, applied herself to the fullest and she has never believed in anything that could not be quantified. She is applying that same approach to this situation now."

"But they're bloody dreams, Lionel! They're not real!"

Lionel's jaw hardened and he took a step towards Peter. "When I held her in my arms at the hospital, she told me what was happening to her. She looked me right in the eyes and told me the reason why she has been so disturbed all this time. And I believe her. I've since had the opportunity to look into her donor's case and I think there are some things about it that are worth having a look into."

Peter clenched his jaw.

"I can't believe I'm hearing this. You have absolutely no proof to back up what you're saying! You're letting her ramble around the bloody countryside, distressing people who deserve to be left alone and causing all sorts of trouble for the authorities."

Peter turned away from Lionel again.

"You haven't been here to see what she's been doing to herself all these years," he continued, his voice shaking. "Christ, she's been so withdrawn. So hyped-up on drugs. You've seen her breakdown for yourself!"

"But have you ever asked her *why* she's relied on drugs?" Lionel countered.

"You're indulging a fucking fiction, Lionel. You're going to destroy her."

"You asked me here to help," Lionel said quietly. "I'm helping her."

At that moment, the entry door rumbled aside revealing Casey standing there, an anguished look on her face. Both men looked in her direction and felt a wash of guilt.

"What is going on?" Casey's voice quavered, her eyes raw.

Peter dropped his head down to the floor. Shame and grief overwhelmed him. Lionel just stood there awkwardly.

"Casey, I'm so sorry," Lionel whispered.

"I can't stay here," Peter said. He marched across to the counter and snatched up his keys. He turned to Casey, but he could not look at her directly. "I'm sorry too, Casey."

Stepping through into the hallway, Peter turned back to Lionel. "Who are you doing this for, Lionel? For her? Or for yourself?"

He didn't wait for an answer. Turning on his heel, he disappeared down the steps.

LIONEL SAT BEFORE the darkened screen of Casey's computer. He rubbed his eyes under his glasses and sighed heavily.

He was still smarting from the confrontation with Peter. Casey was locked in her bathroom. They had barely spoken since Peter had walked out. The air had been thick with tension.

He lifted his hand towards the power switch on the monitor and he let it hover there for a long moment. Lionel had never been overly computer savvy and he was pretty sure that he wouldn't be able to make sense of Casey's custom built machine now.

You're indulging in a fucking fiction!

Peter's stinging rebuke echoed. It stung because a part of Lionel knew that his son-in-law was right. Yet, the more he thought about it, the more he wanted Peter to be wrong.

He *needed* Peter to be wrong.

His finger descended toward the power button, but before he touched the surface the screen abruptly flickered to life and Lionel blinked at a welcome screen.

"Welcome, Lionel," an emotionless female voice greeted. "Please touch your thumb to the scroll pad."

Lionel blinked. He complied, reflexively, moving his hand down and positioning his thumb on the keyboard.

"Identification confirmed. Please proceed. Would you like to commence a secure session?"

"A secure session?" he mumbled aloud. "What on Earth is that?"

Leaning closer, Lionel examined the window which had popped up. Two icons, one with 'Accept' and the other with 'Decline' were displayed there along with some smaller text underneath which he could barely read. Something about a secure network, encrypted browsing, external defence. He knew how diligent Casey was in maintaining her privacy.

Touching his finger to the screen, Lionel pressed 'Accept.'

A browser window opened and Lionel was directed to a search engine.

He focused in on the blinking cursor.

What to look for…

The Pleasant Festival had kept circling in his thoughts all evening.

He tapped the keyboard and watched as a procession of results came up. He touched his finger to the first entry: the official website for the music festival.

A brightly coloured page with a carnival themed design flashed up. Lionel noted that it was advertising for next year's event. Searching the page for a description, he found an 'About' section and clicked through.

'*The Pleasant Festival: an annual celebration of grassroots Australian contemporary music, theatre, cabaret and comedy held in March each year in the seaside town of Queenscliff, Victoria. Since its launch six years ago, the Festival—affectionately known simply as "Pleasant"—has become a hugely popular event on the live music calendar, attracting acts both local and international to the crisp beaches of Port Phillip Bay.*'

Lionel examined the remainder of the site, viewing several picture galleries and press releases on the festival. It was all fairly stock standard information. Nothing caught his interest.

Returning to the results, Lionel scanned them again and saw little that warranted further exploration. He scrolled up to the top of the page and tried another query.

'Pleasant Festival 2012'.

The results seemed to be no better but he went through them anyway, holding out hope for a sliver of anything that might lead them closer.

This time, he noted several links to news items that referenced Saskia's accident and he followed these, only to find that they contained the information they were already acquainted with.

He scrolled to the top once more and saw the image search option. He tried that, causing a slew of results to flash up: pictures of the Pleasant Festival, both official as well as ones taken by attendees. Adjusting his glasses, Lionel leaned in close and carefully examined each image in turn.

There were a lot of group shots and selfies, the kind that usually end up on social media. But often these were the kinds of images that offered the most information. He'd trawled through thousands of images like these in the past, when he'd been working on difficult cases. In remembering that, Lionel chuckled under his breath. This task was usually the most boring one.

He paused, glancing over his shoulder at the bottle of scotch on the kitchen counter. He stood and went over to the fridge, put some ice into a glass, then splashed a generous lug of the scotch over it.

May as well settle in.

Lionel became lost in the images. Time drifted past his notice as he examined countless photos, looking for something. *Anything.*

Somewhere in the early hours of the morning, he sat back and took off his glasses. He rubbed his tired eyes. Knots of tension had gathered in his shoulders. He reached over to massage his right shoulder, wincing as he did so.

Looking out through the glass onto the balcony, he saw Casey huddled up in one of the lounge chairs, a blanket draped around her shoulders and down over her body. Her head leaned to one side and, though he couldn't see her face, he knew that she was asleep.

Asleep for the first time since he'd been here.

Sighing, he turned back to the computer.

He had gotten nowhere with this. Not that he really knew where he was headed.

The images had blurred into a prosaic mass of young faces, revelling in the party atmosphere of the seaside, brightly coloured lights and fireworks, musicians and performers. He couldn't be sure what he was seeing in them anymore.

Absently, he reached across to his glass and lifted it to his lips, not realising that it was empty. He cursed silently, glancing across at the bottle. He raised one brow in muted surprise as he decided to pour one more glass. As he drew it to his lips, he could feel the warmth of the alcohol coursing through him.

His hand brushed over the keyboard as he pushed back on the stool to stand. The screen flickered as it proceeded to the next page of images. He cursed, having lost the page that he was reading.

As he looked down, hoping to reverse his unintended action, his eyes floated across the new gallery and he stopped.

Something caught his eye toward the bottom of the page. He squinted against the bright light of the screen, spying a face that appeared familiar.

He centred the thumbnail, then tapped it. A larger rendering of the image loaded.

Lionel's stomach plunged.

He was looking into the eyes of Saskia.

Posing coquettishly, draped over the front of a car, she reminded Lionel of a model one might find in a glossy automotive magazine.

Lionel snapped up his glasses and peered closer, unable to believe what he was looking at. He flipped open his notebook to a page where he had stapled a photocopy of a newspaper article that had Saskia's picture. He compared the two. It was unmistakable.

Then, another bolt of realisation struck.

Her companion.

Adopting a similar pose, the young woman leaning suggestively against Saskia gradually came into focus once Lionel had positioned his glasses correctly. He recognised the girl as the friend from the photograph that Casey had snapped in Saskia's bedroom.

It was Shelley Agutter.

He drew his hand up to his mouth as he examined the photograph. He could not make out the registration plate of the car they were posing with as it was obscured by Shelley's legs. But, all at once, Lionel realised just what sort of vehicle he was looking at.

A low-slung pair of headlights that tapered into the grille.

Highly polished chrome rings, partially obscured by Shelley's leg, captured the glint of the camera flash.

Interlocking chrome rings.

"Casey," Lionel called into the darkness, his voice hoarse.

On the balcony, Casey stirred in her chair. Her eyes fluttered open at the sound of his voice.

"Pa?" she responded.

"You had better come and look at this."

Shaking herself awake, Casey dragged herself from her chair and threw on her dressing gown. Stepping through the doorway, she approached Lionel, rubbing the sleep from her eyes, but she snapped to alertness when she looked over his shoulder at the computer screen. Lionel looked up at her. He tilted the screen so she could see it more clearly.

Casey's eyes fell across the image. Her jaw dropped.

Saskia and Shelley together. The garish lights of a party. Striped tights and fairy wings.

The car. The Audi.

Casey's knees buckled. All the air left her lungs. Her head swirled as the full realisation of what she was looking at dawned.

"That's it," she whispered shakily.

The line snaked from the courtyard cafe cart well into the thoroughfare. From her vantage point, Casey could still see the cart. Her eyes were focused on the counter where Shelley Agutter was serving.

Casey had set out well before dawn, this time on her own. Her resolve was fuelled by the realisation that Shelley was hiding something significant. In her hand, Casey clutched a piece of paper, a printout of the image her grandfather had discovered last night.

The Audi was no longer a nebulous vision. Shelley had been in the company of that Audi and quite possibly the owner of it. She had told the police nothing of it. There was nothing in the reports Lionel had viewed that mentioned Shelley speaking of a car of this or any sort.

Casey looked down at the image as the line moved forward. There was no mistaking it. The two best friends. The Audi.

She knew, Casey thought, trying to contain her anger. *She knew all along.*

The line moved closer and Casey moved with it until she was right next to the cart, mere feet from the counter. Shelley hadn't seen her.

As she collected money from the customer she was serving, Shelley Agutter caught sight of Casey out of the corner of her eye. Her face hardened immediately. Fumbling with the change in her hand, and dropping some on the counter, she picked it up and handed it to the young man.

Casey watched her resolutely.

And then she was before her.

"I thought I told you to leave me alone," Shelley said as discreetly as she could.

"I know about the Audi," Casey said calmly.

Shelley froze. Her hand shook and her mouth fell open.

Casey watched Shelley stonily. "The night of the accident. There was a car. An Audi."

"How do you—?"

"Know?" Casey finished for her. She slapped the picture down on the counter.

Casey leaned over the counter. "We need to talk."

Ashen faced, Shelley turned to her colleague. "Nathan…"

Nathan turned and saw her expression. He frowned.

"Can you cover for me?"

He nodded, gazing worriedly in Casey's direction then back at Shelley. "Are you all right?" he mouthed silently.

Untying her apron, Shelley nodded hastily and hung it on a hook behind her. She glanced at Casey, her eyes filled with fear. "Come with me."

CHAPTER 24.

As Casey followed Shelley away from the courtyard and onto The Walk, she noticed how nervous Shelley appeared. She frequently glanced ahead and behind them, as though afraid she was being watched.

Turning off The Walk, Shelley led Casey to a trio of benches tucked away in a quiet nook at the rear of the mansion. Shelley gestured to one of them and Casey sat down.

"Okay. If you're not with the police or the media, then who are you with?" Shelley asked, he voice shaking. "Were you at Pleasant?"

Casey stiffened. She knew she would have to tread carefully.

"I wasn't at Pleasant. Like I said to you before, my name is Casey Schillinge. I'm looking into Saskia Andrutsiv's accident."

Shelley frowned, confused.

"How could you *possibly* know about that car?"

"You didn't say anything to the police about it," Casey countered, deflecting Shelley's question. "Why not?"

Shelley wrung her hands in her lap, then clutched them together in a vain attempt to hide her fear from Casey. She shrugged.

"I..." Her voice barely broke above a whisper. "I was scared."

"Scared? Did you know who was driving that car?"

Shelley looked directly at Casey.

"No," she said determinedly. "I don't."

"You knew she was in that car, the night of her accident. She didn't leave the Pleasant Festival alone, did she?"

She tensed at Casey's persistence and shut her eyes tightly.

Casey considered her words carefully.

"Shelley, the police never closed Saskia's case file," she said, softening her voice. "It remains unsolved because they don't have any fresh leads that might help them solve it. If you know something, I can take it to them. I can protect you."

She paused, touching her tongue to her lower lip.

"But, I can also point them in your direction if you won't help me. You're scared of something. I can see that. Help me to understand what it is."

Shelley looked back at Casey with a tortured expression, only to meet Casey's own determined visage.

"Don't you think Lesia deserves to know the truth?"

Shelley blinked, stunned by the mention of that name. "Lesia? How do you…?"

Shelley didn't finish her sentence. She sensed that Casey must already have spoken to Saskia's grandmother. "How is she?"

"She seems okay," Casey replied. Then she frowned. "You haven't seen her recently?"

Shelley looked down at her hands once more. "Not since the funeral. I haven't been able to bring myself to. Anyway, I doubt she would want to see me. It was my fault what happened to Saskia."

Casey leaned forward, softening her expression further. "Shelley, if you know something that can help—that can get to the truth—*please* tell me."

Shelley hesitated. A weariness descended over her. The bulwark she had erected to protect her was crumbling. She regarded Casey and in that moment, Casey thought that Shelley Agutter appeared decades older.

"I-I just wanted to take a trip down the coast," Shelley began, biting the inside of her lip. "Sass and I…we needed to blow off a little steam. She had been through a really hard time with her Nana but things were finally starting to look up. Pleasant seemed ideal."

Casey drew a notebook and pencil from inside her bag and began to take notes as Shelley watched her.

"I got a couple of tickets from a friend. The plan was that we were going to meet up with a group from Melbourne Uni, pitch some tents near the Festival and just have a great time. And we did, at first. Everyone was happy. A couple in the group had brought some weed—nothing serious—but it put us all in the mood." Shelley's voice trailed off. She drifted into her memories. "On the Saturday, we all walked along the beach from the campsite to Pleasant itself and took in the concerts. The atmosphere was amazing."

The lines on her forehead deepened with the pain of her memories.

"We were so happy, Sass especially. She really let her hair down, more than I'd ever seen her do before. She deserved to, you know?"

She looked to Casey as if seeking some sense of understanding and Casey, for the first time, offered an empathetic smile.

"Anyway, it was in the evening—Saturday night—when this *guy* just kinda turned up out of nowhere."

"A guy?"

"I don't know who he was. I'd never seen him before. None of us had. Except..."

Shelley paused and looked down.

"It was like...Sass knew him. She seemed shocked that he was there. It was weird. He turned up in this expensive car. It impressed the hell out of the others. But it bothered me."

"Why?"

Shelley held her hands out, palms up. "I had this bad vibe about him and like, Sass never kept anything from me. We were close. She never told me that she was seeing anybody."

"Can you describe him?" Casey asked.

Shelley shrugged and bowed her head. "We were all pretty out of it, myself included. There was lots of, you know, *stuff* on offer that night. I can't be certain what I remember of him specifically. Except to say he seemed *intense*."

Shelley reached across and took the photograph from Casey.

"I don't know who took this. When he first showed up, we were all clowning around and showing off in front of his car because it was so expensive-looking. Sass played along with it for a bit but I could see she was uncomfortable. It was like, the longer this guy was around, the more she didn't want him anywhere near us. She eventually led him away from the group."

"Where did they go?"

"Not far. Down to the beach. We all went back to partying at the main stage. It seemed like they were gone for ages. I was getting worried so, eventually, I went looking for them. When I found them, they were arguing."

"Arguing?" Casey asked. "About what?"

Again, Shelley shrugged her shoulders and she tensed with frustration.

"I don't know," she said, scratching her head harshly. "It was really awkward. I think she wanted him to leave. He was really cagey about something. And then suddenly, something changed in Sass. It was like, he'd convinced her to go with him."

"Convinced her?"

"She saw me looking at them. She came to me and said she had to go. She wouldn't tell me where. I was beside myself. I mean, this guy that I've never met turns up out of nowhere and all of a sudden, she's going off with him. It wasn't like her. It was like I didn't know her."

Visible grief bubbled forth and Shelley seemed to collapse under the weight of it. She lowered her head, supporting it in her hands as she cried softly.

"That was the last time I saw her alive."

"Why didn't you go to police with this?" Casey asked breathlessly.

"Because," Shelley retorted. "We got busted that night for possession. 'E' was freely available and most of us were pretty wasted. It all happened right in the middle of Saskia going with him. I couldn't remember half of what I'd seen. But I also…" Shelley clutched at herself. "I started getting these phone calls a few nights after the accident. Threatening phone calls."

"From this guy?" Casey asked incredulously.

"I don't know! They were creepy, distorted…I guess so. But it wasn't just the calls. I was getting messages into my pigeonhole at uni. Clothes were going missing from my line. I had a couple of break-ins although there was no sign of anyone forcing their way in. Somehow they were able to just get in. Things—awful things—were being left there. Someone actually *shit* on my bed—more than once. It went on for a few weeks. I felt like I couldn't go to anyone about it. Eventually, I had to get out. I left Melbourne. I put my studies on hold and just left."

Casey took a moment to comprehend the gravity of Shelley's account. She had no reason to deny that what Shelley was saying was true but it left her facing the reality of another apparent dead end.

Looking down at her notebook, she flipped the page, examining what she had written. She saw a note that read, 'student papers'.

"Lesia said that Shelley had some kind of trouble with her visa."

Shelley blinked through her tears and looked at Casey. "I didn't think Lesia knew about that. She was so sick. We deliberately kept it from her."

Casey leaned forward. "Would you tell me about it?"

Shelley took a deep breath in and blinked back her tears.

"Sass got in a mix-up with the Immigration Department. She'd been working extra hours at the uni cafe to cover the bills while Lesia was undergoing chemotherapy. They were in danger of sinking under debt. Turns out Saskia was in breach of her visa conditions. She got reported and then, to add to the insult, they took her away. Department officers came to the school and just… *took her*."

Shelley's lip trembled.

"Where did they take her?" Casey asked.

"The detention facility at Flaxley Park," Shelley answered. "They didn't say anything immediately but they later told Sass that until the situation was sorted out, she would have to remain in detention. It was terrible. They treated her like a common criminal."

Casey scribbled furiously on the page, which annoyed Shelley, but she continued.

"Fortunately, Saskia's support officer told us he was sure it could be sorted out quickly. That's why we didn't tell Lesia. We figured it was all just a big mistake so we told her that Sass had to go away on a field assignment. I sat with her in the hospital while she was having her treatment."

"Risky," Casey said flatly.

"It was. But then, all of a sudden, Sass was out. Just like that. I got a call from her to say she was free to come home. I went and picked her up myself."

Shelley's expression tightened.

"It was after she was released that I first thought something had changed in her. I couldn't put my finger on it, but I suspected she might have met someone in the detention facility. I broached it with her but she was really aloof. She wouldn't say anything. But I definitely sensed that she was seeing somebody."

"You think it was him?"

Shelley nodded. "I do. Whoever it was, she kept him secret. Things were weird between us for weeks. But then, suddenly, she changed again. I think it went cold between them. She kinda came back. She was like her old self again. Then, she was…gone."

Quiet settled between them. A breeze picked up, causing the paper in Casey's hand to flutter. There was nothing left to say. Shelley slumped back in her seat. Having unburdened her secret, she seemed exhausted.

Casey considered the information.

Suddenly she stood, slinging the strap of her bag over her shoulder. Shelley looked up and sat forward as Casey stepped around the bench, preparing to leave.

"That's it?" Shelley asked incredulously. "What are you going to do?"

"I'll be in touch if I need anything further," Casey answered. "In the meantime, you don't need to do anything. Just continue on as you have been." Casey turned away as Shelley's eyes widened in disbelief.

"But, how can I do that now?" she protested, launching herself forward as Casey began walking away from her. "You come out of nowhere with all of this. How can I be sure you're not putting me in danger all over again?"

"You're going to have to trust me."

"*Trust* you?" Shelley croaked. "Jesus, I don't even know you. Why are you doing this to me—to Sass? What gives you the right?"

Casey stopped in mid-stride and turned slowly back to face Shelley. Her expression was sad, rather than angry. Slowly Casey unbuttoned the top two buttons of her shirt and separated it just enough so that Shelley could clearly see the scar on her chest.

"Because I have her heart."

Shelley blinked at the scar, then at Casey. Her knees buckled.

As Casey turned and strode away, Shelley squeezed her eyes shut, then they snapped open wide. In that moment, she felt something instinctual.

"Wait!"

Snatching up her bag, she rushed across the path, closing the short distance between herself and Casey.

Casey watched as Shelley's fingers searched desperately inside her shoulder bag until they latched onto a small object. Teasing it out carefully, she finally liberated it.

She held it out to Casey. "She gave me this that night," Shelley stammered.

Casey took the small cloth purse in her hand and examined it. It was hand-made, its surface adorned with tiny beads arranged in pretty patterns. She could feel the weight of small change inside it, as well as the crinkling of paper against the hard surface of a credit card sized object.

Unzipping the purse, Casey felt inside it, taking out the piece of paper and the card: a Melbourne public transport card. She unfolded the yellowed piece of paper, a torn rectangle of note paper that bore the fragment of a letterhead in the top right-hand edge. Casey's eyes were drawn to the contents in its centre. On it, hastily scribbled in pen, were a series of six groups of numbers and letters.

SX801244
SX708937
SX394923
SX803254
SX987324
SX293875

Casey stifled an urge to gasp. She felt her tongue swell. Saskia's face appeared in her mind's eye. Her desperation. Her silent plea.

Reciting the numbers together, until Casey mouthed them with her…

Until she understood.

"She told me to hold onto this and keep it safe," Shelley explained. "I don't know what they are but she was *adamant* that I take it."

Casey blinked away the image of Saskia's face, looking up as Shelley began backing away. She held her arms out by her sides. "That's all I have," her voice quavered. "There isn't anything more."

Shelley turned and left Casey alone on The Walk.

Casey let her go, holding the piece of paper before her. She examined the numbers again, her mind numb with disbelief and realisation.

She was trying to tell me, she thought.

And then she noticed something else.

Her eyes were drawn to the top right-hand corner of the paper, where it had been torn, presumably, from some sort of notepad.

Though the logo of the letterhead was largely missing, Casey felt a sudden shock of a recognition at the name printed in bold Georgian font.

And then she felt sick.

It read, 'Slattery & Ger…'

CHAPTER 25

Casey parked the Volkswagen in the lot above the beach and peered through the windshield. Across the grass, she spotted Lionel sitting at the table in front of the jetty. She smiled wearily. He was holding a newspaper in both hands before him, and occasionally he absently lifted a cup of coffee that was sitting beside him without looking up from his reading. He appeared completely at peace.

Getting out of the car, Casey stretched wearily then grabbed her backpack from the passenger seat. She trooped down the steps.

Lionel sensed her presence even before he saw her. He turned and looked in her direction. "There you are," he greeted with gruff cheerfulness.

Folding the newspaper, he set it aside and lifted a second cup of coffee into view, setting it before her as she sat down opposite him. He then lifted an open bag of potato crisps and held it out toward her. Her eyes twinkled as she eagerly dipped her hand into the bag.

"If you had been another five minutes, I would have devoured the entire packet."

"Glad I didn't stick to the speed limit then."

Lionel's brow furrowed until Casey disarmed him with a weary smile.

"So," he ventured. "You can claim quite the achievement. Driving all that way on your own."

"I was *pissed off* enough that the agoraphobia didn't even get a chance," Casey responded.

Lionel's bushy eyebrows flicked up. "And how did you fare?"

"She opened up," Casey slung her backpack down on the seat beside her. "As soon as I showed her the Audi, it was clear to me that she knew."

"Just like that?"

Casey nodded. "Just like that. Actually, I think she was relieved to be finally able to tell someone."

She paused, shaking her head slowly as she collected her thoughts. She took a sip from her cup and looked at Lionel.

"It seems that Saskia was involved with someone. And, we can be pretty certain that he was driving that car the night of her accident."

Lionel's eyes widened. "Wait a minute, Shelley Agutter *knew* him?"

"No. That's the thing, she didn't. Shelley says she never met him."

"I don't follow," Lionel's expression tightened in confusion.

"I think I do," Casey said, taking the photograph of Shelley and Saskia at the Pleasant Festival out of her bag.

"Saskia had been in trouble over her student visa. Something about working more hours than she was legally allowed to. She was reported to the authorities and, because she was deemed to be in breach of her visa conditions, she was sent to the Flaxley Park Immigration Detention Facility pending a review. That was where Shelley believed that she met a guy."

"Someone from the facility?"

Casey shrugged. "Shelley doesn't know. Seems that Saskia was a lot more private than anyone gave her credit for—even with her best friend. Whoever it was, Shelley believes that he had a lot to do with Saskia getting out. I think it was someone in a position of influence." Casey handed Lionel the photograph. "It happened all of a sudden. One minute, Saskia was caught in this legal limbo with no apparent end and then, out of the blue, she got a call from Saskia to come and pick her up."

"Did her grandmother know about any of this?"

"Apparently not. It happened during her hospital admission. Shelley and Saskia deliberately kept the detention from Lesia so as not to worry her."

"That seems rather a risky decision?" Lionel remarked. "What would they have done if she hadn't been released?"

"Well," Casey said. "It's a stretch, but I think that Saskia might have known that things were always going to fall in her favour, especially if this *someone* had a hand in helping fast-track her case."

Casey tapped her finger on the photograph, over the car. "This doesn't strike me as the kind of car that just anybody drives, certainly not a fellow detainee."

"Not likely. They had influence over decision-making?" Lionel ventured, a smile tugging at the corner of his mouth.

Casey leaned forward and stood, stretching her legs. "It's only a theory. I've got nothing really to base it on just yet."

"What happened after? I don't quite understand how Shelley didn't meet this person. Weren't she and Saskia best friends?"

"That's the thing," Casey frowned. "Shelley said she noticed a change in

Saskia after she was released. She became really secretive—or, at least, more secretive than usual. Saskia wouldn't talk about him. She deflected any questions about him. Shelley said it put a strain on their friendship. Then, all of sudden, the relationship with the mystery man went cold."

"Cold?"

"Saskia just kinda returned. Became like her old self again. She still wouldn't say anything about the guy but Shelley was just relieved to have Saskia back. She decided to let it go. And then, that last night down at the Pleasant Festival, he turned up."

Lionel's eyes narrowed and he tilted his head. "I'm confused. I thought you said she never met him."

"No, she didn't *meet him* as such," Casey held up her fingers and wiggled them for effect. "She only saw him from a distance and not very clearly."

Casey paused, swinging her hand around as she searched for the right words to explain herself.

"The group had been taking drugs. Shelley admitted they were pretty wasted, so no one could remember him in any great detail. Her only recollection was that he seemed intense. She became worried when Saskia said that he wanted her to leave the Festival with him."

"And she agreed to go," Lionel said, his voice trailing away.

Casey's expression tightened. Her hand drifted down to her pocket, to the bulk of the small purse that Shelley had given her. Lionel watched as she took out the small object and cradled it in her hands before her. She gulped softly.

"What's wrong, Casey?" he ventured as she opened the purse and plucked a small square of paper from inside. Gingerly, she handed it to Lionel.

"Shelley gave me this," Casey said as she watched him unfold his glasses and place them on.

He frowned, studying the scrawled handwriting.

"Saskia gave it to Shelley, that final night at Pleasant. Saskia was adamant that she take it. But she wouldn't say why. Then she was gone. That was the last time that anyone saw her alive."

Lionel inspected the numbers on the piece of paper, running his thumb down each of them in turn, mouthing the numerals as he went. "These look like...*file* numbers."

"Yeah, but file numbers for what?"

Lionel lowered his hands and gazed at Casey.

"Saskia Andrutsiv was detained in a federal immigration detention facility," he said. "I'll wager that these are detainee case file numbers."

"What would she be doing with case file numbers from a detention facility?" she ventured, as much to herself as to Lionel. "I mean, I get why she would have her own, but why would she have these other numbers?"

"I think it's more reasonable to ask what would *anyone* be doing with case file numbers from a detention facility. I would very much like to know who this person was that Saskia was seeing. He apparently had the means to have her released from Flaxley."

Lionel paused as he looked down at the numbers again. "She got these numbers from him?"

Casey shrugged. Turning slightly, she studied her grandfather as he continued to mull over the numbers.

"There's something else," she said.

Lionel squinted. "Something else?"

Casey reached out and pointed to the letterhead fragment in the top right-hand corner of the paper. He squinted through his glasses.

"You don't recognise it?"

He shrugged momentarily.

"Slattery and Ge…," he began.

His voice caught, in part because there was nothing left to read, but also because the familiarity of the words struck him.

"Slattery & Gerard," he said.

Lionel drew in a sudden and sharp intake of air and he looked up at Casey.

"Edie's law firm?"

"They do legal aid work for immigrants," Casey said. "They have done it for a while. They've represented asylum seekers and visa holders who have disputes over their status. Edie told me herself."

"And Saskia Andrutsiv was one of them?"

Casey's gaze drifted out across the water. Without realising it, her jaw had set hard. "That letterhead would suggest that she was."

Lionel looked up from the note and studied Casey, conflict welling up inside him. "Wait," he continued. "What are you thinking, Casey?"

Casey stiffened and retreated from her grandfather. "I don't know. I just…I was shocked when I saw that."

Lionel abruptly stood from the bench and stepped forward, gripping the piece of paper.

"You can't honestly be thinking that…your mother—*my daughter*—might know something about this?"

Casey flinched at the flash of anger in Lionel's voice.

"I…don't know, Pa. She told me that they had done that type of work, pro bono in a lot of cases. And she said that a lot of that work came about because of Simeera Fedele. When I saw that, I was just—it shocked me. It might be worth asking her."

Lionel glowered at Casey. "I think you are venturing into dangerous territory with your thinking, young lady."

"But, Pa, I just—"

"No!" Lionel snarled, thrusting his finger out at Casey to silence her. She jumped where she sat. Tears threatened her as he turned away and shook his head angrily.

Casey desperately cast her mind back over the conversation with Shelley, the photograph of Saskia and Shelley, the numbers Lionel held in his hand, the detention facility.

The detention facility.

Taking out her smartphone, she opened a maps application and entered "Flaxley Park Immigration Detention Facility" into the search pane.

Lionel turned around and blinked in disbelief. Casey's attention was now firmly concentrated on the device. She scrolled the display with her fingers, centering it over a satellite image of the detention facility.

"What on Earth are you doing?" he probed fearfully, stepping forward. He frowned in confusion as he looked down at the satellite image on the display.

When Casey did not answer, Lionel proffered the square of paper between them, gazing at it as the sunlight splashed across the back of the it and the breeze caught the underside of it, causing it to flutter in his grip.

"I think we should take this to Whittaker," Lionel said.

Casey looked up from the screen. Her expression had shifted. To his utter exasperation, a curious smile tugged the corners of her mouth.

"I think I've got a better idea."

Casey skipped up the warehouse stairs and was already unlocking the door while Lionel followed, exasperated, in her wake.

"Casey!" he called after her, his voice plagued with frustration. "I really think you should slow down and think about this. I believe that Whittaker will take a look at these numbers."

Ignoring him, Casey went to the computer, touching her thumb to the biometric pad on her keyboard. She dropped her backpack to the floor and sat, examining the screen intently.

"Casey," he repeated breathlessly, stumbling through the open door.

"Pa," she said distractedly. "On their own, it's not enough. And, besides, we're talking about a Federal Immigration Detention facility here. If we go to him with this alone, Whittaker will laugh us out of the building." She turned in her seat as he stood before her. "I need more to go on."

"What do you mean more?" Lionel shot back. "You've identified the car. You can prove that it existed and you've extracted new information from Shelley Agutter in the form of *these numbers*. It's tangible, Casey, and it'll be tangible for Whittaker, too. I know him."

Casey paused in the middle of typing and closed her eyes. She breathed deeply to quell her frustration.

"I know *him,* too," she countered. "The picture of a car—it's just a picture and it's not a very good one at that. And the numbers, we can't be even sure what they mean at this point."

"I really don't believe that Whittaker will dismiss—" Lionel began before Casey cut him off.

"You've said it yourself, he's pissed off enough already because of my poking around. Pissed off enough to let Prishna off her leash."

"Prishna?" Lionel's eyebrows rose.

Casey ground her teeth together. "I didn't tell you before, but Prishna confronted me at the college. She told me that Whittaker was watching us. He found out about Lesia Andrutsiv." She shook her head angrily. "If I go to him with this, not only will he rubbish it, but he'll likely force us to stop searching."

Casey turned to him then stopped, realising that she was beginning to lose her patience. She did everything she could to soften her expression. "I need to dig a little deeper. I have to be sure about this."

"By hacking into a government computer system?"

Lionel shook his head and placed his hands on his hips. He knew he was struggling. Casey's dogged streak was rearing itself once again. When he looked up from the floor, his eyes fell across the computer's screen. Casey had brought up a web entry for the Flaxley Park Immigration Detention Facility, located in Melbourne's inner northern suburbs. She began scanning through the address details, making a note of the surrounding geography.

Lionel's eyes bulged.

"Wait...what are you proposing to do?" he pressed, his eyes moving between Casey and the screen. "You can't possibly be thinking of going sniffing around a Federal Immigration facility."

A light bulb went off and she stopped cold. She glanced over at him.

"That's *exactly* what I'm gonna do," she grinned. She sprang from her seat and rounded the desk before Lionel could respond. She bounded up the stairs to the mezzanine, forcing Lionel to follow after her. She disappeared into the guest room before Lionel reached the top of the stairs. He found her on her hands and knees before the wardrobe, rummaging through boxes and tossing various equipment and computer hardware left and right.

"Casey. Think about this for a moment," Lionel pleaded. "Breaking into a federal facility could get you thrown into prison! What do you think you could possibly achieve if that happened?"

Casey took a small black case out from a plastic storage container and unzipped it, checking its contents.

"I'm not gonna get caught, Pa," she said without looking up. "It would be more risky for me to try and hack the federal government network remotely. Their network infrastructure is too well-protected from outside incursions. They would be onto me in a second if I tried to hack them from here."

"Even with your skills? Your hardware? Surely not."

Casey would not be assuaged.

"If I'm onsite, I can access their database and see if those file numbers are still in their system. And I can look around and see who might be in there."

Lionel made a noise that was somewhere between a gasp and a hiss. He rolled his eyes and clenched his jaw.

"You cannot be serious, Casey! It's bloody stupidity. I *cannot* have any part in this."

Casey sprang to her feet. Glaring at him, she brushed past him, black case in hand.

"Fine," she snarled. "Don't then."

"Casey."

"What if he's still there?" she challenged, dropping back down the stairs. "What if this person works there right now and no one realises what he's done?"

"Whittaker will make sure—"

"I don't trust Whittaker," Casey shouted angrily. "I can't even be sure that he's on my side. Hell, I can't be sure if anyone's on my side!"

"Casey," Lionel croaked. "That's not fair and you know it. We're all here for you. Your mother and your father and I. We all just want to help you."

Casey stopped at the bottom of the stairs and wheeled around, snapping her head up at Lionel.

"Are you really? You might want have a talk with your daughter, Lionel. Because I think she knows a lot more than she is willing to admit about all of this." Casey snarled, pointing her finger at her chest in a circular motion.

Lionel felt a sharp pang in the pit of his stomach and he appeared to wilt at her stinging accusation.

"Casey, that's not fair. You're not thinking straight."

Casey levelled a glare strong enough to bore through lead.

"I *am* thinking straight," she hissed, her whispered voice quivering on the edge of fury. "I am the *only* one thinking about this. I've done nothing *but* think about this for three fucking years!"

She wiped angrily at sudden fresh tears.

"I want it to stop and I am going to *make it stop*!"

Lionel held up his hands to placate her but it was no use. "I'm…I didn't mean to…"

Casey turned on him and crossed the living room to her bedroom where she opened her wardrobe and snatched the first decent outfit that her hands fell across. She threw it down on the bed behind her then plunged her hand back in, grabbing a pair of heels.

Lionel gulped. He wanted to move his legs but couldn't.

"Casey," he said pathetically as Casey gathered up her belongings in both arms. She strode through the apartment, unable to look at her grandfather as she made for the door.

"Go home, Lionel," she retorted bitterly. "I don't need you here anymore."

Lionel froze as the door clanged shut behind Casey.

CHAPTER 26

The hand of the assailant came down, smashing through the chest wall with a sickening mixture of blood and bone.

And still she fought to free herself.

Saskia's head twisted in a desperate effort to find a means of escape.

In that moment, Casey and Saskia were looking at one another.

Saskia thrust her free hand out, stretching her fingers as far as she could, searching in desperation for Casey's own hand.

Saskia's face contorted; her lips formed words which Casey could see and understand though she could not hear them.

Help me!

Casey reached out, trying to cup her hands over Saskia's cheeks. Once again, she began reciting letters and numbers.

Casey repeated them back to her in silence until they were repeating them in unison.

S…X…8…0…3…2…5…4…

Saskia's expression became serene. Casey thought she saw a smile.

Then, Saskia's eyes looked over Casey's shoulder. Puzzled, Casey looked behind her hesitantly.

Dark human forms coalesced from the darkness and stood on the road, watching the scene.

Casey gasped as the forms seemed to step forward and come into focus.

Lionel stood there. His expression was taut, plagued with disappointment. Beside him stood Edie, her expression stony. Next to her stood Casey's father. He was shaking his head slowly, his eyes filled with anger. More figures emerged. First Prishna, then Whittaker. Behind them emerged Lesia Andrutsiv, supporting herself on her walker while her nurse shuffled along beside her.

Casey looked back to Saskia who was weeping in terror while the assailant continued to violate her.

What is this?

Casey stood and spun on her heel to confront the audience behind her, all of whom were glaring with accusatory menace at her now.

Why are you here? *Casey's mind shouted in silence.*

Lionel slowly raised his hand and, suddenly, Casey was yanked backwards. She cried out as her body tumbled and rolled violently along the bitumen. Saskia's face, the car, the assailant, her family—all of them disappeared into the gloom.

Clawing frantically at the air, Casey screamed…

Somewhere in the chilly pre-dawn hours, Casey jolted in the confines of the cramped Volkswagen and reflexively clawed at the air in front of her. Her hands slapped against the windshield glass until she realised she had been dreaming.

Shaking her head to rid herself of the dream, she shivered. She drew the blanket up around her shoulders, pulling it tightly against herself and blinked in the darkness. She peered through the windscreen but was confronted by a thin layer of frost that obscured everything.

"Jesus," she hissed reaching out and turning the key in the ignition. The car's engine coughed to life, then Casey reached over and turned the climate control knob all the way over until the warmth from the heater filtered into the cabin. Relaxing into her seat, she cast a glance to her left, to the smartphone that lay on the passenger seat in pieces: the handset, battery and rear cover.

Ever the paranoid cracker, she thought, even though she knew that was only part of the reason for ensuring she couldn't be tracked.

She picked up the handset, hesitating as she looked at the darkened screen. Part of her wanted to call Lionel to apologise for storming out the way she had. But she couldn't bring herself to.

She knew her outburst had been callous, that her accusations had been particularly cruel. She didn't know what she could say to repair the damage. Feeling despondent, she lowered the handset to the seat, hesitated and thought about reinserting the battery so that she could boot it up in case Lionel had called.

She growled and let it fall from her hand.

Closing her eyes, she leaned her head back against the headrest, trying to rationalise her actions and push away her guilt. All she could see in her mind's eye was her grandfather's tortured expression and it caused her emotions to spin out of control.

Everything was such a mess.

Her gaze fell across the copy of the photograph she'd taken with her phone in Saskia's bedroom, clipped to the dashboard vent. She reached out and took it, drawing it to her. In the half-light of the emerging dawn, she gazed into Saskia's features, her worldly eyes, her carefree smile.

What had happened? What had Saskia uncovered?

Casey's guilt was blunted by determination and she batted away her torment.

Pa will have to wait.

Sitting forward, Casey flicked the wiper controls and watched as the blades swung up, removing the rapidly melting frost so that she could see out through the glass.

A four-lane highway separated the vacant car park in which she sat from the austere grey walls of the Flaxley Park Immigration Detention Facility. It stood out some distance away from her, amongst thick eucalyptus trees and dense fog. She could see lights winking from inside, signs of life—of the day beginning. Soon, people would come to begin their day as employees and administrators of the centre and Casey knew she would have to be prepared and ready.

The imposing structure caused Casey to shiver.

Flaxley was described as a lower level facility in the Australian government's federal immigration system, designed to house refugees whose status had already been determined and were awaiting release into the community. It also held visa holders who were in breach of their conditions, like Saskia, and were awaiting the outcome of their reviews.

A nexus of hope and despair.

Casey cast the blanket aside. She needed to get moving.

Reaching into the back seat, Casey grabbed the strap of her bag and hefted it through into the front, setting it down on the passenger seat beside her. She rummaged through the contents inside until her hand brushed over a familiar rectangular object. She drew it out and held it up, then reached for the components of her smartphone. Reinserting the battery and securing the rear cover, Casey turned it over, powered it up, then twirled the rectangular box in her thumb and forefinger.

Roughly half the size of her phone, the small, white object was featureless except for a silver micro USB plug that protruded from one side. Casey slotted this plug into the corresponding jack of her phone, then checked the screen as a notification window popped up.

'*RFID scanner detected. Please wait…*'

Casey built this device herself and had employed it frequently as a tool to test the custom security systems her corporate clients purchased along with her expertise. Casey's brief included comprehensive testing of the security software she had designed and deployed; specifically those systems that employed the use of radio-frequency identification technologies, RFID for short.

Though RFID technologies—particularly those applied to employee swipe cards—were improving all the time, the uptake of the latest versions was patchy at best, especially where governments, concerned more with their budgets than best practice, were concerned.

Her device was able to 'sniff' any unprotected RFID chips embedded in employee identification cards and upload the data stored on them. She would then look for any weaknesses in the system that she could neutralise.

Despite their rhetoric to the contrary, government departments were notoriously lax when it came to the security technologies, often trailing their corporate counterparts by a factor of years. Casey was banking on that fact.

The smartphone's screen transitioned once more and a new notification popped up.

'RFID scan initialised. Ready...'

Casey allowed herself a smile, then she set the phone down and reached into her bag again, taking out a tablet computer and pressing the power button on its side. Checking to make sure that it was fully charged, Casey then placed it down beside the phone.

"Okay," she whispered aloud in the darkened cabin. "We're ready."

A STEADY STREAM of employees was flowing along a path connecting the parking area with the centre. Some walked in groups of three or four, engaged in mundane conversation while others trooped inward on their own. There was a mixture of uniformed personnel: guards, cleaning staff, maintenance staff and ancillary staff along with office workers who were dressed in more formal business wear.

The path flanked a large concrete wall topped with razor wire and was separated by a garden bed populated with uniform shrubbery and leafy saplings. A lone gardener worked about halfway along the path. Armed with a shovel, the gardener, dressed in a pair of tan shorts, matching shirt and a wide-brimmed hat, diligently tilled the soil, ignoring the steady procession of employees, then stood to lift a bag of mulch that lay beside a wheelbarrow. Several employees gave the gardener a wide berth.

Cutting the plastic bag of mulch open with a squat pair of garden shears and tipping it out, the gardener adjusted the right hip of her shorts, upon which sat a mobile phone in a pouch. As the centre staff passed by her, none of them noticed anything particularly unusual about her nor did any of them react to the audible beep that sounded as the device on the gardener's belt scanned each individual identity card that was either clipped to a belt or hanging from a lanyard around a person's neck.

As she emptied the last of the contents onto the garden bed, Casey looked up from her work, angling the brim of her hat down over her eyes.

She watched as the procession filed passed her, oblivious to her presence. They approached the door and dutifully scanned their identification over the reading device beside it before entering the building.

Casey reached for a rake that lay on the ground beside the wheelbarrow and began spreading the mulch out before her. As she did so, she noticed an expensive sedan speed into the car park from the entrance to the centre. Its tyres skidded on the bitumen as it lurched into a parking space close to the centre's entrance and braked hard. Casey noted it was a reserved spot.

Curious, she stood taller while continuing to rake the mulch across the garden bed and she watched as a woman fairly lurched from the interior of the car. Dressed in a smart, figure-hugging business suit, the attractive woman juggled a large handbag and a take-away coffee cup while balancing a phone wedged between her ear and the top of her shoulder. Evidently, she was engaged in some sort of intense conversation.

Approaching the centre through the thinning procession, the woman stopped and stooped down, setting her coffee cup on the pavement while she aimed her keyless remote at the car, locking it, all while continuing her conversation.

Cocking her head, Casey watched the woman as she stood and ended her phone call. Several people nearby acknowledged her as they sidestepped around her. One of the workers stopped and bent down to pick up her coffee cup and handbag for her. Though clearly annoyed, the woman managed to break her taut expression and offer a thankful smile.

"Thanks, Paul," she greeted.

"You're welcome, Ms. Catea," he replied. "Good morning, by the way."

Casey turned slightly and allowed herself to study this exchange. The office worker continued on his way, leaving the woman, Ms. Catea, to collect herself. Closing her eyes and taking a deep breath, she sipped from her coffee cup, then searched inside her bag.

Frustration began to spread across her face once more. Clearly, she wasn't able to find what she was looking for.

Adjusting her smartphone in the holster on her hip, Casey angled herself towards the woman and listened carefully. The smartphone beeped subtly, registering that it had scanned the chip of Catea's swipe card. It was definitely buried somewhere inside the large and expensive leather handbag.

A second office worker paused as she passed by Catea and asked if she was okay.

Catea looked up at the younger woman and offered a pained expression. "I can't seem to find my damned card. Could you swipe me in? I'm running so late and I'll need to empty my entire bag in order to find it."

Smiling sympathetically, the younger woman nodded and flashed her own identification card. "I've got this. Come on. I'll give you a hand."

Together the two women walked towards the entrance and Casey watched as the younger woman touched the reader with her card. The doors slid aside and they disappeared inside.

Casey went back to weeding the gardens.

Returning to the car and ensuring nobody could see her, Casey quickly stripped out of her gardener's outfit. She washed her face, arms and hands with some disposable wipes, and struggled into a white shirt, matching grey jacket and skirt and heels. She clipped her hair back as professionally as she could, and angling the rear-vision mirror toward her, applied lipstick and checked herself.

Not bad, she thought.

Satisfied that she could pass for a 'suit', Casey turned her attention to the smartphone and detached the RFID reader from it.

The woman she had watched on the pavement outside the centre's entrance hovered in her memory. She appeared to carry some level of seniority, judging by the way the other workers had interacted with her. But the critical thing was the fact that one of those colleagues had swiped her in. Officially at least, she wasn't yet logged in with the centre's security system, or so Casey theorized. She believed she had a small window in which to act.

Plugging the RFID reader to the female end of a USB extension cable, she connected that into a port on the underside of the tablet computer, then flipped the device over. Navigating the touch screen, she brought up an application that began displaying the data she had retrieved from the dozens of

ID cards she had passively scanned earlier in her guise as a gardener.

She nodded approvingly as a steady stream of information transferred from the RFID device into the tablet. The system hadn't failed her.

Before the employees had begun arriving, Casey had used the device to scan the centre's own card reading device that was stationed beside the front entrance. She had done this to obtain the cryptographic keys she would need so that the centre's security system would accept the identity card that she was about to replicate.

She had also watched the parking bays for any sign of an Audi that might have belonged to someone inside the centre but no such vehicle had appeared. She kept one eye on the car park now, hoping that it might still show up, but she wasn't particularly confident.

Turning back to the tablet, Casey initiated an algorithm from within the application and waited for it to do its work. It showed her a series of cryptographic keys that she'd retrieved from the card reader. Identifying the correct key, Casey highlighted it with her finger and copied it to the clipboard. She returned to the previous screen to check on the progress of the upload from the RFID sniffer.

A progress bar snaked slowly across the screen from left to right.

"C'mon," she whispered urgently.

Reaching into her shoulder bag, Casey took out yet another piece of equipment: this time, a rectangular device larger than the reader. It sported a fixed cable that protruded from one end and a credit card-sized slot at the other. She plugged its attached cable into a secondary port on the tablet.

Casey watched the screen and saw a new notification flash up.

'Card writer detected.'

She looked out through the windscreen, checking her surroundings and hoping that nobody was taking an interest in her.

Finally, a chime sounded on the tablet and she returned to it, carefully reading lines of code on the screen—each of which were accompanied by names. She looked at the assigned credentials for each one to determine their level of clearance within the centre, eliminating all those that fell below the level of administrator.

Her eyes fell across an entry halfway down the screen and they grew wide.

The name accompanying the entry read "Catea."

She was indeed a senior employee—an *unswiped* senior employee.

"Bingo," she murmured, taking a white, credit card sized object from the bag. She slipped it into the card writer and waited for it to be registered.

The sound of a dog barking caused Casey to jump in her seat and she jerked her head sideways, her eyes darting through the driver's side window. Instinctively, her breath caught in her throat. An elderly man, dressed in a woollen jacket and cap, approached the car, holding onto the lead of an excited Labrador. It was barking at a pair of swooping magpies. He cursed the dog as he passed in front of the car and yanked on the lead in an effort to bring the dog to heel.

He didn't even look in her direction.

Satisfied that he had passed into the distance and she was alone again, Casey initiated a 'write' command on the tablet and waited as the system wrote the information to the card. Casey watched it intently until the application chimed, signalling that it had completed its work.

Drawing the card out, she pushed it back in so that she could check her work. The credentials for the card were displayed in the window, complete with a photo image of the card.

Casey smiled broadly at the familiar face on the screen.

'Josephine Catea. Level 4 clearance. Administration.'

BUTTONING HER SUIT jacket, adjusting the strap of her handbag and straightening her shoulders Casey approached the centre's entrance, adjusting her stride to ensure that she appeared professional. Just another nondescript employee. The heels clicked noisily on the pavement, echoing against the adjacent walls of the centre. Harsh shocks penetrated the balls of her feet.

She hated heels.

Fingers of nervousness clawed at her the closer she got to the doors. She breathed as evenly as she could. All she had to do was: hope that Catea hadn't found her card, gain entry into the centre, find a computer terminal that she could commandeer and access their intranet. She would then run a search on the file numbers Saskia had scribbled down on the piece of paper.

Should be a piece of cake, she thought, stepping up to the reader beside the double glass doors.

Should be…

Clutching the card in her hand, Casey waved it in front of the reader and waited. A blue light on the reader flashed once, followed by singular beep and the doors split down in the middle and slid soundlessly aside.

She was in.

Casey scoped her surroundings, noting the presence of several security cameras situated high up on the walls all around her. She dipped her head, just enough so that she could obscure her features.

To her left was a security desk behind a glass window. A large male guard with a handlebar moustache and a severe buzzcut sat at the desk, a newspaper spread out before him. He was munching on a bacon and egg muffin. Directly in front of her was a reception desk, also behind glass. Two staff members were stationed there: a rotund, middle-aged woman with garish spectacles that sat on the edge of her fat nose and a young man in a suit jacket that appeared grossly oversized for his thin frame. On the right of the main desk was a single door marked 'Administrative Offices' and Casey spied a card reader there. She diverted to that direction.

The security guard looked up at her absently as she passed and flinched as some egg yolk dripped over his hand and down onto his shirt. He cursed himself, looking down as she quickened her step towards the door. Wiping the offending yolk from the belly of his shirt, the guard glanced back up in her direction. He tilted his head and smiled through a mouthful of his breakfast as he admired her legs.

The woman at the desk glanced up from the computer screen she was concentrating on just as Casey lifted her hand to her glasses, shielding her features from view. Her colleague said something to her at that moment and the woman turned in her chair to face him as Casey reached the door. Clutching the ID card in her hand, she brushed it up against the reading device on the door frame.

Here goes.

She closed her eyes, held her breath, and grabbed the door handle.

The woman turned back to look at Casey and was about to call to her.

The reader beeped once and a blue light winked on its panel, then the door's lock released.

Casey slipped through it before the receptionist could say anything. Upon seeing the door open, the receptionist shrugged and returned to her computer screen.

Casey found herself in a large, open office space with the central area occupied by desks and workstations arranged in a grid.

It was busy, with staff sitting at their desks working studiously, making or answering phone calls or concentrating on their computer screens. A couple of groups of three and four people were chatting at different desks further back. To her left and right, flanking the central work area, were individual offices behind floor-to-ceiling glass and blinds that could be raised or lowered as desired. Towards the rear of the office were additional work areas, divided from the main area by cubicle walls.

A couple of people glanced in her direction as Casey entered but nothing about her presence appeared out of place. They returned to whatever it was they were doing.

Now to find a terminal.

Locking her eyes onto the cubicles toward the rear, Casey turned to her left and prepared to walk down the aisle that separated the offices on that side from the workstations in the centre.

A petite young woman stepped in front of her, brandishing a thick stack of manilla folders. The expression on her face hovered somewhere between hope and desperation. Casey blinked.

"Hi," the young woman greeted in an overtly pained voice. "Are you the temp I asked Gareth for?"

Before Casey could respond, the young woman thrust the stack of folders out at her.

"Thank God!" she crowed. "He's lumped a tonne of data entry onto me and I knew I was just going to collapse underneath it unless I could convince him to find me some extra help."

Before Casey could speak, the young secretary turned on her heel and gestured hurriedly as she trooped down the aisle toward the rear of the central work area.

"My regular number two has called in sick again," she continued as Casey juggled the pile of folders in her arms. "Something about her horse being sick and *like*, having to get a vet out to see it, *like* immediately! It's so infuriating."

Turning into one of the cubicles at the end, the secretary shifted some papers aside on the wraparound desk so that Casey could set the folders down. The cubicle itself was small. Several pictures of a woman posing with a horse had been pinned to the wall and a calendar hung next to them featuring pictures of horses. The secretary leaned to her right to switch on the computer terminal then offered the chair to Casey.

"Take a seat. I'll just boot up for you."

She dropped her voice and continued speaking out of one corner of her mouth.

"I'll log you in under my credentials but don't tell Gareth. He can be a whiny little toad and I wouldn't want you to have to deal with him."

Casey sat and waited silently, bobbing her head in concert with the young woman's voice as she continued babbling.

"Oh my God! I totally didn't introduce myself. I'm Cherie, by the way. I'm just a couple of desks down if you need anything. Now, I was assured that you're already familiar with our network."

Casey nodded as the computer completed its start up and Cherie logged her in.

"There you go," Cherie said cheerily. "You're all set. Now, can I get you a coffee? We just got this new pod machine and it makes, like twelve different types of coffee, from lattes to mochaccinos and cappuccinos. It totally disgusted Gareth but we overruled him."

"A latte would be great, thank you," Casey answered.

Cherie beamed and turned to leave the cubicle before stopping abruptly. She gasped.

"*Oh my God!* I completely forgot! I didn't even ask you your name."

"It's Josie," Casey answered with a soft, uneasy chuckle.

"Josie. We have a Josie here in Admin, upstairs. She's nice, but don't ever call her Josie though because she can be a total bitch about—"

"I better get to work," Casey interrupted her gently.

Cherie blinked then blushed.

"Right. Sure. I'm sorry. I'll…ahh…get that coffee for you."

Casey waited a few seconds before peering around the edge of the cubicle entrance to make sure that she was clear. She watched Cherie until she had disappeared from view then, she grabbed the leather bag and set it down next to the keyboard.

That was weird.

Taking out her notebook, she opened it to the page where she had secured Saskia's scrawled numbers with a paper clip. Casey navigated to a search pane and typed in the first of the numbers.

'SX801244'

She hit the Enter key and was confronted with a bold-type, pop-up message.

'Insufficient Credentials. Please Contact Your System Administrator.'

"Typical," Casey hissed. She knew this was too good to be true.

Undeterred, Casey patted the pocket of her jacket, feeling the shape of the ID card there. She took it out, listened to see if anyone was coming, then reached into her bag once more for the tablet and the card writer.

She knew that the identification had included an administrator password which was embedded into the card information. It would be a simple matter of reading that data from the tablet in order to find it.

Casey inserted the ID card into the slot of the writer, then brought up the application she'd used to write the card. Within moments, the card's information flashed up onto the screen. Casey leaned into examine the information and spotted a password right away.

She could hear Cherie approaching from the far end of the office. She grabbed one of the thick folders from behind her and put it down on top of the tablet, then cocked her head to listen. As much as she wanted to, Casey resisted the urge to back up from the desk and peer around the edge of the divider.

Turning back to the terminal, she quickly logged out of the system and returned to the entry screen. Lifting the bulging folder, Casey scanned the tablet's display, desperately searching through the information until she found what she was looking for.

She could hear Cherie's high-pitched laugh not more than a dozen feet away.

She stabbed the password into the login and hit 'Enter.'

The computer flashed up a notification window.

'Logging in. Please Wait...'

"You're filthy, Paul!" Cherie cackled from behind the cubicle divider.

She was coming!

Approaching footsteps.

And then she was there. Casey froze.

"Okay," Cherie said, entering the cubicle and setting a cup down on the desk beside Casey. "I didn't ask you if you wanted sugar, so I just grabbed a couple of sachets. I'm so rude."

Casey turned in her seat and looked up at Cherie with a gracious smile.

"That's fine. You're very kind."

Cherie returned Casey's smile with her own then flicked her eyes at the computer's screen.

The intranet window she had logged Casey into was there, a cursor blinking in the search pane.

"Now, do let me know if you get stuck at all," Cherie said happily. "I'm just a few feet away."

Casey nodded quickly, nervously tugging at her earlobe.

Cherie stepped back then turned and left. Casey closed her eyes, listened to the heart beating rapidly inside her and willed it to slow down.

Calming herself, she carefully extracted her notebook from underneath the folder and set it down in front of her. She entered the file number into the search pane on screen.

'SX801244'

A terse tone sounded from the computer's speaker and a notification popped up.

'Restricted File Access. Contact S. Schutz, Department of Immigration & Border Protection Immediately. Entry Requested Logged.'

Casey frowned.

"What the…?"

She backed up to the search pane and went to the second number on the list. She entered it in.

'SX708937'

Again, the notification flashed, accompanied by the abrupt tone.

'Restricted File Access. Contact S. Schutz, Department of Immigration & Border Protection Immediately. Entry Requested Logged.'

Casey snarled at the computer as she set her finger on the third entry Saskia had scrawled.

'SX394923'

Again, the notification. Again the tone.

Something was wrong.

Casey lifted the folder away from the tablet and checked the credentials of the identification card she had cloned, confirming she had the highest access available to her. Josephine Catea's credentials were sound.

And yet she couldn't access the files.

They had been marked as restricted.

What could that mean?

Casey already feared she knew the answer. There was nothing more she could do here.

She had to get out.

Shoving her gear back into her bag, Casey reached down and yanked the power cord from its socket. The computer's screen went dark.

Casey stepped out into the aisle just as Cherie swivelled in her chair and glanced up at her.

Casey clutched at her stomach and adopted a pained expression, but she didn't stop.

With a concerned look on her face, Cherie stood.

"Are you all right?" she gulped.

Casey stopped in mid stride and hesitated before shaking her head.

"I think…I'm getting my period," she croaked, before pushing past Cherie and making for the door.

"Oh no. Well, we have a bathroom just back this way."

Tripping on her heels, Casey almost broke into a jog as she arrived at the door and pushed her way through it.

Cherie turned to follow her but stopped once Casey disappeared from view.

She glanced sideways at a male colleague who shook his head disinterestedly as he snapped a piece of gum.

"Chicks," he said.

"You're an arsehole, Paul," Cherie retorted.

When the temp hadn't returned, Cherie checked her watch then turned in the direction of the cubicle where she had stationed her. Frowning, she got up from her chair and went to the cubicle to find the darkened computer screen and the pile of folders on the desk untouched.

Annoyed, she headed back to her desk to sort this mess out.

Keeping her head down, Casey left the toilets and stepped toward the foyer. The security guards, who appeared to be checking IDs, had moved away from the entrance and there were now enough people moving back and forth that she could blend in. She reached for her sunglasses and shoved them in place as she walked briskly across the foyer.

Looking out of the corner of her eye, Casey spied the secretary named Cherie standing at the Administrative entrance talking to a pair of male colleagues, one of whom had their arms folded tightly. His expression was stony.

Casey quickened her step and staggered awkwardly on one of her heels. The doors were just a few feet from her.

Cherie's eyes fell across Casey's rear and she frowned.

The doors slid across and Casey was out.

She reached down and kicked off her shoes, grabbing them up in her hand as she broke into a half-walk/half-run along the path towards the car park. She kept her head down. She knew the alarm was probably being raised but she no longer cared.

Looking back over her shoulder, she crossed over the path and onto the bitumen surface.

Without warning, the piercing sound of a car's horn erupted, followed by the screeching of tyres. Casey panicked and stopped in the middle of the road.

She felt the touch of something hard against her legs and she gasped, blinking behind her glasses as she turned to face a burgundy sports car.

What the hell?

Casey looked at the windshield of the BMW. It was completely reflective, giving no indication of who might be inside. Her eyes lingered on the car. The driver's side door clicked open.

She gulped fearfully.

Without thinking, Casey bolted, sprinting across the car park, hissing as she rose onto her tiptoes against the hot bitumen underneath her feet. She made for the line of cars farthest from her. Beyond that was bushland that separated the car park and fence from the road.

Behind her, the driver stepped from the vehicle and looked urgently in her direction.

"Wait!" the driver called after her.

Casey ducked, ignoring the voice as she leapt over a squat barrier. She glanced back fearfully before lurching sideways, making for the cover of a group of eucalyptus.

The heart pounded.

The driver's eyes narrowed.

"Are you all right?" the driver called again, stepping around the front of the car, shielding his eyes from the sun.

The female figure disappeared behind a tree and was gone.

At the sound of a loud and persistent knock at the door, Peter looked up from the newspaper spread out on the table before him.

"Can you get that, love?" Edie called from the bedroom. "I'm still wet from the shower."

Another salvo of knocking caused his hackles to rise, and he stood, grimacing darkly as he marched through the hallway.

"If it's bloody Prishna again…" he grumbled warningly, grabbing the door handle.

Pulling the door open, Peter blinked.

It was Casey.

His eyes narrowed in confusion as Casey stood up straighter. She was clutching a thick notebook in her hand. Father and daughter faced one another in an awkward silence, the memory of Peter's distressed outburst at the warehouse still fresh for each of them.

Casey looked beyond Peter into the house. "I need to speak to Edie," she said flatly.

Hesitating, Casey stepped forward and around her father as he stood aside, allowing her entry.

He followed her into the living room as Edie emerged from the bedroom dressed in a bathrobe. Her hair was still wet. She and Peter exchanged a puzzled glance as Casey stopped in the living room and set the notebook down on the coffee table. Placing her hands on her hips, she paced back and forth. Her agitation was clearly evident. She considered her words.

"What's going on, Casey?" Peter ventured suspiciously.

Casey stopped and looked up, directing her gaze solely at her mother. Without speaking, she bent down to the notebook and unclipped a piece of paper from inside. She held it out towards Edie.

Glancing worriedly at Peter, Edie took it and examined it. "What are these?"

"You tell me," Casey challenged malevolently. "That's Slattery & Gerard letterhead, isn't it?"

Turning the paper in her hands, Edie tilted her head. Her mouth parted slightly and she nodded. "Yes it is. Where did you get this?"

"Saskia Andrutsiv," Casey answered. She placed her hands on her hips.

Peter rolled his eyes and scratched his head. Edie remained still.

"Your donor?" she said.

Casey nodded. "Saskia had these numbers with her on the night she died. I've since discovered that she was detained temporarily at the Flaxley Park Immigration Detention Facility over a visa dispute. We think these are file numbers for detainees. You told me your firm represents immigration detainees."

Edie glared incredulously at her daughter. "*We*?" she blurted. "You mean my father?"

Casey ignored her reaction. "Did you know her, Edie? Did Bill Slattery represent Saskia when she was in trouble?"

Peter hissed audibly and turned away from them both. "Jesus Christ."

Edie's features paled. "What do you think you're doing, Casey?"

"I'm asking questions," Casey snarled. Leaning forward, she plucked the photograph of Saskia and Shelley and tossed it down on the glass surface of the table before her parents.

"Look at her. That photo was taken the night she died. Did you know her?"

Edie gulped with barely-contained anger. She looked down at the image, then thrust her hands out defensively towards Casey.

"I have never met this woman in my life and even if I had, you know full well I can't breach the confidentiality of individual clients. Besides which, what are you trying to suggest?"

When Casey didn't answer immediately, Edie felt sickened. She sensed where her daughter was heading. Her lip quivered and she turned away.

"Saskia gave these to a friend on the night of her accident," Casey continued. "Her friend said that she was afraid."

When Edie turned back to face her daughter, her expression was apoplectic.

"And you think that I might know something about it? This is what you've managed to come up with whilst you and your grandfather have been running around out there playing detective?"

Edie's voice shook. She pressed her hands to her forehead and squeezed her eyes shut.

"They should never have released you from the hospital," she whispered angrily. "You're clearly not well."

"I am *fine*," Casey retorted petulantly. "And I know that I am on to something—something big. I *will* find out what it is."

Peter glared at his daughter. "I think you had better leave," he rumbled warningly. "Right now."

"Dad—" Casey began to protest.

Thrusting his finger towards the front door, Peter started forward. "Get out!" he thundered. "Before I call someone to come and take you out."

Casey wilted before him. She tried to work her voice, but no sound would come out. Edie turned away from both of them and withdrew into the sunroom, cradling her arms against her chest, her eyes swollen and red.

Casey retrieved the notebook, the photograph and the numbers from the table and retreated from the living room into the hall.

"You won't be satisfied until you've broken us completely," Peter said desolately as she stopped to open the door.

Casey faltered there, feeling her own sobs rushing up to overwhelm her. Before they could consume her in front of her parents, she slipped out through the door and shut it behind her.

Peter returned to the kitchen to find Edie still standing in the centre, seemingly frozen on the spot. As he came up beside her, he could see the turmoil etched into her features. Tears streamed down her cheeks and he felt sick. He reached out gingerly, placing his hand on her shoulder but she shrugged it off. It startled him.

"Edie?" he said, his voice cracking.

Edie turned slightly, standing full before him and it made him shiver.

Without speaking, Edie turned on her heel and strode into the hall, where she stopped before the telephone. Peter watched her as her hand went to the receiver and she paused, looking up at her husband.

Her face had become ashen.

"I have to make a call," she said, her voice quivering.

CHAPTER 27

Casey stepped softly up to her apartment door and paused, closing her eyes. Leaning her head against the steel plating, she felt a wash of exhaustion. Everything felt as though it were spinning out of control and she was collapsing under the weight of it. The day had been a disaster. The damage she had wrought seemed irreparable.

As she appraised the door, a sharp twinge of fear prickled across the back of her neck. She wondered if her grandfather had actually heeded her request to leave her alone.

Turning her ear to the door, she listened for signs of life from inside, but could hear nothing.

He's not here!

She almost couldn't bear to open the door. Her arm twitching, she raised her hand and gripped the handle. Sliding the door aside, Casey stepped in and closed it behind her.

Casey could see Lionel reclining in a chair on the balcony. He was holding a book in his hands; the rim of his glasses was visible. Evidently, he was engrossed in the pages.

Relief flooded her, sweeping aside her fear. She was grateful that he had opted not to listen to her. Gulping, Casey set her shoes and bag down on the floor beside the kitchen counter. She looked at her grandfather, assessing whether she should approach him.

Padding on tiptoe through the apartment, she was about to divert to her right and slip soundlessly into the bathroom, but Lionel cocked his head. "Did you find what you were looking for?"

Casey stiffened. Heat flushed her cheeks.

There was no hint of anger in his expression, just concern and relief. Casey began to quiver. Her shoulders slumped and she went limp where she stood. Her eyes bulged with tears.

"I..."

She stepped forward onto the balcony where she dropped to her knees before her grandfather. Her face twisted with sorrow and relief.

"I'm sorry, Pa," she choked.

Lionel sat forward, setting the book aside and he left the chair to gather her in an embrace.

Burying her face into his chest, Casey sobbed. "I'm *so* sorry. I didn't mean to hurt you."

Lionel clucked gently and pursed his lips. "Sssh," he whispered gently, stroking her hair. "It would take a damned sight more than that to hurt me, young lady."

Through her tears, Casey managed a tortured laugh at Lionel's comically gruff tone. She drew back and looked up into his wizened eyes. Though she could sense a residual hurt in them, he was clearly relieved to see her. That went a long way to assuaging her guilt.

"I am so stubborn," she said. "Especially when I grab onto something. I'm like a dog with a bone. I just won't let it go."

"That stubborn streak," Lionel observed. Casey nodded as she wiped her eyes.

Lionel cupped her cheeks in his hands. Any thoughts of anger or frustration he might have felt were swamped by relief that she was here. That she was okay.

"I meant what I said," he said, his eyes narrowing. "You have got to slow down. You can't just barge forward. I couldn't forgive myself if anything happened to you."

Casey nodded stiffly. "I know. I know."

She breathed, allowing her pent-up emotions to flow from her.

"Look," he said, sensing the right moment to move the subject to one side. "The important thing is—apart from your safety—did you gain access? Did you find anything?"

Casey frowned, her gaze drifting away from him. "No," she began.

Curiously, she tilted her head as recollections of her sortie came back to her. She focused on a memory of the computer she'd accessed. Lionel noted her quizzical expression.

"Actually, I don't know. I mean, I got in, but when I entered the file numbers, I kept getting an alert saying that they were restricted."

"Restricted?"

He rose from his haunches and resumed his seat. Squeezing his hand affectionately, Casey let go then took up the seat opposite. She drew her legs up and hugged them to her chest.

"Each time I keyed in the numbers, I kept getting the same message. The files were restricted. It also logged the fact that I entered the file numbers and instructed me to contact the Department of Immigration immediately."

Lionel studied Casey. "But weren't you already in the Department of Immigration or, at the very least, in an Immigration facility?"

"Yeah, and I used Admin level credentials. I should have had access to pretty much anything I wanted."

"Yet you couldn't access those files."

"No," Casey whispered dejectedly. "They may as well have been deleted." Her voice drifted away.

Lionel looked back at her and tilted his neck. "This message," he quizzed. "Did it happen just the once?"

Casey shock her head, studying her grandfather's visage. "It happened for all of them."

"Well," he ventured thoughtfully. "That doesn't mean that there was *nothing* there. You said they were restricted—not deleted. If that is the case, perhaps someone doesn't want anyone looking at those files. Certainly no one at the level of your administrator."

Casey felt a lump rise in her throat.

"Okay, Pa," she interjected, holding up her hand toward him. "That sounds a little too much like something I'd come out with."

Lionel smiled and harrumphed quietly, leaning back in his seat.

"What to do then. What to do?"

Casey shivered unexpectedly as a fresh pang of guilt assaulted her. Her thoughts drifted to the confrontation with her parents. Her expression tightened, her features filling with renewed tension. Lionel saw the change in her, but he didn't respond to it.

"There's something else," she choked as fresh tears threatened.

Casey turned to her grandfather and sat forward.

"I confronted…Edie. I pressed her about the note."

For a long moment, Lionel just stared at her and Casey feared that he would become angry once more. Instead, he leaned back in his chair and blew a noisy breath between his teeth.

"Dear, oh dear, Casey," he hissed wearily.

"I had to show her the note—the letterhead. She didn't deny it was Slattery & Gerard's."

Lionel looked out across the water. He nodded tersely, considering her revelation.

"I don't know what you can possibly expect me to say to that," he answered finally, his expression tinged with resignation. "Except that we need to involve Whittaker. He is better placed to...*handle* this sort of thing."

Casey looked away and bowed her head. She saw a yawning chasm open up between herself and her grandfather, filled with the hurt from Casey's own actions. No matter how legitimate she might have felt those questions she had asked were, was hurting her grandfather like this worth it?

Lionel stood and gazed out across the bay again.

"What are you going to do?" Casey ventured fearfully.

He shook his head slowly, unsure of how to answer.

"I don't know. I...should probably go see your parents. I suspect they'll be just as angry at me for this. Then, I'm going to go see Whittaker."

"Well," Casey began, trying to think. "Let me see Scott first. I'll swing by the bar and show him the photo you found. He has an almost encyclopaedic knowledge of motor vehicles. I'm betting that he'll be able to spot what kind of car this Audi of ours is supposed to be. If he can narrow it down, then we'll have a better argument to present to Whittaker, don't you think? It will make less work for the police."

Lionel nodded, but he did not look in her direction.

"Can I perhaps suggest that you leave it for now," he turned finally, and gestured at Casey's rumpled clothing. "Quite frankly, you look like something the cat dragged in."

Casey blinked at her grandfather. For the briefest of moments, his facade cracked and he offered a wan smile at her.

Her grandfather was right. Her body ached from having been cooped up in the car and she could feel considerable tension in her muscles.

"I guess I've lost the right to protest for now," she said finally, wearily. Slowly, she tipped her body forward and screwed up her face. Raising her arm, she sniffed then sighed.

"You're right. I'm gonna go and have a shower."

"Good," Lionel held his finger to his nose, his mischievous spark returning. "I didn't want to be the one to say it but—"

"Then don't!" Casey exclaimed before smirking awkwardly as she passed in front of him.

The security guard looked up and smiled as the well-dressed woman approached from the central corridor. Crossing the foyer, she nodded to him and he got up from his seat and left the cubicle so that he could unlock the front doors. At this time of day, now that most staff had gone home, the night security protocols took over, meaning that her access card would not work.

As she got closer, the guard noticed how tired she looked. Her complexion was pale. The makeup she usually wore had long worn off. Her shoulders drooped.

"Tough day, huh, Josie?" he ventured, sliding a key into a lock on the side of the door frame.

Nodding, she managed a half-smile as she stopped before the door, waiting for them to open.

She chose to ignore the fact he had called her Josie. There were only a few people who could get away with it.

"You have *no idea,* Barry," she responded wearily.

As the electronic mechanism responded to the key turning and the doors slid softly apart accordingly, Barry looked at Josephine Catea with sincere concern.

"Is everything going to be okay?" he ventured.

"Nothing that a year in the tropics wouldn't fix," Josie answered humourlessly. She offered him a weak smile.

"Goodnight, Barry," she said, stepping through the entrance and out into the evening chill.

"Night," he responded, watching her shrink as she walked along the path towards the car park.

Josephine reached her dark grey sedan and aimed her remote at it. The indicator lights flashed and the interior lights came on. She opened the door and tossed her bag onto the passenger seat, then climbed in.

Starting the engine, Josephine cruised out of the Detention Centre car park and entered the dual carriageway, heading in the direction of the city.

As she adjusted the climate control and turned the audio system on, she relaxed back in her seat and indulged in a deep, if somewhat tense, exhale. She smiled as classical music filtered through the cabin.

The guard's question echoed in her mind.

'Is everything going to be okay?'

She didn't know.

She was still grappling with the shit-storm that had erupted earlier in the day. It had quickly snowballed into something much more urgent.

In the midst of dealing with the temp agency who denied sending the relief administrative assistant at the heart of this morning's security breach, Josephine suddenly found herself having to deal with her superiors in Canberra. After several hour-long conference calls, she was no closer to identifying the person who had accessed the facility's database.

All that had been established so far was that the infiltrator was a young woman, based on the description given by their own employee and that she had said her name was Josie; convenient, given that she had gained access to the centre using the credentials of Josephine Catea herself. How anyone could have done that baffled her. Josephine was never lax when it came to matters of security and she was damned sure she hadn't misplaced her own access card.

The security footage gleaned from the centre's camera system had been no help since the infiltrator had cleverly obscured her features. None of the cameras had been able to get a clear view of her from the moment she'd entered to the moment she'd left.

Whoever this infiltrator was, she knew what she was doing.

Flicking up the indicator stem, Josephine turned right onto another major arterial, then reached across to her bag and felt for her phone inside it. She had deliberately switched it off some time during the afternoon to avoid having to deal with unnecessary calls while she tried to control the damage.

She knew her husband would be trying to reach her; she'd had to delay responding to several messages from him at the height of the drama. Though she knew he wouldn't be angry, he would most certainly be worried sick.

Dragging the phone out and powering it on, she looked at the screen and felt her stomach lurch. Eight missed calls from Canberra in the past hour alone along with a lengthening list of missed calls from other numbers, several media outlets, departmental lawyers, as well as her husband.

"Jesus," she hissed out loud as she scrolled through the list until she couldn't look at it any longer. She slapped the phone down on the passenger seat and twisted her hands on the steering wheel.

A sinking feeling settled inside her. This was going to get a whole lot worse before it got better.

Rubbing her forehead, Josephine absently looked up at the rear vision mirror and noticed a vehicle approaching from directly behind her.

She dismissed it at first and looked away but on looking back, she noticed that not only was it close, it was dangerously close.

Narrowing her eyes in annoyance, she shifted into the right lane, thinking that the vehicle simply wanted her to clear out of its path. However, the moment she settled into the new lane, she realised that the car had moved across with her.

It was tailing her.

Setting her jaw, she glanced at her rear-vision mirror, trying to get a closer view of this sudden antagonist but she couldn't identify either the make or shape of the vehicle.

Suddenly, its headlights switched to high-beam, dazzling her vision and causing her to flinch. Her hand inadvertently wrenched the steering wheel and she swerved violently.

"What the hell?"

The mysterious car nudged her rear bumper several times, forcing Josephine to clutch her steering wheel tightly in both hands in order to steady her car.

Fear plagued her. Her breath quickened.

Snatching her phone up in her hand, Josephine desperately navigated to the call screen for her husband. She prepared to dial but, as she attempted to thumb the green handset icon, the car nudged her more violently this time and she fumbled with the device. It clattered to the floor on the passenger side out of view.

Instinctively, Josephine stamped her foot down on the accelerator in an effort to create some distance between her and the vehicle but the stranger followed suit, closing the distance between them. Despite the fact they were on a major arterial, with the city's skyline growing more prominent ahead of them, there were no other cars in their immediate vicinity that she could see.

Suddenly, the vehicle pulled out from behind her and accelerated, matching her speed as it drew alongside her.

Panicked, Josephine stared through her window.

A burgundy sports car, the familiar symbol of BMW emblazoned on its grille. The car's windows were darkened, reflecting the street lamps in them. She couldn't see through them to identify the driver.

The car swerved threateningly toward her, forcing her to react and wrench her own vehicle away from it.

"What are you doing?" she screamed at it. Her heart was pounding as she fought to maintain control.

Almost as if her question had some effect, the car dropped away, decelerating into the distance behind her.

I've gotta get off this road.

Seeing an exit ramp up ahead, Josephine gripped the steering wheel harder and kept her eyes forward. She would wait until the very last moment and swerve onto the ramp before the other car had a chance to react.

Adjusting her rear-vision mirror, Josephine searched for the other car and found it, continuing to shrink in the distance. She realised then that she hadn't thought to try and identify its registration plate.

The exit ramp rushed up to meet her and, letting her foot off the accelerator, she allowed the car to slow without tapping the brake. She swerved onto the ramp and looked back.

The other car didn't follow.

Confused and frightened, Josephine braked as she came to an intersection, then she turned right crossing an overpass.

Looking left as she did so, she spotted the other car continuing on towards the city.

She raised her hand to her chest and exhaled raggedly, feeling herself beginning to calm.

"What the fuck was that about?"

Looking down to the floor on the passenger side, Josephine spotted her phone laying in view. Ensuring there were no other vehicles around her, she unclipped her seatbelt and prepared to reach for it.

Her car gave a sudden lurch and began to accelerate—despite the fact that her foot was resting on the brake pedal.

Abandoning the phone, Josephine sat bolt upright, grabbing the steering wheel once more as she stomped on the brake pedal. Nothing happened. The car continued to gather speed.

She grabbed at the gear shift lever and attempted to move it to neutral but the lever wouldn't budge. It was completely stuck.

Josephine screamed and began to hyperventilate. She fumbled with her seatbelt, then abandoned it in favour of trying to turn the key in the ignition.

Nothing happened.

The sedan rocketed past one hundred kilometres per hour as it raced along towards a set of traffic lights whose orbs had just flicked to amber.

In anguished panic, Josephine stamped down as hard as she could on the brake pedal once more but the car still refused to respond. Out of control, it raced through the intersection, causing cars approaching from either side to screech and swerve to avoid hitting both it and each other.

Josephine glanced down in terror at the speedometer.

130…140…150…

The engine was squealing now, drowning out her own terrified screams.

Something rattled underneath her and the car responded by jerking crazily. Her hands could no longer control the car and somewhere in her terror, she knew.

Suddenly, there was a twisting of metal from somewhere inside the engine. A shower of sparks erupted from underneath the car and through the gaps in the bonnet.

As her sedan hit two hundred kilometres per hour, flames erupted from the engine bay and began consuming the vehicle as it lurched violently to the left.

Josephine pulled her eyes from the fire before her and grew wide as a light pole rushed up to meet her.

The sedan ploughed into the pole and exploded in a brilliant conflagration of light and fire and screaming metal.

CHAPTER 28

Casey crossed the street opposite the Blue Heeler Bar and approached the side door. Slipping inside, she tentatively scanned her surroundings. Though the atmosphere was still quiet, it was steadily filling with after-five patrons, office types mainly, calling by for a drink on their way home from work.

One of the barmen recognised her as she entered and nodded, then frowned, realising that he'd never seen her this early in the evening.

Approaching him, Casey pointed to her left and up the stairs. "Is he in yet?"

The barman nodded. "He hasn't started his shift yet. He's having a bite to eat."

Thanking him with a thumbs-up, Casey turned and ascended the stairs to the rooftop. Sasquatch was sitting in his favoured spot near the corner bar. Armed with a sharp knife and fork, he was cutting into a large porterhouse steak while watching a TV at the bar. He looked up as she approached, his expression similar to that of the barman downstairs.

"Have you had a joint already?" he remarked gruffly as she pulled out the chair opposite and sat down.

"What's that supposed to mean?" she retorted, plucking a morsel of steak he had just cut from his plate and popping it into her mouth.

Scott flashed her a hurt expression but then he flushed pink, realising what he'd just blurted out. "Sorry. It's just that it's still daylight. It's not like you to be out and about this early."

Casey dismissed his observation and nodded to a young woman behind the bar who held up a beer in her hand, offering it in silent question.

"It's not like me to be doing a lot of things lately."

Noticing that Scott was distracted, she followed his line of sight towards the TV screen.

"What are we watching?"

Scott almost blushed at the question.

"Family Feud," he admitted under his breath. "The news will be on in a minute."

Smirking, Casey took her notebook from her bag and set it down on the table. She took out the Pleasant Festival photo and slid it across the table top. "Could I get you to look at something for me?"

Scott licked his fingers, then wiped his hands on a napkin. He took the photograph from her and examined it. He grinned mischievously, giving Casey a clear indication that he was ogling the girls lounging against the vehicle.

"Nice car," he commented through a mouthful of food.

"Trust you," Casey countered sarcastically. The woman from the bar stepped up to the table and put an ice-cold beer bottle in front of Casey.

Taking a swig, Casey kept looking at him. She was waiting for the penny to drop which, after several moments, it finally did.

His chewing stopped. His eyes narrowed, then went wide. He reached for the pair of glasses which dangled from the collar of his T-shirt and shoved them into place. His breath caught when he recognised Saskia and then again as the detail of the car in the image came into focus.

"Wait a minute, is *this* the car you have been talking about? Holy shit."

Casey nodded.

"How did you get this?"

"What can you tell me about it?" Casey asked, ignoring his question. "You know cars better than just about anyone I know."

Shifting his dinner plate to one side, Scott set the photo down between them.

"Audi. 2011," he began. Bringing it closer to him, he ran his finger across the left-hand headlight, then back along the side where a single door was partially visible. "Coupe. Titanium package."

With the focus of a scientist examining a microscopic specimen, he scanned back along the front, stopping over the registration plate that was partially obscured by Saskia's leg.

He squinted. "Victorian plate. Definitely a Victorian plate…first letter looks like a 'W.' Pity about her le…"

Suddenly, he went silent.

"What is it, Scott?" Casey asked him urgently.

He appeared surprised. "It's an S5," he said.

Casey frowned, shrugging her shoulders. "An S5?" she echoed. "That's… *what* is that exactly?"

"That," Scott said, wiping his goatee. "Is high end, and worth some serious coinage. A hundred thousand before you even consider putting it on the road."

"Okay, so it's an expensive car. There are a lot of expensive cars on the road."

Scott shook his head rapidly. "No, no. Not like this. This isn't the sort of vehicle that just runs out of a showroom. This is special, reserved for a particular kind of buyer."

"A particular kind of buyer?"

"Someone who treats their vehicles like a work of art."

Casey frowned and sipped her beer. "Well, that's good, Scott, but it's still akin to searching for a needle in a haystack."

This time Scott chuckled. "I don't think you're getting me. This is a 2011 Audi S5 coupe with a Victorian plate."

Casey leaned in close to the table top. "Right?"

"Right—and the thing is, there were probably less than sixty of these sold in Victoria at that time. If you're looking to narrow things down a bit, I would bet my house that, of those sixty, a good portion of them are still garaged here in the city. All the police would have to do is run a search through Vic Roads and see which of these cars were sold and registered at that time. They could probably pinpoint the very car even with this obscured plate."

Casey's expression melted into a grin. "Just like that, huh?"

Scott winked. "Just like that."

He watched Casey as her eyes wandered. She became thoughtful.

"You're not going to go to the police, are you." It was less a question than it was a statement.

Casey smiled at him. Plucking the image from his hand, she stood and downed the remainder of her beer in one gulp.

As she did so, Casey glanced absently at the TV screen as a news bulletin flashed on and the image of a woman's face appeared on screen.

A familiar face.

Casey's grip on the beer bottle slackened and she almost dropped it. The colour drained from her face.

"What is—"

"Turn that up," Casey snapped.

Scott reached for the remote control beside him and pointed it at the screen, bringing up the volume of the news reader's voice.

"Police remain at the scene of last night's horrific single-vehicle motor accident that took the life of thirty-four-year-old Josephine Catea. So far, they have spoken to a number of witnesses who were in the vicinity of the accident and our sources understand that they have told authorities the vehicle was travelling at high speed immediately before the crash."

Casey advanced slowly towards the screen as the news reader continued.

"Ms. Catea was a federal government employee in the Department of Immigration & Border Protection. It is unclear at this time whether Federal Police will be assisting with inquiries."

Scott looked worried now. "What is it, Case?"

Slowly, Casey turned. Her jaw was slack. She was clearly in shock.

"It's her."

"Her who?" Scott responded urgently. He stood and stepped sideways, putting a hand on her shoulder.

Casey pressed a hand to her forehead and turned on her heel.

"Scott, I've gotta go. I-I'll be in touch, okay. I've gotta do something."

LIONEL WAS IN the kitchen, preparing dinner when the door rumbled aside and Casey stumbled in.

He turned as she entered. Her face was ashen, her expression taut.

"Have you seen the news?" Casey blurted as she marched across to the TV remote and thumbed the power switch.

Wiping his hands on a tea towel, Lionel came over as Casey changed the station to an all news channel. They were still covering the story.

"It's her, Pa. It's Josephine Catea."

"Josephine who?"

"The woman whose ID card I cloned," Casey retorted, her voice shaking fearfully. "I used her credentials to hack into the Flaxley database."

They watched as the newsreader recounted similar details to the story Casey had seen at the bar.

"Surely, this is just a coincidence," Lionel gulped softly.

Casey levelled a glower at him. "Do you really think that, after what we've discovered?"

Lionel frowned, sensing his granddaughter was right.

Casey continued to watch the TV, noticing that the story had been expanded to include new footage of uniformed Victorian Police milling about at the accident scene along with a fire crew and a lone ambulance. It was being ushered through a cordon where the public had gathered and were watching on.

"This is my fault," Casey gasped. "This is all my fault."

A reporter on the scene was interviewing several lookers-on, then the camera switched back to the smoking ruin of the car, still wrapped around the light post. At that moment, Casey spotted Prishna Argawaal, engaged in what appeared to be a tense exchange between herself, two of her own colleagues and three dark-suited men.

Prishna's eyes met the camera lens for the briefest of moments. Casey could see her expression.

Anger. Frustration.

One of the dark-suited men held out his arms on either side and began ushering Prishna away from the scene. A new group of uniformed officers converged on the car in their place. Prishna appeared to protest but the camera operator jerked away from the scene as one of the dark suits tried to block the lens with his palm.

Casey's eyes narrowed.

"Something's wrong." Grabbing the remote, Casey aimed it at the screen and paused the live footage, just as the man's hand obscured the camera lens. Casey scrolled backwards slightly until she paused it on the final clear image of Prishna.

An idea began to foment.

Turning to the workstation, Casey grabbed her smartphone and scrolled through her phone book.

"What are you going to do?" Lionel asked with mounting concern.

Casey nodded at the TV screen. "Something that is probably totally crazy," Casey remarked.

Holding the phone up so that Lionel could see, she leaned forward. Lionel read the name of the contact Casey had highlighted.

Prishna.

CHAPTER 29

Stepping from her car, Prishna shielded her eyes as she scanned the foreshore in front of Mentone beach. A chill morning breeze whipped off the bay and stung her cheeks. She hissed, then cursed aloud at having to leave the warmth of her car. Her eyes fell across the jetty, where she spied several figures. A pair of early morning fishermen. An elderly gentleman sitting on a bench, armed with a newspaper and puffing blue cigarette smoke into the morning air. A lone figure stood, still further along, leaning against the rail opposite. She was looking directly at her.

Even at this distance, Prishna knew it was Casey. She tilted her head.

Dressed in an oversized hoodie, black leggings and trainers, Casey stood back from the rail and lifted her hand gingerly. Prishna hesitated by her car, sizing up Casey.

If Casey was nervous about this meeting, her body language gave no indication. She appeared calm. Relaxed.

She'd ignored Casey's instruction to come alone. Prishna wasn't about to take any chances. Glancing south along the foreshore, she spotted her partner who had emerged from a line of trees adjacent to a children's playground. He began pacing back and forth.

Reaching down to her belt, Prishna discreetly thumbed the transmit button of a UHF walkie-talkie.

"Stand by, Rob," she said.

Locking the car, Prishna buttoned her jacket and trudged down the steps.

Casey watched as the detective approached to within several feet on the opposite side of the jetty and then rested her forearms on the rail. She gazed across the water at a pair of racing yachts that were cruising past. Lifting the cowl of her hoodie, Casey shifted and put her hands in her pockets. Prishna glanced over her shoulder.

Casey gestured with a nod over at the beach.

"You might want to tell your goon to find a seat away from the play equipment," Casey suggested sourly. "Unless he wants to be confronted by an angry parent accusing him of being a paedophile."

Prishna smiled bitterly. It faded quickly.

"I have to confess, Casey, I'm impressed. I thought you were afraid of open spaces."

Casey noted how tired Prishna appeared. Troubled. There was none of the usual snark in her voice.

"You looked tired," Casey commented. "I saw you on the TV last night."

"Yeah, well. Tiredness is an occupational hazard when you're called upon to investigate a security breach and the apparent victim of that breach turns up dead." Prishna turned around and glared at Casey. "I know it was you, Casey," she challenged.

"Come off it, Prishna. You don't honestly think—"

"*Not* the car accident," Prishna snapped forcefully. "I saw the security footage at Flaxley. You're terrible at disguising yourself. I spotted you a mile away."

"If you're so sure it was me, take me in now," Casey challenged.

"Oh, don't tempt me." Prishna's voice trailed away.

Casey tilted her head, examining Prishna curiously. "The Feds have frozen you out," she observed. "Haven't they?"

To Casey's surprise, Prishna nodded. "It seems that whoever accessed the network at Flaxley with Josephine Catea's credentials has stirred up a hornet's nest."

Prishna paused, gauging Casey's expression. "The question is: what did Josephine look at that caused such a shitstorm?"

"You don't believe that car crash was an accident?"

Prishna considered the observation. "There is...suspicion."

Casey crossed over the jetty and stood beside Prishna. The gravity of what she had caused weighed heavily on her.

"Josephine Catea *allegedly* performs a search for a series of file numbers in a Federal Immigration Department database and not even twelve hours later she is dead."

Prishna shrugged her shoulders. "According to the centre she'd left work late after a long day of dealing with the mess you created."

Casey looked away. She felt sick.

Prishna could sense Casey's guilt. "The official word is, she most likely fell asleep at the wheel."

Casey glared at Prishna. Her eyes were reddened. "C'mon, Prishna. You know that's not true."

Hesitating, Casey reached into the pocket of her hoodie and took out a small square of paper. She handed it to Prishna.

"What's this?"

"That…is what I went searching for yesterday."

Prishna regarded her carefully.

"They're file numbers, Prishna," Casey explained. "My guess is that they're for people who were detained at Flaxley. The moment I entered them into the system, it caused an alarm to trip somewhere and the rest…well, just look at what happened."

"Where did you get this?"

A gust of wind whipped up off the water, causing Casey to push several locks of hair away from her eyes. She looked back at Prishna.

"Saskia Andrutsiv."

Prishna's lips parted in shock.

"Josephine Catea wasn't the only one who died because of those file numbers."

Casey placed the piece of paper into Prishna's hand and gestured.

"You can check the handwriting if you want. I guarantee you it'll match with Saskia's."

"I don't understand." Prishna asked. "What does this have to do with Saskia?"

"I got Shelley Agutter to talk," Casey said. "Turns out she had a lot more to say to me than she did to the police. Saskia gave Shelley those numbers the night she died. She never told Shelley what they were for."

"You're not suggesting that Saskia's death was because…" Prishna said, exasperated.

"You've read her file, Prishna," Casey shot back. "You know very well that Saskia was detained at Flaxley over a dispute with her student visa."

Prishna's eyes narrowed and she nodded.

"Saskia," Casey continued, leaning forward, "met someone there. Whoever that someone was, they found out that she had those numbers and they killed her because of them."

Surprisingly, Prishna nodded. "Shelley Agutter came to the police some time after Saskia's death," she said. "She tried to tell us that she had new information about someone Saskia had spoken to the night of her death. But we didn't pursue it. Shelley Agutter and her friends were deemed unreliable witnesses because of the drugs they'd taken that night."

"Well," Casey said. "Don't you think there's something here worth pursuing?"

Prishna's expression faltered. "I don't know what you expect me to do with these?"

Without warning, Casey snatched the piece of paper from her grasp and held it up between them. The breeze blew across the top edge of it, flapping the paper furiously.

"Cut the shit, Prishna. Saskia had these numbers in her hand and she died because of them," Casey snapped. "Now Josephine Catea is dead because of them. Someone really doesn't want these files to get out. You want to know what they mean just as much as I do."

Crossing her arms over her chest, Casey gnashed her teeth. "You can do some poking in the right places."

Prishna considered the numbers. Casey couldn't believe she was still doubtful.

"Look. You find out what they are and…I'll give you Octagon," Casey said.

For the briefest of moments, Casey saw Prishna's tongue caress her bottom lip and she allowed herself a satisfied smile. She lowered her hand towards Prishna, offering the numbers. Prishna took them.

Casey stepped back, then turned and strode away from her. Prishna remained stationary. The walkie-talkie squawked at her hip as her companion tried to raise her.

"What are you gonna do?" Prishna called after Casey.

"I'm not going to stop," Casey replied, without looking back.

"Casey!" Prishna called after her. "Stay out of this. Let the right people handle it."

Casey paused and glared back over her shoulder.

"Find out what those numbers mean, Prishna."

Prishna looked down at the piece of paper again, then slipped it into her pocket.

I'm not going to stop… Casey's words echoed in Prishna's mind.

"Shit," she hissed aloud. *I don't want you to stop.*

The walkie-talkie continued to squawk incessantly and finally, she reached down. Pressing the transmit button, Prishna watched Casey shrink as she crossed the sand, then climbed the steps.

"Let her go," Prishna said softly.

LIONEL WAS SWEEPING the courtyard when he heard the Volkswagen pull into the carport.

He waited, hearing the engine extinguish then the door open and close.

Casey appeared in the entrance. Her expression was blank.

"So?" Lionel ventured.

Casey leaned against the doorframe and shrugged. "Okay…*I think*. She agreed to look into it. But I had to throw her a bone of sorts."

Lionel's expression tightened.

"Do I want to know?"

Casey sat down inside the doorway. "Probably not. I'm taking a risk but I think Prishna might just come around."

"Sounds like a big risk?" he pried. "But, at the very least, you're doing the right thing in going to her."

Resting the broom against the wall, Lionel put his hands in his pockets. "I forgot to ask you last night, what did your friend Scott have to say?"

Casey's expression went wide and she looked up at Lionel suddenly. "Oh shit," she hissed. "I totally forgot!"

Casey sprang to her feet and bounded up the stairs. Caught unaware, Lionel blinked, frozen where he stood before finally following in her wake.

Entering the apartment, Lionel watched as Casey rifled through her shoulder bag.

"Why are you so pleased with yourself all of a sudden?"

Casey flashed her grandfather a grin as she held up the image of Saskia and Shelley posing in front of the Audi. She strode across to the computer and tapped the darkened screen with her fingers.

"Scott found our needle," she said. "He reckons he's sure of the make. I just need to make sure it's the right one."

"Well, that's good news. I guess."

Casey's fingers danced across the keyboard. "Possibly. I just hope Scotty hasn't lost his touch."

Lionel set his gloves down on the kitchen counter then clasped the back of a kitchen stool, carrying it across to the workstation.

"Pray tell how are you going to do that?" he queried with wearied concern.

She glanced up at him, still smiling, but didn't respond.

Instead, she opened her notebook to a page near the middle and handed it to him to hold for her.

While typing and scanning down a list of numbers on the page, she identified the one she wanted and typed it into a newly opened command window.

Lionel watched as she tapped the 'Enter' key. A flurry of text and numbers scrolled across the screen, their brightness dazzling him. He had no idea what they all meant.

Casey pointed to a drawer underneath the glass surface.

"Open that for me." Lionel complied and looked down onto a small, rectangular box inside. "And hand me that," she instructed.

He lifted it out and watched as Casey opened it, revealing a dozen golden objects inside that looked like small ingots, perfectly aligned in a foam holder. Each of them was inscribed with an alpha numeric code on their surfaces.

Looking down from the screen, Casey ran her finger across each of the objects until she stopped at one in the middle and plucked it out. She held it up for Lionel to see.

It was a USB key.

"We're going for a little trip," she said, plugging the golden key into an empty port on the side of the monitor. Returning to the screen, she pointed at it.

"First, I need the right IP address for the remote system from the notebook. Once I've opened that, I just need to identify the correct port number within that address."

"Oh…kay," Lionel responded, completely flummoxed.

Casey looked at a new series of numbers, pursing her lips.

"Gotta have the correct port in order to sneak inside."

"Sneak inside?" Lionel responded with alarm. "Sneak inside where?"

"Just watch."

Finding what she wanted, Casey tapped in a fresh series of commands, then pressed a small button on the gold USB key. A blue LED winked on its surface. Three words flashed up in the dialogue box.

'Loeffler's helminth deploying.'

"Oh, well that's charming," Lionel grumbled caustically.

The screen flashed violently then went dark.

"Wait for it."

Several seconds ticked by. The screen flashed again and came to life.

Lionel gasped.

'Welcome to Vic Roads Intranet.'

"Did you just hack into Vehicles' registration?" he croaked.

Casey nodded with a satisfied smile. "This kind of network, unlike Flaxley, is terrible for detecting outside incursions. We can snoop around in here freely."

Lionel rubbed his mouth in bewilderment.

"I showed Scott the image you found from the Pleasant Festival," Casey explained. "It turns out that the Audi S5 coupe is a pretty special motor vehicle in Australia."

"You got that from Scott?"

"Oh trust me," Casey said, handing Lionel the image of Saskia and Shelley from the Pleasant Festival. "If there is anything anyone needs to know about cars, Sasquatch knows."

"Okay," Lionel responded as he examined the Pleasant image.

"They were imported in small numbers and were affordable only to a select few. He reckons that there were probably no more than fifty or sixty registered in Victoria in 2011."

Lionel watched on as Casey tapped the vehicle details and the year of manufacture into the search pane, then waited. The instant the results flashed up, Casey hissed victoriously and pointed.

'Showing 58 results of 58.'

Lifting his glasses, Lionel squinted at the screen and examined the information there.

"These are all 2011 Audi S5s?"

"Registered in the state of Victoria in 2011, or thereabouts," Casey said, clicking on the printscreen function. The printer underneath the workstation hummed to life. "Now all we need to do is work out which one is our S5."

Casey took the sheets from the printer tray as they emerged, while Lionel retrieved a marker pen. Casey handed him the printouts and he began to study them.

"Where do we begin?"

"We can start by crossing out any of the vehicles whose license plate doesn't begin with a W."

Seeing puzzlement in Lionel's eyes, Casey tapped the Pleasant Festival image, her finger hovering over the partially obscured plate.

"We're pretty certain that's a W."

"Hmm," Lionel agreed, nodding slowly.

Turning his attention to the page, he scanned down it and began crossing out entries with the marker pen. Within moments, he had excluded every entry on that page. He turned to the next, repeating the same action. Casey smiled as she watched him work.

He had whittled the list down by half in under a minute. The pages which he had excluded every entry he let drop to the floor.

"Okay," he said, checking through the remaining entries. "That's them accounted for. We're down to 23 possibles."

Casey thought for a moment. "We're pretty sure that whoever this person was, it was likely they were based here in the city right?"

Lionel nodded. "It would seem to make sense. We suspect that Saskia was making frequent trips to see this person. She wasn't gone for any great lengths of time."

"So," Casey said. "Let's rule out any registrations that weren't garaged here in the city itself and any rural or regional addresses."

Lionel nodded and returned to the pages, checking each entry's address and crossing out those that weren't in metropolitan Melbourne.

"We now have eleven."

He glanced across at Casey and couldn't help but smile.

"Eleven possibles. Now what?"

Casey leaned back in her seat, thinking.

Eleven possible registrations from that year.

"Dammit," she whispered.

Lionel held his hand up, waving it steadily.

"Okay, wait a moment," he began. "Let's look at what we have. Saskia met this person. Is there any way we can establish how she met with him?"

A light bulb flashed on in Casey's head and she gnashed her teeth together victoriously. "There is."

Opening the bottom drawer of the cabinet, Casey reached in and pulled out a bizarre, box-like object that had a cord snaking out from within two exposed circuit boards. As she set it down on the glass surface in between her and Lionel he noted a thin slot that was roughly the size of a credit card at the opposite end of the contraption.

"I'm not even going to ask you what this is," Lionel remarked as he inspected the upper most circuit board with its exposed chips, LEDs, resistors and miniature roadways of metal in between.

Casey plucked up the end of the cable and inserted it into a USB port on the monitor. A green light on the circuit board winked to life and blinked steadily.

Casey pointed at her shoulder bag on the kitchen counter. "Hand me my bag, Pa."

Lionel complied and watched as Casey took it and reached inside, taking out Saskia's beaded purse. Casey unzipped the purse and took out a rectangular card.

She held it up. It was Saskia's public transport card.

Tapping the surface of the card, Casey pointed at the bottom corner of its upper surface, upon which Saskia's name was printed.

"See this?" she said. "This bus card is a registered card."

Casey handed him the card and gestured at the box. He slid it into the slot until they both heard a soft click. The green light flickered on the circuit board, then went solid.

"It's embedded with a chip that stores data," Casey explained as she turned her attention to the laptop and started manipulating screens with brisk finger taps and keyboard commands. "The data is supposed to be secure but, with a little tinkering, I should be able to access it."

"What's stored on it?" Lionel asked.

"Mundane stuff usually. Transaction history, remaining balance. But, because Saskia had it registered with the Public Transport Authority, it'll link with the card owner's account on the PTA web portal. That'll give us access to the travel history of this card."

Lionel smiled at his granddaughter. "*A-ha*," he mused.

"The tricky part is breaking the encryption on the chip," Casey added.

"I can't imagine that will be too much of a hurdle for you." Again, Casey smiled out of the corner of her mouth.

Casey studied the reams of data that scrolled downwards in quick succession, tracing her finger beside a long list of indecipherable code until she stopped at a line near the bottom.

Highlighting a string there, she copied it, then switched over to the public access website for Public Transport Victoria. Ignoring the login screen, Casey instead brought up a separate command window over the top and pasted the code there.

"Now," she murmured, her finger hovering over the 'Enter' key. "Let's see what we can…*see*."

Hitting the key, the browser window transitioned directly into Saskia Andrutsiv's account page.

"We're in," she clapped her hands.

Scanning this new page, Casey spotted a travel history tab and tapped.

"We should be able to see the last six months of her travel."

"That's good, but what exactly are we hoping to find?"

"Saskia never told Shelley who she was seeing and she baulked whenever Shelley offered to drive her to this guy's place. My hunch is that she used public transport to meet with him and I'll bet it was where that car was…"

Casey scrolled through the history. Many of the entries covered travel between the university and a stop just near Lesia Andrutsiv's home. There were also a handful of entries between both the Andrutsiv house and the university into the city centre. Interspersed among these however, were journeys from the university to another location in the eastern suburbs of Melbourne. Casey cocked her head.

"Look," she said briskly. "This one."

Lionel leaned in and peered through his glasses.

"Faraday Street, Carlton travelling to…Cotham Road in Kew. She took a bus for part of the journey, then transferred to a tram for the rest of it."

"Kew," Lionel remarked. "Rather a luxurious suburb. Lots of money there."

Scanning the list, both Casey and Lionel bobbed their heads in unison as they counted the entries: one, two, three, four, five, continuing on down the page until they reached the bottom. Clicking over the page, they counted at least a dozen more. The last transaction was recorded two weeks before her death.

"When exactly was she released from the centre?" Lionel queried.

Casey flipped through to the pages of her notebook to where she had scribbled notes whilst talking to Shelley Agutter.

"October 2011."

Lionel traced his finger back up the screen.

"These trips occurred with almost clockwork frequency from October… right up until late January the following year."

"And then they stopped," Casey added. "Completely."

Lionel bowed his head thoughtfully. Turning in his chair, he retrieved the printout of the vehicle registrations and plucked a black marker from the desk. He scanned through the pages, marking lines through the remaining entries on the list.

Casey watched him. "What are you doing?"

"A final process of deduction," Lionel responded. Lionel continued over the page where he eliminated two more entries. "Where did those tram journeys terminate exactly?" he asked.

Casey entered the details of the tram stop from Saskia's travel history in a search bar overlaying the satellite image. The screen scrolled from left to right over the built-up areas of the city.

"Stop 41," she answered. "Cotham Road."

"Okay," Lionel began, pausing to check back through the pages. "I've dispensed with most of these entries. Let's focus on five, no, six vehicles that were registered at the time of Saskia's death. All were registered to inner city addresses extending from the bay side northwards.

Glancing between the page and the satellite image displayed on screen, he pointed over Casey's shoulder.

"Only...*two*...were registered to addresses in the Kew area."

"She wouldn't have taken public transport if the address weren't convenient," Casey mused.

"No," Lionel agreed. "Kew is quite a pretty suburb to walk in."

He set the page down on the glass between them and circled one of the entries. "Number 5 Arbelside Avenue, Kew," he declared.

Casey leaned in and examined the page, then looked back at the screen, centering the image over a large house on a leafy, tree lined street.

"Let's get a closer look at that one," Lionel said, resuming his seat next to Casey.

Placing a cursor over the street immediately in front of the house, Casey switched to street view.

They were now looking at a two-storey house that was partially obscured by thick trees and dense foliage behind a tall fence. Casey squinted, trying to focus on the front of the house through hanging branches.

Large awnings were drawn down over the windows of the upper storey and on closer examination Casey noted that they appeared tattered and torn in places. The cladding on house itself appeared to be dirty, falling into disrepair. Zooming out, she refocused the image on an empty carport in front of the house. The timbers of the structure appeared to be rotting. Weeds sprouted from the cracks between brick paving stones.

"It looks terrible," she remarked.

Lionel nodded slowly. "It does. Terrible and unoccupied. How old is this image?"

Casey checked the image capture date at the bottom of the screen. "December 2013."

Lionel referred back to the print-out. "It says here that the S5 at this address was registered to a Marco Davich."

Casey switched to another window and tapped out 'Marco Davich' then 'Arbelside Avenue' in the search pane. The subsequent results flashed up and she studied them until her eyes fell across one that caused her expression to tighten.

Clicking on the text 'Death Notice', a new page opened.

"Marco Davich. Born 4th February 1936 and died 11th November 2010."

"A car registered to a dead person," Lionel mused.

"An *old*, dead person," Casey added.

Lionel tapped the desktop.

"What are you thinking, Pa?"

"I think we should take this to Whittaker," he said solemnly.

Casey clicked back to the image of the house, gazing at it intently.

"Casey, don't even think about it."

Her jaw tightened.

"It would be good to get a closer look at that house. I've got a bad feeling about it."

Lionel forced down a lump in his throat.

"I have a bad feeling about it too. But don't you think we've had enough? This is tangible. I believe we can get Whittaker on board with this."

"And what if we can't!" Casey blurted out angrily, slapping the desk with her hand, causing Lionel to flinch.

Immediately regretting her action, Casey stood up and paced towards the balcony before turning back to face her grandfather.

"I don't think he'll believe us, Pa," she said, rubbing her forehead in frustration.

Her eyes darted between the computer screen and her grandfather. There was a fire in her eyes. Her teeth were clenched together.

"I have to know. Whoever this person is, they've struck twice. First with Saskia and now with Josephine Catea," she breathed. "It's my fault."

Lionel held his hands up in front him, desperate to calm her.

"You can't stop this on your own," he said as softly as he could. "Look, I believe you. I think exactly the same way. But we must do this properly and let others take over for the very reason you've just pointed to: Josephine."

Lionel grabbed a newspaper from the kitchen counter. He held it up, showing her the front page. The fiery image of a burning vehicle was splashed across it, with firefighters desperately trying to extinguish the blaze.

A wash of guilt came over Casey and she faltered where she stood.

"You weren't responsible for this," Lionel responded. "But you've stirred up something—something evil—and we must tread carefully. For your own sake, because I don't want this to end up happening to you."

Casey couldn't respond. Only the sound of the computer's fan punctuated the quiet.

Finally she slumped down onto the sofa and drew her legs up, folding them to one side.

"I know you want it all to stop," Lionel said. "The nightmares. Saskia's memories."

She nodded tensely, processing her grandfathers words, angry that he made so much sense. Finally, exhaustion appeared to overtake her. She looked up at Lionel.

"Okay," she said simply. "Call Whittaker."

Lionel tossed and turned in his bed, unable to relax, unable to fall asleep.

Despite repeated calls to St. Kilda Road and leaving urgent messages, Farnham Whittaker had not yet returned any of their calls.

Lionel had done all he could to distract Casey, reassuring her that this was the right course of action, but his efforts had been mentally exhausting. Casey was like a caged animal, spending the entire rest of the day constantly going over all the evidence they'd managed to collect. All the while, the satellite image of the house at Arbelside Road remained on her computer screen.

Somewhere in the early hours, Lionel rose from his bed, went to the bathroom, then trudged downstairs to the kitchen.

Careful not to make a noise, he flipped the range hood light on over the cooker, then took a glass from an overhead cupboard and poured himself a glass of water. He stood before the sink, leaning against it as he sipped quietly, closing his eyes and rocking gently.

In his reverie, he set the glass down on the edge of the counter. As he took he hand away, the glass tipped and fell. He didn't react in time and the glass smashed on the tiled floor at his feet and he snarled in the darkness. Then he paused.

He detected no sign of disturbance from Casey's room. No sound at all. He stiffened and rose to his feet quickly, listening carefully. A knot tightened in his throat as his worst fears bubbled to the surface.

Stepping around the broken glass, Lionel nearly ran out of the kitchen, past the Modigliani on the wall. He peered around the corner, through the gap between the wall and the wardrobe, into Casey's room.

The bed was empty.

CHAPTER 30

Slowing as she passed by a trundling Melbourne tram, Casey spied the street sign up ahead and signalled. She turned from the busy Cotham Road onto the much quieter Arbelside Avenue.

She continued at a slow crawl as she scanned the leafy, residential street. Ahead, a tall brush fence came into view on her left, illuminated by the orange glow of a street lamp. Her eyes fell across a brass numeral affixed to the fence beside a pair of gates and she gulped softly.

Number 5, Arbelside Avenue.

Casey drew the Volkswagen alongside the kerb and leaned across to peer out through the passenger window. Despite the darkness, she could just make out a dense border of thick foliage behind the tall fence that appeared to run along the entire width of the property. The foliage and the fence combined to form an impenetrable barrier, preventing her from seeing the house beyond.

Casey frowned as her foot hovered on the brake pedal. Even though all the evidence indicated that the house was empty, it was physically impossible to confirm it from this vantage point.

She decided to drive on a short distance to ensure she was clear, and then doubled back and brought the car to a stop on the opposite side of the street. She extinguished the engine and sat in the darkness.

In the glow of the street lamp, she could just make out the top of the terracotta tiled roof through a gap in the fence at the corner of the property. Unlike the neighbouring houses, which were well lit from within, Casey couldn't see anything comparable from Number 5. It was as dark as a tomb.

Releasing her seatbelt, Casey took hold of her rucksack, then checked the street ahead. Another tram rumbled through the intersection, while over her shoulder the avenue behind her appeared empty.

Guilt prickled the back of her neck as the memory of Lionel's face nagged at her conscience. His pleas for her to pause and consider the risks of plunging headlong into the unknown echoed in the cabin.

She winced, reminding herself of the fiery conflagration that had been plastered all over the news bulletins, reporting Josephine Catea's accident.

Saskia's face also appeared from the depths of her nightmare.

They were images that had taunted her for so long, that had made her life a living hell. If there were a chance that she could stop them—a chance that she could extinguish them once and for all—she knew had to take it.

She had to free herself.

Casey opened the door and stepped out into the night.

Across the street, the laneway she'd noted from the satellite image was separated from the property by a tall, corrugated iron fence. From her angle of approach, the lane disappeared into the darkness. Casey hurried across the street and scooted into the shadows. Grabbing her phone from inside the bag, she activated its flashlight and held it inwards so the beam played over her stomach.

The sound of a dog barking nearby startled her and she peered down the cobbled path. At the end of the lane she could see an orange glow, similar to the street lamp at the front.

Stepping out from the shadows, she made her way along the front of the property.

The brush fence stood roughly seven feet tall. Casey could not see any gaps in it that would allow her to see through into the property. Looking down by her feet, she noticed tall clumps of grass, weeds and thistles pushing through the bottom of the fence. Signs of neglect?

Continuing along the fence, she came to the pair of gates that were constructed in an identical fashion to the fence. As she cast the light over them, she noted a pair of square holes in the structure, positioned side by side. Her eyes widened as she bent down to see if she could see through. It was then that she noticed a thick chain snaking through the gaps that was secured on the inside by a sizeable padlock. In the darkness, she could just make out the silhouette of the house from the light pollution of the city behind it. There were no lights coming from inside.

No signs of life at all.

She turned and headed back along the street to the laneway where she stopped and shone the light down into the gloom. The lane ran the entire depth of the property, a good one hundred and fifty feet. At the end, where it was lit, there appeared to be another lane running along the back.

Slipping into the darkness, Casey flanked the fence and emerged at the rear. She quickly scanned both right and left, seeing several garages backing out into the lane.

Casey inspected the rear fence of Number 5. Like the other fences, this one was a tall, corrugated iron structure. There was a single gate at the very corner from where she had emerged, while further along she noted a large roller door for the garage. She went to it and tested it, though she knew it would be locked.

Returning to the corner beside the laneway, Casey shone her light on the single gate. This gate too was secured by a thick chain and padlock.

I'm not going to get past this.

Directing her beam up, Casey saw that the top of the fence was clear.

Looking around her, Casey searched for something to stand on. She spied a large, lone wheelie bin further down the lane. She went to it, taking a hold of its handle and grunting as she attempted to move it. It would not budge.

Grabbing it in both hands and recruiting as much strength into her arms as she could muster, she tipped it at an angle, then pulled. Its stubby wheels yielded to her grasp and the bin finally moved. The contents inside it rattled noisily as she hefted it across the cobblestone and she winced as she tried to move it as gently as she could. The dog nearby responded to the tinkling glass inside the bin with ferocious barks.

Casey cursed to herself.

Finally, she wielded the bin into position, then scanned the laneway urgently. The dog continued to bark, however, after a minute or so, it went silent. No one came out to inspect the commotion.

Cautiously, Casey climbed onto the bin and balanced herself, before gripping the top of the gate and looking over.

The rear of the property, like the front, was similarly shrouded in darkness. As she directed her smartphone's light into the yard, Casey saw an overgrown lawn that stood at least three to four feet high. There were garden beds that had long been neglected and rubbish was strewn everywhere. A single red brick path snaked into a courtyard.

As she played the light beam over the house, Casey gasped when she saw a light beam shining back at her. Panicking, she ducked down out of view, shoving her phone against her body.

"Shit," she hissed, afraid to look up for a long moment. Eventually, she risked a quick glance over the top of the gate and saw nothing but darkness.

Puzzled, Casey lifted her light and shone it into the property again, the beam playing over a series of tall, glass window panels that formed an observatory at the rear of the house, much like the sunroom at her parents' home.

A wash of relief came over her.

"My own bloody light."

Shaking her head, Casey looked to where the garage stood. A large pile of junk was stacked against it: timbers, old garden tools and what appeared to be car wheels whose rubber tyres had perished. For a moment, she was reminded of her warehouse.

If she were still doubting that the house was empty, the scene here convinced her that, more than likely, it was.

Shining the light down at the ground inside the gate, she saw that it was clear enough for her to climb over and drop down safely.

Clutching the phone between her teeth, Casey grabbed the gate and pushed off from the bin, swinging her left leg over the frame, followed by her right. With a final push, she vaulted down onto the path.

Appraising the garage, she spied a window constructed of three panes beside a door. Skipping through the minefield of debris and rubbish, she approached it and raised her phone's flashlight.

A thick layer of grime coated the glass panes. Reaching out, Casey pulled her sleeve over her hand and carefully rubbed out a porthole, removing as much of it as she could before peering inside.

Though her view was significantly impaired by dust on the inside of the glass, she could see a similar collection of junk. Playing the beam over the interior, her eye was drawn to an object occupying the centre. Covered in what appeared to be a large canvas tarpaulin, it was definitely a large object. She traced her tongue along the outer edge of her bottom lip thoughtfully.

What is that?

Her pulse quickened. The heart pounded and she grabbed the material of her shirt over her chest.

Stepping back, Casey appraised the door beside the window which was blocked by rusted garden implements, a pair of old shovels, pick axes and a sledgehammer. Moving them aside, Casey tested the handle.

She screwed up her face. *Of course it's locked.*

Locking her eyes on the rusted sledgehammer beside her, she bent down and grabbed it. Immediately beside it she found the tattered remnants of an old potato sack. Considering the window panes, then the material on the ground, she grabbed it and shook it, ensuring there were no spiders lurking inside the folds of the material. She wrapped a portion of it around the end of the hammer, hoping the material would muffle the sound of the steel hitting the glass panes.

Cringing as she held her fist up, she turned side on, angling her head away from the window.

Here goes nothing…

She struck the bottom pane, shattering it on her first try. Flinching as shards fell on the ground before her, she jumped clear. The noise of the smashing glass caused the nearby dog to bark furiously and Casey hissed. It continued on for almost a minute until a male voice cut through the night.

"For Christ's sake, shut up!"

The dog fell silent. Casey waited for several seconds then, satisfied that she was safe, she moved in to inspect her handiwork.

Unwrapping the potato sack from the hammer, she wound it around her forearm before reaching slowly through the open window and angling her arm around to the inside of the door. Casey gingerly touched the inner mechanism of the door handle. Though the metal felt solid, the bar and latch assembly itself moved loosely in her grip until she felt the locking mechanism prevent it from turning any further. If she could pry the door open with something, Casey felt sure the locking mechanism would bend and possibly collapse.

Looking down at the rusted tools on ground, Casey's eyes fell across a thick, rusted crowbar. Picking it up, she quickly assessed it, then wedged it in between the door frame and the door itself.

Satisfied that it was in the best position, Casey steadied her grip on the crowbar and pulled back on it as hard as she could.

At first nothing happened. Cursing silently, she adjusted her stance and tried again, putting as much power into her wrist and hand as she could.

Interminable moments passed.

The crowbar finally levered outwards, widening the gap in the door further. The latch inside groaned in protest, the rusted metal yielding under pressure until it bent inwards completely. The door frame also whined on its hinges until something popped and clattered noisily to the floor inside.

The door swung open and Casey stumbled back, dropping the crowbar. She blinked into the darkness beyond. Collecting herself, she opened it further and it creaked on its rusted hinges.

Casey slipped inside and was confronted by yet another pile of junk separating her from the tarpaulin-covered object in the centre of the garage. Shining the light around her in order to avoid tripping, she stepped forward until she was close enough to the canvas that she could kneel down before it.

Setting the phone down on an old cabinet behind her, she angled the beam over the tarpaulin. The shape underneath it was definitely automobile-sized.

Acid crept up the back of her throat and singed her tongue.

She took a hold of the bottom edge of the tarpaulin in her grip, squeezed her eyes shut then lifted the canvas.

Low-slung headlights, angling in towards the centre.

A grille that swept down over the front, encompassing the registration plate.

Four interlocking rings of polished chrome.

There was no mistaking it.

Casey stood up and staggered back.

She blinked hard in the fractured light.

Steadying herself, she stepped down the right hand side of the Audi S5, taking the tarpaulin with her, peeling it back from the navy blue surface of the car until she had uncovered it completely.

Images from the nightmare flickered before her eyes as she dropped the canvas to floor then returned to the front of the car and stood before it.

Saskia's face…

The assailant…

Beams from the headlights, piercing the darkness…

Casey read the license plate: W-ZC-23S.

She was numb. Tears stung her cheeks. Her breath came in ragged gasps.

This was it. The car that had plagued her dreams. The car that Lionel had found almost by accident. The car that had carried Saskia Andrutsiv to her death on Lasterby Road.

Looking down, Casey noted the right headlamp was cracked and glass was missing. There was also a slight depression in the body just underneath the bottom edge of the headlight.

Casey touched her hand to the cold surface. She shivered, wondering if this was where the car had struck Saskia, the final blow that had sealed her fate and Casey's.

Her hand shook. Her emotions spun. First grief and deep sadness, then a surging, white hot anger.

She glanced over her shoulder.

The house beckoned, coaxing her.

Would there be answers inside? The final pieces of this whole tragic puzzle?

Turning on her heel, she stepped back to the door of the garage, pausing to retrieve the crowbar that lay on the concrete floor. She gripped it tightly, her knuckles turning white as she marched across the overgrown lawn towards the house.

Caution had left her now. In its place was an iron will.

Dropping down onto the patio, she scanned the glass observatory, identifying a pair of double doors in the gloom. Aiming the light at them, she choked up on the crowbar then shoved it full force into the crack between the two doors, splintering the timber frame as she wrenched it to one side. There was a loud crack as the locking mechanism protested but quickly yielded and broke away from the frame. One of the glass panes cracked under pressure. The doors swung inwards.

Casey lowered her arm, maintaining her grip on the crowbar as she listened for signs of life.

Satisfied that there were none, Casey stepped into the darkness.

She had failed to notice that, on the door frame, a small, green LED began to flash silently.

Casey moved deeper into the house. Like the yard, it seemed that this place had become little more than a storage facility. Through the sunroom from which she'd entered, Casey found herself in a living/dining room. Like the car, much of the furniture had been covered with sheets. The air was stale and tinged with the odour of rodent urine.

Beyond a hallway entrance, Casey stopped to run her finger along an exposed side table, tracing a line through a layer of dust. Particles were swept up into the air where they danced in the beam of the smartphone light.

A number of photo frames stood on this side table. Casey bent down to inspect them. One showed a portrait of a couple, roughly the same age as Casey's parents, posing together. The man appeared European, possibly Italian. Dressed in a shirt and tie, he bore a warm smile as he held the hand of his partner: an attractive, stately woman with cropped hair and angular features. Casey's eyes lingered on her face. She thought she saw something familiar. Eventually, she drifted across the accompanying photos. The same couple appeared in several more frames, this time posing with two children—a boy and a girl. Again, Casey saw something familiar in the subjects there, but she couldn't determine what it was. Leaning in, her eyes drifted over the faces of the children. The boy had shock of ebony curls framing a button nose and a beaming smile. The girl beside him, with long, black hair tied back from her face, bore a pensive expression as she clutched the hand of the woman who held her lovingly close.

Casey squinted in the half light, her eyes gravitating towards the boy in one of the pictures.

Who is that?

A shard of glass from the broken sunroom door suddenly dropped and smashed on the floor behind her, causing Casey to jump. She wheeled around, blinking furiously, expecting the worst, but no one appeared to be there.

Turning away from the photo frames she looked ahead, noting the front door of the house at the end of the hall and a staircase on her left. Approaching the stairs, Casey cast the light through doorways on both sides of her: one that led into a bedroom, another to a sitting room. Like the living area, the furniture that occupied them was covered.

At the foot of the stairs, she cast the light up into the gloom, hesitating, cocking her head, listening for any signs of life. All she could hear was her own breathing.

Gripping the crowbar tighter, she ascended as quietly as she could up the stairs, pausing at the top and sweeping the beam left and right.

To her right, at the end of the hall, a door was slightly ajar. She headed towards it, angling the light's beam downwards. On her right was another open door and, as she regarded it, she stopped. Her nostrils twitched as a fragrance touched them—a fragrance that seemed familiar.

Resting the crowbar on the door, she nudged it and peered around it into the darkness beyond. It was a master bedroom whose window looked out onto the front garden. Slipping inside, Casey noted a king-sized bed. It had been made up with sheets and a quilt.

The bedding had been kicked back as though someone had risen from it but had neglected to make it. Casey lowered the crowbar to the floor and ran her hand across the rumpled bed. The sheets were creased as though someone had been sleeping in it.

The fragrance she'd caught earlier was stronger here. It was coming from the bed. Casey racked her brain trying to place it. It was definitely masculine, an aftershave perhaps. She couldn't put her finger on where she'd encountered it before.

Looking up and around, Casey noted a wardrobe, and a table and chair with a man's suit jacket draped over it. Unlike the covered furniture elsewhere in the house, these were completely uncovered, yet not dusty.

Her skin prickled.

Someone has been here. And recently.

She backed out of the room and focused on the door at the end of the hall. Fingers of tension crept up her spine, bringing with them a sense of urgency.

Approaching the door, she pushed it open and directed the light into the room.

And gasped.

The room was a home office, a study—and it had been thoroughly trashed.

There was a desk that sat before a large window. Its drawers had been removed and up-ended. An accompanying chair lay on its side before it. To her left, Casey saw a large bookcase whose entire collection had been dumped in a large pile on the floor. A filing cabinet beside that had been similarly trashed. Its drawers were hanging precariously; papers and folders spilled from them.

Setting the crowbar down, Casey stepped over the mess and shone the light at the desk.

Several folders from the filing cabinet had been set down here and were laid open as if someone had been reading them. Underneath one of these folders, Casey spied the edge of a newspaper and she lifted it out from underneath.

An entire portion of the front page had been cut from it. She examined the date on the masthead. It was the edition from two days ago. Playing the light across the desk before her, Casey searched around until she looked up at the window. The missing front page had been taped to the glass. Her eyes fell across the fiery wreck of a burning car and her stomach plunged.

Josephine Catea's car.

Placing the light down, Casey returned to the file folders on the desk. The contents of the papers inside were incomprehensible to her at first but, as she picked up a sheet from one of them and began reading its contents, Casey began to recognise terms on the page. Blood results, physical examination, immunisation profile.

She frowned.

She picked up another sheet from an adjacent folder and scanned its contents, seeing similar terminology contained within it.

She picked up another.

And another.

It was the same.

What were these medical reports?

Though it had the air of officialdom, something about the piece of paper told Casey that this wasn't something that had been produced by a government agency. Retrieving the phone and holding it up in her hand, she sifted through more sheets of paper until she found one that had a logo printed on it. She brought it close.

Elyria Medical Services.

Directing the light down, she examined the discarded papers on the floor. On every loose page she saw there, Casey found the same medical terminology printed on them.

And then she noticed something else.

Picking up another page, she examined it and found a series of numbers printed; numbers she recognised.

SX801244

Saskia's scrawled note flashed in her mind's eye and her breath left her all at once.

Casey dropped to her knees and sifted through the pile, checking to see if any more sheets contained the same number on them.

She found one. Then two more. Then another two.

Setting the phone down on the chair and angling it so she could see, Casey examined the pages, noting their page numbers and sorting them accordingly until she was looking at a complete report.

It was headed: Preliminary Medical Examination - IMA Candidate No. SX801244, Flaxley Park Immigration Detention Facility.

Casey's pupils dilated. Her blood turned to ice.

Through her burgeoning shock, Casey quickly read through each page, searching for the name of the candidate and the person who had examined that candidate.

The candidate's vital statistics were featured on the first page. Age: 22 years (approx), Gender: female, Country of Birth: Sri Lanka.

Casey noticed at various points throughout the report someone had scrawled notes in red and circled portions of the printed information. She read through one section, containing what appeared to be a blood profile, toxicology screen, liver and kidney function. These last two had been circled and notes made to one side.

"No apparent history of drug use. Kidney function excellent. Liver function excellent..."

The last line of the note had been underlined.

"Ideal candidate for procurement. As per instructions, refer for follow up with Sonmez to arrange for inbound client. Recommend repatriation to the chamber..."

A creeping horror suffused Casey and she felt her chest begin to tighten. She read the last lines again and again, not trusting her own eyes that what she was reading was actually there.

"Ideal candidate for procurement...Follow up with Sonmez ... Recommend repatriation to the chamber..."

Fresh tears stung her eyes as she struggled to read on. The name of the candidate did not seem to appear anywhere on this page nor anywhere else.

But the examiner's name did.

Dr. M. Davich.

"Jesus," Casey whispered raggedly.

Her eyes drifted back to the scrawl beside the blood results and the mention of Sonmez.

"*Sonmez*," she sounded the name out loud.

Something about it seemed familiar to her, as though she'd heard it before. But she could not recall where.

Shaking her head, she read through to the last page, only to find that it finished in mid sentence.

The report was incomplete.

Casey searched the floor around her, looking to see if she had missed a page. She picked up what looked to be a fragment from another report but she couldn't see an identifying number on it. Picking up the phone, she cast the flashlight across the room and into the corner where a bin stood in the corner. An electronic contraption sat on top of it.

It was a paper shredder.

Casey scrambled across to it and lifted the shredder component off of the bin and peered down into it. It was filled with ribbons of A4 paper.

She pulled out a handful of the paper, even though she knew what it was.

Shining the light back at the newspaper report stuck to the window, Casey felt sick.

They know, she thought.

Whoever it was, they knew and now they were trying to cover it up.

Flipping her phone over, Casey brought up her home number and dialled it.

Lionel answered almost immediately. His voice was plagued with worry.

"Casey. What on Earth are you doing?"

"I found the car, Pa," Casey said, trying to contain her emotions, while keeping her voice low. "We were right. Arbelside Avenue is it. This is the place that Saskia was visiting."

There was silence at the other end of the phone.

"There's more, Pa. I've found a lot of stuff here…papers. Records."

"What sort of records?" Lionel asked urgently.

"Medical records," Casey choked, holding up the document she'd collated in her hand. "There is a whole bunch of them here but someone has started shredding them. I think they know somebody is onto them."

"Wait a second…*medical* records," Lionel countered breathlessly. "I don't understand."

Casey adjusted her grip on the phone and fought back her tears, her grief and her anger.

"Okay. The file numbers that Saskia wrote down; I think they were for asylum seekers that were being held at Flaxley Park Immigration Detention Facility. Each of them were given medical examinations on arrival by a private contractor called Elyria Medical Services."

"Okay," Lionel said. "That's not uncommon for private contractors to provide assessment services for the government."

"I've found reports for at least two of those file numbers here. I'm guessing that the rest of them are here too."

"But what on Earth would they be doing there? In a private residence?"

Casey dropped her head and began to shake. Tears fell on the papers in her hand.

"Pa, there's writing on the reports. Handwritten notes."

"What kind of notes?"

"They were screening these candidates…these particular candidates."

Lionel gulped as Casey's voice trailed away. He could sense her anguish.

"What, Casey?" he urged her. "What is it?"

Casey sat up straighter. "Organ harvesting," she said finally. "Someone wanted these people's organs."

The import of her words did not strike Lionel immediately. Within the silence that followed, a horrible realisation began to dawn on him and he felt his legs buckle. He reached out and grabbed the back of the sofa.

"Casey," he stammered. "Is there a name on the report? Can you see a name of a doctor or specialist?"

Casey nodded, flipping back to the first page. She directed the light beam at it, squinting as she scanned the name she had found earlier.

"Davich," she said.

"*Marco* Davich?" Lionel queried.

Casey nodded slowly. "Yeah."

"Our dead Marco Davich," Lionel muttered, trying to comprehend what Casey had in front of her.

"Elyria Medical Services has a dead man working for them," Casey said softly.

"So who is the impostor?"

"I don't know. There's a name scrawled in the notes. I think it's a name at least. Somebody named Sonmez. But I can't see…" She held the report up again, examining the logo for Elyria Medical Services at the top of the first page. "Pa, I've seen this Elyria Medical Services logo before," Casey squinted in the light from her phone. "In fact, it looks *way too* familiar."

"Elyria Medical Services," Lionel repeated.

His eyes narrowed as a flash of recognition passed through him. A fragment of a memory registered and he focused on it, trying to recall where he had encountered it before.

"I think I have, too."

"Casey, get out of there now. I'm going to call Whittaker."

"No, wait," Casey countered sharply. "We should contact Prishna instead. I've already thrown her a bone and—"

Suddenly, a loud bang followed by the smashing of glass downstairs cut Casey off. She whipped her head up, dropping the phone. It bounced on the cushioned surface of the chair, coming to rest with its flashlight beam pointed at the ceiling.

"Casey!" Lionel called out.

Casey slapped her hand to her mouth, stifling the urge to gasp. Dropping to her knees, she scrambled across the floor and cowered behind the door.

"Casey, what's happening?" Lionel shouted.

Cocking her ear to the gap between the door and the door frame, Casey gulped. There was a long moment of silence followed by the sound of footfalls on the broken glass.

Oh, Jesus!

CHAPTER 31

Fighting against panic, Casey realised the smartphone's light was still shining in the darkness. Pushing the door to the office closed, she winced as it squeaked on its hinges before stopping just short of closing completely. Casey reached out for the crowbar, dragging it to her, then she made a desperate grab for the phone, killing the light and shoving it against her ear.

"Pa, someone's here!" she whispered frantically. "Someone's downstairs!"

Lionel felt sick.

"Casey, get out of there," he growled. "Get out of there now!"

"I can't."

Lionel paced around the kitchen counter. Beads of sweat broke out on his forehead.

"Casey, you have to do some—"

Without warning, the line went dead.

"Casey!" Lionel shouted. "Casey!"

Casey clutched the neck of her shirt as a series of loud thuds sounded on the stairs.

Her eyes flicked around the study. For a fleeting moment, she entertained the idea of escaping through the window, but dismissed it just as quickly. It appeared to be painted shut and, in any case, she doubted she would have enough time to get to it.

She was utterly trapped.

How could anyone have possibly known?

She could hear someone moving slowly towards the door now. Squeezing her eyes shut, Casey grabbed the crowbar in both hands.

"I know you're in there," a male voice growled.

Casey's eyes snapped open. Her breath caught in her throat.

She recognised the voice.

"There's nowhere to run. No one is coming for you."

Casey felt her stomach lurch. A vortex of images flashed before her. Images from both the nightmares and from her memories—her recent and real memories.

A conversation.

He leaned in and gently drew down the sheet so that he could examine the cables. In the process, he inadvertently brushed his forearm over her chest…

She shivered and blushed even more acutely…

"You're seeing the boss today?"

"Yeah, this afternoon at three."

"He does like his data."

Casey couldn't bear to believe it. She began to shake.

Saskia's face, pleading with her through the lightning flash inside the nightmare.

The gloved hand in the nightmare; plunging into her chest; cascades of blood…

The intruder was outside the door. It moved as a hand rested upon the handle.

Casey steeled herself.

The door swung open and Casey shifted just enough to allow it to complete its arc.

The intruder stepped into the room behind a powerful beam of light.

Casey held her breath, praying that he wouldn't hear her. The torch light swept around the room as the intruder searched for her. She did not dare look around the door frame to see who it was.

She already knew.

Suddenly, her phone vibrated noisily in her pocket and, as she was wedged behind the door, it vibrated against that too, amplifying the noise so that the whole door became the phone's ringer.

Oh fuck!

His fingers appeared at the edge and, before she could react, he wrenched the door back and shone the blinding light directly at Casey. Though dazzled by the beam, Casey could still see him.

She recoiled.

Francis Arlo.

A single, interminable moment of shocked recognition passed between them. Time slowed to a crawl.

Neither one could move.

Without warning, Arlo whipped his arm up, closed his fist and swung hard at Casey. She whipped her head to her right as his fist crashed into the wall beside her, shattering the plaster board and slashing the skin across his knuckles as it struck a wooden beam inside the cavity. The torch fell to the floor.

Arlo yelped in pain as Casey dropped to her knees and rolled from her hiding place.

Grasping the crowbar in both hands, she sprang to her feet, planting them well apart as she raised it over her head, preparing to strike.

Arlo gasped, seeing her in the half-light from his torch, wrenched his arm free and propelled himself backwards, crashing directly into her midsection.

Casey felt the wind knocked from her and the crowbar fell from her hands. As she collapsed back, it struck her on the side of her head and she saw stars.

She crashed down onto the paper shredder behind her, shattering the electronic component of the machine. Sharp fragments pierced her skin and drew blood. She cried out again.

As she struggled on the floor, a sudden and intense pain exploded inside her chest, sucking the breath from her once more.

The room began to spin and she felt sick.

Arlo did not wait. Recovering, he spun around and braced himself in the middle of the room before spying the fallen crowbar. He lunged for it, grabbing it up in his hand, then he grabbed the torch and shone the beam directly at Casey.

As she flailed impotently on the floor before him, shielding her eyes from the beam of light, Arlo looked down on her, his expression hovering somewhere between sadness and apoplexy.

He shook his head. "You think I'd be stupid enough not to secure this place in the event of an intruder?" he snarled.

Casey's voice caught in her throat. She shook uncontrollably as the pain in her chest grew more intense, robbing her of breath.

Arlo lurched towards her, a crazed fury in his eyes.

"You couldn't leave it alone, could you?" he hissed. "You just had to keep pushing."

Casey spat at him.

"Why," she croaked, struggling to speak against crushing waves of nausea. "*Why!*"

Grief and rage collided within her. She could not comprehend that before her stood the man who had helped save her life. The man Fedele had once called his natural extension. She had trusted him. Had been grateful to him.

She had respected him.

This very same man was the monster from her nightmares—Saskia's memories. The memories that had been given to Casey from the very moment

Saskia's heart had begun to beat inside her chest.

Arlo stood over her, glowering, his jaw clenched, armed with the weapon. The very realisation of her nightmares.

His eyes were filled with hatred and evil. And yet, there was something else.

They were filled with fear.

He raised the crowbar over his head.

In that moment, Casey saw past the torch's blinding light. She saw where he was standing in relation to her.

In one swift movement, she folded her legs up and drew them tight against her body. Dropping the torch, Arlo gripped the crowbar in both hands and sucked in a loud, deep breath.

Casey screamed as she kicked out as hard as she could, her legs propelling towards Arlo like hydraulic rams.

She struck true in the centre of his groin with so much force that Arlo was flung backwards like a rag doll. Striking the wall behind him, he roared in agony as he crumpled to the floor, clutching his groin.

Casey was on her feet in an instant. No sooner had Arlo drawn himself up into a sitting position, she struck again, flicking her right leg up and ramming it directly into his face. The sound of breaking bone mixed with his anguished cries as his nose shattered and bent sickeningly to one side.

Casey would not be assuaged.

She came at him again and again, kicking him as hard as she could, screaming in animalistic fury. Blood poured from his ruined nose. Deep lacerations opened up under his right eye and his chin. A tooth dislodged and flicked up into her cheek.

Her barrage was relentless. The intensity of her anger detonated like a nuclear bomb. Three years of pain and anguish spewed forth in the fallout and he was powerless to stop it.

As he tried to raise a hand up to his face, Arlo's cries grew more desperate.

And then they stopped.

And then she stopped.

She stumbled back. Arlo's hand dropped. His head slumped forward. He continued to moan into the fractured darkness but it was clear he was close to unconsciousness.

Her breath was ragged. Recovering the fallen crowbar, Casey stumbled back and spat on Arlo's inert form. She felt her phone vibrate and her hand dropped to her side, plucking the device from her pocket.

Looking at the screen, she blinked and allowed herself to feel a crackle of relief. There was a 'message received' notification from Prishna.

Glancing down at Arlo, Casey pitched the phone at him, hitting him in the side of his face.

"You're done, Francis," she said bitterly. "They aren't coming for me. *They're coming for you*!"

Casey backed away, supporting herself against the desk as she fought to slow her breath. All at once, her emotions overcame her. Tears streamed down her cheeks and she sobbed in the darkness. Her adrenaline-soaked strength collapsed as she raised a hand to her face.

Without warning, Arlo erupted from the floor and pitched himself at her, striking her hard with a closed fist. The blow knocked her sideways as she crashed against the bookcase.

Disoriented and panicked, Casey felt the room tip sideways and she thrust her hands out in front of her, swinging at the air to protect herself from him.

The expected attack never came.

Instead, Arlo threw open the door to the study and leapt through it, striking the door frame with his hip and shoulder.

In her faltering consciousness, the realisation came to Casey.

He's escaping!

Forcing herself to action, she lurched to her feet and started forward, only to stagger as she vomited on the floor.

There was a crash and a roar of agony from Arlo as he stumbled on the stairs and fell hard through the decrepit banister rail. The sound of smashing glass followed, compelling Casey to look up.

Her stomach spasmed twice, then three times. Casey steadied herself against the door then bent down to retrieve her phone from the floor, its screen flashing with another incoming call from Lionel.

This time, she stamped her thumb against it and shoved it against her ear as she staggered forward.

"Casey!"

"I've got him," Casey growled through clenched teeth. "I've got him and he's on the run."

"Stay where you are, Casey! Prishna's on the way!"

Casey tripped down the stairs. The front door had been wrenched open and hung precariously from a single hinge. The stained glass panel had smashed and shards were scattered on the floor.

Beyond the door, two piercing headlight beams punctured the darkness. The sound of a car's engine screamed to life. Skidding to a stop on the tiled verandah, Casey looked down and through the windshield of a deep burgundy BMW sport coupe. Casey gasped in horror, realising that she recognised the car. It was the same one that had very nearly hit her at Flaxley. Shaking the realisation away, she locked her eyes onto Arlo's face, bathed in a red glow from his dashboard lights.

"I can't!" she cried out. "He's leaving. Arlo is escaping!"

At the other end of the line, Lionel's voice caught in his throat.

"Who did you say?"

"It's Arlo, Pa!" Casey screamed. "*It's Francis Arlo*!"

The coupe revved hard and careened backwards before Arlo wrenched the steering wheel down, spinning it to one side and lining it up with the entrance to the property. The car shot forward, its tyres spitting out white gravel.

Casey bounded down the steps, wincing from the pain in her leg where he had kicked her. Through the gates and onto the street, she watched Arlo's car speed towards the intersection as she staggered towards the Volkswagen, pointing her remote at it and wrenching the door open.

Several people from neighbouring homes had come out onto the street at the commotion. Casey ignored them as she started the car and gunned the engine as quickly as she could.

The Volkswagen leapt forward and fishtailed along the street as she took off after Arlo.

CHAPTER 32

Lionel jogged towards the Blue Heeler Bar.

The young doorman at the entrance frowned as he approached, gesturing to his colleague who glanced at the somewhat desperate-looking old-timer.

Stumbling at the kerb, Lionel growled. He unzipped his heavy parka and loosened his tie before glaring up at the perplexed doorman. The doorman stepped in front of the entrance with his arms folded. His expression hardened.

"I have to see someone," Lionel croaked, his chest heaving. "It's urgent."

"Don't you think it's a little past your bedtime, old man?" the doorman observed sarcastically.

Lionel bent forward and put his hands on his knees, gulping again in an attempt to catch his breath.

"You don't understand. I…"

At that moment, the side door to the bar opened and a third doorman stepped out into the night air. He exchanged a suspicious glance at his colleagues who looked back at him and shrugged.

"This one causing trouble?" the newly arrived doorman asked.

"Seems grandpa here is out for a good time," the younger man remarked. "I was just suggesting that he might be better off tucked up in his nurs—"

He never finished his sentence.

Lionel pounced, raising his forearm and using it like a ram against the younger man's throat, shoving him hard against the wall. His colleagues were caught by surprise; both by Lionel's action and the strength of his hold. The doorman flailed helplessly. His eyes bulged as he struggled to breathe.

Lionel whipped his head up at the two stunned doormen.

"Sasquatch," Lionel snarled, his arm shaking against the chest of the doorman. "I need to see Sasquatch *now*!"

As abruptly as he had erupted, Lionel released his hold. The doorman collapsed forward in a fit of coughing. Lionel grabbed him under both arms and gently held him up while he recovered.

The two accompanying doormen exchanged confused looks, then one of them seemed to understand. As Lionel patted the younger man's back, his colleague stepped back and opened the door.

"Come in. Come in quickly," he stammered.

Supporting the younger man up the stairs, Lionel deposited him in a chair just inside the door, then looked to his colleague who pointed up the stairs and gestured for him to follow.

Emerging onto the rooftop, Lionel scanned the bustling garden, his eyes locking onto Scott who was circling the dance floor area and greeting a number of patrons. Without waiting, Lionel squeezed the doorman's arm and nodded his thanks. He strode across the crowded dance floor, pushing his way through the young crowd as if they were of no consequence. Scott looked in his direction and blinked, first in surprised recognition and then with concern.

Lionel stepped around a nubile young party-goer and nodded.

"What's wrong," Scott said over the din. It was less a question than a statement.

"Casey," Lionel replied grimly. "She's in trouble. She's found the car."

Scott's jaw dropped. "Shit!" he managed to whisper, glancing urgently to his right towards the bar in the far corner.

"I need your help," Lionel continued, his voice faltering.

Scott nodded and rounded his arm around Lionel's back, gently shepherding him through the throng and over to the bar.

"Claire," Scott called to the young barmaid. "Where's the Lurch Monster?"

"Dunno," she apologized. "Downstairs I reckon."

Scott grimaced and thumped the bar with his fist as he looked to Lionel. Then he nodded and glanced back at Claire.

"I gotta go," he said. "Tell Lurch it was urgent."

Claire frowned in confusion at first, then she regarded Lionel who looked at her with a worried expression.

"Okay," she said. "I'll let him know."

Scott turned and took Lionel's elbow. "Come on. Let's go."

Ignoring the traffic, Casey sped along Cotham Road, weaving across the lanes to avoid getting caught behind cars, trucks or trams. She punched the horn repeatedly in a desperate attempt to alert them to her presence, causing chaos in her wake as vehicles skidded across the road to avoid being hit, before responding in kind with their own horns.

She punched the steering wheel, cursing herself over and over for allowing Arlo to escape. She'd had him subdued. He was helpless. Yet, somehow, he'd been able to recover.

The more she admonished herself, the more her emotions spun. Fresh tears stung her cheeks and she wiped them away furiously.

It was Arlo? How could it be Arlo?

Forcing herself to focus, Casey scanned the road ahead of her, searching desperately among the smattering of vehicles for Arlo's distinctive coupe. She spied several luxury cars, one of which closely resembled his. But Arlo's was nowhere among them.

A set of traffic lights flicked to red ahead of her but Casey ignored it. Gripping the steering wheel harder, she planted her foot. The Volkswagen's engine whined in protest but shot forward like a bullet, weaving in between a car and a commercial truck ahead of her. She punched the horn over and over again as she sped through the intersection, causing approaching vehicles on both her left and right to brake desperately.

Casey did not look back.

A tram emerged ahead of her and she raced up behind it before swinging wide on its left-hand side. Her eyes locked onto a sports car several yards ahead.

It was him.

Adjusting her grip on the steering wheel, she dropped a gear and floored the accelerator once more, putting on a fresh burst of speed.

The speedometer's needle twitched wildly, passing ninety, then one hundred, then one hundred and ten kilometres per hour.

Somewhere in her mind, a rational thought admonished her.

This is insane. You are going to get someone killed.

Casey wiped her eyes again, crushing the thought. She would not allow him to get away. She shot past another tram, gradually closing the distance between herself and Arlo until a car's length separated them. She flicked on her high beams.

Blinding light punctured the cabin of Arlo's car and reflected off the rear-vision mirror directly into his puffed eyes. Shouting, he yanked reflexively on the steering wheel, causing the BMW to fishtail.

Knifing pain shot through his ruined nose and Arlo almost lost control. In desperation, he stabbed the brakes, slowing just enough to recover. His action closed the distance between himself and Casey and with a sudden, deafening crash of metal and plastic, the Volkswagen ploughed into the BMW's rear, obliterating the plastic bumper of Casey's car and crumpling the rear of

Arlo's in a shower of sparks and smoking tyres as each car braked to avoid a catastrophe.

Arlo pitched forward violently in his seat until his seatbelt went taut and flung him back, whiplashing his neck in the process. A fresh trickle of blood dripped from his nose.

Reaching across to the multi-function display in the centre of the dashboard, Arlo navigated to the car's phone controls and pressed a voice command function.

"Call Consulting Suites!" he shouted in a ragged voice.

A message flashed up on the display.

'Calling Consulting Suites.'

A dial tone filled the car's speaker system, followed by a click, then a deep voice at the other end of the line.

"Speak!" it ordered. "Where are you?"

"We have a problem," Arlo spluttered through sprays of blood. "The safe house has been breached. The back up files have been discovered."

"You didn't destroy them?" the voice retorted incredulously.

"I d-didn't have time! I thought I would be oka—"

"But you weren't, Francis!" the voice thundered. "You were lazy and now you've allowed our work to be uncovered."

"I'm sorry," Arlo stammered, his voice cracking with emotion. "I'm being pursued now. She is coming at me."

The was a moment of silence at the other end of the line followed by, "She?"

Arlo nodded. "Yes. It's Schillinge."

Another screech of metal pierced through the cabin as the Volkswagen again shunted hard into the back of Arlo's car. His hands were flung from the steering wheel as the BMW careened across the roadway and mounted the kerb where it heavily glanced a tall brick fence.

Arlo cried out in terror, wrenched the wheel hard to the right and angled the car back onto the road. No sooner had he recovered, that the car swerved wildly across both lanes, directly into the path of an oncoming tram.

"NO!" he screamed, yanking down on the steering once more. He wrested control of the car and it jerked away from the tram at the last moment.

Searching his mirrors, Arlo spotted Casey's car. It was still firmly on his tail.

The voice at the other end bellowed, "Where are you now!"

Shaking his head, Arlo dropped his hand to the centre console, flicking the touch screen with his finger and bringing up a satellite image.

"Heading east. Out of the city. I'm close to the freeway."

"Keep going. Lead her away and I will try to contain the damage here."

"What the fuck am I supposed to with her?"

There was another pause at the other end of the line as Arlo flicked his eyes down at the screen then back up on the road ahead.

"You're close to bushland and the river. Get off the main road. Get her into that bushland. Finish her."

The voice disconnected abruptly.

Arlo gulped in the confines of the cabin then winced in pain from the action.

"Damn it!"

As he wiped fresh blood from his upper lip he looked ahead, spying a major intersection approaching. Steeling himself, Arlo checked his mirrors. She was still there. As they closed the distance to the intersection, the lights changed to amber.

He was going to have to time this just right. Tapping the brake pedal, he slowed the car just enough and began to count backwards silently.

Casey saw Arlo's single remaining brake light wink. She reacted in anticipation as she saw the intersection looming.

As the traffic lights blinked amber, she looked down and spotted the flashing red and blue lights of a police pursuit car rushing towards the intersection from the opposite side.

"Oh shit!"

Arlo must have seen it too, for, as they swallowed up the last few metres of road, the BMW lurched to the left, sliding into the intersection as the traffic lights turned red. A white commercial van waiting to cross over entered the intersection, right into the path of the pursuit car.

Casey stomped on her brakes, shedding speed and spinning her wheel to avoid catastrophe. Arlo snaked back and forth, his rear tyres finding purchase as the BMW shot forward out of harm's way. The pursuit car collided sickeningly with the van while Casey's Volkswagen managed to corner the intersection, then it surged forward.

Casey grabbed her rear-vision mirror and looked into it, seeing the chaos behind her. Two more police vehicles had arrived at the intersection, while civilian traffic had banked up in all directions.

Slapping the mirror away, Casey grimaced and focused forward.

Arlo's BMW had shot ahead alarmingly, its sleek form rapidly shrinking. Dropping the VW back a gear, Casey gunned the engine and it whined in protest. She feared she would not be able to catch up to Arlo's high performance vehicle, but she had to try.

Ignoring the traffic, Arlo weaved recklessly in between cars and trucks, hugging the inner lane that flanked a median strip. Punching his horn and screaming at anyone who got in his way, the traffic had the good sense to clear out. However one such vehicle, a refrigerated commercial truck, appeared not to see him and stubbornly remained in his path. Arlo screamed in anger as he was forced to brake hard.

As Casey raced along, pushing her car to its limits, she saw Arlo's car wedged in behind the truck. She allowed herself a malevolent grin and pulled hard to her left until she drew alongside Arlo. She glanced through her side window at the BMW. His own tinted windows revealed nothing. Suddenly, a turn-off emerged up ahead and the truck pulled away to the right, opening up the lane in front of the BMW. It jerked forwards but Casey was prepared for it. She planted her foot and although she feared the VW's engine would explode from its mounts, she vowed she would not lose Arlo again.

The suburban landscape rushed past in a blur. The houses and shops and buildings on both sides seemed to close in on them as both cars leapt over frequent rises, issuing showers of sparks as they slapped down again. The traffic around them careened out of their way and sounded their horns in panic at the nightmare rushing past them.

Casey looked further ahead, noticing signs for the Eastern Freeway.

She hissed.

If Arlo made it to the freeway, he would be gone for sure.

She wrenched her steering wheel, slamming the Volkswagen into the side of Arlo's coupe, but he swerved clear. A median strip split the road in two and Arlo drifted across into the right-hand lane. Casey remained where she was, watching on in horror as he belted through oncoming traffic.

And then, suddenly, an overpass loomed ahead. The freeway entrance.

"Oh shit!" Casey hissed as Arlo's BMW swerved across from the extreme right-hand side, maintaining its crazed speed.

He's making for the entrance!

Reacting instinctively, Casey gunned the Volkswagen, putting herself between Arlo and the interchange.

Arlo slammed into Casey's side, crumpling the driver's side door inward and causing her airbag to deploy. Casey was flung sideways from the impact and her head struck the glass of the driver's side door hard that a thin crack opened up in it.

The world tilted before her, but she refused to succumb. Slapping the airbag away, she glared through the cracked glass and saw that her action had prevented Arlo from reaching his apparent goal. However, in a frightening squeal of metal and sparks, both cars careened up onto the overpass, neither one of them relenting as a dozen more vehicles rushed to get out of the way.

The BMW mounted a median strip, launching itself into the air. Casey fought to maintain control as the Volkswagen skipped across the road. Her vision from her right eye clouded and reaching up Casey winced as a deep laceration leaked blood down over her face. Wiping it clear, she looked ahead in time to see Arlo's car as it veered across the opposite lanes. Smoke belched from under the bonnet. Flames licked the bitumen from behind the front tyre.

To her utter disbelief, the BMW poured on a fresh burst of speed, peeling away and racing down the overpass ahead of her.

"Jesus!" she yelled, giving chase.

Casey noticed almost right away that something was seriously wrong. The coupe swerved sickeningly, unable to maintain a straight line. She dropped away from him, creating a safe distance between them as the elevated roadway angled around to the right and dense bushland emerged on either side.

Suddenly, a metallic scream erupted from Arlo's car and Casey skidded to a complete stop. She watched in horror as the BMW veered sharply and collided with a steel barrier fence separating the road from the bushland beyond, obliterating it as it careened forward, completely out of control.

There was a final agonised howl from its engine before it crashed through the fence completely and disappeared from view.

CHAPTER 33

"This doesn't look good."

Scott slowed the van as he approached the turn for Arbelside Avenue. A white and blue highway patrol car was parked across the intersection, its roof-mounted lights flashing brightly.

A lone, uniformed police officer standing beside the vehicle was talking into a radio mic secured to his shoulder. He turned as the van approached and waved for it to stop. Bringing the van to a crawl, Scott nonetheless signalled his intention as the officer patted the roof of his patrol car. A second uniformed officer, a young woman, stepped out from the passenger side.

Lionel fidgeted self-consciously, watching as the two officers approached. Scott lowered his window as the young woman uncoupled a heavy torch from her belt and raised it at them.

"I'm sorry, sir, but this street is closed to all traffic until further notice," she said officiously.

Lionel glanced into the avenue and saw at least a half-dozen more police vehicles parked in the centre of the street. There were patrol cars, vans and even a truck, all with their lights flashing, bathing the street in an eerie glow. As the young officer played her beam over Lionel, he leaned towards her.

"Senior Constable, we need to pass immediately. We were summoned here by Detective Sergeant Prishna Argawaal."

Though the officer's expression remained blank, one eyebrow flicked perceptibly.

She glanced across at her colleague who was also eyeing Lionel suspiciously. Lifting the microphone from his shoulder clasp, he pressed the transmit button. Neither Scott or Lionel could hear what he was saying.

A garbled voice came back over the handheld. His blank expression faltered and he seemed to regard Lionel with surprise. Nodding once at his young colleague, she turned and peered at Lionel. Her expression was one of shocked recognition. For his part, Scott glanced repeatedly between her and Lionel in confusion.

"You can pass through, Mr. Broadbent," she said with something akin to reverence. "D.S. Argawaal is on scene at Number 5. She'll escort you in."

Stepping aside, she ushered the van through. Scott took his cue and crept forward slowly, nodding at both officers.

"What just happened then?" he quizzed Lionel in an incredulous, high-pitched tone.

"Apparently thirty years on the force still carries some weight," he answered awkwardly.

Scott eyeballed him as they continued but said nothing.

The property at Number 5 was a beehive of activity, with dozens of uniformed and plainclothes officers swarming over the house which had been illuminated from the front lawn by two powerful lighting arrays.

As Scott parked the van, Lionel spied Prishna coming towards them through the gate. He opened the door and stepped down. Prishna nodded at him silently.

"Mr. Broadbent, sir," she said grimly, offering her hand to Lionel. "I ahhh…it seems Casey was right. She was right all along. She's made a significant discovery in there." Prishna rubbed her brow in bewilderment.

Lionel looked over her shoulder at the house. "You've confirmed it?"

Prishna nodded. "It's big. It's *very* big."

Scott emerged from the far side of the van and scanned the street, searching among the myriad vehicles for one in particular. Lionel followed Scott's gaze along the street.

There was no sign of Casey's car.

"Casey told me it was Francis Arlo. Dr. Francis Arlo," he worried. "She was in trouble. He was in there in the house with her."

Prishna held out her hands.

"There's no one here now but we've got several patrols out looking for them. We've had reports come in that two cars were seen heading east along Cotham Road within the past hour."

Lionel glanced at a cluster of personnel, who were milling around the laneway entrance beside the house. Suddenly, they parted to allow a large tow truck to emerge into the street. As the entire length of the vehicle came into view, his jaw slackened. Sitting on its back, covered in a thin layer of dust, was a navy blue Audi coupe.

"Jesus," Scott whispered as the tow truck rounded a patrol car and trundled along the street in front of them. Lionel couldn't speak. He could only watch as the manifestation of Casey's nightmares passed by him.

A uniformed constable approached Prishna from the front of the house holding up the microphone of a handheld radio.

"Prishna!" he called urgently. "Central just advised us of reports of a car being abandoned on the Burke Road overpass for the Eastern. Sounds like it's been pretty banged up."

Scott and Lionel glared at each other then turned away from Prishna.

"Route the patrols to that location immediately!" she ordered.

Scott fired up the van's engine as Lionel climbed in and slammed his door shut.

Prishna reached out to signal Lionel to wait, but the officer tapped her shoulder.

"You've got another problem. The Feds are inbound. They're pushing to take over the scene."

Prishna gnashed her teeth. "Get me Whittaker immediately. The Feds are a part of the problem."

"Mr. Broadbent! Please wait!"

Lionel shook his head. "You've got your work cut out for you. I need to find my granddaughter."

The van jerked violently, completing a one hundred and eighty degree turn. Then it tore off toward the intersection.

The crumpled BMW lay on its side at the bottom of a hill below the roadway. Smoke poured from the engine compartment. Sparks crackled inside the cabin while number of small spot fires had erupted around the wreck, but were already dying as a light rain began to fall.

Supporting her injured shoulder, Casey hobbled slowly down the hillside towards the car, watching carefully for signs of life. Fresh blood began to seep from the laceration above her eye as the rain loosened the crust that had formed over it. Her head throbbed. Fresh nausea roiled her stomach. Willing the sensations away, she focused on the car.

As she stepped down onto the flats and came within a few feet of the wreck, she bent down and squinted, trying to see through the ruined rear windshield. The shattered glass obscured her view. She hesitated, gritting her teeth, not wanting to get any closer even as her curiosity pulled to overwhelm her.

Her caution prevailed and she eventually backed away. Circling around the car, she faced the roof, noting its sunroof had been destroyed.

Approaching to within a few feet, she peered into the interior.

It was empty.

Her hackles rose. She rushed towards the car and looked through the open sunroof. There was no sign of Arlo at all. She whipped her head up and away from the car, towards the surrounding bush behind her and then back up the embankment towards the roadway.

Without warning, the white hot pain she experienced earlier ripped through her chest once more and she doubled over in agony. Clutching her shirt front, grabbing the car for support, Casey hissed through clenched teeth, riding the intensity of the pain until it passed.

Blinking furiously, she caught her breath then stood straighter.

What was that?

She stepped back from the wreck and turned.

A fist swooped in from behind and smashed into the side of her face. At the sickening blow, her body spun violently away from the car. She hit the ground, chin-first several feet away, the impact snapping her head up. Eruptions of light billowed in front of her eyes before the world began to tip sideways. A fresh adrenaline surge enabled Casey to keep the unconsciousness at bay and she scrambled across the sodden ground. Flipping herself over, Casey faced her attacker.

Arlo stood near the car. His shirt was torn and covered in blood and dirt. His bloodied face was puffy and bruised. A mighty laceration ran from the middle of his brow and up over his head where part of his scalp had been peeled back like the skin of an orange.

As her spinning vision slowed, Casey noted his left arm was hanging uselessly at his side. Evidently, it had been torn from the shoulder as his car crashed through the barrier fence.

Steadying himself against the car, Arlo panted heavily, his once handsome face dripping sweat and blood. He started towards Casey but he couldn't maintain his balance. He slipped on the muddy ground and yelped in pain. All at once, the fire went out from his eyes. He collapsed to his knees several feet from her, crying out as his ruined arm slapped the ground.

"I've always liked you, Casey," he slurred through a bloodied grin. "Of all the candidates I've ever known, I thought you were the most deserving. In fact, I would have done anything to ensure you received that gift inside you. I did…in the end."

As quickly as his grin had appeared, his face morphed into a mask of anger. "You could have just lived your life!" he screamed. "We gave you a second chance!"

Casey blinked at the pathetic character in front of her.

Fedele's assistant surgeon.

Saskia's killer.

"You know...she wasn't actually dead...when we took her heart," he continued, his voice quivering on the edge of madness.

Casey's eyes bulged in horror.

"She could have lived...had I allowed her to... "

Casey staggered where she stood and she dropped to her knees. The pain in her chest blossomed again, taking her breath away and she clutched at the collar of her shirt.

"From the moment you gave me her heart," she retorted. "You gave me her memories. Her last hours."

Arlo glared incredulously at her. She began to shake uncontrollably.

"She found you out, didn't she? You were looking for asylum seekers to harvest organs from and Saskia found out what you were doing. And you killed her for it!" She stabbed her finger directly at him. "You did it all, *you bastard*!"

Incredibly, Arlo's lips turned up in a bitter smile. He shook his head.

"I underestimated her. I thought the money I offered her would be enough to...*convince* her...just like the others. She wouldn't be convinced. So I had to act."

"The money?" Casey hissed incredulously.

Arlo raised his head and looked at her drunkenly. "Y-you have no idea how b-big this is."

Suddenly, Casey sprang to her knees and snarled as she rushed him, grabbing him by the throat. She no longer feared for her safety and Arlo was too spent to retaliate. She glowered at him, piercing deep into his blank eyes. For a fleeting moment, a vision of the boy in the photograph from the house flashed before her eyes and she gasped, seeing the child's features in Arlo's face here and now.

"Who was Davich?" she snarled, snapping his neck like a rag doll.

Arlo's expression melted into a twisted grin that conveyed agony and insanity in equal measure.

"Family," he gurgled. "A dear and...overly trusting uncle. Easy to manipulate and dispose of."

Something snapped in Casey's head as she battled to comprehend Arlo's horrific admission. "Who's in this with you?" she screamed. "Elyria? Sonmez?

Tell me!"

Arlo cackled as Casey tightened her grip around his neck, choking off his voice.

Francis Arlo no longer cared. That which he had feared for so long—being discovered—was now happening. He resigned himself to it. The only thing that surprised him was that it was Casey Schillinge who had uncovered it.

Fedele's star patient. One of their greatest successes.

"Elyria…was just a means to an end," he wheezed. "It got us the access we needed to the best *meat*. And S-Sonmez?" Arlo chuckled bitterly at the name, then grimaced as he twisted his neck in a vain attempt to loosen it from Casey's grip. "H-he was the real genius," Arlo continued. "The boss and he go way back. Afghanistan was where it all began. Harvesting organs from the battlefield, he called it. Jarsayah Sonmez was his fixer, able to secure the best clients. Wealthy, fat millionaires who were desperate for replacement organs because they had trashed their own. For the right price…*we made that happen*."

Casey struggled to take in Arlo's horrific revelations.

The battlefield? Afghanistan?

A memory flashed before her eyes.

Two soldiers, adorned in heavy field gear, embracing one another in the desert.

As Arlo sank further in her grip, Casey spat on him and shoved him backwards. He crumpled to ground, howling in agony.

"Who's 'we'?!" she screamed, glaring at him as he struggled on the ground in front of her.

She didn't have to ask the question. She already knew the answer. But she wanted to hear it from him. She wanted Arlo to speak the name out loud.

"*Who's we*!?"

Arlo curled up into a ball and began wailing uncontrollably. He had fallen over the edge, into an abyss of madness.

He snapped his head up to stare at her but, as he pointed his finger, Casey realised that he wasn't looking at her at all.

He was looking past her.

Casey spun around and looked up to see a lone figure shrouded in silhouette from the street lamps behind them.

He was holding a gun.

A flash from the nightmare…

"Boss!" Arlo howled before descending into a fit of coughing.

Casey's eyes grew wide. She scrambled across the ground in a desperate attempt to get to her feet. The stranger raised the gun and a single shot rang out into the night. Casey grunted as the bullet smashed through her collar bone sending blood and tissue cascading up and over her face. The impact lifted her off her feet, throwing her backwards where she sprawled on the ground.

She was helpless, unable to move. The pain was so intense that it stole her ability to scream. The world began to spin and she felt herself being sucked towards the edge of darkness.

Her head lolled back and she could see Arlo sprawled like a rag doll on the ground.

His head was turned towards her. The crazed smile was plastered on his face but he gazed at her with lifeless eyes as a powerful geyser of red fountained from the side of his neck.

Casey looked back to see a hulking figure standing over her, pointing the gun at her. She was too stunned to make any sound.

She gazed in horror into a pair of expressionless eyes.

In the half-light, he stepped closer, cocked his weapon and lowered it towards Casey's temple.

This was it.

Suddenly, he tossed the gun over in his hand, grabbing the barrel so that the stock of the weapon was facing towards her. Swinging his hand down, he struck Casey hard above her right eye.

Her world exploded. She felt a pair of powerful hands lifting her from the ground and she vomited as she was jerked into the air.

What is happening!?

Then the veil lowered completely.

Lionel saw the Volkswagen before Scott did. As they approached the sweeping bend of the overpass, Scott's attention was drawn to the mass of police vehicles parked across the four lanes. A pair of fire trucks, two tow trucks and a single ambulance were parked further along while a helicopter buzzed overhead, its powerful spotlight playing across the scene and the bushland beyond. It wasn't until Lionel tapped his arm and pointed at Casey's stricken car that Scott noticed.

"Oh, sweet Jesus," Scott grumbled fearfully.

Lionel stomach twisted.

The road had been cordoned off with police tape and a patrol car and a uniformed officer in wet weather gear walked towards the slowing van, waving an illuminated wand above his head. Shifting down through the gears, Scott began to slow. Lionel grabbed his arm.

"Don't stop."

Scott blinked at him.

"We *have to*," he protested.

Lionel shook his head defiantly. "We bloody well don't! Keep going!"

Retreating from the brake, Scott accelerated and the van jerked forward, its tyres screeching. The police officer stopped waving the wand and stiffened. His eyes bulged and he leapt out of the path of the careening van at the very last moment.

Scott swerved around the stationary pursuit car, bursting through the tape and speeding onward towards Casey's Volkswagen as the startled officer—along with two of his colleagues—gave chase on foot.

Ignoring a further group of personnel rushing towards them, Lionel surveyed the scene, noting the ruined barrier fence and the personnel standing before it. He looked across to the ambulance, hoping to see Casey. She wasn't there.

She wasn't anywhere.

Scott skidded to a stop just behind the stricken Volkswagen and gulped as a dozen uniformed police surrounded them, weapons drawn. He raised his hands and shrank back in his seat.

Lionel took no notice of them.

He threw open his door and jumped down, rushing to Casey's car. His jaw dropped in horror. The entire length of the driver's side had been crumpled inward. The door's window had been shattered and he could see trails of blood on the glass.

He felt sick.

A police constable rushed up behind Lionel, grabbing him by the shoulder and spinning him around.

"Don't move!" he screamed. "On your knees NOW!"

Lionel blinked at him as a second officer took hold of him and swiftly wrapped his leg around Lionel's, forcing him to his knees.

Lionel winced in pain as he thudded to the road.

"STOP!"

The officers flinched at the sound of the voice.

Lionel looked up as Farnham Whittaker appeared on the roadway from the ruined fence opposite.

"Get him up now!" Whittaker barked.

The police officers blinked and withdrew as Whittaker pushed in between them, shielding Lionel from the weapons that were trained on him.

"Everybody back down!"

The group complied, withdrawing their weapons slowly and stepping back.

Scott cautiously opened his door and stepped down, holding his hands out as he sidestepped to Lionel's side.

"Lionel," Whittaker began tersely, helping him to his feet.

"Where is she?" Lionel cut him off, turning back to the car and slapping the bonnet.

"We're searching the surrounding bush and down by the river now but we…ahh…haven't found—"

Lionel's eyes drilled deep into Whittaker's. "*She's not here*?" he exclaimed, his voice shaking.

"Look, Lionel. There's a body at the bottom of the embankment. Bu—"

Before Whittaker could finish, Lionel pushed past him and marched towards the ruined barrier. Pausing at the top, he looked down and saw jump-suited crime scene investigators milling about the wreck of a sports car at the bottom of the embankment. A few feet away from the wreck, a white tarpaulin covered a distinctly human form.

"No!"

Plunging down the embankment, Lionel rushed to the tarpaulin. Several of the crime scene investigators turned to block him, but he shoved them out of the way.

His heart in his mouth, Lionel grabbed the edge of the tarpaulin and ripped it back to reveal Arlo's ruined face, staring vacantly up at him.

He stiffened, then staggered.

"Arlo," he gasped.

Whittaker and Scott came up beside Lionel. Whittaker held up his hand to an investigator who had just picked herself up off the ground and was coming towards them.

"Who did this?" Lionel choked.

Whittaker blinked at him.

"Well…we're guessing it was Casey," he started.

Lionel flung the tarpaulin to the ground in disgust.

"Rubbish," he snarled, turning and marching back up the hillside. "Casey has never owned a weapon of any sort in her life. She hates guns."

"I'm sorry, Lionel, but until we can find her..." Whittaker responded grimly.

Lionel fished his phone from his pocket, bringing up Casey's number and dialling it.

"I spoke to her when she was at the house. Her line went dead."

Keying her number, he listened as the ringer sounded over and over.

No answer.

A police constable jogged up to them from the far end of the roadway.

"Whittaker," he called urgently. "You better come and take a look at this."

Whittaker hesitated as Lionel and Scott looked at one another. The three of them followed the constables. A group of police investigators were gathered together on the bitumen, a few feet away from the cordon. They were examining the road surface.

"What is it?" Whittaker barked.

One of the investigators stepped forward.

"Sir, take a look," he said pointing at the road. "The rain has affected it a bit but we've got fresh tread. Someone left here in a big hurry and it was definitely within the last hour."

A solid pair of skid marks extended roughly twenty feet away towards the overpass from where they stood.

"A *third* car?"

The investigator nodded. "We've ruled out the Volkswagen and the BMW. The distance between these marks is too wide for either car. This was something bigger."

"Jesus," Lionel wheezed. "She was taken."

His legs buckled. Scott reacted swiftly, grabbing him around his waist.

Whittaker turned to Lionel. His face was ashen.

"We'll get a patrol on this right away. It's not much to go on though. We need *something*."

Scott steered Lionel away from the group and walked him over to the van. He opened the side door and sat him down in the opening.

Whittaker and the constable followed closely.

"You said you were on the phone with Casey before she disconnected. Did she say anything?"

Lionel shook his head in frustration.

"Have you checked in with Prishna? At the house?" he asked shakily. "She said they found a lot of evidence—papers from a firm called Elyria Medical Services."

Whittaker nodded at the constable who turned away and unclipped his radio from his belt.

Lionel tried to calm himself and remember what Casey had said to him before the line went dead.

He looked up at Scott.

"At the house, when I was on the phone with her, Casey mentioned a name," Lionel stammered, clutching his forehead. "*Something* Sonmez. It was definitely Sonmez."

Whittaker took out his smartphone and tapped out the name on the screen. He showed it to Lionel. "Is this right?"

Lionel shrugged. "I can only guess."

The constable turned to face them while still talking into the handset. Whittaker signalled him and handed him the phone.

"Run that name. Pair it with Francis Arlo's and see if it turns up anything. *Quickly*!"

He turned back to Lionel and dropped to his haunches.

"Is there anyone else who might have known about what Casey was doing? Anyone from among her circle?"

"No one knew she was looking into this. Except you and me and Prishna."

The constable jogged briskly towards them, holding the radio up. His expression was plagued with urgency.

"Sir. Central just ran the name. They said nothing showed up between Arlo and Sonmez."

Whittaker grimaced and scratched his head. The constable tapped him urgently on the shoulder.

"But it did show up something else."

The constable hesitated as he handed a piece of paper to Whittaker who snatched from him and examined it.

He paled visibly. He worked his jaw while Lionel and Scott glared at him.

It was Scott who spoke up. "What is it?"

Lionel sprang to his feet and grabbed the sheet of paper from Whittaker. He looked down at the information and choked audibly. Scott leaned across to see.

Whittaker turned to the constable. "Get onto this," he ordered. "I want special operations at this address *now*!"

As Whittaker turned back to face Lionel, Scott had turned on his heel and climbed up through the open side door into the cabin. He started the van and turned in his seat.

"C'mon, Mr. Broadbent, we're going!"

Whittaker gasped and stepped toward the van as Lionel climbed up into it.

"Jesus Christ, Lionel," Whittaker barked, as Lionel slammed the door in his face.

Lionel took up his position in the passenger seat as Scott revved the engine hard and Whittaker tripped sideways as he lunged towards Lionel's door. He grabbed the edge of the window.

"What the bloody hell do you think you're going to do?"

"I'm going to get her. And him."

Lionel grabbed Whittaker's fingers and peeled them from the door frame as Scott shoved the van into gear. The van leapt forward and circled around. Various police officers scrambled to get clear as it leapt over the median strip and roared away towards the city.

CHAPTER 34

A SWIRLING PALL OF DARKNESS.

No light.

No sound.

Was this the dream?

Casey became aware of an intense throbbing in her head. As she emerged from unconsciousness, her head started to spin sickeningly.

She knew she wasn't dreaming.

Her body swayed as though she were rolling on an ocean and her stomach lurched violently. Even though she was only partially aware, her body shook and she vomited over herself.

Shaking her head, she forced her eyelids open. With great effort, her left eye fluttered open. She noted immediately that something was preventing the right eye from following suit. Confused and angry, she exerted as much effort as she could to move it.

Then she remembered.

A lightning flash. A shard of a memory.

The final blow before the world went dark. The swing of an arm whose hand was clutching cold, hard steel.

From the memory, pain blossomed into the present and she could feel its intensity in the deep cut over her right eye. Congealed blood streamed from it and it had hardened to a thick crust.

With her functioning eye, all she could see was a blinding light that dazzled her; a kaleidoscope of colour through an intense backwash of white.

As she attempted to lift her hand to block out the light, she felt a firm grip around her wrist that prevented her from moving it. She tensed her arms against the bonds that held her. They were stretched out on either side of her body and had been secured to some kind of hard surface.

Her skin prickled. The air was cold and she realised that her clothes had been removed. With the exception of her briefs, she was naked.

Her breath quickened. Her pulse throbbed in her temples.

She attempted to shift her legs but realised that they also were immobilised. Craning her neck, Casey looked down to see that three thick straps had been passed over her chest and hips and pulled tight.

Further down, looking past her bare legs and feet, Casey saw that she was in fact not laying down but had been angled into a semi-upright position: a modern day version of the crucifixion.

The surgical bed on which she lay wasn't so much a bed but an elaborate examination table, the kind one would expect to see in a hospital operating theatre.

She was utterly trapped.

Holding her breath to block out the putrid smell of her own vomit, Casey recruited as much strength as she could, channelling it into her mind and her muscles. She bucked against the leather, crying out angrily.

The heart thumped so violently it felt as though it would burst from her. Dizziness overwhelmed her again and resistance left her. The light began to fade. She wanted to crawl back into the darkness.

Casey! A disembodied voice screamed in her mind. *Wake up!*

With a supreme effort, she fought to stop the world from spinning. Conscious thoughts began to flow.

Where am I?

Casey blinked against the light and, for a brief moment she wondered if she had been brought to the psychiatric unit but she quickly dismissed this. Not even they would restrain her like this.

She became aware of a soft and steady beeping that came from behind her. The subtle hum of a fluorescent light from somewhere above. The mechanised breath of a ventilator beside her.

Casey blinked and scanned her surroundings. She was in a room, a chamber of some kind. There were no windows or, as far as she could tell, doors. She could make out a long, white cabinet and bench along one wall that was overflowing with medical items: surgical tools, fluid bags, equipment. The cupboards were stocked with bottles and boxes of varying sizes, indicative of medicines.

Sitting on top of these cupboards was a collection of large glass jars containing dark gelatinous objects that appeared to be floating in fluid. As her eyes further adjusted, Casey realised they were specimen jars; the objects within them were organs. Human organs.

She felt the urge to retch yet again. In one jar, there was a set of lungs. In another, a bean-shaped pair of kidneys. And another, the bulbous mass of a liver.

She recoiled in disgust and, as she blinked, she looked down past her feet to a stainless steel trolley that stood several feet away from her bed. On it sat a jar that was much smaller than the others on the cabinet. Floating in a yellow liquid was a heart. It was dark and swollen, diseased looking. From the thick vessels that crowned the organ, thin filaments erupted like a hundred stringy fingers reaching into the air in silent desperation.

A worm infested heart.

Casey had read about the worms in textbooks and online medical articles that she had explored after her transplant in an effort to understand what had happened to her.

Could this be her own heart?

Her mind reeled and she pulled her eyes away.

An empty examination bed stood to her left, identical to the one on which she lay. Beyond that, she identified a trio of large cylinders with medical gas labels printed on them. Above her head, Casey noted a vital signs monitor. Waveforms snaked their way across the screen, accompanied by numbers that flicked up and down randomly.

Her vital signs.

Casey followed a thick band of cables down from the monitor until they passed out of view and then reappeared beside her right shoulder where it split into three smaller cables of red, black and white. These were attached to her.

This is it. The chamber mentioned in the notes at the house.

The place where it all happened.

The pain in her chest had returned. She steeled herself against it but, this time, the pain did not subside. It remained, like a hand equipped with razor blades that was pushing down into her chest.

From somewhere inside the walls, Casey became aware of a new sound. A soft, mechanical hum that descended from above. It rose in volume and shifted until it was coming from somewhere ahead. Blinking against the light, she strained to focus.

The wall at the far end of the chamber split apart; a thickening shard of light bled from it as a pair of lift doors slid open. A figure stepped forward.

She couldn't see him, but she could smell him.

The fragrance of his aftershave was unmistakable.

Even in her terror, Casey refused to believe it was true.

"Ah, you're awake."

Simeera Fedele's caramel voice sounded as he entered the chamber and casually walked up to Casey's bed.

She turned her head away and squeezed her eyes shut. Disbelief and grief collided within her.

A gentle hand cupped her chin, turning her head. She couldn't resist. She opened her eye and looked up at him.

Fedele appeared serene. He looked down on her with the same compassion that she had always known. Releasing his grip, he returned both hands to his pockets. His expensive shirt was unbuttoned and still bore the blood spatters from their confrontation.

Casey began to shake. Her pupils dilated. Her nostrils flared.

"How are you feeling?" he asked, infusing his voice with genuine concern.

She remained silent.

Reaching across, Fedele examined the cut over her forehead. Casey flinched, jerking her head away from him but he ignored her. He pursed his lips sympathetically.

"That's a nasty cut. I shall clean that up for you. I don't want it to become infected."

He turned to the bench behind him and began preparing a surgical tray, selecting medical supplies from the cupboards and placing them beside it. He transferred the tray to Casey's bedside and sat down beside her, angling the examination light above them over her face.

"I hope you don't mind but I went ahead and treated your shoulder. The bone is shattered, I'm afraid, but my first concern was the wound itself. It was quite dirty and you've lost a lot of blood."

Her breathing was quick. She stared at him in disbelief and terror.

Fedele lifted a pair of stainless steel forceps in his gloved hand and clasped a square of gauze, dipping it into a chlorhexidine solution before bringing it down over Casey's eye. He began to clean it gently, removing the crusted blood. Underneath, it had already begun to swell; the surrounding skin was turning dark.

As Fedele swabbed the wound, Casey shook even harder. He paused and looked down on her, his expression kind and reassuring.

"Casey, you must calm yourself," he said softly. "I don't want to cause more harm to the laceration. I'm sure you don't either." His eyes danced over the wound as he continued cleaning it. "It's quite deep, almost—no—it is *right down* to the bone. I can see it."

He hissed with concern, discarding the blood-soaked gauze into a bin before collecting a fresh one. Casey opened her right eye as best she could, just as Fedele turned back to her.

He smiled and clucked approvingly. "The bruising and swelling will likely worsen," he said. "But the eye itself seems to be intact."

He continued to work, his manner remaining utterly calm and professional. Her mind screamed as she tried to make sense of what was happening.

Satisfied with his work, Fedele switched tools, preparing suture material and opening a fresh pair of sterile forceps. He secured a small, hook-shaped needle into their jaws, then drew up an anaesthetic solution into a syringe, attaching a fine needle. He turned to Casey and smiled.

"I'm just going to inject some local into the skin around the laceration. These sutures can be quite painful."

Casey winced as the needle pierced her skin. She could feel the anaesthetic infiltrating the tissues around the cut, numbing the area. The pain disappeared almost immediately.

Fedele took the forceps in his hand and lowered it towards Casey. She could feel the pressure of the needle entering her skin; the pull of the cotton through it as he worked steadily, methodically, bringing the edges of the laceration together. He was pleased with his work, pausing every so often to check it, before continuing.

"I'm afraid there will be a scar. Not a prominent one, but it will be there," he said, with a hint of sadness. "It is disappointing. I did not want this to be my last memory of you."

Casey's stomach plunged.

The timbre and gentleness of his voice shifted and, in that moment, she knew.

As Fedele completed the last suture, he snipped the end with a pair of scissors and withdrew, placing the equipment down on the tray. He took an adhesive dressing and applied it to the wound.

When he looked down on her, his expression had completely changed. Gone was the gentle, charismatic and sympathetic surgeon she had always known. His jaw had set. His eyes were dark and chilling. He looked upon her with something akin to disgust and hatred. But there was also disappointment and betrayal.

Ripping the gloves from his hands, he tossed them aside and leaned in close to her face.

"Casey, Casey," he began with a whisper. "You have created such a mess."

Despite her terror, Casey managed to furrow her brow in bewilderment.

"Me?" she croaked.

Fedele nodded.

"It is a well-documented policy—law even—that the recipient of a life-saving organ should not seek to find or make contact with their donor. But you..." His bellicose voice trailed away and he lifted his head toward the ceiling. "You had to know. You had to push. That is your nature isn't it? To stretch the boundaries, go places you should not. I should have seen you coming a long time ago."

Fedele's hand drifted down to the strap holding her right wrist. Pushing his fingers underneath the leather, he grasped it tightly and yanked on it as hard as he could. A lightning bolt of pain shot up Casey's arm.

"The question is how?" He gazed into her eyes, a flicker of predatory curiosity emerging from the hardened stone of his expression. "How did you do it?"

Casey gulped and blinked, forcing herself to think. "Every system has a v-vulnerability. A weak link," she stammered, remembering a sentence from an old cryptography textbook. "All it takes is an algorithm robust enough—*tenacious enough*—to exploit it. Eventually the vulnerability will be exposed, drawn out and eliminated."

Fedele nodded and allowed a bitter smile to form. "Arlo," he said wistfully.

He stood and moved to one side. Nodding his head, he slowly walked the length of the chamber in front of Casey, hands in his pockets.

"He was always a vulnerability," he ventured thoughtfully. "But easily manipulated, particularly where money was involved. It did, however, make him effective...for the most part. In the end, Arlo couldn't decide which world he wanted to occupy. He was drawn to the power of the enterprise and how it fed his ego. He wanted the good things but he lacked discretion. Arlo's vulnerability lay in his inability to commit to one path. Thus, the flaw in this system was...exposed, as you say."

Fedele smiled, as though impressed by the genius of Casey's deduction. "Clever girl."

Casey watched him continue to pace. Slowly, patiently.

"By eliminating this vulnerability, the system remains intact," he continued. "This is the expertise for which you are so highly sought after, isn't it? But there is still an external threat."

Fedele stopped pacing directly in front of Casey and turned to face her. He extended his finger. "*You*. All that is left then is to eliminate you."

Casey tensed as he stepped towards her. He began to unbutton his shirt.

"You can't."

"Oh?" Fedele challenged her mockingly, removing his shirt completely and tossing it to one side. "Once you are gone, there will be nothing left. You, after all, have a rather fatalistic personality. A troubled young woman with a long history of psychiatric illness and drug abuse stemming from your inability to adjust post-transplant. You have already made a significant attempt on your own life. It is well-documented. A suicide is very easy to construct. Particularly when you are a surgeon of my calibre."

Casey watched in horror as Fedele removed his belt and unbuttoned his trousers, allowing them to fall to his knees. He was naked underneath. His erection throbbed visibly as he stared at her.

"But you can't," she repeated. Fedele frowned, tilting his head. "You have been exposed," Casey continued. "Arlo was more formidable than you thought."

She paused, to allow the import of her words to stop Fedele as he began to approach her.

"He kept notes, records and diaries. I saw them. He exposed you at length. About what you were really doing in Afghanistan. Your links to Jarsayah Sonmez. How you were harvesting organs from captured enemy combatants for profit and how you both agreed to continue the operation afterwards. He kept it all." Casey noticed Fedele's features flicker involuntarily and he seemed to falter where he stood. "The clients Sonmez procured for you in Indonesia and South East Asia," she continued, her voice taking on a note of bitter defiance. "How you facilitated Arlo's position with Elyria Medical Services so he could provide health checks for asylum seekers: your donors. How you used your connections with the government to secure those donors in exchange for payment. Arlo kept it all."

Casey let her muscles relax.

"The police are coming for you, Fedele. You can't do anything more."

A thick silence descended between them. Casey closed her eyes, the sound of the monitor above her head echoed distantly. Defeat began to seep into her.

Without warning, Fedele's expression changed and he snarled, swooping towards Casey until his face was centimetres from hers. Casey blinked in shock. His teeth ground together noisily, threateningly. The muscles in his jaw were so taut they quivered.

"Oh, but I can, Casey," he seethed, peppering her chin with his spittle. "I can do *plenty*."

Reaching down, Fedele traced a finger between her naked breasts and down over her belly to the top of her cotton briefs. Clutching the material in his fingers, he grimaced and with a surge of strength, Fedele tore the briefs from Casey's body, tossing them aside. He stood back and looked down upon her naked form. His hand dropped to his thickening penis and he stroked it while licking his lips.

Casey attempted to look away in revulsion.

She could see he was losing control; a state that she doubted he had rarely, if ever, experienced.

Her revelations had caused something to snap and he was now beyond reason, beyond the veneer of the powerful, charismatic and influential heart surgeon.

Leaning in again, Fedele lowered his hand to her chest and traced a finger across her right nipple toward the scar.

"I gave you a gift, Casey. All you had to do was move on with your life."

"Saskia wouldn't let me," Casey whispered with resignation. "From the moment you gave me her heart, her torment became mine."

Fedele blinked. He withdrew from her, gazing upon her with revulsion.

"These *dreams*?"

He looked away, shaking his head incredulously, then turned to the medical cabinet along the wall. Slowly, methodically, Fedele opened a drawer and took out something from inside. "Perhaps then, it is time to end your torment."

Without warning, the muffled sound of a smartphone rang out from an adjacent drawer. Fedele stopped what he was doing and wrenched the drawer open angrily, snatching the phone from inside and holding it up.

He glared at it as the sound of thrash metal rock music assailed him from the handset's tiny speaker. For the briefest of moments, Casey felt a surge of hope.

Sasquatch!

Fedele pressed the power button on the side of the handset to extinguish the noise but the phone kept spewing sound forth into the room. He thumped it against his palm, becoming apoplectic. Still the phone wouldn't silence.

Casey began silently counting to herself.

1…2…3…4…

Fedele wheeled around and glowered menacingly, thrusting the handset out at Casey. "How do I shut this fucking thing off!"

...6...7...8...9...

Infuriated by her silence, Fedele flung the phone across the room where it smashed against the wall opposite, disintegrating into several pieces. The offensive noise was silenced.

Casey turned her head away from Fedele as he continued to rage. Her eyes were drawn to the ruined remains of the smartphone which had fallen underneath the second surgical bed.

She smiled.

A small, bright green LED winked to life and blinked steadily.

Scott's van leapt over a fall in the freeway, becoming airborne for a moment before smashing down onto the bitumen in a shower of sparks. The City Link tunnel entrance loomed ahead with flashing signs warning drivers to slow down, but he ignored this, instead dropping back a gear and accelerating. The engine whined in protest and the van shot forward like a bullet.

"Get out of the bloody way!" he roared, mashing his hand on the horn as cars ahead weaved out of the way of the careening van.

Lionel clutched a handle above the door while bracing his other hand against the dashboard in front of him.

We're going die on this Godforsaken roadway.

"Do you even know where you're going, Scott?" he protested.

Scott glared at Lionel as he swerved around an SUV, then hesitated.

"I don't know! I never come to these millionaire suburbs."

"You need to slow down," Lionel countered evenly, trying to calm him.

Reluctantly, Scott tapped the brake, slowing only slightly. He shifted into the right-hand lane, which had been closed to traffic but he ignored the warning signs hanging down from the roof of the tunnel.

Adjusting the volume knob on his police scanner, Scott listened to the chatter they were following. Patrol cars had apparently converged on the Toorak residence of Simeera Fedele.

"Damn it. They beat us to the punch," Scott cursed angrily.

"No," Lionel countered suddenly, raising a finger. "Listen."

"...Negative, negative Central. Suspect is nowhere to be found. Suspect is not at this address."

Lionel and Scott glared at one another.

"Where else could he have taken her?" Scott protested.

Lionel's expression tightened.

"She could be anywhere," he whispered.

Scott flicked his gaze at the phone sitting in the dashboard cradle.

"I've gotta try her again, Lionel. If there is any chance…"

Scott quickly tapped the screen, bringing up Casey's number then pressed the dial icon.

Both men waited.

Whereas before it had gone straight to her voicemail, this time, the phone rang through.

Lionel and Scott looked at one another intently. Then, suddenly, the phone went silent.

"Shit!" Scott hissed, grabbing the handset. He prepared to redial, but was interrupted when an app opened on-screen.

He blinked in confusion. Then disbelief.

"It's her!"

Lionel frowned and sat forward. "What? She's dialling you?"

Scott shook his head. "No. She's not dialling me. Her phone is…"

He didn't finish his sentence.

Shoving the phone at Lionel, Scott wrenched the gearstick back. The van fishtailed, its tyres screamed on the bitumen until they gained purchase.

Lionel held the phone in his hand, trying to focus on the screen as the van reached the limit of the tunnel's descent and was now rocketing back up towards the exit.

On the screen, an icon flashed on and off.

'GPS signal acquisition pending.'

"What, Scott? What on Earth is it?"

Scott waved one arm insanely in the air. His face was as red as a beetroot.

"GPS! GPS!" he spluttered.

Lionel glared at Scott. "Bloody technology. I don't understand!"

"*We need a fucking GPS signal!*"

The tunnel exit came into view ahead of them, while the lane they were in became accessible again to the traffic ahead of them. Scott rammed his fist down on the horn and hollered out through his side window.

"MOVE OUT OF MY FUCKING WAY!"

The van erupted from the tunnel and into the Melbourne night. Scott yanked the steering wheel down, veering sharply across four lanes through a gap in the traffic. A massive rig loomed from behind as he entered the extreme left lane. Its air horn roared in protest. There was a piercing scream of metal on metal as the massive bull bar of the rig clipped Scott's taillight, obliterating it and crumpling the metal housing. The van shuddered and hopped violently but Scott quickly accelerated away from the truck as it braked.

"Jesus!" Lionel hissed as he struggled to hold onto the smartphone, nearly dropping it. "What is this? I don't get it!"

He squinted at the screen with its flashing message.

'GPS signal acquisition pending.'

Suddenly, the message changed.

'GPS signal acquired... Standby for location'

"It's Casey!" Scott blurted. "She put that on my phone ages ago. It's a tracking app that locks onto her phone if ever she's in trouble. She was worried that if her grey hat work ever went south, she might need it. It's like a failsafe thing."

Lionel shook his head. "This will lead us right to her?"

"To her phone, yes. Just cross your fingers and hope she's got it with her."

A satellite map of the city flashed up, with an orange dot in the centre and a blue dot that was mere millimetres above it.

"There!" Lionel snapped, pointing at the screen. He showed it to Scott. "We're practically on top of her."

"Hang on," Scott growled with a sardonic smile as he sped toward an exit ahead of them.

Fedele closed his eyes, exhaling slowly as he brought his rage under control.

Casey looked back towards him and flinched as he lowered his head and looked directly at her. The corners of his lips turned up in a beatific smile. Endorphins flowed through him, stimulating him, washing away his anger.

He sidestepped towards the cabinet and resumed his task, taking wrapped medical trays from the drawers and placing them on the stainless steel trolley. His still naked body began to glisten with sweat and Casey watched him in horror. Her right hand stiffened and flexed in the leather strap but she knew there was no hope of breaking it.

Fedele went to a sink and turned on the tap. He began washing his hands methodically, using a surgical sponge to soap his hands and arms, scrubbing them as thoroughly as he would as if he were preparing for the operating theatre. The process took minutes. He said nothing. He did not look at her. Casey could only watch.

The intense pain exploded once more from within the heart and ripped across her chest. It was ferocious enough that it took her breath away. She gasped, but stifled the sound in case Fedele heard. She squeezed her eyes shut.

Fedele finished his task then raised his arms, using his elbows to nudge the tap lever off. He turned and approached Casey, keeping his arms raised, waiting for the air to dry them.

"If you are not prepared to value the gift which I have given you," he remarked coolly, "then you do not deserve it."

He sat down on the stool once more and inspected his arms, satisfied that they were sufficiently dry. Drawing the trolley towards him with his foot, he began unwrapping the instruments and arranged the surgical tools on the sterile surface. He took a packet containing sterile surgical gloves and lay them open on the tray.

His practised movements were calm with no hint of impatience or fear. Pausing in his preparation, he turned and leaned in close to Casey, his intense eyes boring into her. She tensed, twisting her head away from him as best she could.

"You leave me no choice but to take the heart from you," he breathed menacingly. "And *I will* take it from you." He smiled and began applying the surgical gloves.

"You won't get away with this," Casey snarled in a final, if hopeless, act of defiance.

Fedele merely chuckled. "I already have."

Rotating on the stool, Fedele armed himself with a scalpel blade and held it in his right hand with the delicacy of an artist. Electric motors whirred underneath her as Fedele adjusted the bed's height. Casey felt herself lowering. He reached above her, taking a leather strap that was out of her view. Pulling it taut over her forehead, Casey felt her head snap down hard as he secured it to the bed.

"We're not going to need an anaesthetic this time," he mused gleefully.

The tension in Casey's muscles grew, reaching their zenith in a final act of defiance. But she could no longer hold them. Her mind swirling, she let them go; her body slumped back into her bonds. She succumbed to the inevitable.

"Take it, you fuck," she hissed. "I don't want it anymore."

CHAPTER 35

"Left!" Lionel shouted at Scott as he held the smartphone in one hand while shaking his other hand through the window.

Scott weaved in and out of the traffic, ignoring the potential disasters as the van hopped crazily around one street corner after another. Once clear, it roared onward. Scott glanced over at the smartphone screen, checking the destination marked by the blinking dot.

"Christ! At this rate, we're gonna be led right back to where we started!" he growled. "Are you sure you're reading that thing right?"

Lionel threw his arms up, then just as quickly grabbed the base of his seat as they careened through yet another intersection. Cars, trucks and motorbikes skidded and swerved across the road while drivers punched their horns in anger.

Lionel squinted down at the screen. His eyes grew wide. "It's just ahead! We're closing to within 500 meters!" He showed Scott the screen.

"That doesn't make sense," Scott growled. "Surely this can't be right."

Suddenly, he jammed both feet on the brake pedal. Smoke poured from the van's tyres as it came to a screeching halt. Grabbing hold of his seatbelt, Lionel recoiled in horror then shut his eyes until he was sure they hadn't hit anything. Looking up, he saw traffic in front of them had squealed to stop. Several drivers had leaped from their cars and were shouting abuse.

"This is not good," he murmured ruefully.

Ignoring the commotion, Scott wound down his window and peered out into the night, directly across from where they stood. He looked upon an ultramodern office complex of sandstone and tinted glass that stood back from the street on an elevated strip of land. A driveway rose up from the street alongside the building. The complex was flanked on either side by very grand and expensive residential properties.

Grabbing the phone from Lionel, Scott glared at the screen and confirmed that they were right on top of the location marked by the blinking dot. He scanned the darkened building desperately for signs of activity.

"This isn't Fedele's home," Lionel remarked.

"No, it's not," Scott replied.

He fired up the engine and shoved the van into reverse. The tyres squealed on the bitumen once more, forcing Lionel to brace himself.

"What on Earth?" he wheezed as the van leapt backwards and then sideways. Scott lined the van up so that it was facing the office building.

Scott jabbed a finger towards the front of the office complex, where it met the street. Lionel followed the direction of his finger until he found himself looking at a polished chrome sign attached to a sandstone column.

'Mr. S. Fedele MBBS, MS, FRAC, FCSANZ - Heart and Lung Transplant Surgeon.'

Revving the engine, Scott glanced across at Lionel.

"Hang on!"

The van pounced, screaming up onto the driveway. As soon as they were clear of the road, Scott jerked the steering wheel. The van lurched sideways, aiming it at the massive glass window.

Lionel gulped, but he had no time to react as the wall of glass rushed up to meet them.

Fedele snarled as he wrenched down on the leather strap securing Casey's right wrist, then he leaned across her, pressing his naked body against her as he repeated the action with the strap on her left. Pain knifed down the length of her arm from her shattered collarbone and tears bulged in her eyes. Her terror gave way to despondent grief.

Fedele pounced up onto the bed, straddling her and glaring at her with a maniacal grin. Any remaining vestiges of the consummate clinician she had known him to be had disappeared into this monstrosity.

Glowering with a primal intensity, he rubbed his muscular body against hers as he grasped the scalpel, dragging the flat surface of the blade down her cheek. Casey began to sob.

The strap holding her head slipped backwards, but Fedele did not react. He was drunk in his experience. He so treasured harvests like this one: young, beautiful, alive in his arms. Saskia, Casey and countless, nameless others. He cherished his gift; to take life and to give it. And it gave him immense pleasure to savour this last, final moment.

Casey shut her eyes as she shook uncontrollably, feeling his slick erection pressing hard against her hip, moving across her belly and coming to rest between her legs.

And then…

An apocalyptic explosion erupted above their heads.

The van smashed through the window, obliterating the huge glass panel as it powered deep into the interior of Fedele's consulting suite. It ploughed into the long leather couch, splintering it into a dozen ragged pieces and pitching the ruin into the air before it crashed down onto the glass coffee table. As Scott reacted, planting his foot on the brakes, the van smashed into Fedele's desk, catapulting it backwards into the bookcase which exploded and opened a deep cavity in the wall panelling behind it.

The van finally and abruptly shuddered to a stop. Lionel and Scott were flung forward in their seats. Scott yelped as his large, muscular frame struck the steering wheel while Lionel gasped as the seatbelt locked against his chest and ricocheted him back in his seat.

As the chaos subsided, both men looked up at each other, then through the windshield at the destruction they had wrought. In the wall cavity, electrical wires flashed and sparked. A ruptured gas line erupted in flame.

Scott's eyes bulged as he flung his arm out at Lionel and grabbed his shoulder.

"Duck!"

At, that moment, a second explosion ripped through the chamber, causing it to shake violently. Fedele fumbled on top of Casey as a fireball belched from the elevator shaft and flames crawled hungrily across the ceiling above. He thrust his head back to see the doors of the elevator rip open as their electric mechanism failed. The elevator carriage itself had fallen downwards as debris fell from above.

He lifted his head and listened to the unfolding chaos. In doing so, he extended his neck directly over Casey's face and she found herself looking at his glistening skin and bulging veins.

All thought left her mind in that instant.

Except one.

Unleashing an ear-splitting scream, Casey jerked her head up, biting hard and deep into Fedele's flesh, locking her jaw like a vice around his neck. Fedele howled, first in shock and then in terror as he struggled against her, his arms flailing on either side. Reflexively, he dropped the scalpel from his hand where it clattered uselessly to the floor as he clawed at the sides of the bed in an effort to pull himself free.

Casey would not let go.

Conjuring as much hatred and fury as she could muster, Casey sank her teeth deeper, tasting blood, feeling his skin and flesh tearing. A sudden rush of maniacal exhilaration flooded through her and she smiled gleefully, shaking her head from side to side.

Fedele was impotent, unable to free himself. His cries of anger reverberated around his evil chamber, bouncing off the concrete walls, echoing into the air vents, carrying themselves up the elevator shaft.

Blood welled around Casey's lips. It poured into her mouth, over her tongue. The taste was unbearable. She sensed she must be close to his jugular vein.

Fedele began to hyperventilate, hissing between clenched teeth as the room began to spin. He felt his own blood pumping from his neck and he wailed like a stricken animal, caught in the fatal grip of a predator.

Thrusting downwards with his palms, he searched desperately for the edge of the bed. He found it and, with a huge convulsion, he tore himself free from Casey's grip. A chunk of flesh remained between her teeth and a huge spray of blood blossomed between them both.

Fedele fell from the bed and crashed to the floor. Crying out in agony, he flailed uselessly as blood poured from the gaping wound. He slapped a hand to his neck in a vain effort to stop the flow. Casey spat the disgusting flesh from her mouth and craned her neck to look at Fedele's naked form writhing on the floor. She then did something unexpected.

She laughed out loud.

Fedele tried to stagger to his feet in front of the elevator shaft, but he slipped on the slick floor and fell, hitting his head hard against the concrete. He lay back, adjusting his grip on his ruined neck while trying to slow his breathing. He could feel himself slipping into unconsciousness.

He had to finish this.

As he rolled onto his side, his body turned towards the ruined elevator shaft where flames continued to lick from the interior and into the room.

Fedele grabbed at a wheeled trolley and pulled. The trolley upended, its contents crashing to the floor. The glass jar containing the diseased, worm-infested heart smashed beside Fedele, splashing liquid all over his outstretched arm. The flames from the elevator shaft touched the preserved organ and the flammable liquid and to his horror, Fedele's hand and forearm were instantly consumed by flames.

Fedele screamed, watching as the skin of his hand blistered and begin to melt like a wax candle. His fingers stuck together, forming an angry mass of burning flesh that resembled a macabre mitten. Shaking himself from his shock, he desperately slapped the limb on the floor over and over in a futile effort to extinguish flames that would not yield. The skin blackened and hissed as the flames licked hungrily at his arm, then jumped across his flank and abdomen as he tried to get away from the pool of liquid. Fedele continued to roll, howling as the fire threatened to consume him until, finally, he managed to smother the flames under his own body.

Scrambling into a sitting position on the floor, he held up his arm and glared at it stupefied. His left hand been reduced to a blackened, melted stump that continued to hiss and smoke.

Fedele shrieked at the ruined limb.

Panting wildly, Casey peered over the sides, searching for him as she suddenly heard new noises above her head.

"HELP ME!"

Cradling his ruined limb, Fedele's head lolled to one side and he blinked, spying a glint of metal on the floor across the room.

He managed a smile.

The scalpel.

With great effort, he rolled over and scrabbled to his knees, pausing to steady himself before rising to his full and formidable height. He staggered to the bed, supporting himself against it. Then he lurched towards the scalpel.

Casey watched in stunned horror as Fedele bent down, snatched up the surgical instrument in his functioning hand, then turned to face her. Blood cascaded from the wound on his neck.

Casey blinked.

Fedele grinned once more.

"Oi! *Fuck face*!"

A large shadow fell across Fedele. In an instant, a wooden beam held in a pair of massive, tattooed arms, swung and struck Fedele in the centre of his chest. There was a sickening crack of breaking bone as the impact lifted the surgeon off his feet and threw him back against a pair of oxygen cylinders on the wall.

Scott lunged forward, placing himself between Casey and Fedele. The shocked surgeon looked up through bulging eyes. Flipping the length of hardwood deftly in his hand, Scott adjusted his grip then leapt forward unleashing a devastating swing that crashed into the side of Fedele's head, snapping it sideways. He slumped to the floor unconscious.

He turned in time to see Lionel come to Casey's side, and Scott flung the length of timber aside and went to them, helping Lionel undo the leather straps.

Emotion overwhelmed Casey all at once.

She broke down in wracking sobs, wrenching her arm free and reaching out for her grandfather who embraced her tightly. He kissed her forehead tenderly.

"It's all right, Casey. It's all right, it's over now," he repeated softly, as tears filled his eyes.

Scott released the last of the straps then grabbed a blanket from a shelf. He wrapped it around Casey's shoulders as she sat up and collapsed into her grandfather's arms, allowing the exhaustion, the grief and the relief to rush forth.

On the floor, Fedele began to gurgle softly. His head lolled back, but none of them reacted.

From the ruined elevator shaft, several heavily-armed tactical response officers dropped into view and fanned out into the chamber, their weapons drawn. Upon seeing the trio at the bed and the unconscious form slumped on the floor across from them, the lead officer signalled to his men to hold.

Casey looked into the helmeted face, but she did not react. Instead, she watched as Scott stood in front of them and pointed the squad to Fedele's inert form against the far wall.

It was over.

CHAPTER 36

A HOSPITAL BED.

Another hospital bed.

Her eyes were closed. A large, round pad covered her right eye, concealing the angry bruising underneath it. A dressing covered her collarbone. Her arm was immobilised in a sling.

Lionel sat beside Casey's bed in a reclining chair. He was dozing, snoring softly. A pair of glasses hung precariously from the edge of his nose. He hugged a newspaper to his chest. Scott was slumped on a painfully small sofa opposite, scanning his smartphone's screen.

A TV screen, mounted on a strut that descended from the ceiling, flashed imagery at them. Its volume was muted; the remote lay on Casey's blankets.

The door to the room clicked open and a young nurse stepped inside. Regarding Scott, who looked up from his phone and smiled at her, she tiptoed over to Casey's bedside and checked the pump that was delivering IV fluids into Casey's arm.

Casey stirred. Her visible eye fluttered open and she glanced up. The nurse flushed pink.

"I'm sorry," she whispered apologetically. "I didn't mean to wake you. I just wanted to check your pump."

Casey smiled weakly.

"It's all right," she croaked softly. "I wasn't asleep."

The nurse gave the plastic flask a jiggle then, satisfied, she turned to leave.

Her eyes went up to the TV screen just as the mid-morning news bulletin flashed up.

She gasped as a picture of Casey appeared on screen.

"That's you!"

Casey looked up, feeling around for the remote. She pressed the volume button. The sound of the male newscaster caused Lionel to wake with a start. He jolted upright in his chair and glanced around, disoriented. Scott struggled up from the sofa and came over.

'...Federal Government in Canberra is in crisis this morning following revela-

tions of a highly sophisticated organ harvesting ring, which was uncovered by a young Melbourne woman, allegedly operating from within the Federal Department of Immigration & Border Protection.'

Lionel lifted his glasses into position as the introduction transitioned to a female anchor while images of Simeera Fedele, Francis Arlo and a third man whom Casey did not recognise, appeared in a graphic beside her.

"Federal and State Police Authorities have been mobilised in the wake of stunning revelations of the ring which is reported to have been operating for several years and has potentially involved hundreds of victims."

Casey reached out to Lionel, who took her hand in his. He squeezed it gently.

"I don't recognise that third man," she remarked.

Lionel squinted at the screen. "Someone from government perhaps?" Scott shrugged his shoulders.

'Authorities in Canberra have swooped in on the offices of the Parliamentary Secretary to the Federal Immigration Minister, Mr. Simon Schutz, arresting several staff including the Secretary himself as well as seizing computer hardware and documents. Here in Melbourne—in what has been described as a shocking development—world-renowned heart transplant surgeon Mr. Simeera Fedele has been reportedly taken into custody in connection with the organ harvesting ring. We take you now to a live press conference in Melbourne where the Victorian Police Commissioner, Keith Moodie, is about to make a statement.'

The shot transitioned to a press conference. Several police personnel flanked the Police Commissioner himself, who sat down at a desk before a packed audience of journalists.

Casey identified Farnham Whittaker on the screen, while Prishna Argawaal was in the background, standing to one side of the auditorium. She looked on as the Commissioner prepared to speak.

"Good morning," the Commissioner began, coughing into his closed fist. "I'll make a short statement after which I will accept a small number of questions."

A murmur rippled through the audience, then silenced as the Commissioner continued.

"This morning, Major Crime Detectives working in partnership with Australian Federal Police have made several arrests in connection with an apparent organ harvesting operation that was operating here in Melbourne. Our initial assessment, based upon evidence which has been uncovered thus far, is that it was highly organised and that the Flaxley Park Immigration Detention Facility has been identified as a hub from where...candidates were sourced."

The Commissioner paused as he adjusted his glasses and checked the notes in front of him.

"Now, I can confirm that those arrests include heart transplant surgeon Mr. Simeera Fedele as well as Mr. Simon Schutz, the Federal Parliamentary Secretary to the Minister for Immigration and Border Protection."

The audience erupted into excited chatter while several journalists peppered the Commissioner with a barrage of questions. He raised his hand, calling for silence. Once the tumult had dropped away, he gestured to a young woman in front of him.

"Commissioner, there is speculation that the Parliamentary Secretary was facilitating the fast-tracking of asylum seeker claims so that they could be used as organ donors for wealthy overseas clients. Further, it is being suggested that he was receiving significant financial incentives for doing so. Can you confirm this?"

The Commissioner shifted in his seat and looked down his nose at the reporter.

"It is too early to speculate on the exact roles of each of the suspects. I would suggest that you direct that question to my Federal counterpart," he responded tersely.

He gestured to another journalist who was wielding a smartphone in his outstretched hand.

"Indonesian media sources are reporting that authorities in Jakarta have arrested and charged a prominent doctor with conspiracy in connection with this organ harvesting operation. Do you have any comment regarding that?"

The Commissioner nodded. "Our Federal counterparts have been liaising with Indonesian authorities and yes, a person of interest has been taken into custody."

"What can you tell us of reports that a colleague of Mr. Fedele's, a Francis Arlo, was found murdered last night and is there any connection between this death and the death of Ms. Josephine Catea?"

Casey shivered at the mention of Arlo and she squeezed Lionel's hand tighter. On the TV screen, the Commissioner nodded and glanced sideways at Whittaker, who spoke up.

"Francis Arlo's death, along with Ms. Catea's, are being examined as part of our investigation," Whittaker responded. "Mr. Fedele is cooperating with us.

That is all we're prepared to say at this time."

The Commissioner nodded at another reporter who looked at Whittaker.

"What can you tell us about the reports that a patient of Mr. Fedele's, a Miss Casey Schillinge, was the one who uncovered this apparent conspiracy?"

Whittaker glanced sideways at the Commissioner who wove his hands together on the table in front of him. He glowered at the journalist.

"We have no comment," Whittaker said.

The journalist pressed further. "Was she, in fact, responsible for the security breach at Flaxley Park?"

"Again," the Commissioner rumbled warningly. "No comment."

An aide to the Commissioner stepped up behind him and whispered something in his ear. He nodded and stood.

"Ladies and gentlemen, thank you. That is all we have for you at this time."

The chattering rose again as the police representatives filed from the auditorium. Reporters continued to fire questions as the television switched from the press conference back to the news anchor in the studio.

Casey pointed the remote control at the TV and switched it off. She did not want to hear anymore. Nor did she want to see anymore. She squeezed her eye shut against a burgeoning anxiety. Scott, Lionel and the nurse regarded her with concern.

"Are you okay?"

She nodded wearily, lifting her hand to the bandage covering her eye.

"Yeah," she responded with barely a whisper. "I just…need it all to *stop*."

Casey retreated within herself, pushing against the gathering adrenaline surge and the accompanying memories of the past few days. Of her confrontation with Arlo and… *with him.*

She couldn't bear to even think his name. Her stomach rolled as she fought to block his face out.

The nurse looked to Lionel, who smiled thankfully, then she retreated from the bed. Opening the door to the room, she looked into the faces of Peter and Edie who were just about to knock.

The nurse stepped to one side, holding the door for them as they entered the room. Opening her eye, Casey watched them both. Her expression was empty.

Edie hesitated and dropped behind Peter while he approached Casey's bed gingerly. He acknowledged Scott with a nod.

A moment passed as he looked down upon her awkwardly. Casey couldn't be sure whether her father was shocked by her appearance or whether he was simply unsure of what to say.

All at once, Peter's eyes glistened, his cheeks flushed red and his lip quivered.

"I've got no idea what to say," he said shakily. "This is all so…"

"Crazy?" Casey finished for him, breaking the ice. Peter managed a laugh in spite of himself.

"*Crazy*," he echoed.

Tears spilled down over his cheeks and he leaned down, planting a tender kiss on her forehead.

"I'm sorry," he whispered, his lips lingering on her skin. "I'm sorry I couldn't understand it. Accept it."

Casey squeezed his hand as he drew back. "I couldn't understand it myself. I just *knew.* I had to follow my gut."

"Just as well you did. Everyone is talking about it. Not in so many specifics of course, but it's big news. Even Angus has heard about it."

Casey's one eye grew wide. "God, I hope he's all right," she said, concerned.

Peter patted her arm gently. "He's fine. We've already spoken to him. Your Mum and I."

Casey turned her head, glancing around her father and across at Edie who remained by the door. Her expression was tense. When her eyes met Casey's she shifted nervously, unsure of what to do. It was Casey who finally gestured, beckoning her to come closer.

Peter and Lionel glanced at one another as Edie approached the bed. Lionel moved to stand, but Casey stopped him with her free hand.

Edie glanced at him earnestly and then regarded her only daughter.

"Stay," Casey mouthed.

Peter gently swung his arm around Edie's waist as Casey turned, wincing as she leaned too heavily on her injured shoulder. She looked up at Edie for a long moment.

"There was a file," Edie said. "Saskia's visa case was being handled by our office. Bill Slattery confirmed it…and I've since turned the file over to the police." Edie paused and reached down to touch Casey's face gently. "You were right, Casey," she whispered. "You were right all along. And I am so sorry."

Casey gazed at her mother, too moved to speak. Finally, she reached out for Edie's hand, taking it in her own. Her grip was firm. "It's finished, Mum," Casey said quietly.

Tears welled in Edie's eyes and her lips turned upward in an emotional smile. She nodded, leaning into her husband, resting her head on his shoulder.

"I know," she whispered. "I know."

She held onto her daughter's hand as tightly as she dared.

THE BREEZE WAS stiff as it gusted in off the bay, whipping up whitecaps that coasted in on the current and crashed against the pylons of the jetty, sending salty spray up and over the rail. Thick clouds crossed the sky. To the south, they were especially dark and foreboding, while to the west, approaching sheets of rain dropped in wide swaths to drench the earth.

As Prishna raised the collar of her jacket, she grimaced at the approaching storm. She could only hope that this meeting would be over and done with soon. She would give it five more minutes.

Turning towards the shore, Prishna looked up to see the headlights of a familiar black van as it pulled into the parking area above the beach.

Finally.

The doors opened and she watched as Casey walked cautiously down the steps, supporting her still immobilised left arm with her right. As she crossed the sand and stepped up onto the jetty, Prishna noted that she still wore a pad over her injured eye but had concealed it with a pair of large sunglasses.

Prishna walked along the jetty as Casey approached until she stopped a dozen feet away.

"How're you feeling?" Prishna greeted in a neutral tone.

"Better. Glad to be out of that bloody hospital." She cracked the faintest of smiles and nodded at Prishna who hugged herself against the wind. "I hope you weren't waiting too long?"

Prishna returned Casey's grin with her own. Her eyebrows rose accordingly. "Not too long. Though I doubt we'll have much time before that front reaches us."

Casey glanced at the approaching rain. A few drops stung her cheek.

"So, you're the toast of the Melbourne press and the force," Casey said. "I hear you're in line for a commendation…and a promotion."

Prishna maintained her smile. "Nothing gets past you, does it," she responded evenly. "Why am I not surprised?"

Prishna turned her head to allow the wind to blow her hair clear from her face. "You've uncovered enough material to keep us in work for a very long time, Casey. They're talking about establishing a dedicated task force. It has exposed a lot of highly placed individuals not only within the Federal Government but also overseas." Prishna exhaled audibly. "Who would have thought it? Organ harvesting right here in Australia." Even now, she found the very mention of that fact difficult to process. "It was a huge operation, you know. Wealthy clients desperate for healthy organs were paying up to one million dollars for Fedele's services."

Casey's jaw stiffened. Now it was her turn to shake her head.

"Jarsayah Sonmez, Fedele's colleague from Afghanistan, found the clients," Prishna continued. "Fedele conspired with Arlo to identify donor candidates at Flaxley. Then, Schutz inside Immigration would fast-track their paperwork and facilitate their release. Once they were in the community, they and their records simply disappeared."

"Animals," Casey hissed, her voice shaking with anger. "They better crucify Fedele for this."

Prishna studied Casey knowingly.

"I imagine that there's going to be opportunities for you to contribute further. I know Whittaker is already talking you up."

Casey's glared at Prishna incredulously. "Oh no. I am staying right out of this one," she retorted, her expression hardening. "I am well and truly fed up with the whole thing."

Prishna nodded. "I can understand that. You do realise that you will probably be called to give evidence. Thanks to both yourself and your friend up there," Prishna gestured with a nod towards the car park where she could see Scott standing beside the van, his hands shoved in his pockets. "Simeera Fedele is likely to make a full recovery. He will stand trial."

Casey stiffened at the mention of his name and looked away from Prishna, out across the water. "We'll see, I guess."

Prishna noted the effect the mention of his name had on Casey and she nodded in understanding. "We'll see," she echoed. She reached into her jacket then, and took out a folder. She held it out to Casey.

Casey blinked and took it hesitantly.

"Saskia's case file," Prishna said. "*Amended.*"

Casey regarded the folder in her hand nervously.

"Francis Arlo facilitated Saskia Andrutsiv's release from the Detention Centre. He identified her as a candidate and then initiated a relationship with her in order to manipulate her, as he had done with the others. However, unlike them, Saskia wasn't swayed by his charms. She became suspicious of

Arlo and we believe that she discovered what his real motives were. She must have uncovered quite a bit. She began to fear for her safety. She ended the relationship with Arlo, but he wouldn't accept it. Fearing that she would reveal all, he confronted her at the Pleasant Festival and tried to convince her with more money, more inducements."

"And she went with him anyway," Casey said bitterly.

"Probably because she wanted to stop him once and for all," Prishna answered earnestly, turning towards Casey. "Forensics have examined the car. Despite the time that has passed, they've determined that there probably was a struggle that night. Saskia attacked Arlo. She gave as good as she got. We've since found out that Arlo was significantly injured the night of her death. No one ever put it together. Until now."

"What a waste."

Prishna tilted her head. "Not entirely."

Casey frowned as Prishna rested her hand on Casey's.

"Nothing you can do can bring Saskia back and you can't punish yourself because of it. The fact that you received her heart was just the way the cards fell. There was no conspiracy there. You were next on the recipient list and Saskia was the next donor."

Casey looked down at her feet. Prishna detected great sadness in her.

"Saskia has given you a gift, a *precious* gift. It's your obligation to her now to honour it and her memory by living your life to the fullest. That's the only thing you owe her."

The wind dropped a little as both women allowed a quiet to descend between them.

"So. I guess, all that leaves then is our agreement."

Prishna looked back at Casey. "Octagon?" she ventured.

Casey nodded with resignation.

Reaching into her windbreaker, she took out a small rectangular object and turned it over in her fingers. Prishna noted that it seemed to be fashioned entirely from gold.

It was a USB key.

Flicking it up, Casey pinched it between her thumb and forefinger. She held it out towards Prishna who regarded it, then took it, laying it in the centre of her palm.

Printed onto its surface was a small octagon.

"It's all there," Casey said sourly. "Everything."

Prishna kept staring at the key in her palm.

She took it in her other hand and held it up. Then, placing one hand on the jetty rail, she leaned back and flung the USB key as hard as she could into the air.

Together, they watched it drop towards the ocean until it was swallowed up by the waves.

Casey blinked at the water. "You do know that was pure gold, don't you," she remarked.

Prishna brushed her hands with an expression of mock satisfaction and turned, walking past Casey.

"That's a shame," she quipped as she left the jetty. "Come on. We're going to get rained on."

CHAPTER 37

Casey reclined on the sofa with her feet up, balancing a tea cup in her lap as she regarded the Rothko painting.

The pairing of colour seemed different to her now. Her antipathy towards it had dissipated. Where once she had considered it pretentious and intimidating, Casey looked at the two distinct blocks of colour with none of her former angst. The way the earth-like brown at the bottom rose upwards and gradually evolved through a subtle band of red in the middle then soft orange hues towards the top touched off a flurry of new thoughts about what the image might be and she allowed herself to ponder them.

It could have been anything really. Its abstraction was striking, powerful even. For now, it most resembled the sky. The longer she stared at it, the more the print reminded her of morning.

For a brief moment, images from the dream teased at the edges of her consciousness, but something told her not to resist them. She allowed them to cross her stream of thought as fleeting vignettes. She considered them without emotion.

She saw herself standing alone on Lasterby Road. There was nothing around her except the sprawling fields, the row of pines whose branches swayed languidly in the breeze. The ribbon of bitumen stretched into the distance, towards an emerging dawn.

Closing her eyes, she winced and lifted her hand to the resolving bruise that haloed her injured eye. She no longer wore the pad to conceal it. The sling that she was supposed to be wearing to support her injured collarbone lay at her feet. It was a bloody ridiculous thing.

Across from her, Kirkwood tilted her head curiously observing Casey's study of the print, as she picked at a corner of the clipboard that rested on her lap.

"I've always had some sort of *thing* for that print," Casey said, before Kirkwood could venture a question. "Even before, when I first started coming here."

Kirkwood twisted in her chair and looked at the Rothko. "Oh? I got the impression that you hated it."

"I did once," Casey admitted frankly. "But, things change."

Kirkwood feigned an expression of mock hurt and both women laughed. "What do you see?"

Casey raised her cup to her lips and sipped thoughtfully. "Beginnings," she offered.

"I suspect Rothko might have thought the same thing when he painted it. I often see that myself. Sometimes, I imagine the sun is just about to rise in the image and that it will evolve."

"Evolve?" Casey questioned, her eyes narrowing. "Into what?"

Kirkwood shrugged. "Who knows. Possibility? Potential? Beginnings? There are endless motifs in his work."

Casey sipped from her cup again, then set it down on the table in front of her. "You feel the same about your work," she said.

Kirkwood raised an eyebrow, clearly impressed. "That's insightful. Yes, I do. Everyone has potential. Even those who might seem the most *lost*. That has been my approach ever since I started in practice. Everyone begins somewhere."

"I figured that," Casey said.

She sat forward, swinging her legs over the edge of the leather sofa and resting her feet on top of her leather sandals on the floor. She clasped her hands together, squeezing them tightly. "So. What do we do now? Where do *we* begin?"

Kirkwood looked down at the notepad. Closing the clipboard, she tossed it on the table.

"We don't need to begin. In fact, we don't really need to do anything. Why don't we just talk instead?"

Casey studied Kirkwood. She pursed her lips.

"Okay," she said, knowing that Kirkwood never just talked. Not that she really minded much anymore.

Kirkwood began. "Do you have any plans?"

"I do," Casey responded with a hint of enthusiasm. "I'm heading north for a little while. I'm going to take that holiday I promised myself."

"Good." Kirkwood beamed. "Good for you."

Her eyes narrowed as a thought popped into her head. "Wait. How are you going to get there?"

"I'm going to drive…all by myself." Casey took a stilted breath in, as though she still couldn't quite get her mind around the challenge she had set for herself.

Kirkwood's eyes widened and she nodded approvingly. "I *am* impressed. You've gotten yourself a new car already?"

"No, not quite," Casey paused as her lips twisted into a wry smile. "Edie… *Mum* is letting me take hers."

Casey noted Kirkwood's raised eyebrow once again.

"Sounds like progress. You and your mum are…"

"Talking?" Casey finished for her. "Yeah. We're talking. It's good. Nice. She is trying really hard, although I think Dad might have pushed her into agreeing to surrender her car to me." Casey's eyes drifted away from Kirkwood. "I miss my Vee-Dub," she said. Memories threatened.

Distant echoes of smashing glass and screeching tyres.

She stifled them before they could infiltrate further into her mind.

Kirkwood watched her with subtle concern. "They will pass in time. Your memories."

Casey shrugged. "I guess."

Kirkwood studied her more intently, sensing a little of Casey's obfuscation returning. "You're still dreaming?"

"No," Casey responded. She relaxed her shoulders. "No, I'm not. They've stopped. Ever since I stopped him. Fedele." Casey went quiet, though Kirkwood sensed she hadn't finished.

"But?" she prompted.

Casey looked up. Her face tensed slightly. "There are other memories. Her memories."

"Her memories. You mean Saskia's?"

Again Casey nodded. "I am seeing things or, rather *feeling* things. Old memories. Things that I know aren't mine. I assume they are hers."

Kirkwood considered her theory without any hint of judgement or doubt.

"I expect they will pass, too," she offered. "Or maybe they won't. You're in a unique position, having acquired what you have inside of you. It's quite reasonable to wonder whether a part of her has remained with you. The question is whether you can come to a place where you have peace with that."

"I think I can."

"Well then. When you find that place, so will she."

Casey smiled sadly. Her lip began to tremble.

Kirkwood's eyes diverted to the clock on the wall as the hand approached the top of the hour. Casey noticed and felt a pang of disappointment.

"Time to wrap up, huh?"

Kirkwood tilted her head sideways back and forth, considering. "Well, actually, my three o'clock cancelled earlier, so we *could* stretch this conversation for a little longer. If you wanted to."

Casey nodded and smiled more broadly. She wiped at her eyes. "That would be good. I think I would like to stretch this out for a lot longer."

"How much longer?"

Casey glanced casually around the consulting suite. The books on the shelf behind her, Kirkwood's cherished photos, out through the window and the garden beyond. A pair of birds were splashing in the urn again, oblivious to their human observers.

The old angst was gone. The fear. There was nothing left to conceal, nor was there anything that Casey wanted to conceal.

It felt good to be here. Safe.

Turning back to Kirkwood, she relaxed back into the sofa and put her free hand behind her head.

"Oh, I'm a basket case, Geddie Kirkwood," Casey said with a mischievous grin. "This is gonna take ages."

Kirkwood laughed and poured herself a glass of water from a pitcher on the table.

"I'm very pleased to hear that, Casey Schillinge."

Lionel stood in the centre of the courtyard behind the warehouse. Armed with a broom, he swept the pavement, stopping to lift a garden hose that snaked across the courtyard from a nearby tap towards a large pot containing a small orange tree.

The courtyard had been transformed. Gone was the accumulated mess, refuse and discarded ephemera of Casey's failed attempts at raising her own garden. In its place, courtesy of Lionel's handiwork, was a pristine retreat, the centrepiece of which was a brand new outdoor dining setting and matching day bed. All around him was a revived garden consisting of low maintenance fruit trees, hanging baskets and colourful flowers. A vine grew from a trellis along one wall, promising a lush green backdrop in the not-too-distant future.

As he scooped up a final pile of dirt and leaf litter, Lionel stood and admired his project. From the carport, he heard the sound of a car boot closing. He turned just in time to see Casey step into view. She wiped beads of sweat from her brow.

"That's it," she said. "I'm packed and ready. All's I've left to do is to...fill the tank."

Lionel noted her hesitation. "You know you can still probably catch that flight up with me if you want. You don't need to drive all that way."

"Fly?" she croaked, lifting her finger skyward. "You'd have me—a recovering agoraphobe—fly?"

Lionel's cheeks reddened visibly and he flashed an awkward smile. "No, of course not. It's just that it's a long drive to do on your own. Even if you weren't, you know..."

Casey giggled and leaned in to plant a reassuring kiss on her grandfather's cheek. "You're making a total hash of this, aren't you?"

Placing her hands on his shoulders, she squeezed them gently. "I'll be fine, Pa. I *am* fine. I'm looking forward to this. Six hours on the road, I figure I'll make Hambledown just in time for dinner."

Lionel checked his watch and nodded thoughtfully. It was a little after 8AM.

"My flight is at three. You may actually beat me there if you head off now."

Casey clasped her hands together with eagerness. "Right," she declared.

Casey scanned her little courtyard as she checked off her mental list, ensuring there was nothing left she needed to do.

All at once, she stopped as she took in the tranquil space Lionel had created for her. She became wistful.

"Thank you," she said softly. "For *everything*."

Lionel put his hands in his pockets and looked down at the ground with a bashful grin, scratching at the bricks with the side of his shoe. He was never good with receiving praise.

"This was easy, Casey."

Casey flicked her head towards him. "You know what I mean, Pa. You gave me the kick in the arse I needed. Pulled me out of that awful hole I'd dug. If you hadn't..."

Lionel nodded slowly. He gazed at his granddaughter. "You would never have given up, Casey. Somehow, you would have found a way. But, now it's time to stop and take a well-earned breather."

Casey leaned in and rested her head on her grandfather's shoulder.

"There is one more thing I need to do," she said.

Lionel raised his finger and turned around to a shelf behind him. He retrieved a posy of flowers from it. She inspected the bright pink and deep red rose blooms, interspersed with purple delphiniums and lilies.

"Will this do?"

Casey brought the posy to her nose and inhaled its scent.

She closed her eyes and smiled.

"They are perfect."

THE VAST CEMETERY stretched out all around her as she pulled the car to a stop on the narrow roadway leading in from the outside. Scott's black van followed a few lengths behind. As she turned the key and withdrew it from the ignition, Casey ruminated that at any other time in the last few years she would not have coped at being in a place as huge as this. She would have lost her nerve in an instant.

Stepping from the car, Casey raised her hand to shield her eyes from the sun as she regarded Scott, who joined her on the kerb. He was dressed in his black trousers, matching shirt and jacket with the logo of The Blue Heeler Bar emblazoned on it.

Casey smiled. "Thanks for coming," she whispered.

"I'm glad to," Scott replied nervously. "Though we might not want to dally too long. I'm no bloody good in graveyards."

Casey inspected her surroundings, noticing a smaller garden down a gently sloping hill, well hidden from the service road. It was connected by a long path that ran between the tightly arranged headstones.

Scott reached into his jacket and took out a map of the cemetery grounds. He handed it to Casey who had taken a piece of paper of her own out from her pocket. She compared the directions that were written on her piece of paper with the map in relation to where they stood now.

She nodded.

Lesia's directions were unmistakable.

Reaching back into the car, Casey took hold of the small posy of flowers, checking to make sure the buds were intact. Then, locking the car, she signalled to Scott.

The garden was positioned away from the main section of the grounds across a broad expanse of lawn. It appeared separate from the cemetery—a small, independent corner that was circled by trees and containing a much smaller number of gravestones.

Many of them were quite old, Casey noted. Spotted with moss and cracks of age and wear, with little iron fences stained with rust. Other sites were marked by simple plaques.

Searching among them, Casey's eyes came to rest upon a small, dark headstone. It was polished to a high shine. A fresh sprig of rosemary and mint leaves jutted out from a small holder in its top. She knew the moment she saw it that this was the one that she was looking for.

Reaching out, she squeezed Scott's arm and gestured with her head. Scott remained as she stepped away from him and circled around the stone.

She needs to do this on her own, he thought.

Casey stopped in front of the grave and looked down. For a moment, Scott couldn't tell if she had found it, but as he watched her, Casey's eyes became glassy. Her lip trembled.

She gazed upon the inscription that was etched into the stone.

"Saskia Polina Andrutsiv. Born 8th September 1990. Died 17th March 2012. At peace with God."

A portrait shot of Saskia imprinted in metal and housed in an oval frame sat underneath the engraving.

Casey lifted her hand to her chest as a familiar ache rippled across it. A tear trickled down her cheek.

Slowly, she stepped forward and bent down, touching her hand to the top of the headstone.

"We did it, Saskia," she whispered softly.

She lifted the posy and set it down gently on the headstone before kneeling down and plucking a pair of weeds from the grave.

"I kept my promise."

Weeping softly, her tears flowed freely, falling to the soil where they mingled momentarily on the top of some moss, vestiges of grief and gratitude, before seeping into the earth.

The gift was no longer a burden she refused to accept.

Casey's eyes flicked up towards Scott, who watched on from his vantage point several feet away. She was surprised to find his own features filled with emotion. He drew a hand from his jacket pocket and wiped at his eyes furiously, hoping that she hadn't seen him.

Through her tears, Casey smiled. She looked down. Pressing her fingers to her lips, she kissed them, then touched her hand to the headstone once more.

There was so much she wanted to say.

So much…

In the end, she could only conjure one phrase.

"Thank you," she whispered.

THE OPEN ROAD stretched out before her…four lanes of unobstructed freeway.

Lifting her hand to the rear-vision mirror, she adjusted it and inspected the view behind.

The city was already shrinking rapidly into the distance and with it the last echoes of her old life. Casey knew that when she returned, things would be different.

Adjusting her sunglasses, she took in the view on either side. Open pasture stretched out like a luxurious carpet of green, a smattering of cows grazing languidly in the meadow. Beyond that, a ribbon of Australian bushland draped the hilly horizon, fingers of tree branches reached up to touch the brilliant, cloudless blue. As Casey leaned forward and gazed through the windshield, she noted the thin contrail of a jumbo jet threading its way across the sky.

There was no anxiety in this vastness. No fear. Just pure and unadulterated freedom.

A large, green sign up ahead listed the various distances remaining for towns along her route. Hambledown was listed second from the bottom.

575 kilometres.

Reaching over, Casey thumbed the controls for the sunroof and watched as the glass panel slid back. The cool morning breeze tousled her hair and she smiled broadly.

Casey let out a victorious whoop as she shifted gears, gunned the accelerator, and felt the BMW pour on speed. The city shrank further in her rear-vision mirror.

Her heart felt full.

Her heart…

THE END

ACKNOWLEDGMENTS

I'd like to thank the following beta readers: Molly Ringle, Ashleigh Oldfield, Abbie Williams, Graham Adams, Scott (The Sasquatch) Taylor & Laura Laird.

Special thanks to Meghan Tobin-O'Drowsky and Bonnie Donaldson.

I want to single out Scott (once again) for allowing me to create a kick-arse sidekick who was a joy to write.

And, of course, Michelle Halket for her constant support and belief in me.

ABOUT THE AUTHOR

Dean Mayes is an Intensive Care Nurse who is fascinated by philosophy and the paranormal, so his stories weave an element of magical realism with deep humanism. He grew up near Melbourne, Australia, and now lives in Adelaide with his family. Dean loves outdoor cooking, anything to do with Star Wars and (insanely) long-form podcasts.

He is the author of *The Hambledown Dream, Gifts of the Peramangk,* and *The Artisan Heart.*

www.ingramcontent.com/pod-product-compliance
Lightning Source LLC
Chambersburg PA
CBHW030743120726
47947CB00013B/1

* 9 7 8 1 7 7 1 6 8 0 3 8 7 *